Alley Justice

By

T.A. Novak

Enjoy Detroit with JAKE.

T.A. Novak 9/2/2008

© 2012 by T.A. Novak
All rights reserved.

ISBN: 978-0-9885051-3-1 (Paperback)

Library of Congress Control Number: 2012919536

This book is printed on acid free paper.
Printed in the United States of America.

Edited by: Jon McQuinn, and Lori Villarreal

Cover art by: Lori Villarreal

Alley Cop Publishing-Est. 02/08

Dedication

This book is dedicated to the Marist Fathers and to Conrad Vachon who tried their best to teach me something at Notre Dame High in Harper Woods, Michigan.

I would also like to dedicate this to two fine Detroit Police Officers. First, an officer I consider my mentor, Clifford Roberts. Secondly, my dear friend, Richard Dungy who retired as Deputy Chief of Police in Detroit after 25 years of service. Richard died in September, 2015.

Acknowledgements

I don't believe any author can claim that their final work was the result of their efforts alone. This book started as a simple assignment for the Lake Havasu City Writer's Group in Arizona. Their critiques and questions led to the contents herein.

Then too, I am indebted to those who have edited my work. Without their help, the final product would not be what it is—something I can be proud of.

Prologue

June 27, 1968

The green Checker Cab was coming out of Highland Park. It pulled to the curb on Hamilton. Jake watched it stop. A young black male paid the driver and started walking west towards the alley.

"Let me out, Duane! Make a U-turn and head around the block."

He heard Duane in the background, "His shirt's black, not red." Jake ran between oncoming cars. As he got to the alley he saw his man cutting back east. Jake picked up his pace. As Jake got to the corner, the man was re-crossing Hamilton.

He's making sure no one's following him. Jake broke into a run. *Red shirt, black shirt. Witnesses make mistakes.*

Harris Harris, a man with two first names, walked with a spring in his feet and money tucked in his shirt. *Piece of cake. Alarms, hah! Just gotta be in and out. Quick.*

Harris was back in his neighborhood, two cab rides and a mile from the bank he'd just robbed.

Jake saw the black shirt turn into a yard. He ran faster, drawing his .38. The man crossed a street, into another yard, bumping out a wooden gate and back into another alley.

Harris ducked behind three garbage cans; his small automatic in his right hand. *Where'd the cop come from?*

Garbage cans fell when Harris stood. A gold tooth glistened as he smiled. In his right hand was a pistol. He fired two shots. Jake fired simultaneously. Harris spun and fell onto the garbage cans behind him. Jake slumped to the alley floor.

There was a slight twitch in a black shirtsleeve, then nothing. The man was dead.

Somewhere in the distance, Jake heard brakes screeching, then Duane's voice yelling, "Officer down! Officer down!"

In the background sirens were wailing.

Chapter One

July 31, 1971

Orange flames leapt towards the sky, intermingled with the heavy black smoke from the burning tires. The heat pushed Jake back. He took a deep breath and tried to open the door again. The Suburban's chrome handle was glowing hot. His tears were flowing, forming rivulets in the soot on his cheeks. "Debbie, help me! Kids, open the door!" He jumped up as he cried out, "Anne! Jeanette!"

It was his own voice that woke him. This had been Jake's daily alarm for more than a month. He glanced at the image in the mirror on the dresser. Again, he was sitting on the edge of his bed, holding his right hand in his left. He expected to see blisters. There were none. He stepped out of the tangled, sweat-soaked bedding that was around his waist and half on the floor, staggering to the kitchen to start a pot of coffee.

As the water ran, he looked out the window and saw the wheat field that edged up to his back property line. The scene of the fire was a full seven hundred and thirty miles away and happened forty-one days earlier. He had never been near mile-marker 437 on I-80, the spot where the Nebraska State Police said it happened. Though Jake no longer heard the screams of his wife and children in his flame-filled nightmares, he felt that he had been there, maybe unconsciously wishing he had perished with them.

As he filled his coffee cup, he promised himself he would make the phone call he had been putting off. He was healing. Slowly, but still healing. He seemed a little better each day. He knew he would never be totally healed, but he had to move on. He owed his family that much. He had to keep reminding himself that he didn't die with them.

Two hours later, Jake dialed a number from the old tin flip-pad alphabetical directory that Anne had kept from their days in Detroit. Jake hoped the number from three years ago still worked. It started ringing.

————

On September 8, 1971 John Anthony Bush was sworn in as a Detroit Police Officer. His silver shield carried the numbers: 2441. He was pleasantly surprised to discover that his old badge went unused. More than three years had passed since he had turned it in to Lieutenant Orth at the Detroit Police Department's Tactical Mobile Unit.

Jake, as he preferred to be called, was again wearing the blue uniform and the Sam Browne of the Detroit Police Department. A recycled, nickel plated thirty-eight Colt revolver was in the spit-shined holster worn in cross-draw fashion on his left hip. At this short ceremony there was no family in attendance. Jake's dad died in 1965, and his mother had moved to California. Jake knew his wife and children wouldn't be there. He forced the thought of them out of his mind.

A return to the police academy was waived. He was, as they say, "back on the job." Jake left District Inspector Bertolini's office without much to say. He knew his old boss pulled some strings to get him rehired. He quietly got into his '69 Ford pickup and drove to Jefferson and St. Jean, to the Fifth Precinct, his new assignment.

As Jake drove, Jesse Scott's face crossed his mind. Jess was an old partner from Jake's Tactical Mobile Unit days. The last he heard, Jess was working at the Fifth. Jake hoped he still was. He'd understand why Jake had come back to Detroit. The thought of a return would have never crossed his mind had he not remembered an unexpected visit by Jess to Hope, Michigan, two summers before. On a Sunday in July,

1969, Jess had just showed up in Jake's front yard. He said he was out for a Sunday drive, one hundred and thirty miles from Detroit.

Jake remembered when Jesse Scott had given his two-week notice prior to resigning from the department effective the last day of July, 1967. The riot started July 23rd. Since Jess was leaving, the bosses didn't let him on the street. He was left behind to guard the TMU office in the basement of the city garage on Jefferson and Chene. Jess quietly left for Minnesota amid the turmoil in Detroit the last day of the month. Jake never thought he'd see his old partner again.

During that 1969 visit he remembered Jess saying that he had suffered what he termed a "life-altering" event. "My life in Aiken, Minnesota, came to an abrupt end about a year after I left Detroit."

"How?"

Jess, never one for long conversations, went on to unload about his family's move to Minnesota, going into the bulk oil business with his older brother, and how his brother got killed by a drunk driver. "Within a month after that, our house burned down. I started drinking too much. Beth finally had enough and took the boys back to Petoskey, Michigan." Jake just listened. "I've quit the sauce, but it was too late for Beth. So I went back to Detroit."

"Where you working?"

"Number Five. Precinct narcotics."

"Kicking in doors on drug houses?"

"Yeah. I volunteer to be the first in."

"You're nuts." Jake shook his head, remembering his one-time partner and his too-tough-to-die attitude.

"Oh, I might take a bullet. A gold one that'll get me an early retirement—at full pay."

"Think that'll get Beth back?"

"No. But then I can go off and hide in the woods somewhere."

"And you hunted me down to tell me this? Why?"

"Just needed someone to talk to."

Jess drove off and Jake never heard from him again. But that one visit with Jesse Scott came back to Jake when he, too, had a life-changing event. Now, more than ever, he needed to find something to fill the void in his life. Maybe Jess had the right idea.

———

Life was different for Jake this time around. There was no story-and-a-half house with kids running through it and a lawn to mow. Jake vowed to never drive past it, no matter what. There were too many memories. This time his home was a cramped basement apartment with a small kitchenette and a studio couch for a bed. It would have to do until he found something better.

Returning to Detroit hadn't been a hard choice to make; he'd always known deep inside that he'd be a cop until the day he died. Now, there was no one left to explain his actions to. Just fragmented memories remained—distant ones. His subconscious blotted out most of them, except the last kiss from his wife, Anne, and those from his kids.

Yes, the memories still occasionally slipped past Jake's protective subconscious. Deb, Michelle, and Michael had just gotten out of school for the summer. Anne packed them, along with the four-year-old Jeanette, into their new Suburban and took off for a month's vacation to visit Anne's mother and the rest of the in-laws in California. Jake's last image of them driving off still remained somewhere in the deep recesses of his mind. The older girls had painted cardboard signs for the side rear windows, reading, *California here we come.* Michael had mastered using the new CB radio, installed so they could talk to the truckers along the way. "Breaker, breaker—"

Somewhere, buried among the few things Jake saved from his shattered life, was a newspaper article from the *Omaha World-Herald*. It told the story of a family driving west on I-80 and being in the wrong place at the wrong time. A stolen car careened out of control hitting a Chevy Suburban and bursting into flames. All the occupants of the Suburban died and so did the driver of the stolen car.

There was a period of time that summer when he shed too many tears, blaming himself for letting his family go west without him. A part of him died with them. *Maybe the old Jake did.*

Jake tried to remember the love he had for his family and tried blocking out the tragic end to their lives. He didn't always succeed. His loneliness was a constant reminder.

Many times the car thief also crossed his mind. *I hope the bastard's still burning in hell.*

————

When he finally came to grips with reality he made that phone call. It was time to go back to a life on the streets of Detroit. Jake knew where he belonged. Besides his family, what he missed the most was wearing a police officer's shield and feeling the weight of a gun on his hip.

The phone call to Jimmy Gramatico had gotten him a meeting with Jimmy's uncle, District Inspector Anthony Bertolini. A physical by the department doctor got him cleared to be hired, and he breezed through the physical agility test on anger alone.

Now, he was a cop again.

Jake pulled into the lot behind the Fifth Precinct. And yes, he was scared. Correction, apprehensive. He walked through the garage and took a short hallway to the front desk. He stopped in front of the lieutenant that was manning it. "Patrolman John Anthony Bush, reporting for duty sir."

Chapter Two

It wasn't too long after Jake hit the street that his new pistol was in at J&J's Sport Shop. He had worked at the store for a year while in high school and had walked the beat that J&J's was on, Van Dyke, while starting out at the Eleventh Precinct back in '62.

He bought a Model 28 Smith and Wesson .357 magnum after pondering for a while about getting a .41 magnum. But the Model 28 would fire .38 wad cutters, and Jake planned on using the precinct range a hell of a lot more than he had during the 60s. The lucky break he caught in an alley in 1968 was a constant reminder, so was the scar and the distorted left collar bone. He knew the chance of getting shot again would always be there. He wanted to eliminate the luck factor. During his last tour, the Smith and Wesson revolver was the one he liked the feel of, but, *feeding four kids came first*. Jake quickly pushed that thought out of his mind.

New partners every day and a new neighborhood greeted Jake as he mostly filled in on Five-Two and Five-Six for the first month working afternoons. But the radio blared the same type of calls: "Five-two, family trouble at 19340 Burns" or "Five-Six and Five Cruiser, man with a gun at 12207 Kercheval." Jake jumped right into being a street cop again, making a power turn with their Plymouth, heading towards the address on Kercheval.

The Fifth Precinct was one of the busy stations, and Jake did see Jesse Scott once at the station. Jess was leading a car thief into a holding cell. "Hey, Jess. Still working precinct narcotics?" Jake extended his hand towards his old partner as he spoke.

"Nah. The B&E car." Jess squeezed Jake's offered hand. Strong and firm like always.

"You look different, Jake."

"Just older. What happened with precinct narcotics?"

"An opening on the B&E car came up. I grabbed it."

Jake turned, heading towards the garage. "Gotta go, my partner's waiting for me."

———

That was the last Jake saw of Jess until near the end of September. As Jake was leaving for the night, the shift sergeant stopped him. "Bush, see the inspector on the way in tomorrow."

"What's it about?"

"My note just says to have you report to Inspector Mills' office 3:00 p.m. Wednesday."

The next day, as ordered, Jake knocked on the door to the inspector's office. Jess Scott and Sergeant Fox were there with the inspector. "Jake," Fox said, "there's a vacancy on the B&E car. Would you be interested?" Just like that. No introductions, nothing.

Jake looked at Jess.

The inspector answered the puzzled look on Jake's face. "I understand that you were Officer Scott's partner at TMU?"

"Yes sir."

"He wants you back. His regular partner is moving over to Five Cruiser."

"What about seniority?" Jake asked as he looked towards the sergeant, then the inspector.

"We put who we want on the B&E car. Jess asked for you," Sergeant Fox answered.

A precinct B&E car was a plain-clothes assignment and Jesse Scott would be his partner. He didn't have to think about it. A smile crossed his face. "When do I start?"

"The first of October," answered Fox. It was a done deal in less than five minutes.

———

The precinct B&E crew's primary purpose was to look for burglars, thus the name. Naturally, car thieves or any other felons were also on their "put 'em behind bars" list.

Most of the busier precincts had such a crew. When Jake was at Number Thirteen in 1963, they had Fred Greening and Roy St. Onge on the B&E car. Those two cops were a legend within a five-mile radius of Woodward and the Boulevard. It was rumored they might have even put the fear of God in some of the Highland Park and Hamtramck outlaws a time or two. Some of the old timers at the Woodward and Hancock station still talk about some of their alley antics; the most famous of which was when Greening took a potshot out of their car's passenger window at a fleeing burglar and the recoil of his .44 magnum caused him to drop his gun while breaking his right forearm against the roof of the car. The bad guy got away when Greening had St. Onge back up so he could retrieve the gun that was still spinning on the concrete alley floor when they got to it. Fred's right arm was in a cast for two months and his Smith and Wesson spent some time out-of-service getting re-blued, as well as a new front sight and set of wood grips.

The B&E crews used unmarked cars. This was the ultimate street- cop job as far as Jake was concerned. The men assigned to the precinct cruiser crews, known as *The Big Four,* consisted of one in uniform, the driver, and the three others in plain clothes. Those three wore suits or sport coats and mimicked the Jack Webb look, while the guys on the B&E car wore anything down to tennis shoes and jeans.

They were alley cops. They got dirty.

Jake settled on sweatshirts and jeans. If needed, the shirt would cover the handle of his magnum. Jess wore sweatshirts too, but with the sleeves cut off. He liked to show off his biceps.

More than seven years had transpired since Jess and Jake worked in uniform on Eight-Four at the Tactical Mobile Unit. Besides getting older, both men made some subtle changes in their lives. As before, they both came in early, taking notes from the teletypes, updating the stolen car board and keeping their circular book up to date. They had a past they seemed to be running from. The job was their escape. That happens when you don't have a family at home.

Jess and Jake were similar in height, Jake a tad under six foot and Jess just over it. Jake topped out at 190, which was considerably better than the frail 168 he weighed back in '62. His facial features, the nose in particular, had him being pegged as a Slav of some sort. He was Polish. As before, he returned to wearing his hair very short and flat. *Once a Marine, always a Marine.*

Jess was 60 pounds heavier with not a bit of fat clinging to his frame. In essence, he was built like a Bullmastiff, had a square muzzle, and was as muscular. His hair was thinning with a distinct widow's peak.

In his earlier days, Jess did a stint with the Arrows, a semi-pro football team playing up the road in Pontiac. If he was another four inches taller and forty pounds heavier, he would've probably had a chance with the Lions when Joe Schmidt retired.

Upon Jake's return to the department, he had decided he needed to improve his physical conditioning. The local Y filled the bill. Three years away from the job put some weight on him and now he needed to turn the flab into muscle. He quickly got into a three-times-a-week regimen in their weight room. Jess didn't need the visits to the gym, but started going anyway, saying he'd spot weights for Jake. Then Jess decided he needed to burn off some energy too. The difference was that while Jake started out benching 150 pounds, Jess was hefting 250 and not even breathing hard.

Jess was using the basement pistol range at Number Five twice a week and mentioned it to Jake during one of the workouts. Jake knew that he got lucky in the only shootout he was involved in, so he joined Jess. He wanted to become proficient with his new S&W magnum. Jess preferred the department-issued Colt .38 Police Special. They decided to come in fifteen minutes early on Tuesdays and Thursdays and hit the range. It didn't take them more than ten minutes to fire two cylinders into silhouette targets. Jake improved quickly, to the point where Jess was getting a little pissed off as the targets rolled forward and they compared holes. He liked to be just a bit better than anyone else, his football mentality, as Jake called it.

"You doin' extra practice, Jake?" Jess said one time.

"I'll shoot left handed if you want."

"No, just be there blazing if we get in a jam."

———

Jess never asked about Jake's family. He had heard rumors, so he just let sleeping dogs lie. Jake in turn didn't ask about Jesse's boys. He knew they'd be about ten and twelve by now. Jake had forgotten their names.

Lives change. Jake was a prime example. Years ago he was among the faithful at St. Raymond's in his old neighborhood. Now, he hadn't really been to church since the funeral. He tried going one time at Assumption Grotto, but all he did during mass was to ask *Why?* He was mad at God.

Besides, Sunday mornings were best for running around Belle Isle. Jake hated running since Marine Corps boot camp.

11

Now that Jake's only life was *The Job* and running would keep him in better shape, he did it. Secondly, he needed to burn off excess energy as much as Jess did.

———

The first night on Five Twenty-five, Jake showed up wearing a University of Michigan sweatshirt, jeans and a pair of brogans he'd kept from his last tour—black Kangaroo skins. Jake liked them to run in. Somehow he didn't feel comfortable in a pair of sneakers. October in Detroit was already slipping back to cooler temps and rain always threatened. He carried a tan poplin jacket, just in case. Jess looked him over, shaking his head like he disapproved.

"What?" Jake asked.

"Plain stuff works better."

"Not a Michigan fan?"

"It's not that. More like you'd blend in better without that big gold M. People are watchin' us 'n remember stuff like that. Bad enough we're two white guys and obviously cops.

"You didn't tell me we had a dress code." Jake just shook his head. "I'll save it for running on the island."

Jess was leading Jake to their car. "Sometimes I grab one of the dick's cars. Again, trying not to be too obvious. Our regular tank is that blue '69 Chrysler. It's Five's old cruiser painted over. Looks like a cop's car no matter what." He walked to a green Ford parked two down from it.

"Nuts," Jake said, sliding into the jump seat. "Now my blue shirt clashes."

"Call me tomorrow, I'll tell you what to wear."

Jake could tell Jess was glad to have him back as a partner. The small talk told him Jess was happy. They drove off looking for bad guys. Just like old times.

———

A week into working together Jess was slowly driving with his lights out hugging the curb on Kercheval. He slid around any parked cars. It was after nine. He asked, "What's that teletype on a drug store burglary in Fifteen?"

"A silver Plymouth. Man and a woman. Both white." Jake grabbed their book. "We've got a plate number. Nora Robert fifteen-twenty-two. Happened at 6:38 this morning."

Jess drove around the block and turned north on Fairview. "I saw the tail end of a light- colored Plymouth." Jess flicked on the car lights when they got near. A Plymouth was nestled in between two other cars. It was silver.

How in the hell did he see that?

Jake caught the plate number. It matched. The car looked empty. Jake took the passenger side while Jess shined his light into the driver's side.

The beam of Jess's light caught the top of a head low against the driver's side window. He jerked the door open. A white male fell out head first. Jess caught him. There was a woman on Jake's side of the car. He slowly opened the door and caught the woman as she fell out. He lowered her to the grass just beyond the curb.

"Mine's breathing," Jess called out. "How about yours?"

"Same here." Jake flashed his light on the floor and seat. There were pill bottles and torn white envelopes. Prescription envelopes.

Jake got to the radio and called for a couple of station wagons with stretchers. The two occupants of the Plymouth appeared to be in a drug induced sleep. The car wasn't more than a half mile from the drug store they'd broken into. Five-Two-Five didn't use words like *alleged*. The occupants of the car were surrounded by the evidence, thus, they were the burglars.

A tow truck dropped the Plymouth in the Fifth Precinct garage so Jake and Jess could gather all the evidence. As they were tagging the open and unopened prescription envelopes Jess said, "No doubt they started popping pills as soon as they turned the corner leaving the drug store. Stupid drug-infested society we work in, eh?"

"Zonked all day," Jake added. "With the B&E happening this morning."

Jess and Jake bagged and tagged everything that could have been related to a burglary. "Find out anything on the two?" Jake asked as he started going through the car's trunk.

"The male, Richard Peoples, lived across the street from where the car was parked. The car is registered to a Gertrude Schneider. They're running the prints on the woman. It's probably Gertie. Both are in Receiving Hospital's prison ward. Getting their stomachs pumped."

They took the evidence inside to catalog it. That and the report Jake typed finished their night.

Chapter Three

Joe Herbert took the two signed checks that he'd found in the bottom of the cash box, tore them into tiny shreds, put them in an ashtray and put a match to them. The ceiling fan inhaled the tiny wisp of smoke from the ashtray. On the table he had stacks of fifties, twenties, tens and fives. *Twelve grand. That'll get them bookies off of my ass.* Joe took a big gulp of his coffee. *Paid in full Mr. Bloodsucker.* The mask he used was already cut into unrecognizable pieces along with the rubber gloves he'd worn. He had them in a small lunch bag that he planned on disposing on the way into work. He put one of the thirteen bricks, leftovers from a backyard grill he'd built, in the green tin cash box. A quick trip across the Belle Isle Bridge in the morning and the current of the Detroit River would quickly hide it forever.

The next morning Joe was looking in the mirror, making sure his hair was neatly combed. He moved one strand of light brown hair to its proper place with nicotine-stained fingers. His reflection showed him a man whose one-time heavy drinking and two divorces had added at least ten years of wear on his 35-year old body. He grumbled to himself about alimony and the ponies eating away at his paycheck. He was hoping to wean himself off the horses. *Nothin' I can do short of murder about the two bitches though.* Joe attached his clip-on necktie and left for the day, the lunch bag and the green tin cash box in hand. His shift started in an hour and a half. The trip to Belle Isle would add about thirty minutes to his travel time. He was working the day shift this month.

———

Detective Lieutenant Stuart Walker leafed through the stack of armed robbery reports from the previous weekend.

After he separated them by dates, he saw that robberies were down for the start of the weekend. There were only thirty-two reports for Friday, June 4, 1971. Saturday had a bigger pile; he guessed there were over fifty. Sunday had the least amount. *Must be church-going crooks.* He smiled at that thought, knowing all Sundays were usually slow, even in Detroit. The churches really had nothing to do with the amount of crime, but somehow the Sabbath was observed, even if unintentionally.

One report for Friday piqued the interest of the lieutenant. The perpetrator had worn a full over-the-head *Mickey Mouse* mask. Walker snickered a bit, thinking this really was a Mickey Mouse holdup, until he read the estimated take in the armed robbery—$12,000 and change. He reread the report. It had been a stickup at a small neighborhood bar in the Fifth Precinct. The establishment had the abnormal amount of money on hand to cash paychecks. Friday was payday at the Chrysler Plant just down the block from the bar.

Walker returned the report to the pile and grabbed the next one, knowing the Fifth Precinct dicks could handle the initial investigation. They'd call if they needed help. There was a knock on his fourth-floor office door at Police Headquarters. The black stenciling on the glass read Lieutenant, *Detroit Police Robbery Bureau.* Walker dropped the report on a pile and saw through the glass that it was his sergeant, Charlie Barnes, and waved. "Come on in, Charlie."

————

Joe was methodical as he cut up the mask and the rubber gloves, and put both in another lunch bag. This time there were three signed checks that he put a match to. Joe knew he didn't want to mess with those checks and try to get something out of them. His was a cash-only operation. He poured himself another coffee and took a seat behind a bowl of Cheerios. *Two jobs were all I said I'd do.* He took a deep drag on his cigarette and looked at the money on the counter. *Well, maybe just one more.* On his way out to the garage he put a brick in the empty black tin cash box he carried.

———

Detective Lieutenant Walker was going through the robbery reports dated Friday, June 17, 1971. *This is more like it. Must be fifty-some.* The third one into the stack was on another bar holdup. Instead of Mickey mouse, it was Pluto with a nickel-plated revolver, and the bar was on the west side of Detroit. $9500 was the take. Walker grabbed the phone and punched in three numbers. "Charlie, get all the guys together. I'll be out in a minute."

It was ten minutes before Detective Lieutenant Walker found what he was looking for—the robbery report from two weeks before. The twelve detectives working for him were clustered near the coffee pot. Their asses were leaning against desks and file cabinets. Charlie spoke. "Whatchew got, boss?"

Walker read the report from June 4th aloud. A chuckle or two emerged. "Couldn't have been our Mickey Mouse," came a voice from the group. "My kids were watching him that night." More laughs followed.

"We all know it was Bones who was watching Mickey. Not his kids. That gives Mickey an air-tight alibi." More laughter. All the guys called the very skinny Art Roshey "Bones." The name fit. His clothes just hung on him like there was no meat underneath.

Walker let out a shrill whistle and raised his hand, quieting the group. "My first thought two weeks ago was basically the same—a Mickey Mouse bandit. But now listen to this one." Walker read the report from the past Friday night. Pluto was the perp. Walker's crew laughed, but not as much. Walker raised his voice to be heard over the chatter. "It's not a joke when two robberies net over twenty-one thousand." The room went silent. "Who do we have free?" Walker looked around. No one spoke. "All right, Dunlop and Phelps. Hit these two bars. Talk to the bartenders who were on. See if we got a pattern here. Might be the same guy."

"What about the Ames case?" asked Phelps.

"When's it go to court?" Walker passed the reports to Phelps.

"Friday."

"Okay, today, and if need be, tomorrow, check these two bars out and get back to me. That'll give you a couple of days to make sure your witnesses are ready for your case."

Phelps took the reports from Walker. "Let's go, Dun's. I've got tickets to the Tiger game tomorrow."

———

The Detroit Police Robbery Bureau added two more reports on corner bars being held up over the next two months, all on a Friday night when they had extra cash on hand. All committed by a Disney character on payday night. Walker knew he didn't have enough men to be sitting in bars waiting for a holdup. Four armed robberies, all by a cartoon character using a nickel-plated revolver. Two more meetings with his crew and a list was formed. All four bars were normal watering troughs for the workers at car assembly and parts production plants sprinkled throughout the cities of Detroit, Highland Park and Hamtramck. All the reports were of holdups within the Detroit city limits.

After the second robbery, Walker had two of his teams canvass the bars around these types of factories. There were at least thirty bars and counting that said they cashed payroll checks. They said ninety percent of the checks they cashed were just after the afternoon shift on Fridays. Of the four bars that were hit, the robberies all took place within fifteen minutes before a plant's afternoon shift would be coming in with their checks. Even owners of the smaller bars said they had extra cash on hand on payday nights to take care of their patrons. It was a simple deduction: Somebody was casing these bars and selecting the targets.

Walker knew he needed some luck and some extra men if he was going to crack this case. He talked to his counterparts in Highland Park and Hamtramck. They didn't have any reports of holdups by cartoon characters, so Walker knew he wasn't going to get any help from them. Sergeant Charlie Barnes had a crew do a rough count of the auto industry-related plants around town. Six out of thirteen precincts in Detroit bordered on or housed automotive-related factories.

Walker awoke the morning of September 29th thinking about all the territory his guys had to cover to catch one man. They'd have to get lucky, and he didn't like to depend on luck. He was Scottish. *It's the Irish that are into the shamrocks.*

He climbed into his city-owned Ford, hit the key and left for work. He glanced at the fuel gauge as he stopped at a light on Seven Mile. Walker pulled into the first gas station he saw. He spotted an old friend as he pulled onto the ramp. Jake Bush was gassing up a pickup. "Jake, what the hell're you doing back in town?"

Jake looked up and recognized Stuart Walker from his first stint in Detroit. "Hi there, Stu. Where you working now?"

"Robbery Bureau." Stu looked at Jake who was in uniform. "You back on the job?"

"Yeah. Almost a month now."

"What happened?"

"Long story."

"Where you at?"

"Number Five."

"I'm still living at the same place on Hamburg," Stu said.

"Stop by for a drink some evening."

"I'll be working afternoons."

"Doing what?"

"Working the B&E car." Jake hung up his hose. "Joan still taking care of you?"

"Yeah, still feeding me way too much." Stu patted the stomach that wasn't there. He was still slim and trim. Joan kept him that way.

Jake and Stuart Walker walked inside and paid for their gas, then went their separate ways. Stu headed for 1300 Beaubien and Jake towards Jefferson and St. Jean.

Jake first met Stuart Walker when they were both patrolmen. Stu worked at Number Fifteen, and Jake at Number Thirteen. They had a common interest—English setters. When Stuart made detective, he was assigned to Number Thirteen. Jake saw Stu often at work when they both worked there; Stu with the station dicks, as they were called, and Jake in uniform. It had been at least six years since Jake last saw Stu.

———

That chance meeting with Jake had Detective Lieutenant Walker thinking. By week's end he had twelve patrolmen, all assigned to different precinct B&E Car crews drinking coffee with his own men, and twelve additional detectives brought in from six other precincts. Walker's plan was simple: Between his own detectives, the other precinct dicks and the plain-clothes officers, they might be able to snag the "Disney Bandit." Jess Scott and Jake Bush were among the men crowding the robbery bureau room.

Ideas were bandied about: Men in the back room with shotguns, or men playing bar patrons, waiting for the crime to happen and then take the guy down. Simple enough.

Stuart Walker threw out his own idea. "I only have you guys on a limited basis. I think we are dealing with someone who takes his time and picks a target, so I want to use you just one day a week. We've got a list of the bars with the most potential. Charlie Barnes already did the legwork on that. We'll eliminate the four that were already hit—for now."

"You know, it might be a beer truck driver," Patrolman Lameroux chimed in as he poured himself a cup of coffee. "Anybody check the drivers out?"

"Not a bad idea," Walker added. "Already done. There's no one driver delivering to all of the bars that have been hit, so we don't see a connection."

Before anyone else could drag out what he hoped would be a short meeting, Lieutenant Walker said, "Rather than spend a lot of time guessing, I want to cover as many bars as we can for about four hours on a few Friday nights. You'll work with your regular partner. Your job will be to keep your eyes open for anyone who looks like they're casing the place. This guy knows where everything is, and what time to do the job. There's a slim chance we're dealing with a guy who pops in, looks the joint over, then comes back with a mask an hour later. That's always a possibility. It's more likely that this guy would be casing the bar one week and hit it the next. I'm trying to eliminate the guess work. Charlie's got a list of bars with factories nearby and the times the workers at the plants change shifts. So far, all the robberies took place between 11:30 and 11:45 p.m. before those getting off the afternoon shift come in. If we have teams inside eighteen bars between nine o'clock and one on a payday night, maybe we can stumble across a guy casing the joint."

"And what do we bust him for? Being nosey?" a voice rang out.

Barnes shot back, "This ain't no rookie. Maybe if you see something, you can pick the guy out of the couple a thousand mug shots we have on file. We're looking for something to grab onto. Right now we don't have squat."

Walker interrupted, "Or better yet, you might just be there when a bar gets hit."

The thirty-six cops looked around, talked to their partners, and a few questions came up. Walker and Barnes fielded them. Then Walker said, "I got your bosses to commit to four Fridays. Hopefully we'll have our man by then."

"Whose buyin' the beer?" asked Lameroux.

"Buy your own, asshole. If I buy, it'll be soda pop," quipped Barnes.

The final plan was that each pair of officers would call Sergeant Barnes for their assignment by noon the next Friday. Everyone would be working a bar outside of their own precinct—hopefully to keep from being recognized as cops. Each pair would watch and wait for four hours, then call it a night. Walker stressed that there'd be no suits and no fedoras. "Look like a beer-drinking factory worker. Not like a cop."

"Moe, you'd fit in. Fat and—"

Barnes butted in. "Enough of the bullshit. I'd suggest that you don't even let the bartenders know we're doing this. Whoever's pulling these jobs is pretty slick. We don't want to tip our hand."

Walker closed the meeting telling them to see Barnes and give him their home phone numbers. Jess went straight to where Barnes was seated. Jake followed. Jess spoke. "Give us a bar in Number Seven that's high on your priority list."

"Anxious?" asked Barnes.

"No. Just want to check it out beforehand. I like to know where I'm operating."

Barnes ran his finger down the list. "Stan's. Farnsworth and Joseph Campau, near the Dodge Truck Plant. Names?"

"Scott and Bush. Five's B&E Car."

―――――

That night Jess stopped by Stan's Bar while they were working their normal seven in the evening until three in the morning shift. He told Jake it was time to "check the lay of the land." He did that the next night too. On the second night the bartender struck up a conversation with Jess. "You guys are new around here." He put a drink in front of each. The bartender knew from the night before that the one who looked like a Detroit Lions middle linebacker drank Blatz, the other, Vernors Ginger Ale on ice, in a glass, no straw.

Jess nodded. "Yeah, we're looking for a quiet place to shoot the shit."

"It'll be quiet for about an hour. The midnight shift'll be in shortly to tip a few before work. When they leave the afternoon shift will be busting in the doors."

"Name's Jess. This is Jake."

The bartender grabbed the five that Jess held out. "I run a nice place. Not too rowdy, 'cept on payday night."

"Fights?" Jess asked.

"No. Just too much money in their pockets and a lotta beer drinking. Some hot pool games maybe."

The two stops by Jess and Jake had Lenny, the bartender, peg them as two guys staying out of their wife's hair for an hour or two.

―――――

The next Friday night Jake and Jess were sitting at a small round table in a corner near the wall. It was the third night they slipped into the bar. This time they were on the clock for four hours, working for Lieutenant Stuart Walker. It was payday night.

———

Joe's eyes panned the room as he sat at Stan's Bar. *So I screw the working stiffs. So what?* He knew the workers at the Dodge Truck plant liked Stan's. It was walking distance from the main gate. *They can't wait to cash their pissy-assed assembly line checks and have a beer.* Joe's eyes focused on where the bartender retrieved the cash box when he cashed a check.

At least fifty people were crammed in the place. Some took a stool at the bar, some were playing pool and some just grabbed a beer at the bar and went to a table to join friends. All came in to cash their checks. *Yep, there he goes again.*

Joe watched as the black metal box was pulled out and the barkeep counted out some twenties, a ten and two fives after taking the check from the customer in front of him.

"Take out for three Stroh's, Lenny," the guy cashing the check said. The barkeep took out a five and made change from the register. He put the payroll check into the bottom of the tin box under the stack of cash. Lenny put the cash box away.

The man who cashed his check pocketed the bills, grabbed the bottles of beer and found an empty table. Two more guys came in, spotted their friend, waved and went to the bar. They cashed their checks before joining their comrade and grabbing one of the beers on the table. "Stroh's? D'you always drink that cheap shit Wally?" one of them said. Cheap or not, they chugged down a few swallows before sitting.

Joe always came in before the afternoon shift-workers flooded the taverns on a payday night. He wanted to get a good stool at the bar so he could view the action. He always chose bars close to the car plants sprinkled around Detroit and Hamtramck. Joe figured these would be the most productive. He was right. His four previous hits netted him $52,000.

When casing a place, Joe always made sure he wore nondescript clothes—maybe a plain sweatshirt and jeans, maybe a denim jacket. He liked sitting near the end of the bar. He could see all he needed from there. He kept to himself, having a cigarette or two, but this time sipping a Black Label beer. He always ordered something different on each job. Joe's goal was not to set any patterns. He looked like any normal worker, having a beer before heading home from work.

———

Jake Bush thought he recognized a guy who took a seat at the far end of the bar, but didn't know from where. It was just a lone guy who was drinking a Black Label beer. Jake kept his eye on him.

Jess mentioned one guy who came in alone that did not look like a factory worker. A woman shortly joined him in a back booth. When the woman started running her hand up and down the man's thigh. Jess picked someone else to watch.

———

The bartender came up to Joe, "Another Black Label?"

Joe put a five on the bar. "Yeah, one more. Save my spot, I'm goin' to the can." Joe went down the hallway towards the back door and the johns. He knew he had to hang around to make sure Lenny kept the cash box in the same place. Joe laughed to himself, knowing what Lenny didn't realize was next payday, he'd be back wearing a mask, the last one of the five he had picked up at a Halloween store. He chose five masks, again, so the cops had nothing to go on. *Time to get a new batch.* Joe smiled at his own ingenuity for shopping at a mall just outside of Flint, Michigan, an hour-and-a-half north of Detroit.

Jake thought his man was leaving until he saw Lenny put down another bottle of Black Label. His man came back and lit another cigarette. *Where do I know him from?* Jake thought for a minute. *Did I ever bust this guy?* When Jake saw his man return, he nudged Jess on the elbow. "Partner, check the guy out at the end of the bar."

Joe knew that most of Stan's patrons had a beer or two then left for home. Some hung around to play a game of eight ball. It had been a month since his last job. He had been working midnights and that interfered with what he'd rather be doing—planning his next hit. Only one of his days off for the month fell when the auto workers got paid. *No hit and run jobs*, he told himself. He knew he had to case a job right. Careful planning and no shortcuts were important in his line of work. Joe drove around during the daytime, listing targets based on the traffic patterns of the plant workers and the bars they frequented. Most of the workers left their cars in the plant's parking lot and just walked the half block or so to a bar. That's how he chose Stan's. *The stupid bastards all hit the same watering trough even when they finally got to the day shift.* They had patterns. Joe prided himself on not having any.

Lenny started popping tops and filling glasses from the beer on tap, taking just a minute to cash a few checks from the black metal box he kept behind a small cherry-wood refrigerator door under the cash register. Joe watched for a half hour. The box always went back behind that one door. *Perfect,* he thought. Joe's last two hits were on the west side; *it's time for an east side contribution.*

Joe pocketed his cigarette butts from the ashtray, casually dropping them into the blue denim jacket pocket. No one seemed to pay any attention as Joe wiped down the brown Black Label bottle with a bar napkin. *No prints, no traces.* That was his goal since he started his moonlighting venture. He looked like any normal worker, having a beer before heading home. Joe left Stan's by the back door to the alley, counting the steps to where he parked his car on Farnsworth.

"I know him from somewhere," Jake said as they watched the man disappear down the hallway.

Jess took his second swallow of Blatz. "You say you've seen him before?"

"Pretty damn sure. He's slick. Took his butts with him."

Jess grunted and took another swallow of his flat beer. "I think we just saw the Disney Bandit. Tomorrow we'll start looking at mug shots with the dicks at Robbery. Maybe you'll remember where you've seen him."

An hour later Jake and Jess left Stan's. "What time do you want to get together and go downtown?" Jake asked.

"Meet me at the station at eight."

"It's Saturday. Someone going to be there?"

"I'll call Barnes. He gave me his home number."

Jake woke with a start the next morning. He placed the face. "Fuckin' asshole," he muttered under his breath. It was only 6:30. He had time for coffee and plenty of time to think. An hour later, he tucked his Smith & Wesson into his hideaway holster and went to meet his partner. A half hour later Jess was sliding into his truck.

"Well, did you figure out where you remember the guy from?" Jess asked. No hello. Nothing. Right to the business at hand.

"I think so. We'll know more in a bit." Jake drove to Police Headquarters.

"You gonna tell me?"

"Later. After we look at some mug shots."

Jess, not one for long conversations, let it go at that. Because he was sure the guy wiping the bottles off and pocketing the butts was their man. *Just need to catch him at it.* Jess smiled, knowing it was just a matter of time—*maybe next Friday at Stan's.*

———

Lieutenant Walker was just shedding his gray sport coat when Jess and Jake knocked on his office door. Barnes had called Walker and told him one of their crews had a lead.

Jake gave Jess a nudge. "Let the boss know what we saw last night, while I go talk to Barnes." Jake retreated from the doorway.

Fifteen minutes later, Jake came in balancing three coffees. "Barnes said you take yours black, Lieu."

"Yeah, thanks. Your partner says you think you recognized a guy last night. Remember who he is?"

Before Jake could answer, Barnes knocked on the jamb of the open door. He had a thick twelve by eighteen photo binder under his arm. Barnes put it down on Walkers desk.

Jake leaned forward and flipped it open. "Let's first let Jess see if he can pick out the guy we saw."

Jess dragged his index finger over the eighteen pictures on the first page, grunted, then turned to the next. Barnes and Walker sipped their coffees. Jake hung over Jess' shoulder, glancing at the pictures between sips. On the third page Jess stopped. He tapped one picture at the bottom of the page. "This one."

Jake took a closer look. "Yep, that's him."

———

The days slowly dragged by. Then, on Friday night, ten minutes before the shift workers would punch out at the

Dodge Plant, in the alley behind Stan's, Joe slipped on a *Goofy* mask, rubber gloves and pulled out his .38 caliber Colt from his worn work-jacket pocket. He slipped in the back screen door, latching the hook on it to keep out any interruptions, walked past the restrooms, storeroom and straight to the end of the bar. From there he could see the entire barroom and front door. There were two customers sitting at the bar. Lenny was wiping down some glasses.

The bartender glanced up at the movement to his left. Joe lifted the .38 towards Lenny and said, "Don't get stupid. Get the cash box out." Joe knew the mask would muffle his voice. No one could see the smile on his face under Goofy's nose. Lenny hesitated. "From the little door under the register," Joe barked. Lenny pulled out the cash box and slid it down the bar. Joe grabbed it and bobbed the gun barrel towards Lenny, and then at the two people at the bar. "On the floor. Don't move for ten minutes and you'll live to talk about it."

Joe backed down the hallway to the latched screen door. He reached behind and slid off the hook glancing into the dark alley before walking out. He slowly closed the screen door, walked the twenty-five steps to the side street, took a right for a half block and slipped into a gray Ford Fairlane. Joe had taken the dome light bulb out to keep him in total darkness when he opened the car door. He pulled off the mask, cranked the engine and drove off into the night. *Another perfect crime.* At the next corner he turned on his headlights, made a left turn and headed home.

At his kitchen sink, Joe cut the mask and the rubber gloves into little strips and put them into a sandwich bag for a deposit the following morning in the dumpster at work. He laughed to himself. *Who'd check for evidence there? Another one of my ingenious moves.* Only then did he open the black box and count his take.

———

At seven the next morning Joe pulled into the parking lot after a short detour via Belle Isle, parked, grabbed the small bag, strolled by the dumpster and made a deposit. He jogged up the back stairs and into the roll-call room. Some guys were playing pool, some Ping-Pong. He sat near a card table and watched a couple of hands of a euchre game.

Joe felt some movement around him. He looked up into the eyes of Lieutenant Rose. Men in suits were to his left and right. The lieutenant spoke. "Patrolman Joseph Herbert, you are under arrest. You have the right to remain silent—"

The rest of the words faded into the background. One suit removed the pistol from Joe's holster; the other moved Joe's arms behind his back and snapped on a pair of cuffs.

How in the hell?

They led him out of the squad room and down to the front desk at the Thirteenth Precinct. The men in suits were Detective Lieutenant Stuart Walker and Detective Sergeant Charles Barnes.

———

It was Saturday night in the city. The Fifth Precinct B&E car slowly drove east on Warren in the curb lane with their lights out. Jake learned it from Jess. It was Jess's preferred way to drive after dark. "So how come you didn't tell me who the guy was?"

"I wasn't real sure myself. I wanted you to pick out the picture."

"You weren't sure?"

"No, it had been about seven years since I last saw him."

"Still could've said something."

"You said a long time ago I talked too much."

"Touché." Jesse's head turned to the right. "See the guy in the alley?"

"No." Jake swiveled his head. "Now I do."

"Make a U turn and let's see what he's up to."

———

The week before Joe Herbert's arrest, after Jess and Jake had identified the photo Sergeant Barnes placed in the binder of mug shots, Walker and Barnes had decided that it would be best to put a three-car, twenty-four hour tail on Joe Herbert and to let the job go down. Walker wanted all the evidence— the mask, the gloves and the cash box. He wanted to make the arrest this way instead of chancing any gun play in the alley as Joe left the bar.

"I don't like it," Jake said.

"Jake and I can be in the bar—"

Walker cut him off. "He's not going anywhere, except to jail. I want this case gift wrapped. No loose ends."

Walker was right. A search warrant for Herbert's house revealed a stash of cash. A Detroit Police dive team found two of five tin cash boxes in the muck under the Belle Isle Bridge, all weighted down with a single reddish brick that matched a few leftover in Joe's yard. A lunch bag with strips of a Goofy mask and rubber gloves was retrieved from the dumpster in the Thirteenth Precinct parking lot. The bag had Joe's prints on it. What Walker never told Jake and Jess was that the two guys at the bar were his—*Just in case.*

One almost forgotten fact was the newspapers never got wind of the arrest of a Detroit police officer until a week later. It was old news and warranted just a short, one-column-wide blurb on page three of *The Detroit News*, and on page two in *The Free Press*. Walker didn't need to see blaring headlines on a cop being arrested.

Chapter Four

John and Nancy Licavoli, with their teenage son, John Jr., were leaving Saint Jude's Catholic Church after the eight o'clock Sunday mass. For the first time in two weeks the sun was shining. So far, November of 1971 had been gray and dismal, and the weatherman was even talking about the possibility of snow by Monday. As they climbed into their 1961 DeSoto four-door hard top, John heard a voice. "Johnnie, gotta minute?" John stood, looking for the man calling him.

He spotted a figure from years ago walking between cars, a broad, used car salesman's smile under a trim mustache with dark hair combed straight back topping off his thick eyebrows and dark eyes. It was Johnnie's cousin. "Yeah Vinnie, long time no see."

"Still running that tool and die shop off a Warren?"

"Still there." John had not seen his cousin Vincenzo Giacchina in at least five years. He was especially surprised to see him at Saint Jude's. John knew Vinnie and churches didn't mix. Oh, he was Catholic all right, but after his confirmation he'd taken to the streets rather than a church pew.

"How about I drop by and talk tomorrow?"

"Sure. I'm there at seven."

"I'll bring the donuts. Have some coffee on."

"See you then," John said.

John dropped in behind the wheel, turned the key, flipped the park lever and punched the Drive button. He started out of the church lot. "Your cousin Vinnie?" Nancy asked.

"Yeah." John turned onto Seven Mile, heading home.

"Wonder what he wants?"

"Probably a loan. I'll know in the morning."

"Stay clear of him, Johnny. He's no good," Nancy added as she opened the church bulletin and scanned it.

"Who's Vinnie, dad?" John Jr., better known as Packy, asked from the back seat.

"My cousin," answered his dad. "No one you really want to know."

———

John, baptized Giovanni, Licavoli had opened Precision Tool and Die the year before his son was born. He did a lot of small jobs for the auto industry, mainly Chrysler and Dodge. He made a decent living and had fifteen guys working the floor for him for the past ten years.

John had distanced himself from his cousin Vinnie when they were teenagers. Vincent Giacchina had chosen another way to make a living. He started running numbers when he was about fifteen, working for one of the mafia families who controlled things on the east side of Detroit.

Good contracts started trickling in to John's tool and die business once the *Big Four* automakers saw the work he put out. John added on to his shop twice in ten years. The last was a warehouse to handle the increase in his business. He even bought a used Clark fork truck to move some of the heavy stuff.

While Johnny's business took off, Vinnie had been moving up in the ranks, too. He became the muscle for the east side *Family*. Twice, Vinnie had to use more than muscle, nothing that a well-placed .38 slug couldn't fix. Both times it took weeks for anyone to file a "Missing Persons" report with the police. By that time, no one knew where to start to look for Charlie Manetta and Bennie Santina. Vinnie was the only one who knew what was in the duct taped and weighted packages he'd dropped into the shipping channel that wound around Harsens Island. Vinnie cleaned up after himself.

Vinnie had gotten tripped up by a charge of felonious assault that neither he nor the *Family* could buy his way out of. A cop had witnessed Vinnnie swinging a hunk of pipe at a guy who'd been a little slow on paying off his gambling debts. That piece of pipe earned Vinnie five to ten years at the Jackson State Penitentiary when he was sentenced at Detroit Recorders Court. He hadn't been worried about doing some time. Word had already reached the prison long before the gray bus with barred windows arrived at the prison that Vincent Giacchina was connected—well connected. His grandfather on his father's side was *The Don* of Detroit. For sure, nobody fucked with Vinnie.

Vincent made good use of his tour at *Jacktown*, as the prison was known. Of course it was nothing close to the real purpose of time in jail—something called rehabilitation. What he'd learned was equal to a four-year degree from the University of Michigan. Maybe better. He never had to crack a book or attend a class. Prisons are that way. He learned who the right contacts were and a way to increase the *Family's* profits in the Detroit drug trade.

Word got back to Grandpa Tony from Vincent through his attorney that there was a new distribution route from Mexico available to points in Arizona, Texas and New Mexico. All a man with enough cash had to do is go pick it up.

The *Don*, Anthony Giacchina, or better known as Tony G, saw this news as a way to increase his supplies of marijuana, cocaine and heroin while putting an end to the inflated prices emanating from the New York families. Naturally, Tony G tapped Vincent to oversee the construction of the delivery system from Mexico to Detroit once Vinnie got an early parole, all neatly arranged. There was millions to be made—

maybe billions. Tony G didn't hesitate buying the right people.

That's what prompted Vincent's interest in Cousin Johnny's shop. His plan was simple: An underling would steal a certain type of car, drive it to a safe garage and put a good license plate on it, not one that would be reported stolen. Vincent would then find a *mule*, someone who did not even know the purpose of the road trip, to drive the vehicle to southern Arizona or New Mexico, drop it at a specified location, eat bon-bons for a couple of hours, then return the vehicle back to Detroit. It was a simple and fool-proof plan in Vinnie's eyes. At the yet-to-be-determined safe garage, the cargo would be unloaded and the car, like a disposable cigarette lighter, would just become part of the trash found along any alley in Detroit.

"I want to rent the use of your warehouse for a while," Vinnie said as he put a white bag down next to the coffee pot. "I brought some fresh cannolis."

John was pouring two cups of coffee when Vinnie's question stopped him cold. "What do you mean, 'use my warehouse?'"

"I need a place to do some quick work. A new enterprise."

"I use it. There's no room for anything else."

"I'm talking at night. We won't take up any space."

"Vinnie, I don't know what you're into," John said, raising his hand to fend off an answer. "And I don't want to know. The answer is no."

"Giovanni, we're family. Think about it for a while. All we want to do is rent some space. Two Franklins a week."

"There's no thinking. I run a legitimate business." John dumped both cups of coffee into the small lunchroom sink. That was his signal the meeting was over.

The Saturday morning ritual at John Licavoli's house was to back his pristine '61 DeSoto out of the two-car garage, if it wasn't raining, wash and wax it, and put it back for his family's Sunday morning trip to church for eight o'clock mass. John checked the weather. It was a good day to wash and wax the car. He flicked on the light as he went into the garage to lift open the overhead wooden door. The first thing he saw, as the daylight caught the back of the pure black four-door hardtop, was shards of broken glass. He had two broken taillight lenses. *How in the hell?* He walked around to the driver's side, his eyes were drawn to the deep scratch in both doors on that side. When he got to the front of the car, he saw that both headlights were broken. The passenger's side had a deep scratch as well. John's heart sank. His '61 DeSoto was one of the last cars off the line when Chrysler decided to shut down its production at the end of 1960. A DeSoto was the first car he remembered his father driving. John's DeSoto was his way of honoring his father—an Italian immigrant who'd died of a heart attack while working at the Chrysler metal casting plant seventeen years before.

John slowly swept the garage floor, wondering how anyone could get in without leaving a mark, and then, to do this to his pride and joy. *Why?*

On Sunday, John drove his family to church in their 1972 Chrysler Town and Country station wagon. The next day John called a collision shop from his desk as soon as he opened the shop. He made arrangements to have the DeSoto picked up. Minutes later, his phone rang. "Precision Tool and Die," he answered automatically on the second ring.

"How come you didn't drive your black beauty to church yesterday?" It was Vinnie's voice.

"It was you, you son-of-a-bitch—

"Now, now, Johnny. Is that any way to talk to a concerned cousin?"

"You stay away from my house, from my cars."

There was a slight pause, then, "How's that son of yours? What do you call him? Packy?"

A cold chill went up John's spine.

"I'll stop by the shop this afternoon. A cuppa coffee would be nice."

John hung up the phone. His face fell into his hands.

Precision Tool & Die's warehouse became that safe garage Vinnie had been looking for. That afternoon John gave Vinnie a key to the warehouse. Johnny's DeSoto was returned the next week. The tow truck driver said the bill was paid in full.

John Licavoli started finding an envelope of cash addressed to him on his desk every Monday morning. He didn't know what Vinnie did in the warehouse and wasn't going to ask. It was always as he'd left it when he locked the place the Friday before. He opened a separate account at The Detroit Bank and Trust. He didn't plan on using the money.

———

Jess caught a plate number as a Chevrolet Impala was heading the opposite way on Warren—nothing on it. "Grab a U-turn," he said. Jake immediately made the maneuver and gunned the '69 Chrysler. "The blue Chev a block up," Jess added.

Jake saw the taillights on the Chev turning right on Cadieux. He made the same turn seconds later. There was no traffic ahead. No taillights. Nothing.

Jake stopped at the next corner and looked left while Jess looked right on Cornwall. Nothing was moving. "What the hell? Where did it go?" Jake asked. There was no answer from Jess. Jake circled the block, then made a wider circle. They kept looking, driving in wider circles.

"That's the third car that's vanished on us this month," Jake said twenty minutes later.

Jess just grunted a response. He was driving when they lost the other two cars they wanted to check. All three just disappeared. All were Chevys. They were just going to do a quick street investigation. There was nothing on their *Hot Sheet*, but they always found a reason to stop a car. A broken tail light, no light over the rear plate—all good reasons to make a stop and talk to the driver. Or, they'd make something up. You never know what you'll find when you dig a little.

———

Jess and Jake started two hours earlier than their normal shift the day after the last car had disappeared on them. It was cloudy and a light rain sprinkled down as Jess drove. "We need some daylight, if you call this daylight," Jess said. Jake agreed. Jess went straight towards Warren and headed east. "We're missing something." He drove slowly, just looking.

Jake was stymied too. Cars didn't vanish on them. They were that good. Five Twenty-five normally caught what they went after. Now they were stumped.

Jess turned left then right. The first street, New York, was a dead end. According to Jess, Detroit named its shortest street after the Big Apple just for spite. He took an alley heading south, then took the next left and ended up facing a loading ramp at the back of a small factory warehouse. He backtracked, went around the block and ended up in front of Precision Tool and Die at Neff and Munich. The shop was a one-story red brick building facing Neff. To the north was the slightly taller, attached warehouse Jess had stopped behind just minutes before. He parked. "Humph!"

"You thinking what I'm thinking?" Jake asked.

"Probably. The last car, the Blue Impala. We lost it just a couple of turns from here. A left turn, then a quick right and another left would've put it at that warehouse's door and out of our sight. We lost the other two close to here too." Jake just nodded in agreement. "There's something going on in there." Jess put the car in drive, slowly going north on Neff to Warren and made a right turn. He drove south on Herford looking down every alley. For two hours he drove streets and alleys before he spoke again. "That warehouse is the only place that could swallow up a car in a hurry."

––––––––

Vinnie had been involved with his new venture for two months. It took eight days to turn a car around from being stolen off a Detroit street to being ditched in an alley somewhere else. There were two cars that were suited for Vincent's use—the Chevrolet Impala and the Caprice, 1970 through the new 1972s that just hit the showrooms. Their frames were the same. Either model would hold the sealed square black plastic container in front of the gas tank, neatly banded with packing metal straps to the frame. To the naked eye looking under the car, the plastic box with a bit of dirt caked to it looked like it was part of the gas tank. It contained the shipment of the product ordered. Name your poison— Coke, H, or Mary Jane.

The tool and die warehouse was used to pull the plate off a newly-snatched Chevrolet before it took a road trip. When it returned, the *mule* drove to the warehouse after making a phone call—always after dark. The cargo was unloaded with four snips to cut the bands. Vinnie didn't even have to use the fork lift his cousin had in the warehouse. A creeper worked just as good and was noiseless.

Any trash or goods were loaded into an extended GMC Handi-Van Vincent had painted to represent a legitimate business: VHA Enterprises, Inner City Package Delivery. He even put a phone number under the name. The Chevy was then dumped in a distant alley minus one of the ten license plates that Vincent had registered in names taken off tombstones at Mt. Olivet Cemetery. A *Family*-owned used car lot took care of the paperwork with the Secretary of State.

Almost two weeks later, Jake and Jess were cruising the alley on the north side of the businesses on Mack near Belvidere. They were looking for burglars or anything that moved after dark. A blue Impala was tucked close to a telephone pole, backed in. Jake checked one side, flashing his three-cell into the windows. "No plate," he heard Jess saying from the back of the car. It wasn't locked. Jake found the VIN and jotted it down. He made a call to East Side Radio.

"Five-Two-Five, that's a stolen 1972 Chevrolet," was the reply from the radio operator five minutes later.

"Looks like the one we lost a couple of weeks ago," Jess said.

A tow truck took the Impala to the Fifth Precinct garage. The Auto Recovery Squad was notified. They came out and dusted it for prints. It came up showroom clean. Jake added a note to their report to contact him at Number Five once the owner was located.

Two days later Jake had the name and phone number of the owner. He called him. "Mr. Rancourt, this is Patrolman Jake Bush from Number Five. Did you find anything wrong with your car other than a lost license plate?"

"No, just a ton of miles on it."

"Like what?" asked Jake.

"Almost 5,000 miles."

"You sure?"

"Had the oil changed the day before it was taken. Wanna come by and take a look?"

"What's your address, sir?"

Jess and Jake made a quick trip to 20231 Barlow in the Fifteenth Precinct. Bill Rancourt said he might have put twenty miles on the car after the oil change. Jess did the math. The Impala had 4,832 miles put on it since the service work.

———

Jess and Jake were sitting in the Auto Squad early the next morning. They were thumbing through the stolen car reports, listing where they were taken from, when and where they were recovered. Usually a car is stolen one day and dumped the next. Joy rides, burglaries and stickups were the primary reason for stealing a car—unless it was destined for a chop shop. Then it'd never be seen again. Five Twenty-five was looking for cars that had been gone a week or more.

Jake and Jess found four cars taken and then recovered empty that were off the map for a week or more. They noted the names and addresses of the owners. Jake and Jess went to talk to them. Two were on the west side of Detroit; a bit out of their territory.

There was something these owners hadn't noticed; the added miles on the odometer until Jess started asking. All had at least 4,500 miles added while they'd been missing. Three of the cars were Chevy Caprices, the other was an Impala. Three 1970 models, one a '71. All had been recovered without a plate.

Two nights later Jess found Jake in the teletype room talking to Sergeant Fox. "I was just asking about the lack of activity on your log sheets the last few nights," said Fox.

Jess, being the senior man on the crew, told the sergeant what they'd been working on, explaining their trips to the auto squad and what they found out. Fox listened intently. "What do you think?" asked Fox.

"Running guns? Dope?" Jake said. "Those models have big trunks. A couple of bodies could fit in one and there'd still be room for more."

Fox asked where the tool and die shop was. Jess told him. "Let me see if there's a home around there where we can set up a stake-out. If we went in the shop to look around, they'd just move." Fox turned to walk out, stopped and said over his shoulder, "Run with it, guys. But put something down on paper and I'll feed it to the boss. He's getting used to you two making some arrests. It'll put his mind at ease."

Jess said he'd have his "secretary" put something together. He looked at Jake when he said that. Jake took note of the smirk on his partner's face.

There were days Jake regretted taking typing at Notre Dame High in nearby Harper Woods; then again, he didn't. Making out reports in long hand was a bitch. Jake and Jess knew that. Early on, Jake realized Jess was a two-finger pecker. Jake took over typing the reports.

They'd been setting their own hours of late far exceeding a normal forty-hour work week. Mentally, Jake never punched out. He doubted that Jess did either.

Two days later Fox left a note for the crew of Five Twenty-five. A house two doors down the alley from Precision Tool and Die was vacant and up for sale. On the note was the address of a place on Woodhall and the phone number of the real estate company. Jess called the Real Estate One office and set it up for an agent to meet them.

The house was perfect. The back faced the alley behind the tool and die shop. It was a story-and-a-half with an attic window about 150 feet from the warehouse door. They got a set of keys. That night Five Twenty-five's blue Chrysler filled the empty garage and Jess and Jake were sitting on a couple of folding chairs staring out into the night at the warehouse door. A light rain was falling, just enough to make the vacant house damp and about fifty degrees. Winter was closing in. A single overhead light in the alley gave them all the light they needed.

Three nights into sitting on uncomfortable chairs and a couple of full thermoses of coffee drained, a set of headlights stopped in front of the warehouse door. It was a van with some writing on the side. The warehouse door slid open, the van entered and the door slid shut. Fifteen minutes later a dark Chevrolet Impala's lights were shining at the warehouse door. Again the door slid to the side and the Chevy drove in.

Jess looked at Jake saying, "I'm going downstairs and take a peek. Keep an eye on the place," and disappeared down the stairwell.

Jake heard the faint snick of the downstairs door latch. Jake watched for movement at the warehouse. Five minutes later the Impala was backing out of the warehouse and the door was closed. Five more minutes passed and the van pulled out. The driver of the van locked the warehouse door and drove into the night.

Jess's voice came up the stairwell. "Let's go partner." Jake never even heard the door open. Jess, all 250 pounds of him, was like a cat. Jake folded up the chairs and joined his partner. Jess was behind the wheel waiting. He backed their Chrysler out of the driveway, heading to Number Five. "Got a name and a phone number off the van. A plate number off the Impala," Jess said.

Jake checked the *Detroit Yellow Pages* for VHA Enterprises, Inner City Package Delivery. There was no listing for it. He dialed the number Jess had gotten off of the van. An operator's voice came on the line saying there was no such number in service. Jake dialed for directory assistance, asking for a number for "VHA Enterprises," then for "Inner City Package Delivery." He drew a blank on both.

The next day they were in the main office of The Secretary of State on West Grand Boulevard. Their badges got them the name the Impala's plate was registered to: John Yetkevich, at 4420 Chalmers in Detroit on a 1969 Chevrolet Chevelle.

Back at the station Jake looked up the number and called. "Can I speak to Mr. Yetkevich, please?" The female voice on the other end of the line asked who was calling. "Patrolman Jake Bush, Detroit Police Department." Jake jotted notes as he listened. "Ma'am, are you driving a 1969 Chevrolet registered in your husband's name?" He listened, then ended the call. "Thanks for your help, ma'am. Sorry about your husband's passing.

Jess looked up from the copy of the morning's Free Press. "And?"

"The guy died two years ago. He was a Ford man. She doesn't drive."

"Did the Secretary of State say when that plate was registered on the Chevelle?"

"Five months ago."

That night, Jake and Jess were sipping coffee and sitting on folding metal chairs upstairs at the Woodhall house. "Might not be anything going on for a few days," Jake said. Jess just grunted. An hour later a van's headlights were aimed at the warehouse door. Jake stood, knowing it was his turn to get a closer look. He slipped down the stairs and out into the night.

Jake watched as the door slid closed on the van. Fifteen minutes later a light colored Chevrolet Caprice was nosed against the door. It opened, swallowed the Chevy and closed.

In ten minutes the Caprice came out and the van followed. The driver of the van got out and secured the door behind him. Both vehicles were off into the night.

Jess joined Jake. "Get a plate number?"

"Yep." They got into their Chrysler and left.

———

The next morning they were in the Secretary of State's Office. Badges weren't necessary this time. Mrs. Abigail Schmerin recognized them. A call to Lansing got them the information on the plate number. At their precinct Jake made a call after finding the name in the phone book. He had the same results, only the husband had been dead for three years this time. Jess heard Jake's "thank you ma'am" as he hung up the phone. This plate was registered on a Chevrolet Impala, a 1970 model.

"You know you're doing a hell of a job as my secretary," Jess said, with a half-smile on his face. "Making all the phone calls, the reports to Fox."

"Don't press your luck, Kemo Sabe. The least you can be doing is getting me some coffee while I'm on the phone."

"I'll try to remember that next time."

Jake was surprised he was getting full sentences out of his partner.

———

For the next five nights Jake and Jess were hunched over the attic window until daylight, sipping coffee and eating bagged lunches watching the warehouse. Jake was getting bored. Jess didn't talk much, if at all. Finally the sixth night, just past midnight, a dark Chevrolet Impala pulled up to the door. In seconds a van pulled in behind it. The driver of the van got out and unlocked and pushed the door to the side. Both vehicles entered. Jess was moving when the car first arrived. "Stay put," he said over his shoulder. "Watch 'em."

The door closed behind both vehicles. Three seconds later a pebble hit the window. Jake ran down the steps.

As Jake moved alongside Jess in the alley, Jess spoke. "Same plate number I got a week ago. Time to see what they're up to."

Jake took one side of the closed door, Jess the other. They waited for it to open. "Freeze! Police!" Jake and Jess shouted a half beat from one another as they moved.

A car creeper was spinning on the floor, dropped by a guy in coveralls.

"Kill the engine," Jake ordered the guy with a thin mustache seated behind the wheel of the van. Jake's .357 got immediate attention. Mr. Coveralls stood with his hands raised. The driver of the Impala had his hands up as Jess opened his door.

They seemed to know the drill. In seconds all three were prone on the floor, hands on the back of their heads. Jake covered them while Jess located a wall phone. "This is Five-Two-Five, dispatch. Send a couple of cars to Precision Tool on Neff and Munich, around the back. We've got three to go."

————

Jess and Jake stood looking into the one-way window to Detroit's Narcotics Squad interrogation room. On the other side, Detective Sergeant Victor Hasse was taking a statement from the driver of the Impala, a black guy named Alvin Lavender. Vincent Giacchina was in a holding cell. The third man, the one in the coveralls, Giulio Iacovelli, was in another cell on a different floor.

The pieces came together quickly. The Chevy driver, Alvin Lavender, was just that, hired to drive to Sierra Vista, Arizona, to a grocery store and make a call. After an hour eating two apples in a Fry's Super Market lot, he drove the Impala back to the warehouse in Detroit. He had been promised $500 for his time. Not a bad take for a week's work. He said he had been given $200 up front for gas and motels. Anything left was a bonus.

"I don't know nothing about any drugs," Alvin said. "I just took a job driving to Arizona and back, and two phone numbers to call."

Giulio Iacovelli wasn't singing. He only spoke Italian. Detective Joseph Tocco from the Robbery Bureau was called in to interview Giulio. Joseph spoke fluent Italian. Guilio was carrying a passport and it showed that he had been in the States for six months. He had a Rome address. The detective got the man talking. Giulio said he was a chauffeur in Rome for fifteen years, and was hired for his driving abilities. The Rome Police did have a sheet on Giulio. Before he started driving for a Cardinal in Rome; he had a few scrapes. He had been arrested for stealing two cars, a BMW and a Mercedes, before he got the job with the Cardinal. A friend of a friend of Vinnie's had recommended hiring Giulio after seeing him drive the streets of Rome. The *Family* paid a bit more than the Catholics did.

Vincent Giacchina kept his mouth shut after asking for a lawyer. Fifteen kilos of heroin were found in the van, along with the metal bands, the creeper, and a pair of tin snips. Arrest warrants for all were issued by Judge Del Rio. Sergeant Hasse got a search warrant for John Licavoli's house and business—the tool and die shop.

As soon as they knocked on Johnny's door and flashed a badge, Johnny started talking. It only took one look from Nancy and the whole story about Vinnie, the DeSoto, and the use of his warehouse came out. "I never knew what he was doing in there, but knowing Vinne, it had to be illegal."

Cousin Vinnie's home was in Grosse Pointe Park. A Detroit Narcotics team sat by his phone while another crew, armed with a search warrant issued to an officer from the Grosse Pointe Park Police Department, turned the place upside down. Three empty plastic containers with a white powder residue and two reels of banding metal were found in the garage and taken in as evidence.

A call came in to Vinnie's house that evening, answered by one of Hasse's men. Another Chevy was coming home. "Meet you there in forty-five minutes," the cop said to the voice on the other end.

The narcotics crew used Vinnie's van to go to the warehouse. The *mule*, Randy Jackson, was arrested. The Caprice he was driving was towed to 1300 Beaubien, Police Headquarters, with the package underneath intact. This was a load of cocaine headed for the streets of Detroit. The Caprice had made a trip to Deming, New Mexico, for its load.

———

The next night Jess and Jake were updating their car board and circular book. Sergeant Fox came in followed by Inspector John Mills. "Got your report on your surveillance and the subsequent arrests," Mills said. "Too many typos." Jake saw a smile on the inspector's face.

"Were there that many?" Jake asked.

"Too many for a secretary, Mills answered.

Jake took a quick look at his partner.

Mills laughed. "Seriously, I just stopped in to say thanks," Mills added. "To both of you. Maybe this'll get us some good press for a change." The inspector shook Jake's and Jess's hand and left.

Fox filled the crew in on John Licavoli being cleared of any connection with his cousin other than trying to protect his family. Jake and Jess made a visit the next morning to Precision Tool and Die. Over coffee in Johnny's office, Jess jotted down two phone numbers and gave them to Johnny.

"Next week, three years, whenever," Jess was saying, "any hint of a threat to you, your family, your business, just call either one of us."

Johnny had his doubts. The mafia had a lot of reach. These two cops didn't. Jake saw the look in Johnny's eyes and said, "A message was quietly delivered to Tony G. He said he didn't know Vinnie was squeezing relatives. You're related to Tony, aren't you?"

"Yeah. A great uncle on my mother's side."

That night Jake and Jess were back on the streets of Number Five, looking for reasons to stop a car. A glance, a taillight out, whatever. It was their job and they took it seriously.

Chapter Five

Fall turned to winter and frozen gray slush covered the rotting elm leaves next to the curbs. Detroit prided itself on its elm trees. Clouds filled the skies. The sun was seldom seen before and after Christmas. That's just the way winter is in Detroit—actually all of Michigan. Jesse's bi-weekly trips to Petoskey had to be put on hold twice due to the blinding blizzards that hit US 27 and I-75 at frequent intervals between West Branch and Gaylord. Both Jess and Jake lived to work. The trips to the precinct, court, the pistol range or the Y didn't need sunshine. The weather didn't slow the crime rate in Detroit either. It just made things a bit more uncomfortable when the thermometer read near the zero mark.

Jake and Jess met for coffee before hitting the gym every now and then. This was one of those times. There wasn't much talk, just two guys biding time, waiting for their next shift. The boss, Sergeant Fox, did not like them working too much overtime. Both had over two hundred hours of comp time on the books. It was Jake's turn to buy at Biff's on East Jefferson while Jess grabbed a booth and cracked open a copy of yesterday's *Detroit News*. As Jake sat down, Jess pointed out an article on page three of the paper. A guy named Vincent Giacchina died at Jackson State Penitentiary in a yard fight. "Guess if you fuck up twice you've lost your protective umbrella," Jess said casually as he took the paper back. It had been just two weeks before they sat in Judge George Crocket's courtroom and listened to Vinnie get fifteen to twenty years in prison for drug trafficking. "He didn't last very long," Jess quipped.

"I heard Tony G collected Desotos." Jake said as he dipped a plain donut in his coffee. "Maybe he took umbrage with Vinnie messin' with one."

"You're reading way too many books, Jake. Umbrage? Where'd that word come from?" Jake just answered with a shrug.

"Ever hear what happened to the Dago from Rome?"

"Forgot to tell you," Jake said. "Deported as an unwanted alien. He's probably driving for another Cardinal. Catholics always give people a second chance. They call it absolution."

James Bannon, the head of STRESS, *Stop The Robberies Enjoy Safe Streets*, called Inspector John Mills three times wanting to recruit Jesse Scott and Jake Bush for his unit. Mills left a note to have his crew stop in early after Bannon's third call.

The inspector went home at five. Jess and Jake showed up at his office fifteen minutes before he was due to leave. Coming in early was no big deal. They had already planned to do some target practice that day. Jess knocked on the door jamb, and he and Jake entered when they saw his arm wave them in. Mills was just hanging up the phone.

"That was Bannon again," he said as he motioned for the guys to take a seat. "He's been calling, asking if my B&E crew would like a move to his unit. I apologize for dragging my feet. He lit his pipe after carefully tamping down the tobacco with the blunt end of a black Bic lighter. "I'm kind of possessive. I don't want to lose any good men, so I sat on the calls. But, after thinking a while, I figured it'd be only fair to see what you two would want." Mills clenched the briar pipe between his teeth and relit it, taking two short puffs. He fell silent.

Jess looked at Jake and got no response. Jess asked, "Can you give us a day or two to think about it?"

"Take as much time as you want," Mills responded. He wasn't in any hurry. It was Bannon who was recruiting.

———

Kercheval and Mack Avenue were quiet. The day's wet snow turned to ice as the mercury dipped below twenty-five, both good reasons to stay home. Jake turned the midnight blue Chrysler onto Warren, hugging the curb at a snail's pace. The ruts in the frozen slush in the curb lane crunched under the weight of the car, popping like discarded Christmas tree bulbs. One dim street light per block lit Five Twenty-Five's way. The only bright spot ahead was the Clark Station two blocks down. Slowly it came into view as Jake steered around an old Ford that had a flat tire and grabbed the curb lane again. The ice balls crunched under the slow roll of their Uniroyal tires, interrupting the otherwise still night. Five Twenty-five's dark color blended in with the dark brick buildings to their right. The activity on the Clark Station ramp came into view, slowly, growing larger as the Chrysler inched forward. There was a red Pontiac at the pumps. The attendant, bundled up in a heavy pea coat and a fur hat with ear flaps, was finishing filling the tank at the back of the car.

Jake slipped the transmission into neutral and let their car glide. There wasn't any traffic, on foot or with wheels. He and Jess silently watched the movement happening to their immediate left front. The man in the fur hat and pea coat, twisted on the gas cap, returned the hose to the pump, and went to the driver's window to collect. The window opening grew as another character came into view from behind the station's small hut, arm thrust forward. The attendant slowly backed away raising his hands. The new guy was keeping his right hand extended as he jerked open the door on the

Pontiac. He reached in, grabbing a handful of hair, dragged a female from behind the wheel. With a twist of his hips he slid into the driver's seat, slamming the door and bringing the motor to life.

Without a word between them, Jake put their Chrysler into drive, the roar of its 318 engine heading straight towards the fishtailing Pontiac that was bumping over the curb, sliding left, then right on the ice. The driver gave it too much gas and the Pontiac did a one-eighty, jumped the curb across the street, teetered, spun to the right and plowed over the sign at the corner of Warren and Crane. The sign post bent enough to lodge under the left front wheel. The drive wheel whined on the frozen slush. The Pontiac wasn't going anywhere.

The driver jumped out and a bullet smashed through Five Twenty-five's windshield as Jess was slipping out his door, leading with his Colt. Jake flipped the Park lever on the Chrysler, the tranny shuddering with a loud clunk, clunk, clunk and the motor died. A dark automatic swung towards Jess and fire erupted from it. Jess's Colt barked once and Jake fired twice. Jess's shot stood the man upright; Jake's magnum tumbled him backwards. Everything went quiet.

Jess kicked the small black automatic further from the prone body, that of a young black man. Jake trotted over to the woman still lying on the ramp. He reached down and helped her up. The attendant grabbed her other arm. "Ma'am, you all right?" Jake asked. Her wide eyes went from the attendant, then back to Jake, not believing what had just happened within the span of no more than fifteen seconds. That's all it had taken.

The attendant finally spoke, his eyes jumping from the body on the ground across the street to the white men with guns. "You guys STRESS?" With all the press they were getting, it was a logical question. That Unit had been involved in a lot of shootings.

"No," Jake answered. "Just your ordinary Fifth Precinct cops."

Jake could see the attendant's eyes go dull. Maybe he thought he'd get his name in the papers with a STRESS shooting taking place on his watch. "Nuts," was his only comment as he let go of the woman's arm and went to ring up her purchase.

Jake helped the gray haired woman to the only stool in the station. The palm on her right hand was bleeding and she had abrasions on both her knees. He pulled out his hanky and dabbed her hand. Frozen tire ruts in the snow will cut skin. He dabbed her knees to see how badly they'd been cut. Her nylons had holes in the knees, the blood was slowly oozing over her dark skin, glistening a bright red under the overhead fluorescent lighting. "I'll get a car to take you to get those cleaned up."

She reached over and patted Jake's hand. "I'll be all right, young man. I just need to get home to my husband."

"No telling what kind of stuff's on the ramp, ma'am, the scrape on the left knee and the cut on your hand is pretty deep. You need to have a doctor clean 'em up."

"That boy that shot at you, is he dead?"

"I'm afraid so, ma'am."

"Not your fault. When he took to using a gun, he was goin' nowhere." She looked down at Jake as he put some pressure on one of her bleeding knees. "In Mississippi this wouldn't be happening."

"What?"

"White police caring for an old black woman. That's where Lucious and I come from." She looked out through the plate glass window to the Pontiac jammed up over the bent sign post. "Our car—" A tear rolled down her left cheek.

"I don't think it's that bad. My partner's probably already called for a tow truck." As he spoke, a red Dodge truck with flashing yellow lights pulled up to the disabled car at the same time two marked Detroit Police cars arrived. The truck had a hook dangling on the back. She smiled as the tow truck moved the Pontiac off of the sign post.

"Please, let us get you to Harper Hospital."

"Can you take me?"

Jake looked at Jess walking over from the corner. "Yes, the hospital is on the way to the station," he lied. The reports could wait. Jess would understand. "Ma'am, got a number where I can call your husband?"

"Please call me Mary." She paused for a moment and then gave Jake her phone number. "Please don't tell him I'm hurt."

"I'll tell him to get his coat, we'll pick him up."

"You can do that?"

"Someone's got to drive your car, right?"

———

An hour later Jake was pulling into a slot alongside the Fifth Precinct garage. Sergeant Fox was waiting for them, pacing back and forth. When he saw their car he threw down the cigarette he was smoking and stamped it out with his foot. "Where in the hell have you two been? The dicks are scrambling all over; the ME needs your report to finish his. You wouldn't answer your radio. Damn you two!"

Jess just looked over at Jake. Jake shrugged his shoulders and smiled. "Doing some PR work, boss. Mrs. Adams needed to have her wounds cleaned up and Lucious needed to drive their car."

"Who the fuck's Lucious?"

"Mr. Adams." Jake looked at his watch. "Can I get to our report? I go off shift in a half hour."

"Good luck on that," Fox said as he was following them to the report room. "You know you guys are on admin leave for five days while they investigate the shooting." It wasn't a question.

"Even if he shot first?" Jess asked.

"Five days off the street. You'll have to report to 1300 at ten. Sixth floor. The shrinks'll be expecting you. And Homicide will want your guns for a ballistic test."

Jake asked, "Did anyone ID the bad guy?"

"J.C. Miller. Age 19. He's got a recent address on Goethe and a record four sheets thick," the sergeant answered.

"Boss, can you have someone put a new windshield in our car while we're gone?"

"I forgot I've got to make a report on that too," Fox said. "Jake, would you mind typing it for me?"

"Get the clerk to do it. I'm only Jess's secretary."

———

Five days later the crew of Five Twenty-five was back in the saddle. Jess was behind the wheel heading southwest on Jefferson. "Give any thoughts on that STRESS offer?"

Jake turned his head to look at his partner. "What do you think?"

"Too much time off just for shooting a guy. Think of what it'd be like if we were involved in all the shootings those guys get into. I was going nuts. My kids are in school, so there was no making a trip north to see them. I'm staying. You can go if you like."

"Guess you're stuck with me then."

Jess smiled, "How about a plate of ribs tonight? You hungry?"

"Yep."

Jess made a U-turn. "The Rainbow all right with you?"

"Ribs any good?"

"The best in Number Five." The street lights on Jefferson glared through the Chrysler's new windshield. Fox did get it replaced.

"Unless you've got a better place in mind?"

"The Rainbow's fine."

Snow started drifting down. It was too cold for a major snowstorm. That's one of the benefits of the sub-zero temps at the end of January. Fact is it even gets too cold for a lot of snow sometimes. Jake waved at the beat cop walking on Jefferson. The guy touched the bill of his hat with his night stick.

Jake was glad he wasn't walking tonight. He remembered pounding a beat in Number Eleven on midnights when it was minus 24. *Everything was closed and no place to warm up 'til Sergeant Sech had some pity on me.*

"Wanna grab that rookie walking and let him warm up?" Jake asked.

Jess made another U-turn. He was probably thinking the same thing.

Chapter Six

The winter seemed to crawl by as Jake and Jess filled their log sheets by finding fifteen abandoned stolen cars and one that was still rolling occupied by three pimply faced white kids heading for some mischief on Belle Isle.

In April their biggest bust was a small-time burglar who didn't realize that fresh snow made for easy tracking from the back of a TV repair shop on Kercheval to a home on Parkview. Then to add insult to injury, the portable Timmy French made off with hadn't even been repaired yet. When Jess and Jake followed the tracks to the house, the guy was banging on the side of the TV, trying to get the picture to come in. "I only wanted to check the weather," Timmy said as Jess snapped on the cuffs.

"One of these days, mister," Jess said with a smile, "you're going to figure out you're not smart enough to be a crook. The white stuff on the ground should have told you snow was in the forecast."

———

Betty Bynum turned eighteen on April 17, 1972. On June 15th she started washing dishes at the Rathskeller, a nice restaurant on John R and Dakota. It was a special day for her. This was her first job and she was going to be making "a whole three dollars and seventy-five cents an hour," she proudly announced. She was all smiles as her "Daddy" kissed her on the cheek and said goodbye when he dropped her off at work.

Betty was christened Elizabeth Jean Bynum at the New Hope Baptist Church two weeks after she was born in 1954. Her mother, Merrianne, was in labor for what seemed like forever, giving birth to the baby girl, but all the pain was forgotten the moment the nurse placed the squirming baby in her mother's arms.

The baby's father, Lorenzo Bynum, said his little caramel-colored Betty was born smiling. At least that is what he told all his friends and neighbors as he wheeled her around their Detroit neighborhood that summer in her pink and white stroller.

As a year and a half went by, Betty seemed a bit slow to crawl, or even attempt saying "Momma" or "Dada," no matter how hard Zo and Merri tried to get her to mouth those loving words. Zo and Merri just thought Betty would catch up as time passed.

She didn't. At age three, the doctors at Children's Hospital finally diagnosed Betty as having been born with what they called "non-syndromic mental retardation."

Betty grew as a normal child and, with special tutoring, learned to talk. She was nearly four before she walked without teetering. But her "Daddy" and "Mommy," as Betty finally learned to pronounce, loved and doted over her with each step she took and each word she mastered.

At age five, further testing by the staff at the University of Michigan Children's Hospital determined that Betty Jean would not fully develop mentally. The doctors didn't say Elizabeth was retarded, but introduced Lorenzo and Merrianne to a new term—that she was a "special needs" child. Thus, Betty did not attend the regular schools as her playmates and cousins did. She went to special schools. As far as Betty knew, she was living a normal happy life. To her, no one was a stranger. Once she met you, she knew you forever. Zo and Merrianne worried about that, but over the years one or both were always with her.

Lorenzo worked midnights at the Chrysler Jefferson Plant. He was a patternmaker. Merrianne got a job when

Elizabeth was six; working as a teacher's aide in the schools that Betty attended. She did this to be near her daughter as much as possible.

At age 17, the doctors, psychologists and every specialist the Bynums could find, agreed that Betty could lead a somewhat normal life, maybe even existing and working in the outside world. The doctors said that all the tests showed that Lorenzo and Merrianne's daughter had reached her mental maturity. Doctor Pierce put in plain-enough terminology for Zo and Merri to understand: *Non-syndromic refers to intellectual deficits that appear without other abnormalities and could be caused by something as simple as not getting enough oxygen to the brain during childbirth.* Merrianne and Lorenzo had completely forgotten about the long and painful labor so many years before. The doctor said that mentally, Betty would always be 10-to 12 years old. It took a while, but the Bynums finally gave up on the dream that their Betty would someday catch up to others her age. They just loved her all the more.

The schools that Betty attended sometimes found jobs for their slightly-challenged students. They found her a job at The Rathskeller. The only problem was the Bynums lived at 3230 Beniteau, a half block to the south of Mack, and The Rathskeller was at least seven miles away. Lorenzo and Merrianne were hesitant about Betty going out on her own, even if it was just to work. But Betty's excitement pushed aside the fears they had. They wanted to give their daughter every chance to lead a normal life. At first, the Bynums took turns driving Betty to and from work. She finally convinced her parents she could take the bus.

For the first month Zo rode with Betty, and somehow her mom appeared at the bus stop on Woodward for the return trip home. Going to work, Betty took the Mack Avenue bus to

Woodward, then transferred to the northbound Woodward bus, getting off just beyond Highland Park at McNichols. From there Betty had less than a city block walk to her job. The ride home was just the reverse.

The second month the Bynums relented and let Betty ride the bus to work by herself. "I'll never grow up if you don't let me," she cried.

It's not that the Bynums did not want Betty to grow up—she already did physically. It was a hard for Zo and Merrianne not to always be there for her, but they finally felt that they had to let Betty do as much as she could by herself. After all, they reasoned, she could count change and recognized all the stops on the bus route.

Betty's hours were from 2 p.m. until 10. The Rathskeller closed at 9 p.m. Even taking the bus, she would get home by 11:15, just in time to see "Daddy" off to work. After a couple of weeks of their daughter riding by herself, Zo and Merrianne relaxed, not entirely, but just a little until they heard her footsteps on their wooden porch.

———

Jake and Jess kept up their routine, spending three mornings at the Y and two days coming in early to use the precinct range. Between those diversions, Jake found a better place to live just off of Eight Mile and Schoenherr. The place was just a tad bit illegal—three blocks beyond the city limits of Detroit on Georgiana—in the city of Warren. Jess helped him move. Jake conveniently forgot to change his address and since his phone number never changed, nobody would know he was violating Detroit's residency requirements.

About half way through May, Jess wanted to take a longer look at a gray Dodge half-ton coming out of an alley off the west side of French Road at Warren. The brake lights weren't working. The bed of the truck had a blue plastic tarp over it.

The tarp was covering chunks of copper piping, two .22 rifles, three reels of 16-gauge black housing wire and the contents of someone's power tool collection. Waylon Wolt and Jefferson Wilson, both of Flint, were booked for "Investigation, Breaking and Entering" when they couldn't account for why they were coming out of an alley at two in the morning.

Further investigation by the Fifth Precinct Detectives found that Wolt had just been released on parole from Jackson Prison after serving three of a five-year sentence for home invasion in Flint. Their arrests cleared up thirty-three reports of home burglaries in the Fifth, Eleventh and Fifteenth Precincts. A Flint storage facility rented by Wilson held approximately thirty thousand dollars' worth of guns and tools that hadn't been fenced yet. The duo had teamed up to rob from abandoned homes and some occupied ones and backyard sheds. Wolt said three newspapers on a porch let them know the owners were away.

Summer fought its way into Detroit on June 3rd. Just the day before the temperature topped out at fifty-two. On this day the sun came out and it hit eighty by noon, a typical Michigan transition from one season to the next—totally unpredictable.

———

Hakeem Rami Ahmed liked riding the buses in Detroit, and a week after his last visit with his parole officer he was back on the prowl. He knew the best way to find a likely target was to take a bus ride. The fare was only a quarter and transfers would take him as far as he wanted to go to the north, south, east, or west.

Years before, on February 14, 1968, to be exact, a man named Jesse Leander James Jr. was sentenced at Detroit's Recorders Court to serve two to ten years for Assault with

Attempt to Rape. He copped a plea to a lesser charge, a deal that the Assistant Prosecuting Attorney, Joseph Paine, quickly agreed to accept—to "expedite the case." Jake Bush was the arresting officer. It never was disclosed in court that Jesse Leander James Jr. was positively identified by seven of twelve victims. All had been raped at knife-point after getting off a bus after dark.

Jesse Leander James Jr. became Hakeem Rami Ahmed when he converted to Islam the first month he filled a cell at the Jackson State Prison. The "pro bono" lawyers did the paperwork to make the change official. The only reason for the conversion was that nobody messed with any Black Muslim at the prison. He figured that out, after he got jumped on twice the first week he was in there. His first prison haircut got rid of the pomade-laced do he had been wearing the past five years. After the haircut he let it grow to a full-blown Afro, just like the rest of the "brothers of Islam" wore.

On August 10th, 1969, Hakeem got an early release. He was paroled four days shy of eighteen months for good behavior. Hakeem had the name of a mosque in Dearborn on a slip of paper he tossed as soon as he got off the bus on the day he was released. He figured he didn't need any protection on the outside. The new name stayed though. He never liked being named after a father he'd never met.

Hakeem's mother died just after he got out of prison. He inherited her home at 223 Pingree. The Pingree home was a part of what was considered an affluent neighborhood going back fifty or more years when doctors, lawyers and the well-to-do lived in the area.

Hakeem's monthly meetings with his parole officer for the next two years were a waste of time. His P.O. had given him plenty of leads for getting a job, but the only work available to an ex-con was what no one else wanted. "I ain't sweeping no damn hot newspaper warehouse," he said after just one day working at the *Free Press*. It wasn't that he couldn't hold a job—he didn't try. He joined Detroit's bulging welfare rolls. The aftermath of the 1967 riots had the whites moving out in droves and the decent jobs and businesses followed them.

He once had a girlfriend, but a willing sex partner didn't satisfy him. He remembered all too well the high he got when forcibly taking what he wanted from a crying, unwilling partner.

After his final visit with his P.O., Hakeem was hanging around Grand Circus Park where the DSR bus lines converged. Normally he'd ride the Grand River or Fenkell lines heading west, or the Mack or Gratiot lines heading east. Sometimes, just for kicks, he'd take the northbound Woodward bus to Eight Mile to see what he could stumble upon. He had so many choices, and in the first six months he had scored four times. He felt a pulsation in his groin just thinking about the one 50-year old spinster lady that he took near the fairgrounds. He smiled remembering as she cried, "Please don't. I've never—"

Betcha she loved ol' Hakeem, he thought to himself.

———

Jess and Jake took turns with their pre-shift routine. One updated the stolen car board; the other went through the teletypes and updated the circular book. They had been together almost a year. Every now and then Jake would reread the circulars kept in a black binder. He didn't want to miss a clue that he might have overlooked. A new circular caught his eye.

"Jess, take a look at this one." He slid it Jess's way. "A guy raping women taking a bus home."

"Not that story again, Jake."

"I'd bet it's my guy. Eight rapes to date."

"I know, the Tastee Barbeque, 1967. Constantly chewing a toothpick. I can repeat the story verbatim."

"Screw you."

Jess just shrugged and led the way out to their car. He read the circular fifteen minutes later when Jake was grabbing two coffees to go at Biff's. He liked jerking Jake's chain.

The regular workouts at the Y continued. The weight room was all grunt and sweat for them and on Tuesdays and Thursdays they kept up their routine at the pistol range. Jake and Jess both lived to work the streets and kept in shape. They looked at each night on the streets as another chance to slam the door on a "bad guy." The Job was their life.

Jess would head to Petoskey every other set of days off and see his sons. He had that going for him, something to look forward to. Once, he asked Jake what he did on his days off, but never got an answer.

That was dumb. He had forgotten Jake might still be mourning the loss of his family.

In reality Jake spent more time at the gym, the pistol range, and the library when Jess was out of town. He was reading to get away from his own life and into someone else's. That's how he survived.

———

Elizabeth Bynum had been working at the Rathskeller for two months. She loved her job and adored all her co-workers. They were nice to her. She in turn was a good addition to the kitchen staff, always cheerful, always smiling. The first of August had Betty being promoted to the salad table in the kitchen. She was a natural as she sang while preparing the shrimp cocktails, or making little rosettes out of the radishes that added her own little personal touch to the relish trays that the waitresses put on every table after taking their drink order.

The owners, the Kurz family, loved the brightness that Betty brought to their kitchen.

On August 7th, a Friday night, Betty said good-bye to the closing chef at The Rathskeller and took the short walk to her bus stop at Woodward and McNichols. It was a warm, muggy night. Within ten minutes, her bus pulled up, she climbed aboard, paid her fare and got her transfer for the Mack Avenue bus. She noticed it was Ernie driving and said "hello." He responded and waited until she was seated before he continued on his route. She always sat near the back of the bus, watching the lights on the buildings flicker by as she read the ads overhead. The ad for the movie, *Benji*, caught her eye. She loved animal movies and the cartoons on TV. She planned on asking her daddy to take her the next day.

Twenty minutes later she heard Ernie call out "Mack Avenue." That was her cue to stand and move towards the back door. She waved at the driver as she danced down the two steps and off the bus. Behind her another black lady climbed down, followed by a young black man. Betty crossed Woodward towards the Mack Avenue bus stop. The lady walked ahead, and Betty noticed the man following a few steps behind. All three waited and within a few minutes the Mack bus pulled in and stopped. All three boarded. The man and the lady took seats as Betty handed the driver her transfer. She found an empty double seat near the back door. At the next stop two more people boarded. When the bus started up, a man dropped into the seat next to her. It was the man from the Woodward bus. They pulled away from the curb heading east on Mack.

"Heading home?" the man asked.

Betty took a quick look, answering, "Daddy said don't talk to strangers."

"Just makin' small talk."

She answered more firmly. "Daddy said don't be talking to strangers."

"Your daddy's probably right." The man moved to another seat.

Betty was glad because he seemed so nice. She had to bite her lip to keep from talking to him. *Hope I didn't make him feel bad.*

———

For four weeks Jake and Jess had been making a habit of sitting on Mack and watching cars flow in both directions. They made a game out of catching plate numbers as cars went by. They'd already grabbed two occupied stolen cars that way since they started this routine, but that was their secondary purpose. Jess and Jake talked about the bus rapist a few times and decided that they could follow an eastbound bus, trail it slowly with their lights out, and just watch passengers disembark. Jess figured it was a good way to spend a couple of hours a night. "Who knows what kind of scum climbs off a bus," he'd say. People-watching was Jess's forte.

Jess had been Jake's mentor when they worked the TMU years before. Now they were working as a team, each looking for tell-tale signs like a subtle move that piqued their interest. Many times, they stumbled into a burglar or a guy toting a piece. They conducted a lot of street investigations, most of which came up empty, but quite a few "bad guys" ended up behind bars because of Jake and Jess's persistence.

Since Five Twenty-five started tailing buses, they found they could keep an eye on six of them eastbound in two hours. As soon as it started getting dark, they headed for Mack and if nothing else got in the way, they'd follow buses for three to four hours. Both knew that if you didn't look for something, you'd never find it. They picked up the buses as they crossed into their precinct from Number Seven and followed it to the Fifteenth Precinct border.

Just when they were getting bored and tired of inhaling diesel fumes from the buses, they grabbed a purse snatcher right after he knocked down a little old lady when she got off a bus. The kid hadn't gotten a half block with the purse when Jess bowled him over. Jake had to laugh as he watched a tall fat kid being outrun by someone just as big without an ounce of fat to slow him down. Jake was at the wheel and racing to the front to head off the foot pursuit. Jess had the young bull down and handcuffed before Jake got their car stopped. After he was placed in the back of their Chrysler, Theodore Roosevelt Poet said he'd never been hit that hard, but then he never ran into someone like Jesse Scott.

Two months later, Jake was in court when that the purse snatching earned Poet a three to five year sentence. Judge George W. Crockett Jr. said he was tired of seeing the young man in his courtroom.

———

Jesse Scott sometimes bragged that he was half Indian and Jake didn't doubt that for a minute. He had the patience of a man who could survive with a bow and arrow. Following buses was slow and methodical. It took approximately 15 minutes to travel the length of Mack, depending on the number of stops it made. Once the bus hit Alter Road, they'd make a quick U-turn and scoot back to the west end with just enough time to pick up the next bus. As Jess always said, "You've gotta outwait what you're hunting."

He's half Indian all right, maybe more than that, Jake thought.

It was a muggy August night and Jake parked to wait. The 10:15 bus came and Jake hugged the curb, staying about a half block back. It stopped three times to discharge passengers, a guy by himself, then two women, then a lone woman. When Jake hit Alter Road, he made a U-turn to get back to the edge of Number Seven and restart their hunt and stalk routine. The 10:30 bus passed through uneventful. Two guys got off at Cadillac.

———

Betty saw the sign for Lillibridge on her left and pulled the cord to remind the driver that Beniteau was next, her stop. She took the three steps to the back stairwell and got off as the door folded open in front of her. She danced down the two steps, waving at the driver, and started walking towards her house.

A man on the bus watched the girl pull the cord and stand to get off. His heart was racing. He knew to let her get off, then hit the cord two or three times as the bus pulled away, as if he almost missed his stop.

Jake picked up the next eastbound bus at 10:45. They were near the end of their run when the bus signaled for a stop at Beniteau. Jake stayed back. He and Jess watched a woman wearing a white blouse and tan slacks get off. She started heading east as the bus started forward. The bus suddenly stopped. A man jumped off, heading in the same direction as the woman.

Jess slipped out his door without a word, pocketing the Motorola walkie-talkie. He kept close to the buildings on Mack, in a slow trot at first. Jake drove past the moving bus, and turned on his headlights.

Just as Betty reached the alley she heard steps and turned to see the man from the bus behind her. He grabbed her, forcing her into the alley. She got off a short scream as he put his hand over her mouth.

The man pushed the girl against a board fence, holding her with his knife at her throat. "Shut up, bitch," he whispered. He took his hand from her mouth, tugging at his belt, then at her slacks. He could feel his erection screaming to be let loose. The girl's eyes were wide; she was trying to cry out, but had no voice. "Hey, daddy's girl, did he tell you about this?" The man let his hardened cock flop out of his open trousers.

"Freeze Asshole!"

The man turned, knife in hand and his penis out. He stumbled and ran. The girl started shrieking. Betty stood, crying and shaking. Jess grabbed her. "You're Okay. You're Okay. I'm a cop. The girl hugged Jess tighter, sobbing uncontrollably.

Jake heard Jess's voice over the radio, "He's running north in the alley—"

Jake took a right, then another putting their unit into the mouth of the alley. Wham! Jake put the car onto its nose. He watched a body as it slid across the hood and off the left side of his car, hitting the corner of a garage.

Lorenzo was standing on his porch, waiting for his smiling daughter to come home. He heard brakes squealing in the direction of Mack Avenue and jumped from the porch running. Headlight beams to his right caught his attention.

Lorenzo saw his Betty with a man. "Take your hands off of my baby!" he shouted.

Jesse Scott turned and showed his shield. "Police officer," he said, handing the shivering girl to the man.

She leapt into her father's arms, wailing, "Daddy, Daddy!" The man and daughter clutched each other, crying and kissing.

"Daddy's gotchu baby. Daddy's gotchu."

Down the alley Jake slowly got out of his car. At his feet lay a man with an Afro. A pool of blood growing underneath his head.

Jake reached into his car and grabbed the mike from under the dashboard. "Radio, have Five-Seven-0, meet Five-Two-Five, in the alley east of Mack and Beniteau. Officer involved accident. Better send an ambulance too." Jake bent over and felt for a pulse. There was none. He walked down the alley and joined Jess comforting Lorenzo and Betty Jean Bynum.

There wasn't a ninth rape victim added to the Women's Division Circular. The last one published was re-sent to all precincts and bureaus with the word "Apprehended" in bold red ink stamped at an angle across the page.

The dead man was identified as Hakeem Rami Ahmed, age 29, by the identification in his wallet. The Women's Division showed photos of Hakeem Ahmed to the recent rape victims among a deck of other photos of black men with Afros—all picked out Hakeem as their rapist.

Two days went by and Jess and Jake were slowly cruising the curb on Kercheval. Jess spoke first. "You're awful quiet, Jake."

"Thinkin'."

"You're not feeling bad about running the guy over, are you?"

"Nope. Just wondering if the girl's all right."

"She'll be fine." Jess changed the subject. "Did you hear the guy's prints put another name on the coroner's report?"

"Yep. Jesse Leander James, Jr. My man from 1967."

"He won't be coppin' a fuckin' plea this time."

"For sure." Jake smiled. *Maybe there is a God.*

Lorenzo and Merrianne Bynum drove Betty to The Rathskeller so she could quit her job. She didn't want to ride a bus anymore. The owners of the Rathskeller made a call and found her another job closer to home. The owner of the Roostertail, Joe Schoenith, was a personal friend of Mr. Kurz. This restaurant was a real swanky place on the river, ten minutes by car from Betty's house. Betty was back smiling at everyone, and loving all her new coworkers. The alley was just a bad dream.

She did get to see Benji. Jake called the Bynums to see if he could take her. She reminded him of daughters lost so long ago.

Chapter Seven

Normally the Fifth Precinct's B&E Car was on the street Tuesdays through Saturday nights. The bosses either shut the unit down on Sundays and Mondays, or they'd fill it randomly with two other officers if all the regular cars had bodies in them. Vacations happen. Jess was taking two weeks off the second half of August, planning on spending time up north with his sons, twelve-year-old Tommy and Billy who turned ten in April. Jess's parents live on Black Lake and Jess looked forward to fishing and swimming with his sons.

Sergeant Fox assigned a 22-year-old rookie to work with Jake while Jess was off. His name was Remington Southworth, a June graduate of the academy. When Jake saw the assignment board, he went straight to Fox's office. Fox obviously expected the visit because he started talking before Jake got half way in the door. "I thought you'd appreciate me finding you a partner bigger than Jesse Scott." Jake just stood dumbfounded. "Now, before you get bent out of shape I have a reason for using the kid."

"I don't like it."

"Jake, just hear me out. Two of the other guys assigned to a beat are black. The bad guys would make you as cops as soon as you hit the street."

Jake took a seat. "Hell, they know we're cops anyway with the car we're driving. Give me one of the others; a guy with some time on the street. This Southworth just graduated from the academy."

"It's just for two weeks." Fox looked over at Jake, the corners of his mouth curling into a smile as he leaned back in his chair. "You can give him a hell of a lot more street experience than rattling door knobs on a beat would, right?"

Jake shrugged. "I'll give it a try." *Sly bastard, appealing to my ego.*

Jake left the sergeant's office saying that he shouldn't be surprised if their numbers fell off.

———

August 17th was a Thursday and Jake grabbed the key for the precinct pistol range. He sent a target downrange and emptied a cylinder into it. As he reloaded to shoot a second cylinder, the door opened behind him. Jake glanced over his shoulder. A tall, beefy guy with red hair and a face full of freckles walked in, took the next stall, donned a set of ear muffs and moved a silhouette downrange. Jake fired six wad cutters from his .357 and hit a button to bring up his target. He was done with his 12-shot routine. The redhead next to him shot six rounds with the .38 he was using, reloaded and snapped off six more. Jake looked downrange and only saw one hole in the silhouette—a very large one. The redhead ran his target up as he flipped off his muffs.

"Nice shooting," Jake said as he pulled his own target off of the clip and replaced it with a new one. Eight out of twelve of Jake's holes were nicely grouped. The other four were a little higher and to the right, just above the X ring. Still killing shots, but not as good as those on the target the guy next to him shot at.

"Sergeant Fox said you'd be down here. Guess I'm a bit late," the redhead said.

"I take it you're Southworth." Jake watched the man's target move up to the shooting bench. Southworth's group was half the size of a half dollar, each hole touching another.

"Name's Remington. And you're Jake Bush." He extended his hand to shake. Jake took it, quickly noticing the vise grip that went with the hand.

The two left the range, climbing the stairs to the main floor of the precinct. "What all did Fox tell you about me?"

"That you're down shooting on Tuesdays and Thursdays about 5:45." Southworth pulled the door handle at the top of the stairs. "That you were street-wise and to pay attention to what you say." Jake stepped by Southworth and led the way to the teletype room.

A half-hour later the stolen car board was up to date and so was the circular book. Jake had Remington reading the last three days of teletypes, pointing out the ones they should make some notes on.

"These two are from the next precinct over, Number Seven. And this one's from Thirteen." All were street holdups with decent descriptions. "The bad guys don't know precinct boundaries, so it's good to see if there's something that'll stick in your mind." Jake pointed out a man wearing a red do-rag who was wanted for a robbery. He'd gotten a watch and wallet while brandishing a knife. "Make a note of the watch type in case we see a guy with a red do-rag."

Jake was getting plenty of nods out of his rookie partner "What do people call you?"

"Remington'll work."

Jake shook his head. "That's a mouthful. How'd you get a name like that?"

"English aren't supposed to have a sense of humor. My father did. He said I was named after the pump shotgun his soon-to-be father-in-law carried the day my mom and he got married."

"He serious?"

"No, not really. I was born two years after the wedding. But my dad never did answer any question straight out. He always had a smart answer for everything."

"You're talking about him in the past tense."

"Yeah. He died three years ago. A dirt bike didn't make a turn in Utah. He was on it."

"Sorry. I didn't mean to pry."

"No problem. He lived on the edge. 'Full throttle' my mom always said." Remington went to the blue Chrysler they were using. As he grabbed the passenger door, he said, "Dad never did anything slow."

Jake took the wheel. "Time to teach you what the academy never did." They stopped five cars in two hours and talked in between on the why he stopped one car and not another. They ate, then stopped a few more. Somewhere during that first night Southworth mentioned "Uncle Beau" as he talked about becoming a cop. Jake let him talk, but remembered the nameplate on his boss's door. "Sgt. B. Fox." The lights came on. Now Jake knew how he got assigned a raw rookie. *Sneaky bastard,* was the term going through Jake's mind. *Beauregard, as in B. Fox.*

Remington was quickly picking up the ways of the street. The English kid's innocent-looking face—freckles and all—did not look like it belonged on a police officer. Any bad thoughts Jake had about nepotism were shit-canned when one 200 pound asshole balked at Remington's request that the man should get out of the car and put his hands on the roof. In a half heartbeat, large hands grabbed material. Compliance to the order was immediate as a body was extricated through an open driver's side window. *Maybe Uncle Beau knew what he was doing after all.* Jake smiled.

Jake's only problem was the name his partner preferred. Jake thought of calling the kid "Red" a time or two, or maybe "Shotgun," but decided against it. Remington was big enough to be called what he wanted to be called.

Three occupied stolen cars and a burglary arrest within the first week sold Jake on the rookie. *Hell, Jess may even like the kid.*

The two weeks flew by. Jess was due back the next day. Jake's thoughts were pushed aside when a black Buick 225 crossed in front of their car as they waited for the light to change at Warren and Conner. The driver quickly looked away as he passed across the front of the unmarked police car. Jake knew the driver made them as cops. All Jake could see in the split second was that the driver was black and had a fancy "do." Jake fell in behind the car and checked the plate against their car board. Nothing. At Mack the light changed to red and the Buick glided to a stop. "No brake lights," he murmured. The light changed and the Buick proceeded south. Jake pulled around the car and Remington motioned the driver to pull over, holding his badge high so the driver could see it.

Jake took the left side of the Buick while Remington took a position to the right rear of the car. "Can I see your license, please?" Jake took it and the registration the man handed him. "Mr. Arnold, your brake lights aren't working. Can you step out of the car, sir?" Jake guided the man to the back of the Buick. "Safer to talk here." Their Chrysler had its warning lights flashing and the late evening traffic on Conner wormed around the two cars. Remington started searching the Buick from the passenger's side.

"That man ain't gotta right to go in my car."

"Relax, Mr. Arnold. If everything's cool, you'll be on your way. He's just taking a quick look. You aren't carrying a gun are you?" Jake turned the man around and did a quick frisk. The man was clean.

Southworth came to the back of the Buick. He held a red cloth in his hand. "Found this among the scrunched up White Castle bags. What kind of a watch does he have on?"

Jake turned Arnold's left wrist and moved his shirt sleeve up to take a peek. "Bulova. A nice expensive one."

Southworth took a set of cuffs out of his belt and started snapping them on Joseph Arnold's wrists behind his back, whispering in Jake's ear. "Red do-rag. Bulova watch. Holdup in Thirteen a couple of weeks ago."

Remington walked Joe Arnold to the Chrysler, placed him in the back seat and then called for a car to transport the Buick to Number Five.

At the station they found the teletype on the armed robbery. Joseph Arnold was booked for Investigation Robbery Armed. The red do-rag and a Bulova eight-diamond watch were tagged and held as evidence. Remington typed the report while Jake got him a coffee.

Jake smiled as he and Remington Southworth walked to their personal cars in Number Five's lot. "Hey Red, good working with you. The dicks should make our man on that holdup. I'll tell your uncle Beau that you can fill in on our car anytime."

The Southworth waved. "Keep that uncle shit under your hat. And it's Remington, ol' man."

Two days later the Number Thirteen Detectives called to say they made Joseph Arnold on the robbery. Fox put through the papers for a citation for the crew, Remington's first.

———

"Well, how'd it go, Jake?" Jess asked as they met in the teletype room.

"Didn't even know you were gone." Jake tossed the car board to Jess so he could update it while he checked the teletypes.

"No really, how'd the rookie work out?"

"All I'll say is you should ask for him next month when I take my vacation. Now let's hear how the visit with your kids went."

———

Jake's vacation came and went with Remington Southworth filling in on the car. Jess never said a word on how those two weeks went, but then, Jess normally didn't say much anyway. Jess and Jake were done booking a suspected burglar when Southworth and his partner, Jim Bookens, working one of the uniform cars, were bringing in a drunk driver. Jess just looked up and said, "Hi Bob" to Remington and acknowledged Brookens with a nod. Jess and Jake moved to the report room to finish the paperwork.

Jake threaded in the three-page report form into the Underwood typewriter as Jess poured two cups of coffee. "Still black with one sugar?"

"Yep. Hey, where'd the name Bob come from?"

"The new kid?" Jess pushed a cup towards Jake. "I was thinking of calling him 'the Bobbie' since he's English, but that's about as long as calling him Remington. Just started calling him Bob. It's much easier."

"When I asked how I could shorten his name up, he said he preferred Remington," Jake said.

"He likes Bob. Turns out Robert is his middle name. So Bob it is."

"Hear any more on whether Fox wants to make our car a full seven-day unit?"

"Said maybe after the first of the year. Everything's on hold until then."

Jake was thinking Remington would be a good fit on the car if it went seven days. He finished typing the report on their arrest and yanked it out of the machine. You never did say how the trip up north went."

"I think Beth and I may work something out."

"You getting back together?"

"I'm hoping. I'm looking at a piece of property up near Utica."

"That'll be a long drive."

"Not as far as Petoskey."

"Hope it works out." Jake knew Jess missed his kids. But he could see them once in a while. Jake was jealous. Young smiling faces emerged in Jake's mind. He pushed them away as the words *Mike would be*—snuck in.

———

Reginald Mills had been assigned to the TMU since 1968. He replaced Jake Bush on Eight-Four. There was a time Reggie thought he'd never realize his dreams—wearing a badge for the city of Detroit. It took him three years to land a job on the department. He had joined the Marines right out of high school. Upon being discharged he returned to Detroit and put in his application to the department. Written tests were never a problem for Reggie. Two months later the oral review board told him that they wanted to see a work history before they would consider hiring him. This confused Reggie at first, since two of his high school friends, who also went right into the service from high school, had been hired that summer by the Detroit Police Department. His two friends were white. That was the first time Reggie wondered if his race came into play.

In the Marines he made rank quickly. Reggie's parents, his dad a draftsman at Fisher Body, and his mom a grade-school teacher, always told him to work and study hard, and he could be anything he wanted in life. There wasn't a "poor me" bone in his body. That's just how he was raised. Now he wondered.

Reginald got the Detroit Police the work history they asked for. He went to work at the Tank Arsenal in Warren, working for the U.S. government. A year later, he reapplied. This time the oral board did not like the neighborhood where he and his wife, Linda, were living. The panel thought that Woodrow Wilson and Collingwood was not a suitable area, so Reggie found another apartment closer to the Tenth Precinct, in an area that Reggie thought was actually less desirable than where he lived in the Palmer Park Precinct.

But Reggie was determined. His third trip before the review board brought different results. On July 10, 1961, Reginald Mills started the Detroit Police Academy. Reggie actually thought they finally hired him because he was so persistent and had run out of excuses not to hire him. Upon graduation, Reggie was assigned to the Twelfth Precinct. He was proud to be one of the nineteen percent Negroes on a 5,000-man department.

In 1968, his move to the TMU brought a change in the way his fellow officers treated him. He was now part of an elite group of men who were judged by how well they served as police officers, not by the color of their skin.

As of September 5, 1972, Reggie had been at the Tactical Mobile Unit for over four years, was near the top on the Sergeant's list, and had earned thirteen citations for meritorious police work. He and Linda now lived in the Eleventh Precinct in a nice brick home on the corner of Spencer and Lantz. Their children, a son and daughter, were excelling at school. He was happy that he'd persisted. He loved being a cop.

Reggie and Linda had just gotten out of a PTA meeting. On a whim they stopped at Buddy's Pizzeria on Conant just off of Six Mile to pick one up and surprise the kids. Buddy's was their favorite—pepperoni and mushrooms with double cheese—a square one. Reggie ordered a cold beer while Linda had a Coke to sip on while the pizza was in the oven. They were in a booth against the wall.

It was just past eight and there were about ten people in Buddy's when a loud voice boomed out, "Everybody on the floor! This is a stickup!"

Reggie looked over his shoulder. The voice belonged to the man at the front door holding a pistol in his hand and wearing a nylon for a mask. Looking to his left Reggie saw another man at the bar with a pistol in his hand and no mask. He was black.

Linda started moving to the floor, looked at Reggie, and knowing what he was thinking said, "Please Hon, just do as they say." Reggie resisted the urge to draw his off-duty pistol and joined his wife on the floor.

The man at the bar emptied the cash register and moved from prone body to prone body, dumping a purse, or grabbing a man's wallet. Reggie's eyes moved back to the front door. Slowly Reggie turned his head towards the man grabbing cash out of wallets and purses. He was only ten feet away by then. Reggie heard Linda's whisper, "Please Reggie. For me. For the kids." Reggie felt his wallet being lifted.

"Shit!" The robber said when he saw the badge pinned inside the wallet. He pulled Reggie's pistol from its hideaway holster.

Linda then heard, "Uncle Tom mutha fucker," and three reports sounded from the snub nosed pistol—Reggie's pistol. His body just shuttered as all three bullets hit him in the back.

Linda screamed as she held her husband in her arms while the two men ran from the bar.

Two hours later, the Homicide and Robbery Bureau detectives were still going over the crime scene. Lieutenant Richard Dungy, Reggie's boss at the TMU drove Linda Mills to her home on Spencer to break the news to their children. The lieutenant's attempted words of comfort were drowned out by her heart-wrenching sobs

"I should have never stopped him," she bawled. "He never had a chance."

A $300 robbery at Buddy's Pizzeria put an end to the life of a good cop. A black man who dreamed of one day being a sergeant, a lieutenant or even more, on a department that didn't want him in 1960. Now, it was a department that mourned the loss of one of their own—killed in cold blood just because he was a cop, a black cop. The shooter called him "Uncle Tom." And no man wearing blue or carrying a badge saw any skin color. Reginald Mills finally was one of them.

———

Jake and Jess were among the mourners at the Antioch Missionary Baptist Church on McDougal. They proudly wore their uniforms. In the front pew sat Linda Mills, her son, Reggie, Jr., and her daughter, Carol, as every man, including the Police Commissioner, John Nichols, walked slowly past the casket. An hour later, a twenty-one gun rifle salute broke the silence at the Calvary Cemetery as Reginald Mills, Badge #3215, was laid to rest.

Jess and Jake silently drove their unit back to the Fifth Precinct. The fire within them burned. Though neither Jess nor Jake had ever met Reginald Mills, each knew they buried a brother officer that day. Both were thinking the same thing: *Somewhere there's someone who knew who the two men were, and one of them executed a cop.*

Any cop who worked the street for any length of time had a snitch or two who might know someone who knows something. Jess had three. With no discussion between them, Jess went to see Tommy Lee Watson, a small-time pimp who had four girls working along Kercheval. His second stop was an apartment that LeRoy Watson, a two-time convicted car thief, who lived on Jefferson near Biff's restaurant. Maybelle Reams was his third stop. She was a street whore, whose life Jess saved two years before. She worked the corner of Mack and Beals. All heard the same message: "Anything you hear, anything you know, I want to know. Just call Number Five and ask for me. I'll find you."

Jake knew a couple of guys who owed him from his days at Thirteen and the TMU. They ran a blind pig. Jake figured it might be still going strong. He had Jess drive to John R and Piquett, and sure enough, the Leaman brothers' candy store and upstairs after-hour joint was still in business. He went inside to visit Pappy Jack and Lannie.

"Sure brother," Pappy Jack said as Jake left him with his number at the Fifth Precinct. "We'll keep our ears open."

Jess drove off. "What do these two owe you for?"

"Saved their asses when some guys were holding up the place on a New Year's Day."

"Sure they'll call?"

"They will. They owe me big time. They'll call if they hear anything."

———

Two days later Jake found a note when he checked their box at the station. There was just a phone number under his name. Jake dialed it.

"It's your dime," said the voice on the other end.

"This is Jake Bush. You left a number."

Three seconds of silence followed. Then, "Pappy Jack said to pass this along." Another silent moment passed and Jake heard a match ignite and someone take a puff. "A white guy named BJ Lloyd was doing a lot of talking at my table last night. Talking about someone popping a cop. Someone he knows."

"Know where this BJ lives?"

"On Chene. Above a beauty parlor. That's all I know."

"Who's this?"

"A friend of the Leaman brothers." There was a click and the line went dead. Jake jotted down the phone number in his notepad. He could get the name behind it if he needed to.

In an hour he and Jess were cruising Chene in the Seventh Precinct. There was a slight drizzle and the street lights blinked on. They found two beauty parlors. Both had apartments above. The parlors were closed. There were no name tags under the buzzer at either apartment.

"Any ideas?" Jake asked.

"Sit and watch. There's a rib place across from the first one. One of us can watch for traffic from there, the other can use the car to watch this one."

"I'll be four blocks away ordering ribs." Jake grabbed the walkie-talkie and put it on his belt under the black windbreaker he was wearing.

"I'll drive you."

"I'll walk. How long we gonna watch?"

"'Til the rib joint closes."

"Sounds good." Jake slammed the car door and walked north on Chene. He pulled his raggedy Detroit Tiger hat down to shield his eyes from the mist.

In an hour Jake was on the radio to Jess. A black couple left the apartment he was watching. "We struck out here." Jess told him to bring him an order to go and a coffee. Jake got two orders and two coffees and hoofed it back to where Jess was parked. The rain was coming down just enough to give him a chill. Jake saw an extra head in their car. Jess had someone in the back seat. Jake stepped into a vacant doorway to keep the bag he was carrying dry. He knew Jess had seen him walk up. He waited until he saw Jess wave out the window

"Meet Bee Jay Lloyd, not initials, just letters," Jess said as Jake slid in the jump seat.

Jake looked at BJ as he hung over the seat and set the bag with ribs and coffees on the back seat floor. BJ was a slightly-built white man, at least three days since his last shave, probably longer between baths from the smell of him. He wore a raggedy long sleeve blue polo shirt and dirty jeans. His hands were shaking as he tried lighting a cigarette.

"Jake, come around and drive. I want to talk to this piece of shit." Jess moved to the back seat his feet straddling the bags of ribs and coffee and pushed BJ over behind the passenger's seat like he was a speck of dirt. It didn't take any more effort. "Ditch the cigarette. We don't smoke in here." Jess didn't wait for the man to react. He just snatched it out of his mouth and pitched it out the window.

"Man whatchew fuckin' with me for?" BJ's eyes flicked around, looking out the back window, then out the side, then at Jess. "Officer, I don't know nothing about a cop getting killed."

Jake dropped the Chrysler into drive and went north on Chene.

"Jump on the freeway and head east," Jess said. Jake took the ramp and headed towards Conner. "Clean the carbon out of it while BJ and I have a nice conversation."

Jess put his arm around the man. "Jezus, when'd you last shower?" Jess pulled his arm back. BJ hugged his door. "Let's get back to who shot the cop."

"I tol' ya, I don't know whatcher talkin' about," BJ whined.

"Wrong answer. We know better." Jess put a grip on the man's left kneecap. "How fast you goin', Jake?"

"Sixty."

"Get it to eighty. I think our man's thinkin' about jumping."

"No I ain't."

"I see it in your eyes, BJ. Now I want some names. Who shot the cop?"

"I don't know nothing."

Jess reached past the man and popped the door handle, flooding the Chrysler with the hiss of wet tires slapping the tarred expansion joints. Jess grabbed the bag with the coffee and ribs and threw it out. BJ's head turned and watched the white bag bounce off the blacktopped shoulder and into the lane behind them. The grill on the next car caught it on the second bounce.

"I don't have all day," Jess growled." Names. Or you're going to jump out."

"I'm not jumping—"

Jake yelled from behind the wheel, "Don't jump, mister. I'm doing eighty."

"I'm not trying—Oh fuck!"

"That's not what the people behind us are going to see." Jess put his left hand on the man's knee, his right on BJ's shoulder and added some pressure.

"Please don't!" The road noise got louder.

"Names."

Jake adjusted his rear view mirror so he could see in the back seat.

"I don't know any," BJ wailed.

His eyes flicked to Jake, then back at Jess. Jess started pushing. The door on the Chrysler swung wider. His eyes went back to Jake. "Hey, don't let him do this to me." BJ tried grabbing Jess's shirt. "Please, slow this fuckin' car down. He's pushin' me out."

Jake's eyes went to his rear view mirror. "Jess, how far you think he'll bounce?"

"Hold it. Hold it. This ain't funny."

"Names." Jess gave him another shove. BJ's right leg tried to brace against the back of the front seat. The whack-whack of tires on the tarred joints drowning out BJ's pleas.

"I'm at eighty-five, Jess."

BJ was part way out his door. "Tate! Ronny Tate." Jess pushed a little more. "An' Darrel Bowers." Jess pulled BJ back into the car. The wind blew the door shut and Jake eased off the accelerator.

"Now wasn't that easy?" Jess brushed off the man's jeans. "Next question. Where can I find Tate and Bowers?"

BJ grabbed his chest, hacking and coughing. "You want fuckin' addresses?"

"That's the idea. Unless you want to hang out that door again?"

"You weren't going to let go."

"Try me, asshole. A cop was killed. I don't play games. I want answers."

BJ's head pivoted around as if he was looking to see if anyone was listening. "I don't know where the white guy hangs out. Bowers shoots pool at Shorty's on MacDougal."

"Tate's white?"

"He and Bowers pulled the job."

"How'd you hear about them?"

"Bowers stopped at my place two nights ago. Man, he's scared. Looking for some dope. Beggin' for a hit. I lined him up with my man. Once he was high, he just kept talkin'." BJ's eyes darted from the windshield to his side, then out the rear window. "Shit, now I'm in the fuckin' middle of this."

"Then Bowers is the guy who popped the cop?"

"Yeah. The cop's the one who put him away. Bowers said he had to put him down. Knew he'd recognize him."

"Where's he live?"

"Jezus Christ, man—" Jess popped BJ's door open. "On Ferry off a Mt. Elliot," BJ blurted out.

"Show us."

"You nuts? I'm dead for fingering him."

"You're alive because of it. Now show us where he lives."

Jake took Mt. Elliot to the north and turned left on Ferry.

"Second block up. On the right," BJ mumbled. "Upstairs. The house with blue shutters."

Jake drove slowly past the house BJ had pointed out. The wipers on their Chrysler pushed the small raindrops out of the way. He saw the house with the dark shutters. There was a sliver of light on the side of an upstairs window. Someone was home. Jake circled the block.

"You sure that's the house?" Jess asked.

"Yeah, that's it."

"Only one way in?" Jake asked.

"Yeah. Stairs off of the front porch," BJ answered. "How you gonna know he's home?"

"You're gonna ask him to let you in."

"Me? Oh no man. Ain't I done enough?"

Jess grabbed BJ by the throat. "Just tell him you got another dime hit for him. He answers, you're done."

"You'll let me walk?"

"Yeah, you can walk."

Jake pulled the car into the alley. The three got out and walked back towards the house BJ said Darrel Bowers lived in. The downstairs was dark. Jess led the way up the stairs to the apartment above. All three, BJ, Jess, and Jake, stood on the landing, listening. Jess put his ear to the door. He nodded and mouthed, "TV." Jess prodded BJ with his .38 and nodded.

BJ knocked on the door. "Darrel! Open up!" Silence. BJ rapped harder. "Hey Darrel, it's BJ. Jus' seein' if you're all right."

The third time Jess hammered on the door for BJ.

BJ yelled,"Darrel, it's me, BJ."

"Man, whatchew want?" A muffled voice asked from behind the door.

Jess whispered. "Bowers?" BJ nodded. Jess followed with a shoulder full force on the door. His second lunge broke it open. Footfalls ahead took Jake and Jess towards the back of the small living room past the blaring TV with guns first. They followed the noise.

"Police," shouted Jess. The sound of breaking glass and a scream followed. The shade and glass from the window at the back of the room was missing. Jake and Jess looked out onto the yard below. The dim light from the alley behind the garage showed a figure, wrapped in a curtain and a window shade, crumpled below.

Jess and Jake ran down the stairs and around to the backyard. The figure lay in a heap. His neck was twisted so his face was looking back at them. An empty look. He was obviously dead.

"Where's BJ?" Jake asked. He then walked to the front porch and knocked on the main door of the house. After pounding on the door for five minutes, an elderly man answered. He was in his robe and pajamas. Jake used his phone.

BJ was long gone. He was nowhere to be found. Jess and Jake secured the scene. In ten minutes three-cell flashlights were bobbing all over the neighborhood. Uniforms and suits filled the yard. Flashbulbs popped from every angle. Finally the body of Darrel Bowers was zipped into a black rubber bag and taken to the Wayne County morgue.

The morning news on WWJ broke with the story that an eyewitness had come forward claiming that two Detroit policemen had thrown a suspected "cop killer" out of the suspect's second-story apartment window.

BJ Lloyd had reappeared.

By noon the Detroit News and Free Press were putting together their columns, and all the TV stations had reporters scrambling to 1300 Beaubien. Jake and Jess were there sitting with the detectives from the Homicide Bureau answering questions concerning BJ Lloyd's accusations.

One phone call, among the many, that came in that day to Police Commissioner John Nichols' office was from a man named Ronald Tate. He said he wanted to turn himself in to the commissioner before "the cops threw him out a window."

Commissioner John Nichols formed an incident review board made up of four prominent Detroit citizens and four ranking police officers. Patrolmen Jesse Scott and John Bush were put on administration leave pending the findings of the review board.

Two weeks and hours of testimony later, only one fact was conclusive—Darrel Bowers, Negro male, age 29, of 2234 East Ferry died of blunt trauma to the head and neck area caused by contact with the ground after a fall from the second story of said address. Toxicology reports from the Wayne County Medical Examiner also determined that Mr. Bowers had an extremely high concentration of a mixture of cocaine and amphetamines in his system. The testimony of BJ—no names, just letters—Lloyd revealed that he had *assumed* that Darrel Bowers didn't jump through the bedroom window, and that he, BJ Lloyd had in fact fled the address on East Ferry as officers Bush and Scott broke through the door to the Bowers' apartment.

Nothing was said about BJ's wild ride in a blue Chrysler on the Ford Freeway. BJ knew his word wasn't worth a damn after lying about seeing the cops throw Bowers out the window. *Then too*, he thought, *they know where I live*.

Officers Bush and Scott were reinstated to full duty on September 30, 1972. Five Twenty-five was again cruising the streets of the Fifth Precinct.

Chapter Eight

On December 15, 1972, Ronald Tate, white male, 31, pled guilty to the robbery armed at Buddy's Pizzeria and an added count of second-degree murder in the death of Patrolman Reginald Mills. The prosecuting attorney's office was willing to accept the lesser murder plea because they had nothing beyond circumstantial evidence that linked Ronald Tate to the robbery and the murder of the officer. Tate said he was pleading guilty because he was in on the robbery, but had nothing to do with the death of Officer Mills. He said he was a marked man and figured he would die at the hands of the police and that's why he turned himself in. Judge James Del Rio sentenced him to life in prison.

Jake and Jess were having coffee and donuts at the Donut Hole two blocks from the Y when the story hit the *Detroit Free Press*. The innuendoes were still there about two police officers "suspected" of throwing Tate's partner out of a window when trying to arrest him. As Jess read the story, he commented, "Well, at least they spelled Scott and Bush right."

Jake snickered, "Even the *Free Press* couldn't screw up names like that."

"You don't read the paper much, do you?"

"Don't plan on it either." Jake changed the subject. "Hear anything more on putting our car on the street seven days a week?"

"Not a word."

"Any news from Petoskey?"

"Beth and the boys moved in to a house down here three weeks ago."

"You never said you bought a place near Utica."

"Didn't I? Beth found the place. It's off of Van Dyke and M-59."

"You happy?"

"Yes."

"I noticed a change in your attitude. Now I know why."

"You did?"

"Of course not. I'd get more reaction out of a chair than you. Damn, my partner gets back with his wife and kids, moves into a house, and—"

"Jake."

"Yeah."

"You still talk too much."

Jake shrugged his shoulders. "What can I say? See you at the range tomorrow?"

"Yep."

"Five bucks I beat you."

"The Bobbie's coming. My money's on him."

———

Rodney Blubaugh was reading the morning *Free Press.* The lead article mentioned the slate of candidates running for mayor. He went into a coughing fit when he read the name of Colman Young. "Black fuckin' Communist," he screamed. He hacked up a big oyster, probably caused by smoking two packs of Camels a day.

Rodney was 35, mostly bald and weighed in at 350 pounds. He owned a small-appliance repair business on the east side of Detroit. He never married, deciding against marriage because he said women only wanted to change a man. He was content being just the way he was.

The reality was that back when he was attending Denby High, even the homely girls thought he was the most repulsive male on the planet. His nicotine-stained teeth and excessive body odor were immediate turn-offs to any teenage girl. As he aged, his personal hygiene habits never improved and neither did any female's perception of him. His sex life consisted of the monthly delivery of his *Playboy* and *Hustler* magazines.

Rodney joined the Army two days after barely graduating from high school. He was almost twenty because it took him an extra year to earn the required passing grades in math and science. "Thank God for Dees," Mrs. Vandangle, the Denby principal said when she finally watched his fat ass waddle out the door for the last time.

Blubaugh's three-year enlistment in the Army had him bouncing around the southern U.S., going from one base to another—not by choice. He was transferred five times because he hated answering to non-white NCOs and the Army had a lot of them. Quick transfers were their way of handling the problem. Private Blubaugh's last duty station was Fort Benning in Georgia. He was a month short of his three-year hitch when they discharged him. Rodney didn't have enough time left to bother with a transfer. The paper he carried said nothing beyond the standard meaningless "Honorably Discharged," as he headed home.

Rodney quickly landed a job at the Chrysler Assembly Plant on East Jefferson. By the following December he was fired for "fighting with fellow workers." The Chief Steward for the UAW saw no sense in filing a grievance on his behalf since the midnight shift Union Steward was the one on the receiving end of the beating at the hands of Rodney Blubaugh. The victim ended up in the hospital for two weeks with a severe concussion and a broken arm. That union steward was black, and Blubaugh still didn't like non-whites, period. The midnight assembly line at the Chrysler plant was predominantly Negroes, and Blubaugh hated them all.

After he got axed, Rodney found himself opening up a small-appliance repair shop on Morang near Kelly. His business started out slow, but grew steadily over the years. He might have big and clumsy looking, but he could sure figure out how to get something to work if he replaced enough internal parts. Though he never made the money that Chrysler had been paying, he made enough to afford his Pabst and pizza diet. What he liked best about his line of work was that he didn't have to deal with the "niggers." His neighborhood customer base was pure white and he liked it that way.

Rodney, being an independent business owner, fell into a daily routine by spending the first two hours in the morning at Millie's Diner sharing his thoughts with about ten or eleven other locals who dropped in for a cup of coffee, maybe breakfast on occasion, but mostly to discuss the state of Detroit under siege. "There's a black plague taking over this town," was his normal daily parting shot as he tossed fifteen cents on the table for Beverly, the waitress, and left the diner to open up his repair shop at nine.

On a spring morning in 1973, he was telling his cronies at Millie's that "a nigger named Coleman Young was running for mayor. He's going to win if we don't do something."

"What do you think we should do?" asked Marv Thergold, the plumber who had a shop across from Millie's.

"Start arming yourselves. Get ready for the fuckin' war," spat out Rodney. The group just looked away, or changed the subject. They were talkers, not doers.

The morning *round table* and Rodney got into discussions like this because of the never-ending articles on police brutality in the papers ever since the '67 riot. "All written by liberal black ass-kissing reporters," according to Refrigerator Rodney—as he was dubbed by the roundtable crew. Then too, there were weekly articles about the "white flight" to the suburbs, as the papers called the collapsing housing market. Rodney put the *Detroit Free Press* and the *Detroit News* on his personal shit list. He stopped taking both papers.

One particular morning Rodney asked, "So I'm asking you guys again, whatcha doing about being pushed out of our own town by these black bastards?" Blubaugh looked around at the faces at the big oval table. No one answered. Rodney pushed away from the table, grumbling as he left. "Bunch of chicken shit assholes is all you are."

What the gang at Millie's did not know was that the month before Rodney Blubaugh had submitted a "Permit to Purchase" and a request for a concealed weapon permit with the Wayne County Sheriff's Department. The mailman, just the day before, had brought the approval for him to get the . 44 magnum that he'd been eyeing. Rodney was a business owner and, as stated in his application, carried large sums of money at times. That was a bit of a stretch, but he figured no one at the Wayne Sheriff's Department would know otherwise. Rodney thought that if he was going to war, he wanted to be well armed.

When Rodney picked up his new pistol, he bought three boxes of ammunition and planned on knowing how to use it. Within a week he rented an abandoned farm up near Brown City that had two small rows of apple trees behind a deteriorating barn. Just past the trees was a grassy mound created by old farm debris and decomposed horse shit. *Perfect for setting up my private range,* he thought. The closest neighbors were a mile in any direction.

The more Rodney thought about "those yellow bastards" at Millie's, the more he was driven. Rodney bought three sets of the largest army fatigues he could find at Silverstein's Army Surplus on McNichols, along with a World War II German helmet, two bayonets—one Japanese, one German—

and a cosmoline covered 1903A3 Springfield Rifle for $39.95. Again he grabbed three extra boxes of 30-06 ammo for the rifle.

When he was putting away his most recent purchases, he saw that one of the sets of fatigues was from France. He rolled them up and tossed them in the garbage. They only cost $3.95, so he wasn't out that much. *I'll be damned if I'm surrendering like they did.*

His last purchase was a 1950 Studebaker pickup that he painted olive green in the old shed at the farm near Brown City. The paint was among the cheap stuff he found in five gallon pails at Silverstein's. He brushed it on and it ran a bit, but he figured war vehicles don't have to be pretty. The final touch was the white stars he hand-painted on each door. He moved the Studebaker to his own garage in Detroit when the paint job was dry—in the middle of the night, naturally. He wanted it handy when the war started.

Two months later, and the rest of his "war fund" spent on "C" rations stored in the old farmhouse, Rodney Blubaugh thought he was ready to wage war. There was a store-front office on Kercheval covered with placards and a banner touting Colman Young's run for mayor. Rodney found the campaign office as he was delivering a rebuilt washer to a place on Montclair, *the only whites left in the neighborhood.* Rodney shook his head as he unlocked his old Dodge half-ton. *Niggers'll steal you blind in broad daylight if you let them.* Of course, Rodney didn't feel too threatened. At his weight, not too many would-be crooks would take on a might-be Sumo Wrestler—one that had a .44 magnum tucked between the crack in the center of the worn-out bench seat.

After midnight, on a Monday, Rodney rolled out his olive drab Studebaker and in fifteen minutes meandered east on Kercheval. He stopped just long enough to put three shots from his Colt .44 mag into the plate glass window. *Fuck you Coleman Young* were the words in Rodney's mind as he turned two corners and headed back to the Morang and Kelly area. He closed his garage door on what he had dubbed his *War Machine.*

Teletype 5-3677 was issued city-wide: Wanted for investigation on a random shooting in the Fifth Precinct, an old model army truck with white stars on the doors.

———

Things were slow for Five Twenty-five. They nabbed a stolen car here, a small time burglar there. They filled their time backing up a hot run or two every night. Number Five had their share of "man with a gun" runs, or "prowler in the alley" broadcasts. Jess and Jake kept up the routine at the Y and the range. Jess didn't talk about how life was going with Beth and the boys, so Jake just kept his questions to himself.

———

The next two days Rodney Blubaugh bought copies of the *Free Press* and the *News.* He read each front to back. There was no mention of the windows being shot out of the Coleman Young campaign headquarters. At Millie's, Rodney let most of the others chatter about the state of the City of Detroit. Three of the regular guys always listened to talk show blather on their AM radios and they didn't mention anything about windows being shot out. Wilson Pratt brought in copies of *The Michigan Chronicle* from time to time. The first time he did so Rodney asked, "What the hell you bringing in that nigger paper for?"

"To see what the other side is doing," Wilson countered. Rodney had no answer for that.

Today he was hoping Wilson was still reading *The Chronicle.* When Wilson excused himself to make a trip to the john, Rodney followed. "Still getting the Chronicle?"

Rodney asked when he knew it was just the two of them crammed into the two-hole room.

Wilson looked around and stuttered a bit, "W-Why'd you ask?"

"You were right. We should know what the other side's doing. I'd like to see the last few issues if you still have them." Rodney really wanted to see if there was any mention of the windows at the campaign headquarters.

Wilson felt relieved that Rodney was seeing things his way. "I'll drop them by your shop today."

"Thanks. And keep this under your hat. Don't let the other guys know I'm reading *The Chronicle*."

"Yeah, sure."

––––––

A week later Wilson mentioned there was a black couple being shown a house on Roxbury. "What?" Rodney asked. *Jezus. That's three blocks from where I live.* He caught the name of the real estate company that was offering the house for sale.

That afternoon he thought he'd recon the area. He in his Dodge drove slowly through the neighborhood and, in particular, on Roxbury. Two houses northeast of Yorkshire, there was the sign for Penn Realty. The bottom line on the sign read: "An equal opportunity realtor." Rodney drove around the block three times, and twice through the alley. His recon was complete. He knew the house, front and back.

Two hours later Rodney had two Molotov cocktails ready with rag wicks. He laid out a set of fatigues, a pair of airborne jump boots and a helmet, then he took a nap. At three in the morning Rodney tugged on the fatigues. He couldn't bend down to tie his boots, so he just wrapped the extra-long laces around the top of them, stuffing the pant legs in the open tops. He stopped for a glance in the full length mirror on the bathroom door. *Fit and ready for action,* he mused to himself as he pulled the chin strap tight on the German helmet.

In reality he looked like an over-stuffed hunk of knockwurst in an olive drab casing rather than a soldier. Rodney rolled his *War Machine* out of the garage. The two cocktails were in an old milk crate wrapped in bunched-up newspaper to keep them from rattling on the floor of the passenger's side of the Studebaker. He drove east on Havermill to Roxbury then turned left into the alley beyond and doused his headlights. He counted the streets as he crossed Corville, then Whittier after making the little jog in the alley. The one alley light hanging in the middle of each block gave him just enough illumination to negotiate between garbage cans. He used his emergency brake to stop behind the target so his taillights wouldn't blow his cover. There was no dome light in the Studebaker so he felt around and grabbed each bottle by the neck, one at a time, and slid out. He knew from his recon that one cocktail was for the unattached garage and the other for the wood porch on the back of the house. He lit the wick on both with his Zippo and tossed the bottles. He turned his back on the erupting flames and waddled out to his idling truck. He flicked on the lights and drove out of the alley, heading west, taking the shortest way home to hide the *War Machine.*

The July 3rd edition of *The News* carried a short article on a house fire on Roxbury and that the Arson Squad was working on the case. The next day's *Free Press* ran basically the same story adding that remnants at the scene confirmed the use of a Molotov cocktail in the fire, and that the vacant house was up for sale. The house and garage were a complete loss.

Teletype 15-3892 was issued city-wide: Stop for investigation. An older army half-ton truck, seen in the vicinity of an arson fire in the Fifteenth Precinct. Detain for the Arson Bureau.

———

Jake was making notes on the teletypes as he took them off the machine and put them on the spindle that held the teletypes in order. The newest were always on the top of the pile. Jess was working on the stolen car board. "Jess, got a teletype on an army truck that's maybe connected in an arson."

"There was something on a truck like that near where some windows were shot out a few weeks ago," Jess answered.

"Same guy, probably." Jake flipped through his notes. "Yeah, olive drab truck with white stars on the doors."

———

"Hey, did you guys see the article in the *News*?" Wilson asked as he grabbed the coffee Beverly had just poured. "About a house fire?" That got the table's attention. "That's the house I told you about that someone was showing to a black couple."

"Can't buy what ain't there," snickered Marv.

Rodney just smiled. *I don't need them for my war.* He tipped the waitress a quarter as he left the table. Beverly saw the coin hit the table and wondered what made him happy for once.

The article in *The Chronicle* two days later announced that mayoral candidate Coleman Young would be addressing the congregation at People's Community Church located at Woodward and Pingree the following Wednesday, July 25th. Rodney's heart rate climbed as he read the article.

That weekend he went to his farm to practice. Once home, he altered his *War Machine* slightly. The white stars on the doors were sprayed over with three cans of olive drab paint.

He knew they made the truck too obvious and too identifiable.

In the two days before the planned Coleman Young appearance Rodney spent his evenings on recon, in his Dodge wearing his blue denim work clothes. He wanted to check traffic patterns, get the lay of the land and a feel of police presence in the area. He hadn't really spent too much time on Woodward beyond downtown.

The direct route from his house on Somerset and Havermill via I-94 was nine and eight- tenths of a mile and took him seventeen minutes. He wanted to stay off the freeways on the way to the church. Detroit's expressways were ditches, dug through the city with limited options to get on and off, and full of fender benders. Besides, he wanted to have time to think as well as make sure he didn't have a tail. *When you're at war, you have to stay one step ahead of the enemy.* He chose a roundabout route traversing Cadieux, Harper, Chalmers, Mack, Mt. Elliot and E. Grand Boulevard. Oakland to Holbrook was the final leg to Woodward. One left turn and the church would be there on his right. Total travel time was twenty-five minutes. The People's Community Church was a large structure, covering almost a city block. He settled on tossing two cocktails, one on the north end, the other as he rounded the corner onto Pingree. *Hit 'em hard and run* was the plan. He wanted to scare the shit out of Coleman Young.

The route he chose to return home would be as direct as possible. Speed and time would be essential to get off the city streets and stash the Studebaker. He ran the route twice, Second Avenue to Clairmount, making a left, then another onto the Lodge Freeway heading south, then cutting east on the Ford and getting off at Cadieux. His return time was nineteen minutes without exceeding the speed limit.

The Coleman Young appearance was scheduled to go from 7 p.m. until 9. Rodney planned on hitting the church at 8. It would still be light, but he hoped most of the people would be inside listening to their savior, Mr. Young, and no one would be able to ID the truck. He knew his cocktails probably wouldn't catch anything on fire, *but it'd sure scare the bejesus out of them.* Rodney smiled at that thought.

Rodney enjoyed playing war. The only thing he wished was that one of the guys at Millie's would have showed a little guts and teamed up with him. It would have been easier having someone drive while he lit and tossed the cocktails. The church would be on the passenger side. He knew it wouldn't take but ten seconds to drive what equaled a city block, toss two bottles and turn onto Pingree and get the hell out of there. That's why he made the trip to the farm. There he practiced with gasoline-soaked wicks in empty bottles. The Zippo stayed lit while balanced in his ash tray and he could light the wicks and do a left-handed hook shot over the top of his truck. *Yeah. I can do this by myself.*

Jess wrote July 25, 1973 on their log sheet as Jake pulled the blue Chrysler onto St. Jean. They headed north. "Any place you want to go, Jess?"

"Kercheval."

"I like Mack. We'll get Kercheval next."

"Then why ask?"

"To get you talking." Jake headed towards Mack and turned right.

Rodney had his cocktails packed in scrunched-up paper balls in the milk crate resting beyond the floor shift on the Studebaker. Just in case, he had his Springfield rifle loaded with a full clip with one in the chamber, muzzle pointed down. It was only an arm's length away; his German helmet was nestled on the seat next to him. He threw an old army blanket over everything just in case. In between the split bench seat rested the Colt .44 magnum with its grips barely showing. He was ready. Rodney eased the Studebaker out of the garage and headed for Morang. His heart was pounding.

———

Five Twenty-five was at Mack near Chalmers heading east. Jess spotted two men in the bus stop just beyond the light. "Jake, let's talk to those two." He pointed at the men.

Jake spotted the men Jess was looking at.

Both were carrying jackets and since it was 70 that evening, the cops were curious. Then too, the men were black and heading in the direction of Grosse Point Park, an all-white neighborhood.

Jake pulled their unit to the curb.

———

The *War Machine* turned right onto Harper and after a few minutes Rodney signaled for a left turn onto Chalmers. The old Studebaker didn't have turn signals, so Rodney used his left arm, extending it straight out with a cigarette hanging between his fingers. He made the turn and took a couple of puffs on the Camel before snapping it out the window. He hacked up an oyster and spit it out while grabbing another cigarette. The Zippo sat neatly straight up in the ashtray. Rodney grabbed it and lit the next cigarette dangling from his mouth. Two puffs later, Mack Avenue was ahead and he signaled with his arm for a right turn. The light turned red for him. He glanced across the street. A blue Chrysler was in the bus stop and two whites, obviously plainclothes cops, were talking to two black men. Rodney chuckled to himself; *them cops got their own war going on.* The light changed and Rodney made the turn, heading west on Mack.

Jess was jotting down the names and addresses of the two men on their log sheet. James Bradley, age 32, and Sylvester Adams, age 30, were on their way to St. John's Hospital at Mack and Moross. Their ID's showed that they were maintenance men at the hospital and were working a ten-hour shift. At six in the morning it tended to be a bit cool, thus the jackets. The Mack bus was just pulling around the blue Chrysler and Jake flagged it down for Bradley and Adams. "Sorry if we inconvenienced you guys," Jess said as they hopped on the bus.

Jake was just opening up his door when he looked west and saw the back of a dingy green truck. "Jess, jump in!" Jess didn't ask why, he just climbed in his side. Jake hit the gas and made a quick U-turn. He had a red light, but blew it without getting T-boned.

"We in a hurry?"

"An ugly green pickup. Olive drab." Jake snaked to the left around three cars in front of him, cut back in and hit the next light red. "Shit." Jake looked left. It was clear.

"Clear on my side," Jess snapped. The tires bit as Jake floored it. They heard brakes squealing as cars just missed the big, blue Chrysler. The olive drab truck was a half block ahead.

The street noise caught Rodney's attention and his eyes shot up to his rear view. "Damn," he muttered as he saw a blue Chrysler swerve into the turn lane behind him. It was making up ground. Rodney turned right on St. Jean, then left on Canfield. As he made the last turn he saw the blue Chrysler behind him. "Fuck this!" He made a quick left on Beniteau.

Jess keyed the mike. "Radio, this is Five Two-five, we are in pursuit of an olive green pickup, south on Beniteau—" The

Chrysler slid sideways, tires chirping as they dug when Jake tromped on the accelerator.

"Car in pursuit, repeat your location."

"South on Beniteau from Canfield, heading towards Mack."

"Repeat your call number, please."

Jess didn't key the mike. "Fuck! We're in a chase an' he wants an essay." Jake swerved around another car. Jess spoke calmly into the mike. "Five Twenty-five. We're driving a blue Chrysler four door if you really want to know."

Jake was gaining on the olive green truck. Jess spoke into the mike again. "The truck's wanted in an arson, Radio. Driver may be armed."

Rodney had his eye on the road ahead and saw the alley as he neared Mack. He took a fast left, hit the alley ramp hard, bouncing the milk crate with the cocktails. The blanket fell to the floor and the butt of the Springfield slid into his right arm. He crossed St. Jean, again, bottoming out the Studebaker. A car braked hard as Rodney blew through the street. He started screaming at the top of his lungs. "Coleman Young, you cocksucker!"

"Five Two-five, what's your location?"

"Alley north side of Mack. He just crossed St. Jean."

Ahead, Jess and Jake could see the green truck bottom out again as it crossed Gladwin. "There's nowhere he can go." Jess yelled. There was a factory ahead and the alley dead-ended into a twelve-foot cyclone fence.

Rodney put the *War Machine* into a sideways slide when he saw the fence. He grabbed a Molotov cocktail with one hand and reached for the Zippo. It was gone. Rodney saw it harmlessly lying on the floor on the passenger's side, just under the Springfield's barrel. The *War Machine's* passenger door was fully exposed to the blue Chrysler screeching to a stop twenty yards away.

Jake rolled out his door, banging into two garbage cans against a light post. His magnum came up, zeroing in on the green truck's open passenger window. Jess leapt out his side, his back hugging a brick building. He looked for a target. Both saw a head wearing a helmet and the man sticking something under his chin.

Whomp! The top of the Studebaker erupted. A blob of red jettisoned out the frayed cone in the top of the truck. The helmeted head flipped to the side, then down. The Colt gripped in the man's right hand fell onto his left leg. Rodney Blubaugh's war was over.

Black police cars came from everywhere as Jake and Jess slowly inched towards the ugly, green 1953 Studebaker. Each had their pistols palmed, ready to fire. There was no need.

The Fifth Precinct sergeants called for the Medical Examiner, a crew from Homicide, and after seeing the Molotov cocktails, the Arson Squad.

Jake pulled the report out of the typewriter and slid it towards Jess to read and sign. "Wonder where he was heading?"

Jess shrugged. "To torch something or someone."

"Looked like he was going to war. The loaded rifle, the helmet, military fatigues." Jake took back the report and signed it himself. "Ready for lunch?"

"Where?"

"You tell me. You're senior man."

"Let's go to Shakers."

Jake slid in the passenger seat so Jess could drive.

The morning *Free Press* ran a story above the fold with pictures of Coleman Young shaking hands as he left the People's Community Church the night before. Estimates ranged from 1500 to 2000 people had been in attendance. The reporter noted that in his opinion Coleman Young was just about assured of being elected the next mayor of Detroit. The paper was lying in the middle of the *Round Table* at Millie's.

"Wait 'til Rodney sees this," said Marv as Beverly poured him a cup of coffee. "Where in the hell is he this morning? He's late."

"Probably gearing up for the invasion after Coleman's rally last night," said Wilson Pratt. Larry and Steve grabbed chairs and sat as Beverly poured. There was just one empty chair. It was Rodney's Blubaugh's usual place. No one dared to take it.

The afternoon edition of *The Detroit News* carried a short story on page two. The front page was full of articles on Coleman Young. The story on page two read: "The Detroit Police attempted to stop a vehicle at approximately seven last evening for investigation in the area of Mack and St. Jean. The vehicle fled. After a brief chase, the driver of the vehicle committed suicide. A police spokesman said that they wouldn't release the person's name pending notification of next of kin."

The next morning's *Free Press* carried a similar story on page three, adding the name of the victim, detailing the arms seized in the vehicle, and stating that no evidence had been found indicating the man's intended target.

Jess put the paper down, took a sip of his coffee and looked at his partner across the table. "Rodney apparently was going to war, but nobody knows where."

Jake just nodded.

Chapter Nine

Jake stuck his head in his boss's office. "Hey Sarge, remember that commando nutcase back in July?"

"Yeah."

"Anyone ever find out where he was headed?"

Fox looked up from the reports he was rummaging through. "Just that they found a ton of white supremacy shit in his house. Nothing more."

"Just thought I'd ask." Jake waved and headed off to the range. Jess was probably waiting.

What Fox said about the literature was the first Jake had heard about the suicide they witnessed. Jake told Jess when they were through at the range.

"Lots of crazy stuff going on, Jake," remarked Jess. "Oh, by the way, here." Jess handed Jake a small envelope.

"What's this?"

"An invite to a Halloween party that Beth is planning."

———

A half hour later they were ready to hit the street. "I don't do parties." Jake said as he slid into the jump seat of their car.

"It's Beth's way of showing off the new house. She's hoping you'll show." Jess drove off into the night.

The air was damp. The rain had finally stopped. Some leaves from the elm trees were slowly drifting down in the breeze, hastened by the weight of the rain that had been falling for two days.

Jake opened the envelope and read Beth's card and her note. "I don't do costumes."

"Neither do I," Jess answered. "They're optional. By the way, the boys said they'd like to see you."

"I'll think on it." Jake looked at the date again. "October 28th?"

"Yeah, a Sunday night. Our night off."

A pink 1970 Lincoln caught Jake's eye. It was a bit late going through the light in front of them. Jess had seen it too and was already moving into the turn lane before Jake needed to say anything.

Five Twenty-five stopped the Lincoln on Conner just two blocks past Mack. The late red light was a reason to stop a car and all they needed to start their night. There were two men in the Lincoln. Jess approached the driver; Jake positioned himself near the right. It was a Mark III, the top of the line put out by Ford Motor Company.

"Can you two gentlemen get out of the car, please?" Jess took the license offered and opened the door so the driver could get out.

"What seems to be the problem, sir?" the driver asked as he climbed out from behind the wheel. The passenger got out of his side. He kept silent.

"Come to the back of the car," Jake called out to them. Both headed for Jake, who was stationed between the Lincoln and their own Chrysler.

The driver was white, the passenger black, both in their thirties and wearing work clothes. They approached Jake while Jess started shining his flashlight under the seats. In five minutes the short investigation was over. The names were logged, along with the license plate number, the time and location. The men said they were going to work, a late shift at a furniture repair shop off of Gratiot and Harper.

The Lincoln's taillights faded as Jess made a U-turn.

Jake was thinking. "Jess, did you notice the driver's shoes?"

"Like what?"

"Different color paint on them. Like overspray. Then the other guy had burn holes in his pants from the knees down."

Jess made another U-turn and had the tires squealing as he buried his foot into the gas. "Damn Jake, we're getting sloppy. Where did they say they worked?"

"Gratiot and Harper."

Jess headed that way. "Burn holes, like from doing some welding and the paint. Doesn't sound like any kind of work at a furniture repair shop." Jake checked the names and addresses on their log sheet. "Call *Radio* and get a registration check on that Lincoln."

Jake manned the radio while Jess slowly cruised by the first block at the corner of Gratiot and Harper. Jake hung up the mike. He compared what information *Radio* relayed back to them. "Plate's registered to Dean Millspaugh, our driver, but not on the Lincoln. It belongs on a 1970 Chevrolet."

"And there's no furniture repair shops, a block either way here," Jess said five minutes later after he checked the area. "We've been had."

"They lied, and we just took their word. Why?" Jake was craning his neck, hoping to catch a glimpse of the pink Lincoln.

"'Cause we weren't thinking like cops," Jess answered.

Jake dropped the clipboard between him and his partner. "Yeah, we were probably thinking of what kind of costume to wear to Beth's party."

"Just why'd they lie? That's the question." Jess pulled into a White Castle on Gratiot. "Let's get a coffee and think this out."

———

At the start of the shift the next night Jess and Jake were parked a block down from 1372 Newport, the address on Dean Millspaugh's driver's license. They sat for four hours and didn't see a light on in the house or any traffic moving. "Maybe he moved," Jake offered to break the silence.

Jess just grunted.

The following night they were a block south of 1502 Manistique, the address *Radio* had given them on the registration. The early sunsets of October made it easier to watch the house. Within an hour, a pink Lincoln backed out of the driveway. "Took the plates off of his Chevy I'll bet. Now let's see where he goes." Jess followed a block behind, with no headlights until the Lincoln turned onto Mack. Three blocks later the Lincoln turned onto Lakewood. Half a block down it stopped. Another got in the car. "Looks like he just picked up his partner, Sam Malone. Grab an address, Jake."

Jake jotted down the number as Jess drove by the house where Millspaugh had picked up his passenger. "Maybe heading to work, like the other night." Jake picked up the mike and called Eastside Radio. "Radio, this is Five-Two-Five. How about a wants and warrant check on two men—" He gave the radio operator names, birth dates and addresses they had gotten the night before.

Jess kept his lights off when he could and stayed as far back as he dared as the Lincoln drove to Warren and took a left. Five Twenty-five's Chrysler blended well with traffic behind the Lincoln. Twice Jess hit red lights, but negotiated through the traffic to keep the Lincoln in sight. The pink car turned right on East Grand Boulevard. Traffic was thinning, so Jess gave the car more room. At Concord the taillights on the Lincoln disappeared. "Shit!" Jess banged the steering wheel. He pulled their car to a stop. Jess and Jake both stared into the darkness. The only thing looming in the distance was a water tower with red warning lights slowly blinking on top of it. The tank was within the confines of the old Packard Motors Plant.

"Radio calling Five-Two-Five."

"Go Radio," Jake said into the mike.

"Nothing on either Millspaugh or Malone."

"Thanks Radio. Five-Two-Five out." Jake hung up the mike. "What'd you think?"

"Tomorrow we'll check with the detectives. See if they have records." Jess slowly drove around the massive abandoned auto plant. "Somewhere in there is a pink Lincoln," Jess said.

"My thoughts exactly. Wanna take a walk?"

"We're deep in Number Seven, you know?"

"Did precinct boundaries ever bother us before?"

"Let's go." Jess pulled into an alley next to a set of railroad tracks, turned off the key, grabbed his flashlight and followed Jake, who was already crossing the tracks.

"Place has been empty for years." Jess whispered.

Jake let out a "Uh-huh," and stood still for a moment. "An uncle of mine, Uncle Rein, worked here. A draftsman, I think. The end of the fifties is when it folded."

What the pair did not know was that the Packard plant covered about thirty-five acres spread out on both sides of East Grand Boulevard. Both sides of the plant were connected by a windowed viaduct over the Boulevard at the fourth floor level. When it had been running, over 40,000 people were working there on any given day with shifts that ran around the clock. Back in the 40s and early 50s, within the confines of the compound, were multiple indoor garages, two schools, a department store and a grocery store. The place that now remained was just a run-down skeleton of what it used to be.

Jess remained silent. He was looking for where a pink Lincoln could disappear. Jess and Jake let their night eyes guide them as they walked around the mammoth old plant. An hour later they were on their second tour around the building to the south of the Boulevard. A cyclone fence was stretched across a tunnel-like opening that faced East Grand Boulevard. There was a gap that Jess found. He squeezed in. Jake followed. It was a maze in there. As they slowly looked over the thousands of windows, some broken out, some not, flashes appeared to illuminate one. They crept closer. The windows were painted over, but flashes of light pierced the night from within. "Our welder," Jake whispered.

"Yep." Jess motioned for Jake to follow. They retreated to the blue Chrysler parked more than a city block away. Jess turned on the engine and flipped on the heater after a few minutes to take the chill out of the air. He just sat there, thinking.

"Somebody's using the old plant for something," Jake said, breaking the silence. "At least part of it."

"Well, we now know where our Lincoln disappeared."

"Now what?" Jake turned the heater on high.

"Two guys and a bunch of lies. Why?"

———

Dominic Macetti lived a layered life. To the city of Detroit, he was the owner of the long empty Packard Motors property. The real owner of the plant was an off-shore company named VanSet, presumably based in Costa Rica. VanSet was actually the layer above Macetti. The company had been looking for a name on the title that said, *Mafia*, but without any real mafia ties. VanSet was a Dutch company that wanted to expand their interests in the U.S. VanSet's lawyers had found Dominic. By having a mafia sounding name, if there were any investigations, whoever had questions would be looking in the direction of Italy, mainly Sicily, rather than towards the Netherlands.

Dominic turned 42 in 1973. He had jet-black hair that topped his six-five frame. His broad smile had a thick black mustache that hid his top lip. Once he passed the 40 year mark, Grecian Formula was needed to keep the gray in check. Armani suits filled his closet and he preferred Florsheim wing tips.

Back in his Detroit Western High School days, Dom learned to keep someone between him and whatever scheme he was into. He started out loan sharking. He was the money behind the associate who did the actual business. That way, if anything happened, Dom was out of the picture. Just before graduation, he had to put some pressure on some seniors who would soon be off to college. Ralph Brunk, Dom's associate, took the fall for that one when the school started investigating. Brunk's diploma was withheld. Macetti got his.

After high school, Macetti was involved in other loan ventures. He expanded into money laundering, then property management schemes and finally property acquisitions. The term *Slumlord* fit him well. He bought apartments and properties on the brink of decay, put a couple of bucks into them, and hung out *For Rent* signs. But he always remained one or two layers away from being the man in charge. He liked someone else's name mentioned when building inspectors or bill collectors started looking for the man behind the code violation, or to get a bill settled after being six months in arrears.

Dominic Macetti was 38 when VanSet found him. That's when the Packard property became his—sort of. There was a slight misstep when Dom was 40. Uncle Sam had him for not filing his federal taxes for ten years. He paid the fine, but had to take a vacation on the taxpayers' dollar for eighteen months. He served his time at the Federal Correctional Institute, in Milan, Michigan.

With time served and lesson learned, Dominic now paid his taxes on time with as many loopholes as his accountant could find. He was back in business.

———

Don and Wayne Schutt were brothers. They were 50 and 52-year old bachelors. Don was the eldest. He was built like a Boston bulldog, broad-chested, no more than five-eight and wore thick glasses. He had meaty arms from wielding a hammer and the tools used to bump out dented fenders for as long as he could remember. Wayne was a little thinner and carried the air of a bookworm. He did the finer work in the collision business, like the masking and painting. He had the patience. Don didn't.

In the late 60s the Schutt brothers quit working for someone else and bought a collision shop on the west side of Detroit. They called it *Bump and Grind.* The shop was within a half mile of DRC, short for the Detroit Race Course, at Schoolcraft and Middlebelt Roads. *Bump and Grind* was also just a short drive from *Busts are Us* on West Eight Mile, a place that Don Schutt couldn't stay away from. Don was the one who chose the name of the bump shop.

Many a night, six days a week in fact, Don sat nursing a Coke as the topless ladies entertained on the stage six feet away. *Michigan Liquor Laws prohibited topless and nude dancers where alcohol was served.* Don always wanted a seat where he could smell the sweat and perfume of the heavily-endowed beauties. That aroma caused a few ejaculations when a table dance was too much for him. A time or two he talked one of the dancers out for a little fun after hours. A $100 for three minutes of his grunting and her oohs and aahs in the back seat of his '57 Cadillac was all he needed. Most of the time, he was much happier with his hand under the table. *Who needs a wife,* he often thought.

Wayne preferred the horse races. He hit it big three times in the first year on the Daily Double. When the Trifecta was introduced with the promised bigger payoffs, Wayne was there six days a week. He loved the smell of fresh dirt mixed with a bit of horseshit.

Both businesses—the DRC and Busts are Us—were dark on Mondays. Don spent the downtime perusing *Hustler* and *Playboy* magazines, while Wayne pored over the previous five days' worth of *The Daily Racing Form,* hoping to find the tip that would let him hit it big at DRC. Then, when the track's ninety-day season was over, he'd make his way to Hazel Park, and then to Northville Downs. He liked the runners, but in a pinch, the sulkies attached to a horse had to do. He liked playing the horses as much as his bother Don liked tits.

The brothers did their own bookkeeping. By 1969, their addictions and short-changing the U.S. Government—the IRS —had *Bump and Grind* in the hands of the National Bank of Detroit. In addition, a year-long court case got Don and Wayne a cell for a year with an added five years of probation. The good thing was that they were able to spend their time at the federal prison in Milan. It was close to home.

In 1972, through connections made in the Milan prison, they found Dominic Macetti who purportedly owned the long-abandoned Packard Motor Plant. Dominic had a plan that they liked. Don and Wayne Schutt unofficially leased a part of the plant that still had electricity, air and all the utilities necessary for them to re-open a collision shop. The old Packard painting department fit their needs. After a walk-thru with Ralph Brunk, Dominic's old high school associate, they agreed on the terms—a three-way split, 40-30-30. Macetti was to get the bigger piece of the pie.

Dominic Macetti had much bigger ideas than gouging insurance companies for accident repairs. Auto parts were in high demand, especially replacement parts for hot-selling cars. Then too, there was a market opening up for "refurbished" cars in Mexico and South America. Macetti put up the money to redo 75,000 square feet, just a miniscule part of the 3,500,000 square-feet one-time auto plant that had him listed as the owner. The Schutt brothers may have only wanted to re-open a collision shop, but Dominic talked them into going into what he hoped would be a very lucrative business—a chop shop. Dominic had the connections and the Schutts, the know-how.

Within a year Wayne Schutt hired Sam Malone and Dean Millspaugh. Sam had been a welder at a GMC Plant. Millspaugh had been a painter trained at the Ford Motor Company. Malone had done a bit of time for helping on a safe job, and Millspaugh did two years on some stolen check charges. Both had been sent to the Schutts by Macetti.

———

The next four nights Jess and Jake climbed the water tower at the Packard Plant. They dressed for the cold and damp October air and in black. Jess handled the field glasses, Jake the note pad. By the end of the second night they located the concrete ramp just west of Concord and the metal overhead door behind which cars disappeared. It was within the walls of the plant. That's where they focused their attention. Sometimes the moonlight was good enough to see the make and color of a car, but license plates were beyond the capabilities of Jess's hi-powered binoculars. Two repeating cars over the four nights were the pink Lincoln and a dark Buick. They came and went nightly, the Buick was always first to arrive around nine and leaving at four in the morning. Jake kept a record of the number of cars in and out.

Jess and Jake were sitting in Fox's office before going to the range the following Tuesday. Fox started the conversation. "What've you two been up to? Your damn log sheets are blank."

They told him about the Packard Plant.

"What the hell're you doing in the Seventh Precinct?"

"Just following up something that started in our backyard," Jake answered.

Fox played with a paper clip, mumbled under his breath a bit, then said, "You're right. Sounds like a chop shop to me too." Fox checked his rolodex and wrote down a number. "This is Frank Pruent's number, an inspector at Auto Squad. Call him in the morning. Keep me posted on what's going on."

"Thanks boss," Jess said as they got up to leave. In a half hour Jess and Jake climbed into their Chrysler.

"What's the agenda for tonight?" Jake asked.

"To stay warm. That fuckin' water tower was cold."

"Scary too."

"What'd ya mean, scary?"

"I've never been that high off the ground." Jake turned up the heater. He was still chilled from the previous four nights.

"I've never met a Marine who said he was scared." Jess chuckled as he drove into the night.

"I said scary, not scared."

The next day Jess and Jake were sitting in front of Inspector Frank Pruent on the second floor of 1300 Beaubien. They filled the Auto Squad boss in on everything they had observed.

"All circumstantial evidence," Pruent said.

Jake handed the onion skins he had on Millspaugh and Malone. "These are the records of the first two guys we stumbled across. A safe man and a guy sent up for check forgery."

Pruent looked over the records. "Is there a place where you guys can get some license numbers, makes and models of the cars?"

"The water tower is out. Can't get plate numbers from that high up," Jake said as he got out his notepad. "Got dates, number of cars in and out, some makes and colors if you want them. Some nights it was just too damn dark to make things out, even with field glasses."

"Hang on to that when we go for a warrant," Pruent said as he looked at his roster of men posted on the blackboard behind him. "How 'bout I give you a man, while I get ahold of someone in the Detroit Planning Commission. Maybe I can get the prints for the building."

"Buildings," corrected Jake. "There's a lot of buildings in that complex."

"First, let us scope out the place in the daylight," Jess said. "Maybe we can find a place better suited to getting plate numbers, makes, and colors. That kinda stuff."

"Somewhere on the first couple of floors," Jake chimed in.

Jess jerked his chin towards Jake. "He didn't like the water tower."

"I'll have my man find some infrared camera equipment. You find the spot to set up and we'll do some filming." Pruent made a few notes for himself. "Think you can check the place out without tipping your hand?"

"Can you get us some city credentials?" Jake asked while he wrote down some notes. "A couple of tape measures and a clipboard can get us around the place all right. I read where the mayor said he'd like to demo the place."

Pruent nodded and looked at Jess, "What'd you think?"

"I think the chop-shop is a night-time operation, so we should be able to nose around."

The next day Jess and Jake were dragging a 300 foot Stanley tape measure around the outside and inside of the old Packard Plant. The ID badges pinned to their coveralls said they were working for *The Detroit Building Code and Enforcement Department.* They purposely stayed away from the area they thought was too close to where they thought the chop shop might be operating. They were looking for a location to set up the camera—somewhere across from the ramp and the metal rollup door.

Debris filled room after room and one building seemed to be in more deplorable shape than the one they'd just left. "No wonder the mayor wants this place leveled," mumbled Jake. He counted three dead dogs in various stages of decomposition in two of the buildings, five places where the homeless set up a shelter using old mattresses dragged in from somewhere, and triple layers of crushed boxes where a body had undoubtedly been curled up for a night or two.

A second story window of an old office seemed to be the likely choice for their stakeout and camera. Jess sent Jake out into the compound to make sure he could read the credentials Jake wore from inside. As Jake turned towards the windows, a man rode up on a ratty, old Schwinn bicycle. Gray tipped curls poked out from under a Detroit Pistons cap. He was wearing a white shirt with a small gold badge pinned to it and patches on his arms that read *Ames Security.*

"Can I ask whatcher doin' in here?" The man with the badge said.

"Takin' some measurements for the city. They're gonna tear the place down," Jake answered. "And who might you be?"

"Jethro Ames. Ames Security. And the owner said nothin' 'bout the place being taken down.

"Well this is just preliminary work, Mr. Ames. The city is working on a deal to buy the property, and my partner and I are doing a cost-analysis for an economic feasibility study." Jake saw Jess approaching out of the corner of his eye. "Jess, this is Mr. Ames of Ames Security."

The security man turned to see Jess, carefully reading the ID badge he was wearing. "If'n they tear this place down, what they gonna do with the few tenants still using the place?"

Jess shook the security man's offered hand. "How many are there?"

"Don't rightly know. Building 120, behind us here, is in use, but I've got orders not to snoop. Some hush-hush after hours project, Mr. Macetti said. Then there's a small ad firm across the Boulevard. Two others that I know of in the main office part. My job's mainly to keep the riffraff out. You know what I mean."

"We've seen the used needles and stuff on the second floor. You've got a tough job."

"Mosta my time is chasin' hooligans off, tryin' to spray paint walls an' stuff."

"How often you see Mr. Macetti, the owner?" Jake asked.

"Only seen him once. The day he hired me. Big fella. Black hair. 'talian lookin' wearin' a nice suit"

Jake visualized Jethro's description. "How's he pay you then?"

"Get a check in the mail every first of the month. Delivered right to my home."

Jake scratched a note in his pad. "How do you contact him if you see anything?"

"Phone. Only I don't talk to him. It's some answering service. Just tell them what I see. One time there's these punks givin' me some trash talk 'n threats. Dialed the number, told the girl what's goin' on. An hour later a car shows up with three guys who look like they play for the Lions. The punks ain't been back since."

Jake tapped his clipboard. "Got that number handy, my boss'll want to give him a call, set up a meeting once we finish our feasibility study."

"It's in my head." Jethro rattled off the number. "LA 9-2455. Tell them you got a message for Mr. Macetti."

"How about an address and phone for you, in case we need it?"

Jethro Ames gave Jake an address on Mt. Elliot and a phone number. "I work outta my house," he added.

"Thanks Mr. Ames. Now we've got to get back to our measuring."

The old man on the bike peddled off, taking the turn around the building at Concord.

"Think the old man bought the 'Economic Feasibility Study' bullshit you threw at him?"

"Hopefully enough where he doesn't call Macetti about us being here." Jake started stretching out his 300-foot tape. "How 'bout you go back inside and see if we picked the right spot to set up surveillance."

"Already done," Jess answered. "We'll get a good look at what's coming and going into Building 120."

"Good thing Jethro had that building number. It might help if Pruent comes up with the blueprints. Now all we gotta do is figure out how to get the equipment and us inside without Jethro seeing us."

"Got that figured out. We call him to meet us somewhere and get the stuff in while he's peddling his bike there," Jess answered. "A seventy-year-old man on a bike don't get around too quick."

"I kinda like the guy. A one-man security company still trying to earn his keep," Jake said as he reeled in the measuring tape, tucked his clipboard under his arm and followed Jess to their car.

———

Two days later Inspector Frank Pruent assigned Jimmy Prill, a patrolman, to work stakeout with Jake and Jess. Jimmy was on limited duty, assigned to the Auto Squad, and knew how to use the infrared camera.

The three officers loaded up the equipment, using a gray Ford borrowed from the Building Code and Enforcement Department, complete with a city logo on each door. At a pay phone, Jake called Jethro Ames. Jethro was at home, a good thirty minutes by bike away. Jake set a time to meet another thirty minutes later to give them time to set up.

Two Marine Corps duffle bags carried the camera, tripod, and miscellaneous equipment that Jimmy said they'd need. Surprisingly, the two wall plugs still had juice going to them. "Great," Jimmy said. "I've got battery packs if I need them, but power is better." Jimmy was left to install a padlock on the door, to keep the riffraff from stumbling onto it accidently.

"We'll be back to get you in no more than half an hour," Jess told him as he and Jake left for the walk to their city car.

Jess and Jake met Jethro Ames at Palmer, by the railroad tracks. Jake thanked him for being available on short notice. "Just had one question. The railroad tracks. Are they part of the parcel owned by Macetti, or are they owned by the railroad?"

"Can't really answer that. I just watch the buildings. Two checks a day that Mr. Macetti asked for. He never mentioned the railroad tracks."

"Well, sorry to inconvenience you Mr. Ames. Thought you'd know."

"No problem. Due for my second round anyway."

Jake held up his hand, stopping the man as he started to mount his old bike. "I'm curious as to what Mr. Macetti's reaction was about us being here?"

"Never called it in. He said not to bother him unless someone was messin' with the property. You weren't messin' with nothing."

Jake smiled and looked at his partner. "We'll tell our boss about you and pass along your number, in case the city buys the property. They'll need a man like you looking out for their interests."

"Thanks. I'll get to my rounds." Two skips on thin legs later the man in the white shirt wobbled off on his bike. Jake and Jess drove their Ford towards the buildings across East Grand Boulevard to pick up Jimmy Prill.

————

At precisely 6:15 the next night, a van stopped on Concord just south of East Grand Boulevard. One man carrying a rucksack slipped out the side door and ambled towards the skeleton of the south building, part of the Packard Plant. The same van dropped off two more men dressed in dark clothes at two different places. It was a cloudy October, and the change from daylight savings time the week before brought long shadows and looming darkness. Jake was the first, slowly making his way to the one set of steps to the planned stakeout room. Chunks of plaster crunched under his brogans. He stopped as he neared his destination. In what little ambient light that was left he saw two young men huddled around the door with the new padlock. They were using a piece of rebar, prying at the hasp.

"What the hell you guys doing?" Jake barked.

The rebar fell to the floor as the two men whipped around. "Who the fuck're you?" a man in a black do-rag asked. The two spread out. Both were black. Do-rag had on a dark jacket, jeans and tennis shoes. The other had on a gray sweatshirt under an unzipped plaid hooded jacket.

Do-rag retrieved the metal bar; the other grabbed a hunk of two-by-four off the floor. The light penetrating the broken windows behind Jake was fading and he thought of the three-cell flashlight in the rucksack; he sure could use some light.

Jake did not want to blow their whole setup, so using his pistol was out. He reached into his rucksack, his hand finding his light. "I'm from Ames Security."

"Your white ass ain't workin' for Pop Ames. We're the night shift," Do-rag spit as he said it. The two inched towards Jake. "You best get your ass outta here."

Jake flicked on his light. Their hands shot up to cover their eyes. The man in the hooded jacket recovered and shuffled two steps forward. "Macetti said the place was ours."

Do-rag moved forward too. "I think this piece of shit'll look good beat to death next to that dog down the hall." Teeth shone behind the smile in the beam of Jake's light.

"Maybe it'll be you next to that dog." Jess's voice came from Jake's left.

Do-rag and his friend's eyes flicked from one white man to the other.

Jess held a nickel-plated revolver aimed at the man with the board. "Now on the floor or buy a fuckin' bullet." The barrel of Jess's pistol caught what little light there was as he waved it.

Metal dropped as another flashlight brought more light to the hallway. Jimmy Prill was behind the light, a pistol firmly in his hand.

"Man, what's goin' on?" Do-rag spoke as he went to the floor.

Jess stepped forward, a flashlight in one hand, his .38 in the other. He kicked the rebar one way and the two-by-four another. "Jake, did Dom say anything about a couple of black punks working midnight security?"

"Not a word." Jake answered.

"Call him." Do-rag butted in. "He knows me. I'm Bone Dog."

"I think we should just shoot the muther fuckers." Jess nudged Do-rag with the toe of his shoe. "What's his number, asshole?"

Do-rag gave the number. "He'll vouch for us. We work for him."

"We got a job to do guys," Prill chimed in.

Jess nodded. "Hands behind your backs." He put a boot to the one closest to him. Jake grabbed a roll of duct tape out of his rucksack. Wrists and ankles were secured. A large patch went across each of the men's mouths.

While Jake and Jess were doing this, Prill had his room open and had the camera rolling as bodies were dragged into the room. "Your pink Lincoln just showed up," Prill whispered.

Jess grabbed the field glasses. "Same license number."

Jake knew it by heart and jotted it down.

Two more cars pulled up the ramp. They stopped long enough for Jess to relay plate numbers to Jake. In the next two hours ten more cars pulled up the ramp and into the open overhead metal door on Building 120. A time or two a car's pause was not long enough for Jess to read the plate number, but make, color, and a partial number would suffice.

"Holy shit," said Prill. "They've got a mass production going on in there."

"Yeah, and we have our friends on the floor behind us to blow our cover." Jake looked over and could see the two sets of eyes darting about. The dim portable light Prill had set up gave Jess, Jake and Jimmy just enough light to operate with. Every time a car pulled onto the ramp, the camera rolled.

At nearly four in the morning the metal door rolled open. The pink Lincoln was nosing onto the ramp. "Must be wrapping up for the night," Jess said. "A black Buick is next. Jake you got a number on a black Buick?" It stopped long enough to padlock the door.

"Got numbers on two dark Buicks."

"Call *Radio* and have a car stop this one. Must be who's running the show. Give the operator both numbers."

Jake pulled out the portable Motorola. "Five-Two-Five calling Radio."

"Go Twenty-five."

"We need a car in Number Seven in the vicinity of Concord and the Boulevard to make a stop for us."

"Is there a car in Number Seven near Concord and the Boulevard? Five-Two-Five needs an assist."

"Seven-Six, radio. What do they need?"

Jake relayed the information on the car with two possible plate numbers, adding that they should just make a routine stop and get the names and addresses of the occupants.

The three cops packed away their equipment. "What about our two guests?" Jimmy asked.

"Shoot 'em," Jess said.

The eyes of the two started darting around.

"Think Pruent can keep them out of circulation for a couple of days?" Jake asked as he was about to radio for the van to pick them up.

"I'm sure he can," Jimmy said. "And away from phones." He helped lift Do-rag, alias Bone Dog, to his feet.

Don was driving his 1970 Buick Gran Sport while Wayne padlocked the overhead door. "When's that load of parts being shipped?" Don asked as Wayne slid into the seat beside him.

"Dom's man, Ralph, said a truck would be by tomorrow. 'Bout one or two."

"Good, I have ten pallets of transmissions and rear ends taking up too much floor space." Don put the car in drive and coasted down the ramp. "Call him back and tell him to send two trucks. I've got a ton of radios and fenders. Also tell him his Charger is ready. I need it out of the way."

The Buick rolled onto the Boulevard and headed to the west side of Detroit.

"How many cars did he send us today?" Wayne asked.

"Too many if he doesn't start shipping some stuff."

"I'll call him."

Red lights flashed in the Buick's rearview mirror. "What the fuck is this?" Don muttered as he slowed the Buick and pulled to the curb. The police car pulled in behind. Don watched as a cop in a dark blue tunic approached his side. Don rolled down his window.

"Sir, can I see your license and registration, please?"

Don dug out the papers. "Is there a problem officer?"

"Need some ID from your partner, too."

Wayne reached for his wallet and leaned over to hand it to the waiting officer.

"No, no real problem," the officer said. "Just an odd time of the night to be out cruising. Nice car, by the way."

"Thanks," Don replied. "Odd shift at the plant the last few weeks. Behind on orders."

"Where's that?"

"A little place that feeds Chrysler. Near Belle Isle."

That seemed to satisfy the officer. "Be right back."

"Why do you think he stopped us?" Don asked.

"Two white guys in a black neighborhood," Wayne answered casually.

The cop returned. "Here guys, thanks." He handed Don Schutt the two licenses and the registration. "Just so you know, a couple of whores on Gratiot said some white guys stiffed them. They said it was two dudes a bit younger than you guys though." The officer went back to his car.

Don put the car in gear and continued west. "That reminds me, brother. Mind if I whip onto John R and see if Yolanda is still out. I could use a quick head job."

"Not with me in here. I'm not into watchin'."

"Chicken shit." Don drove on, just glancing down John R. Yes, Yolanda was leaning on a light pole at Milwaukee. "All work and no play they say—"

"Forget it." Wayne leaned his head against his window and dozed off.

————

Seven-Six and the crew of Five Twenty-five met at Biff's across from the Belle Isle Bridge for a coffee and to exchange information. "They were just some guys we were tailing from our side of town. Didn't want to tip them off," Jess explained to the two officers. When they went to leave and the two in blue tried to pay for the cinnamon rolls Jake had ordered with the coffees.

"My partner's got it guys, thanks." Jess looked at Jake and smiled.

Jake got out his wallet and pulled out a five. Seven-six waved and drove off. "How did I get to pay?"

"The guy who orders, pays. House rules." Jess smiled again and slid in behind the wheel.

"Let's have Pruent pull the records on Donald and Wayne Schutt tomorrow." Jake said. "See what we're dealing with."

Ralph Bunk relayed the message from Wayne Schutt to Dominic. "They said your Charger is ready."

"Pick it up the next time you deliver a car."

Just two weeks earlier Dominic saw that one of his guys latched on to a 1971 Dodge Charger R/T and was going to deliver it to the shop to be cut up. It had a black vinyl top over a red body. He gave his man orders to have the Schutts repaint it, changing the red to Burnt Orange. He wanted that car for himself. Dominic Macetti always wanted something that would smoke rubber when he hit the gas. The 440 Magnum engine that came standard on the R/T and its 370 horses could do that.

Inspector Frank Pruent was presiding over a meeting that included Lieutenant Richard Dungy of TMU, Lieutenant Pierce of the Seventh Precinct, five of his own patrolmen and finally Jimmy Prill, Jake and Jess. He filled everyone in on the chop shop operating at the old Packard Plant. "We're going to have to raid the place tonight," he was saying. "I've got two guys I've been juggling, keeping them away from a phone. We've run out of time."

Jake and Jess knew that Bone Dog and Willie Peebles would blow their operation out of the water. Jess turned his head towards Jake and whispered, "Tol' you we shoulda shot them."

Jake just shook his head. Sometimes he didn't know when Jess was joking or when he wasn't. Pruent would have to let them each make a call. One for sure would be to Macetti and for sure, he'd shut the operation down.

"At 2:30 a.m. we close the place down." said Pruent. "Lieutenants Dungy and Pierce said they'd have enough men to assist with the raid. Whatever we get by that time is what we'll fly with." Pruent ended the meeting. He asked Prill, Scott, and Bush to stick around.

"Tonight I want you guys back out there. Film everything you can, get plate numbers and whatever. At two-fifteen shut it down. You three got the rollup door. The guys from TMU, my guys and number seven will cover the other three ways out."

He assigned the mission the name *Night Watch*. For any radio communication, the Seventh Precinct is Night Watch Seven, TMU is Night Watch Eight, The inside guys, Jake, Jess and Jimmy, were given Five for a call number. "The Auto Squad will be one," added Pruent. "Any questions?" There were none.

It was 7 o'clock and quite dark when the black Buick with the Schutt brothers unlocked the rollup door. The pink Lincoln followed fifteen minutes later. At 8:00 p.m., 9:32 p.m. and 12:38 a.m. a Buick, Chevrolet and a Cadillac climbed the ramp and the rollup door was opened for them. Jess called out the license numbers of each to Jake. Prill caught it all on infrared film.

Ralph Brunk was the driver of the last car, a green 1972 Cadillac, to pull into the Packard Plant about half past midnight. His job was to pick up the other two drivers and the Charger.

"Give me about an hour or so," Wayne Schutt said. "Have a coffee. The Charger'll be ready then. I just riveted a different VIN plate in the driver's side door post and need to clean up the paper and tape."

At 1:00 a.m., Pruent's voice was heard over Jake's portable radio. "Night Watch One here. We've got two Freightliner box trucks at the back loading dock. When they leave, a couple of TMU crews will detain them away from the area."

Forty-five minutes later, Pruent reported that both trucks were stopped at Palmer and Mt. Elliot, and the drivers were in handcuffs.

"Night Watch Five, Shut it down," came the order from Pruent at precisely 2:15 a.m. Jimmy started taking down the camera while Jake and Jess moved down the stairs to take up positions near the ramp 150 yards away.

It was exactly 2:16 a.m. when Ralph and the two other drivers climbed in Macetti's Charger to leave. The engine growled when Ralph turned the key. The tires chirped a little as he put it in drive. "Watch them horses," said Wayne, leaning in the window. "Dom'll get pissed if you get a ticket on the way home." Ralph waved and eased towards the ramp.

———

Jimmy Prill slid the camera and tripod into the canvas case and zipped it closed. He started putting away the rest of their gear when he saw the rollup door rise. In the moonlight he saw a car drive down the ramp and into the night. He couldn't be sure, but he thought it was a Dodge Charger. He couldn't make out the color.

"And Jess has the fuckin' radio," he mumbled to himself.

In minutes, red and blue flashers filled the night. Building 120 was raided by men from TMU, Number Seven, Auto Squad, and Jess and Jake. The four men in the building were arrested.

Inspector Frank Pruent read them their rights as handcuffs where tightened on the wrists of Donald Schutt, age 52, Wayne Schutt, age 50, Dean Millspaugh age 31, and Sam Malone, 33. Jake was logging all this information for their report.

Jess looked at Jake as he was writing. "Jimmy tell you about the Charger that got away?"

"Yeah. He was smart enough to grab a partial plate though. Should have left him the radio."

Jess just shrugged.

Tuesday, October 23, 1973, Jake and Jess climbed the stairs coming from the range. They passed Fox's door and saw him in there. Jake knocked.

"Well, well. What the hell we got here? You planning on hanging out at your home for a while?" Fox stood and smiled.

"For a while," Jake answered. "I put a copy of our report in your box."

Fox motioned to a couple of chairs. Jake braced for an ass chewing. "I hope you two don't get big headed, but congratulations are in order. Inspector Pruent called Mills today. That's the biggest bust they've had in ten years."

Jake and Jess beamed. Jake spoke. "Just like pulling on a loose piece of yarn on a sweater. We just kept pulling to see where it went."

"You didn't get the big guy, I heard. Somebody named Macetti."

Jake said, "Sweater came apart too fast before we could put him in it."

"Okay. I understand, but how about sticking around our place for a while. The burglary numbers are going up."

"We've only been gone for a week," Jake answered.

"Ten days," Fox retorted.

———

Jake found Jesse's house out in the sticks and he didn't know how. It was three miles past Twenty-five Mile Road and two more to the east of Van Dyke. Jess was right; they didn't have signs at all the corners yet. But Jess described it well. "It's a ranch type home with a big-ass scarecrow hanging from a light post in the middle of the yard." Jess also mentioned to watch out for the dog. "He'll piss on your leg if you stand around too long." Jake growled at the dog that came running out from behind the house. It turned and ran with its tail between its legs. There were about four cars in the driveway besides Jesse's.

Against his better judgment, Jake did dress up for the Halloween party, sort of. He found a loud green plaid sport coat at a Salvation Army store and a fedora to go with it. He hoped to pass himself off as an Irish used car salesman. *For Tommy and Billy,* he told himself. He didn't have the courage to find a rubber mask to compliment his attire; he just went with a Lone Ranger mask. As he went to ring the doorbell, another thought hit him as he waited for someone to answer. *Jake, you look like a fuckin' idiot.*

The door opened and Beth, dressed as a sultry blond in a leopard-skin jumpsuit, put a big hug on him. "Jake, I'm so glad you could make it." She led him in the door.

There were about ten to twelve men and women inside wearing various costumes and at least a half dozen kids running around. Three of the youngsters were dressed as Superman and so was one of the grownups—the one and only "I don't wear costumes"—Jesse Scott.

Tommy and Billy ran up to see "Uncle Jake." It had been a few years. They still remembered him, mask or not. As they tugged at his arms, he had flashes of Deb and Michelle playing with him.

Beth grabbed Jake by the arm before the faces of Mike and Jeanette appeared. "Jake, this is someone I want you to meet. My friend, Edie."

He was glad for the interruption.

"Hello, Edie." Jake tried to smile as he held the hand of a 200 pound witch draped in black with a wart on her nose. He could tell the wart was phony, he didn't know about the rest. The witch smiled and Jake saw a twinkle in her eye.

The witch spoke. "Beth told me so much about you. You're Jesse's partner, right?"

"The only one who would have him, I guess." Jake paused. "Besides Beth, that is."

Chapter Ten

It was Devil's Night in Detroit and Five Twenty-five was rolling in their dark blue Chrysler. Jess was driving. As usual, he headed out for Kercheval. Jake propped the car board in its place. "The pyromaniacs are gonna be out tonight."

Jess just grunted in acknowledgement. Five minutes later he spoke. "What'd you think of that witch the other night?"

The full sentence surprised Jake. He just shrugged. "What's to think?"

A smile crossed Jess's face. "You spent a lot of time talking to her."

"She's nice to talk to."

"Get her number."

"No."

"Why?"

Jake shrugged again.

"Here." Jess handed Jake a piece of paper.

"What's this?"

"Her number."

"Jess, I—"

"Take the note. Beth's orders." Jake pocketed the piece of paper without looking at it.

"Do what you want with it," Jess deadpanned. "I'm just the delivery boy."

"All units Ten-five's in a chase. Go ahead Ten-five."

"South on the Lodge, heading towards the Ford."

"Repeat the description on the car Ten-five."

"Black over burnt orange Dodge. He's taking the eastbound Ford. He's leaving us—"

"All units, going east on the Ford, Ten-five is in pursuit of a—" Jess hit the gas and headed towards Conner as the radio chatter kept all cars abreast of the chase. At Conner, Jess turned towards the Ford Freeway.

"Radio this is Eight-fifteen. We're behind the Dodge, still heading east."

"Seven-ten's got the off ramp blocked at Mt. Elliot."

"Eight-fifteen, radio; we need a couple of cars ahead of this maniac. We can't keep up."

The radio operator responded, "Is there a car that can block the off ramp at Van Dyke?"

"Fifteen-two's got that."

"Eight-Six-0 and Eight-eighteen are on the Ford at Van Dyke awaiting the Dodge." Jake recognized Dungy's voice. Jess took the ramp at Conner.

"You got 'im Six-0. He's comin' up on your ass."

The radio was silent for a minute.

"Box 'im in. Box im' in." Again, it was Dungy's voice.

Jess slowly descended the down ramp at Conner. Two cars from Fifteen fell in behind. Jake was twisted around looking for headlights and the TMU's blue flashers. He waited for an update by radio. Jess was crawling along at twenty miles per hour.

"Radio, this is Eight-Six-0. We have the driver in custody."

"Might as well get back to the quiet of Number Five," Jess mumbled. As he took the next ramp off the freeway, they could see streaks of red and blue flashers bouncing off the walls of the Ford freeway behind them. Jake knew Jess's heart rate was up, the same as his. A chase does that to every man working the street. If it doesn't, you're not a cop.

———

Other than the chase, Devil's Night was the same as it had been for the last few years—hundreds of vacant homes were torched. Jake reflected on the 1950's, when the guys in his neighborhood, Jake included, would engage in more benign pranks—ringing doorbells and running away. Others may have gone so far as to toilet-paper their neighbors' trees. Jake passed on that one.

As Jake patrolled the streets of Detroit in 1973, Devil's Night meant the little pranks had grown to full-blown arson. Five Twenty-five's radio blared out calls for "Meet the Fire Department" at addresses in Number Five, Seven and Thirteen. Jake hoped all were vacant homes that wouldn't be a big loss.

Jake and Jess stopped a total of thirty-three alley walkers and corner loiterers, and not one matchbook was found in the 100 or more pockets turned inside out, nor any of them had a hint of a gasoline-laced cologne. The cigarette-smoking detainees had lighters. No matches. Sniffing hands and clothes weren't in Jess and Jake's normal search procedure, but they did exactly that all night long.

Jake was tucking away their stolen car board and info binder in his locker. Jess came in the door two minutes later and opened his locker across the aisle. "Last bit of advice, Jake. You should call Edie. Her costume was a good one."

Jake started to say something, stopped, then closed his locker. "I'll give it some thought."

———

Fox had left some papers in the box for the crew of Five Twenty-five which Jake grabbed on his way through on Halloween night. There was an update from Inspector Frank Pruent of Auto Squad. After the normal "thanks for your good work" blather, the note went on to say: One of the men you arrested at the Packard Plant, Dean Millspaugh, was also charged with "Unlawfully Driving Away an Auto" and

"Possession of Stolen Property." His pink Lincoln was previously white and stolen on September 11, 1973.

The next item of interest was on the black and burnt-orange Dodge the TMU was chasing on October 30th. It was driven by a Dominic Macetti. The car had been reported stolen two weeks before and repainted. Someone forgot to change the VIN on the car's firewall to match those by the windshield and on the driver's door post. Mr. Macetti was charged with Felonious Driving, Reckless Driving (with life endangerment), possession of stolen property and UDAA.

"You ain't gonna believe this, Jess. The man behind the chop shop, Macetti, was nailed for driving a stolen car." Jake laughed.

Jess took the note out of Jake's hand to read it. "Humph," was his only comment.

There were eight more pieces of paper in the box for the crew of Five Twenty-five: Four subpoenas each for Patrolman John A. Bush and Patrolman Jesse Scott. They were to appear before Judge George Crocket at Detroit Recorder's Court to give evidence in the preliminary hearings for Donald Schutt, Wayne Schutt, Dean Millspaugh, and Samuel Malone, on November 1, 1973, at 8am.

"Looks like we're going to spend a lot of time in court tomorrow, Jess."

"Comes with the job." Jess pocketed his subpoenas.

———

Sunday evening Jake paced the floor. He spent all day Thursday and Friday in court; most of the time just sitting and waiting while the lawyers and the prosecutor filed one motion after another. The night before, Saturday, Jess and Jake both took the night off on "Court Time." Fox complained that they had too much on the books and Saturday was a good day to burn at least eight hours of what was due them. Jake picked up three books at the library. He read *The New Centurions* that night, a novel by an ex-cop from Los Angeles.

Sunday morning Jake ran around Belle Isle. It gave him time to think. Later, that Sunday's football game didn't keep him interested. He went out to pick up a pizza before half-time. The Lions ended up beating the Forty-Niners, but he found himself starting Wambaugh's second book while the announcers droned on. Three times he put the book down and picked up the phone. Three times he changed his mind. At 8:30 that evening, he dialed the number that was scribbled on a crumpled piece of paper. On the third ring a female voice answered. "Hello?"

There was a long pause. "Edie, this is Jake."

"Jake, it's good to hear from you." He could hear her giggle.

Jake breathed deeply. *There, the ice is broken.* "I've been meaning to call—"

Fifteen minutes later the call ended. He smiled as he read his notes. Cops take notes when they talk on the phone. Even a personal call. The lady's full name was Edith Ruth Douglas.

Jake went back to his book. A half page later he put it down.

———

The following Tuesday, Jake shot the best he ever had since Jess and him started going to the range. Jake then breezed through the teletypes and updated the stolen car board before Jess could return with two coffees. At 7:00 on the nose, he was behind the wheel of Five Twenty-five. He drove straight to the alleys behind the south side of Mack, then moved to the alleys on the north side. All the while he drove, he talked about the books he read, the state of Belle Isle while he ran and the impending frost warnings for the night.

Two hours went by and Jake unceasingly talked. Jess let him ramble. They checked the businesses on Kercheval, front and back, then Jake returned to Mack Avenue. He was in his second alley on the south side. "Hold it," Jess mumbled. As the car slowed Jess was out his door. Jake threw the Chrysler into park and was out with his flashlight and their portable radio. He saw the same flash of lights that Jess had. Jess went to the back door and looked in.

"I'll cover the front," Jake whispered. He broke into a run, took the side street and around the corner at Mack. He guessed that he wanted to be four doors to the east. He slowed, peering in store windows as he crept. The second store down, a shoe store, looked okay. The next, a grocery store, took a while, but he saw no movement. Then he peered in the big plate glass window on the front of Rexall Drugs. He saw movement. Jake stared into the dark store interior. *There.* He saw it again. Someone was inside. Jake keyed the mike on the portable. "Radio, this is Five Twenty-five. Need a couple of cars at—" He backed away to catch an address. "3274 Mack. We've got a B&E man inside."

"Cars in Five, Five Twenty-five needs some help at 3274 Mack, B&E in progress."

"Five Ten's on the way."

"Five-Two's right around the corner," came a second response.

Holmes and Radcliff from Five-Two drove up and dismounted. "Guys, take the rear. Jess is there alone. They jumped back into their unit and drove around the corner.

Jake heard the radio operator relaying Two's message telling Five-ten to go to the front of the Rexall store. Jake heard their car pull in behind him as he was watching a dark figure try to climb some shelving in the middle of the store. Jake pressed his light against the plate glass window and his beam broke the darkness just as shelving gave way. Boxes fell, and a body hit the floor.

"Can one of you guys radio the desk and get the owner here?" Jake asked the arriving crew. "I think our man came in through the ceiling and can't get out." Maleck went back to their unit to make the call.

"Jake. Up here." Jake looked up. Jess's head was hanging over the top of the brick wall above him. "Call the owner and get him here to open up."

"Already happening."

Jess's head disappeared from view. Three different flashlight beams slowly panned the inside of the drug store through the plate glass windows. The man inside was sitting down where he fell from his make-shift perch. Jake keyed the mike. "Radio, any word on the owner?" Jake's beam stayed on the man. He looked closely and recognized the wrapper. "He's eating a damn Hershey bar." Maleck and his partner chuckled in the background.

"Five Twenty-five, the owner's on the way. A half hour out."

"Hey!" It was Jess again. Jake craned his neck and looked up. "What the hell's taking so long?"

"The owner's on his way. Relax. The guy inside is eating candy bars."

"Tell him to send a couple up this way. I'm getting hungry."

Jokes outta Jess? Jake couldn't believe it.

A half an hour passed and Jake thought the guy on the inside was on his fifth candy bar. A white Ford pulled in behind the black Detroit Police car. A man with a jangling set of keys came up. "What's the problem, officer?"

"Need you to open up. Someone's inside eating all your candy." Jake shined his light on the recessed door so the man with the keys could unlock it. The first thing the owner did was hit the light switch. In the middle of the store sat a black male, who said his leg was broken, atop what was once the top shelf of a rack in the candy department. The owner, Mahendra Patel, unlocked the back door to let Jess and the crew from Five-two inside.

"Mr. Patel, can you check the pharmacy area?" Jess said. "I don't think the guy came in to just eat your candy."

Five-ten's ride was a station wagon with two folded stretchers behind the rear seat. Maleck wheeled one in while Bill Franks, his partner, looked for something to splint a broken leg. Under arrest was Dwight Lamont, Negro male, 23, of 2374 Hampshire. His jacket pockets were filled with pills. Jake got a couple of bags from behind the counter to put the evidence in while Mr. Patel tried to determine what they were. There were red ones, yellow ones and blue and white capsules.

"You get to count those," Jake said to Jess.

"Me?"

"Car rules. I type the reports, you tag the evidence."

Jess started counting. There was no arguing. Those were the rules he established when Jake came on the car.

Further questioning revealed that Lamont had dropped into the store by levering up the A/C unit with a large pry bar. Lamont readily admitted that he hadn't thought of how he'd get back out. He said he turned the lights on to see if there was a way without tripping the alarm.

Jake let out a little laugh when he heard that. *Yeah, half of what we do is by accident.* Five Twenty-five just happened to be in the alley at the time the lights were briefly on.

After the splint was put on Lamont's leg with the help of repatriated Ace bandages and some shelving splinters, he was hauled off to Detroit Receiving Hospital as a prisoner of the Detroit Police Department.

"Jezus Jenny, Jake. What the hell were you so cranked up about earlier? I was ready to put a sock in your mouth."

"I called Edie."

"And?"

"We had coffee last night."

"So?"

"So you were right. It was a good costume. She's about a hundred thirty with a nice set of legs."

"Shit. Now I've got a love-sick partner."

"Who said anything about love? We just met. Remember?"

"It's gonna be a close election next Tuesday." Jake waited for an answer from Jess. There wasn't any. He steered their Chrysler around two parked cars. "You talking tonight?"

Jess broke his silence. "I don't talk politics."

"Do you talk about anything?" Jake didn't get an answer.

Jake was slowly driving alleys behind residential streets with his lights out. Occasionally they'd pick up an abandoned stolen car that way. A half block ahead a set of taillights went on and a car started to move. Jake turned on his lights. The car ahead sped away, taking a right on the first cross street. Jake mashed the gas and made the same turn. Two blocks and a left turn later, Jake saw the car brake hard, the driver's door open and a man out running. Jake bailed out with his feet churning. He knew Jess would climb behind the wheel and try to head off the runner.

The man cut to the right over a fence. Jake went over the same fence and was twenty yards behind. The man took a left across the front yard of a house and Jake was gaining. At the side street it was a pure foot race. Jake's strides brought him closer. The man cut left around a house. Jake took the corner. Whomp! Jake was thrown to the ground. All he could do is grab clothing and hang on. A fist caught Jake alongside the head. Another caught him in the shoulder. Jake hung on with his left hand and started pummeling whoever he had ahold of. One second Jake was under the man, the next, he was on top. Jake felt a hand at his pistol. Jake reached for it.

"Whoa! Whoa, man!" The man's hands flew up in surrender.

Jake reached for his cuffs and secured a right wrist, twisting it behind the man's back. In a second he had the other cuff on. "On your feet," he gasped. Jake slowly turned to see where he was and tried remembering how far he chased the guy.

"What's with the cuffs, man?"

"They go with the badge. You're under arrest." Jake's heart rate started coming back down.

"I didn't know you was the m'fuckin' po-lice!"

"In the flesh." Jake flashed his badge and led his man under the street light. He was at the corner of Goethe and Montclair. Jake kept a tight grip on the guy. Jake had to look up at him, he was at least five inches taller than Jake. The man was black, bald and his ears stuck out like small radar dishes—too big for his head. He was about 35 and had two teeth missing.

"I thought you was Amelia's ol' man."

"Who's Amelia?"

"Frank's wife."

"Who's Frank."

"A guy from work. Only thing I knew was a white guy was chasin' me."

"Frank's white?"

"Yeah."

"I'm not buyin' that shit."

A block down Jake saw the lights of his car as Jess turned the corner. Within a half hour Nathaniel Glass sat in the bullpen at the Fifth Precinct, while the car he ditched was carefully searched in the precinct garage. Jess took care of the search. There was nothing in the car that would keep Nathaniel in jail. Jess didn't tag the half gross of rubbers he found in the glove box.

Jake was on the phone with the Wants and Warrant's Division. Nathaniel was then fingerprinted and held for the Fifth Precinct Dicks on a report Jake titled: "Hold for Investigation." Jake was hoping the man's fingerprints and mug shot would reveal a long record, maybe another identity, something that would make the foot race and punches he took worthwhile.

The next day Jake got a call from Detective Rodney Peaks. "Prints, nothing. Record, none. Sorry Jake, I guess he was just banging Reggie's wife as he said. You just happened to drive up as he was leaving." Peaks let out a little chuckle. "You want to come down and talk to him before we boot him?"

"No. Just tell him to stay away from other men's wives. He could get shot."

"He says he realized that when he felt the pistol in your belt. The one phone call he made was to his preacher. I think he's repenting."

Jake ended the conversation rubbing the knot on his head, wondering if he got in a few good licks that Nathaniel would remember.

The November, 1973 Detroit mayoral election pitted the recently resigned Police Commissioner, John Nichols, against

Coleman Young, a black social activist, who was first elected as a Michigan State Senator in 1964. Coleman Young was put in office by the slim margin of 16,741 votes. Jake voted for Nichols, but was hoping that Young's election would somehow revive the dying city.

The elm trees were all but bare as mid-November came and went. A few remaining leaves hung on until the bitter end, like some of the residents, people like Jake and Jess who cling to the hope that Detroit would rise from the ashes still smoldering after the '67 riot.

Jake called Edie before going to work the next day. He didn't talk politics.

———

Jess was parked among fifteen or so cars in an apartment parking lot. Jake added a pack of sugar into the cup of coffee, stirred it and took a sip. It was November 21st. The Lions were playing the Redskins at noon the next day, and Jess, Beth and the boys were joining Jake at Edie's house for Thanksgiving dinner.

Jake was a bit nervous. Other than a few phone calls and one night out for coffee, Jake wasn't really ready for a full-blown dinner with kids and all the family stuff that goes with a holiday meal. Edie said she had two boys, Hank and Sam. It had been a long time since Jake's last family-type holiday meal, but with Jess and Beth there, he thought he could handle it.

Jake picked up the field glasses and scanned the parking lot at the Chatham supermarket across Jefferson. The air was damp and cold. Rain was predicted. Maybe some frost. The store closed at nine, and Jess wanted to just watch things until then. He thought it was a good change of pace. The store was crowded with last minute shoppers scrambling for overlooked things they needed for the holiday meal.

Yams. Anne always wanted yams and cranberry sauce.

Jess said that shopping carts with unattended purses were good targets at a supermarket. For some reason women assumed things were safe under bright neon lights, while jostling around thin aisles with stocked shelves.

Jake broke the silence. "You know, one of us with the portable radio on foot somewhere out there—"

"Good idea." With that Jess grabbed their Motorola walkie-talkie and slid out his door.

The radio in Five Twenty-five scanned Eastside Radio and had a separate frequency where Jake could talk to Jess and vice versa. With Jess on foot, that meant Jake had to be near the radio. He grabbed the binoculars and focused on the Chatham store's lot.

———

Jess became a shopper. He went into the store and grabbed a cart. Ten minutes later, in the baking aisle, he overheard the tail end of a conversation coming from the next aisle.

"You two just wait outside. When you see me coming out, I'll be behind the mark."

Another voice said, "Where do you want us?"

"Somewhere close, but not too close. Whoever's in front of me's got the cash."

Jess left the cart with the Cheerios, bag of pancake mix, and dish soap in the aisle. He didn't see who was doing the talking, but knew he had to be outside. *Whatever's going down, will happen outside.*

He went to the first car near the store entrance and fiddled with the trunk like he was unlocking it. Seconds later two men came out the door following a woman pushing a cart. They waltzed around her. Both were black and around 20. The taller of the two was bare headed and wore a red nylon jacket. The second man had on a pork-pie hat and a heavy black jacket. They walked to a dark-colored Ford in the lot. One of them opened the trunk.

Jess walked back towards the entrance and cut around the corner of the building. There stood an older black man lighting a cigarette. He had on a white Chatham apron and a white hat with red trim. Jess flashed his badge. "Stay here and smoke while I borrow your hat and apron."

The guy almost choked on his first puff. "Whatchew talkin' about?"

"Quick, the apron and the hat. What're you supposed to be doing out here?"

"Gatherin' the carts."

"I'll do that for you. You stay outta sight. Smoke two or three cigarettes if you have to." Jess donned the hat and apron. "I'll let you know when your smoke break is over."

"Sounds good to me." The man grabbed a discarded cabbage crate and sat on it.

Jess shuffled around the corner and started collecting carts. He saw the two men still at their Ford. Jess stayed a row of cars away, looking for a stray cart here, another there.

———

Jake spotted Jess collecting shopping carts in the lot. Jake dropped the glasses mumbling to himself, "What the hell?" He checked again. Yes, it was Jess, his gray sweatshirt under an apron bearing the Chatham logo on the bib and wearing a funny white hat with red trim. Jake figured he could leave Jess to his own devices especially since he didn't have a clue as to what he was up to. Jake scanned the lot from one end to another. Nothing looked out of place.

"Jake!" It was Jess's voice over the radio.

"Go."

"Check the two guys beyond where I've got the carts pointed."

Jake swung the field glasses to where Jess left a line of empty carts. The lights from beyond the plate glass windows and the large sign over the top of the store illuminated the area. Jake spotted two men alongside a dark Ford right where the carts were pointed. They were fifty yards from the store's entrance. The trunk was open. One man, wearing a red nylon jacket, leaned into the trunk and rummaged through it for a second or two, closed it and joined a hat-wearing friend at the side of the car.

"There's a third inside the store." Again, Jess's voice.

Jake fixed his binoculars on the two. They started moving slowly towards the front of the store. Jake saw a glint of something alongside the right leg of the man who had been in the trunk. Jake looked for Jess. He couldn't see him. Jake keyed the mike. "Watch the guy in red. He took something out of the trunk." Jake slipped out of their Chrysler and ran across Jefferson.

A couple came out of the door pushing a shopping cart. The man had an afro; the woman had a shawl covering her head. The man was stuffing something into his wallet. Close behind came another man, his hands were thrust deep into the pockets of his black coat. Jake didn't know where Jess was, but knew something was going down.

Jake weaved in and out of parked cars, keeping his eyes on the couple pushing their cart. To his left, he saw Red Jacket and his hat-wearing pal. They were walking straight towards the couple. The man wearing the hat lunged, knocking the woman away from the cart and to the ground. Jake was 50 feet away, drawing his magnum and running.

A gun came up in the hand of Red Jacket. His eyes were on the woman's companion. "The wallet, mutha fucker." His pistol moved slightly just as a shot rang out.

Red Jacket fell.

"Freeze! Police! Jake yelled.

From out of nowhere Jess was airborne, throwing a body block at the man with the hat. In one motion he scrambled up and drop kicked the guy just to make sure he was out of commission. Number three, Black Jacket, looked at Jess, then to Jake, and for a way to run. Jake's pistol swung towards the man's chest. "Don't even try." Jake took another step. "On the ground, asshole!"

The man made the right choice. He got on his belly with his hands over his head.

The man in the afro bent over to help the woman up. "Kate, you all right?"

"What's goin' on?" she asked.

"Don't know."

Jess flashed his badge. "I'll be right with you." He bent over and checked Mister Red Jacket. He was writhing on the ground, crying. He was hit, but alive.

Jess flipped his cuffs to Jake. Jake cuffed pork-pie hat, then Mr. Black Jacket.

Jess keyed the mike on his portable. "Radio, this is Five Twenty-five—"

Sirens wailed and red lights flashed. Fire rescue carted Red Jacket away. Jess's bullet had gone in the right side of his chest and out the back shoulder blade. The man's good arm was shackled to the stretcher. Patrolman Southworth rode in the ambulance with the prisoner.

Five Seven-0, a pair of sergeants, had the intended victims in their car and were taking notes. Detectives were on the scene interviewing witnesses.

Jake tapped Jess on the shoulder. "How 'bout getting outta the damn apron?"

"Forgot." Jake could see a little red rise on Jess's face. "Be right back."

Jess jogged to the corner of the store just past the door. "Hey, smoke break is over." He tossed the hat and apron towards the man and walked back to the crowd of cops and people.

———

The Lions were getting mauled by the Redskins. The saving grace was that Beth and Edie had the table set. Any empty space was filled with bowls of yams, mashed potatoes, green beans, and cranberry sauce. Jess had the steaming turkey in front of him and was wielding the carving knife. "Billy, your turn to say grace," he said.

Billy reached over and grabbed his brother's hand. Edie grabbed Jake's with her left hand and her youngest son's hand with her right. Billy started, "Bless us, oh Lord—"

It had been a long time since Jake heard those words. Only it wasn't Billy's voice he heard, it was Debbie's. A tear welled in his eye.

Chapter Eleven

The Detroit Lions were shut out by the Redskins, twenty to zip in that Thanksgiving Day game. At seven that evening Jake and Jess were rolling in their blue Chrysler. Jake's mind was elsewhere, thinking about how well behaved Hank and Sam were for five and seven year old boys. They didn't pay attention to Jake spending a lot of time with their mom, but then, they were busy rough-housing with Jess's two boys.

On their only coffee date, Jake had told Edie how he'd lost his family among a few tears. Correction, lots of tears. Edie, in turn, had filled Jake in on her life. She had an ex-husband somewhere. She hadn't seen him since the divorce three years before. Her child-support checks came straight from Anheuser-Bush, the company her ex worked for.

The street lights flickering on Mack brought Jake back to the present. "Thanks for being there today, partner."

A grunted response was all Jake heard.

"I mean it. I don't think I could've done the Thanksgiving thing alone."

"Maybe that's why Edie invited us."

Jake checked the plates on a Ford that crossed in front of them at Warren, a subconscious move that both he and Jess did as they drove the streets of the Fifth Precinct. Jake laughed to himself, thinking how many times he caught himself looking at a license plate as he drove to or from work only to realize he didn't carry a stolen car board in his 1969 rust-riddled Ford.

Jess's voice broke Jake's train of thought. "It's time you stopped mourning, Jake."

"What do you know?"

"I don't, but then two years seems long enough."

"When did you become a psychologist?"

"Today."

Jess talked and Jake liked it. It might be only in bits and pieces, but it was a start. That's what he liked about Edie, she talked and listened.

A red Camaro with a blonde behind the wheel cut Jess off and made a right turn onto Conner. She was going somewhere in a hurry. Jess took the turn and went after her.

––––––

Laurie Stutkiewicz was quite a looker as she'd struggled through her four years at Pershing High. Over the course of those years she'd found out that some male teachers were subject to delusions of grandeur if she sat a certain way, flashing her long legs, or exposing just a bit of cleavage. It was those little things that had earned her a "C" in the few classes that she was teetering on flunking, or, at best, getting a low "D." She remembered one stubborn old codger—he was forty-two—who was flunking her in chemistry until a couple of trips to her knees in his after-hours lab convinced him that she was really an "A" student.

What she didn't realize was that once school was out, she had to actually produce to earn a paycheck. She got a job as a cashier at J.L. Hudson's when she was 19. The second time her register was short, they quietly let her go. The shortages amounted to $175. Her manager, Mrs. Penny Bridgman, thought Laurie couldn't count. In fact, Laurie used the money to improve her wardrobe. She liked to dress flashy.

Her next job was at Progressive Electric, a small electrical supply company, doing clerical work like billing the contractors and checking the accuracy of invoices. One little dalliance, with her skirt hiked above her waist and panties around one ankle after closing time, earned her a move up to the company's one and only desk in the Accounts Payable department.

In six months Laurie miss-sent three checks to herself that she neatly forged for her own personal use. Hanging paper and forging checks became a way of life for her. She was good at it. If a boss questioned some missing funds, a quick screwing would get her a reprieve for a month or two, but not forever. In three years she had five jobs.

The early seventies was a good time for a well-endowed, pretty young miss with killer legs to find employment. The human resource people, predominantly males, were the easiest to convince that she was the right fit for their company. Laurie's biggest conquest was while she was employed at the Burroughs Corporation, working at their Third Avenue offices in Detroit. It took auditors a year and a half to realize that Laurie was up to no good. She lost track of the number of times a lifted skirt in a storage room stalled their probes. One day, she simply didn't show up for work after being tipped off by a gracious recipient of her sexual expertise. Laurie knew the ugly schmuck was in love with her. "Thank you," she'd whispered as she kissed him good-bye. Laurie Stutkiewicz simply disappeared. She became Laurie Stark. A new driver's license and social security card said so. There was no Mr. Stark.

Jess pulled alongside the red Camaro when the female driver finally stopped for a light at Jefferson. Jake flashed his badge and motioned for the woman to pull over. She turned onto Jefferson and into the bus stop.

"See what her story is, Jake," Jess said.

"She cut you off, not me."

"Yeah, it's probably safer that I talk to her."

"What'd ya mean by—" Jake's words faded into an empty seat as Jess walked to the driver's side of the Camaro. Jake had to hustle to cover his side of the car, a procedure he and Jess had learned years before during their TMU training. Whether the driver was a woman or a man—one cop took the driver, the other covered him by watching through the rear window from the passenger's side rear fender.

Jess talked to the girl for a minute or two, then walked back to Jake. "Get a name check on this woman." He handed Jake her driver's license.

"What's up?"

"There's something about her I don't like."

Jake reached in his open window for the mike and called the radio operator.

Five minutes later *Radio* came back with, "Nothing on Laurie Stark, DOB 5/15/50. That plate is registered to her on a 1973 Chevrolet Camaro.

"Thanks, Radio." Jake raised his voice. "Nothing on her."

Jess asked the woman to get out of her car. "See my partner, ma'am." She brought her purse as she walked to the front of the Chrysler.

"What the fuck's going on?" she asked over her shoulder as she saw Jess start to search her car. "I don't like being treated like a common criminal."

Laurie walked with an exaggerated swing, making sure everyone could see the entire package. Jake motioned for her to join him on the curb. By then, Jess was going through her glove compartment and under the seats in her car.

"Ma'am, please open your purse."

"What'd ya think, I gotta gun?"

"Never know."

"I don't like—"

Her words were cut off by a whistle from Jess. Jake saw him throwing a thumb towards the station. Jess had found a reason to run Laurie Stark in.

Laurie flashed a broad smile. "What's it gonna cost me? Two quickies just to hear you say, bye-bye pretty girl?"

Jake slowly backed to his car, reached in the door for the mike and keyed it. "Radio, have a car meet Five-Two-Five, Conner and Jefferson. We've got a car to go in."

"What the hell's going on?" Laurie complained as Jake took her purse and started slipping on a set of shiny handcuffs.

"Ma'am, you're under arrest."

"What for?"

"You name it. Being too vulgar? Accosting a police officer? We'll make something up if we have to." Jake turned the woman and guided her into the back seat of the Chrysler.

Jess showed Jake what he'd found. "These were in her glove compartment." He fanned three more drivers' licenses with different names on them.

Five-Ten showed up. Maleck had Remington Southworth with him. Jess asked them to run the car into the station. Maleck looked into the back of the Chrysler and only whispered, "Wow!"

That prompted Remington to take a look. Laurie Stark looked like she belonged on the big screen. She had long blonde hair and was wearing a tight white blouse under a loose black leather jacket. If being handcuffed behind her back didn't show enough, she made sure her chest was thrust fully forward so that any of the four cops looking didn't have to overtax their imagination.

Jess knew what Maleck and Southworth were thinking. He smiled and flipped Remington the keys. "Clear your mind, kid. You've got a car to drive."

The Fifth Precinct was set up so that when someone walked in the front door a thirty-foot wide mahogany desk stood about twenty feet in with a wall and maps behind it. The desk normally had a lieutenant in the center with a patrolman clerk on one end and maybe a police cadet manning the switchboard. More often than not, there was a sergeant behind the desk too, if he wasn't out on the streets checking on his men. Jake and Jess brought Laurie Stark in through the garage and over to the front desk.

Lieutenant Archbold frowned when he looked up and saw the crew on his B&E car bringing in a woman wearing handcuffs. He ordered them removed.

Well excuse us, Jake thought as he took them off. The lieutenant then spoke to the blonde. "Sorry ma'am," he said. "Please have a seat there while I see what these officers have." Jake moved Laurie to a straight-backed chair in a corner near the front door of the station house. He stood next to her while Jess talked to the lieutenant.

Sergeant Ryan and Patrolman Wilson, the clerk, made sure they got their eyes full of the legs and cleavage sitting just fifteen feet in front of the desk, while the 18-year old cadet, Bill Philo, spilled his Coke while trying not to be caught looking. Laurie was well aware of the attention she was getting and posed accordingly, smiling as the cadet left the desk to find some dry trousers.

Jess handed the lieutenant a crumpled piece of paper and a couple of other small items. The lieutenant looked at them and shook his head. "Ma'am, step forward, please." Laurie moved to the desk with Jake at her side. "We're going to have to hold you while we check a few things out. Can you explain having four drivers' licenses?"

The woman's face reddened. "I want to call my lawyer."

The precincts in Detroit did not have holding facilities for women, so Five Twenty-five transported Laurie Stark to the Women's Division on the eighth floor at 1300 Beaubien. It was there that she was fingerprinted and put in a holding cell. Laurie didn't really have a lawyer; she had to get a number out of the *Yellow Pages* to make her one call.

Back at the station, Jake typed up the report. It read: One arrest, Investigation of Uttering and Publishing. Arrested: Laurie Stark, W/F, DOB May 5, 1950. Address: 755 Somerset, Gross Pointe Park, Michigan. In parenthesis, Jake typed: May also use the names Laurie Smart, Laurie Ann Simms and Laurie Samson.

Under tag number 5-134589 in an evidence envelope, Jess put one crumply check drawn on the National Bank of Detroit by the Burroughs Corporation. The date was unreadable. It was made out to Laurie Stark in the amount of $4200. There was no signature in the appropriate spot.

Jake noted on the report that the check was found balled up under the driver's seat in a red 1973 Chevrolet Camaro by Patrolman Jesse Scott. The Camaro, bearing license number AR 3445 was registered to Laurie Stark of the above mentioned address.

The envelope under tag number 5-134590, contains four State of Michigan driver's licenses. The one bearing the name of Laurie Stark was on her person.

All four licenses had the same Michigan ID number: S125 973 051 052, and all had the same picture and the same birth date.

License # 2 issued to Laurie Smart of 13930 Rex, Detroit, Michigan; License #3 issued to Laurie Ann Simms of 922 Oakland, Highland Park, Michigan, and #4 issued to Laurie Samson of 11634 Collingwood, Detroit.

Jake was tired of typing and hoped the Check Squad would be able to sort things out. Five Twenty-five had four good reasons to arrest the woman.

———

Jess and Jake were at the Y pumping iron the next morning. Jake took hold of the 250 pounds Jess was benching. "What made you want to search her car?"

"She did everything except take off her underwear."

"Tempting?"

"Not really. See what it got her?"

Jake slid onto the bench and looked up at the barbell Jess was ready to spot for him. "Mind taking off about 50 pounds?"

"Whimp." Jess smiled and took two 25-pound discs off.

"By the way," Jake said before he started his reps, "if she gets a halfway-decent lawyer, they'll throw out the search."

"I know. But she's cooling her cute little ass in jail for a while, isn't she?"

"You noticed?"

Jess didn't crack a smile when he said, "I'm not dead."

"Sometime I wonder."

———

Two days later, just before they hit the street, a call came into the Fifth Precinct desk. The clerk called out, "Jake or Jess, pick up line four."

Jess took the call. Jake watched Jess nod his head a few times, then smile. "Thanks for the info, Mallory." Jess hung up the phone.

"Well?" Jake watched Jess walk past him heading to their car.

Three steps later he stopped and turned. "Your girlfriend Laurie had a fifth last name—Stutkiewicz. That's the one she was born with."

"You're shittin' me."

Jess continued. "Her prints matched the ones taken when she hired in at Burroughs. She burned Burroughs for a few thousand dollars. There were three Uttering and Publishing warrants out on her, one under the name Stutkiewicz, one under Simms and the last one for Samson."

"Bet she can't screw her way out of those."

Jess slid in behind the wheel. "Mallory said she offered."

For some reason, a pretty smile came to mind as Jake climbed in their car. *I'll have to give Edie a call.*

———

A week and a half went by and only two snow squalls blew through Detroit, though the temperatures dropped into the twenties at night, putting a damper on foot traffic. Jake thought that winter was getting an early start, but then, he remembered this was Michigan. Jake started wearing a navy blue corduroy parka halfway through the month, while Jess put on a nylon windbreaker over his usual non-descript sweatshirt. "Don't you ever get cold, Jess?"

"It's not cold yet."

Jake cranked up the heater thinking, *if twenty-four isn't cold, I don't know what is.* Then he remembered one Thanksgiving when he was about 12. A foot of snow had fallen on the city. *Maybe this isn't so bad.* He knew he could dress for the cold, but didn't look forward to the snow. Jess and Jake finished November stopping about twenty cars a night, all for naught. They picked up three abandoned stolen cars, all in alleys. There were a few B&E dwellings, but they normally occurred on the day shift and they worked strictly nights.

"By the way, did Fox say anything about that drug store B&E?" Jake asked.

"Yeah."

"When?"

"A week ago."

"Thanks for telling me."

"What's to tell? He's in jail and his prints cleaned up nine other jobs."

"Just nice to know sometimes."

————

December started just as slow as November ended. "Mind if I ask you a question, Jess?"

"As long as it isn't too complicated." Jess's flashlight hit the car board to check a plate going the other way. He didn't go after it.

"How'd you and Beth get to know Edie?"

"They both sing in our church choir."

"I never knew you went to church."

"I don't talk religion. That a problem?"

"Let's see, no politics, no religion. What *do* you talk about?" Jake waited. Jess didn't bite.

Jake started talking since Jess wasn't.

"You see in the paper where we're now the minorities in Detroit?"

"Who're we?" Jess checked another plate on the board.

"The whites. Us."

"Who says?"

"The *Free Press*. Just a little blurb that says by the end of November, 1973, the blacks now outnumber the whites in Detroit."

"It doesn't affect me," Jess said.

"It will."

"How?"

"The demographics of this city. You will be affected."

Jess looked over towards Jake and glared. "I said I don't talk politics."

"This isn't politics, just facts. One, Coleman Young is our new mayor. Two, we are now in the minority. Besides shutting down the STRESS Unit, Young says he will totally integrate the supervisory ranks of the police department."

"I don't take promotional exams anyway."

"You ever listen to our mayor?"

"No."

"He's a reverse racist, if there is such a term." Jake let out a sigh. "One day we are going to have to justify why we even stop a car if there's a black driving it. And it's going to be our mayor that's behind shit like that. He hates whites."

Jess cranked his head around. "Go around the block."

"See something?" Jake made the turn, then another.

"A guy tucked into the alley. Let me out here, and go a block up. He might be coming out of the other end."

Jake turned the corner onto Pennsylvania, doused his lights and coasted to a stop near the alley on the south side of Warren. He waited, watching the mouth of the alley. Jake noticed that their portable radio was off the seat, so he knew Jess had it. Three minutes passed before Jake heard the radio. "Come east, Jake. Lights on. We need to flush him out."

Jake flipped on the lights and drove the Chrysler slowly into the alley. Three buildings in, a dark figure broke from his left, running east, then cutting south in the alley away from Warren. Jess came out from behind a garbage can within fifteen yards of the fleeing man.

Jake cut a right on Cadillac and headed south. Just as he was going to race to the next corner the dark figure broke from between the houses and across the front of the Chrysler. Jake threw the lever into park and was out running. He could hear the clank, clank and final clunk of the transmission as the car died behind him.   Ten more yards and Jake dove, tackling the man. Ten seconds later, Jess was helping him handcuff the man. He had two pry bars, wearing them like a pair of pistols, holstered in his belt. In a jacket pocket was a leather zippered case containing twelve various-sized lock picks. The man had no wallet, no identification and wasn't talking.

Jake's report was titled "One arrest, Investigation B&E." In the body of the report Jake noted the location of the arrest of one John Doe, black male, approximate age, 32, along with a physical description. Jess put the pry bars and the set of lock picks in a large manila evidence envelope and tagged it.

"Guy's been around," Jess said as they hit the street again.

"Seems so. Bet his prints'll put a name on him."

"Probably two or three." Jess flicked off the lights on the Chrysler and crawled down the curb on Kercheval to finish off their night.

On the second Monday in December Edie was sitting across from Jake at a back table in a little place called Shakers, within the confines of the Fifth Precinct. Jess and Jake were regulars at the place. If it wasn't for breakfast before or after their workout at the Y, it was for a taste of Pigeon's daily special just after hitting the street. It was Jake's kind of place. He wasn't much for candlelight, fancy waiters, and a bottle of wine chilled in a silver ice bucket. In fact, he didn't like wine.

Beth was keeping an eye on the boys for Edie.

"The place might not be fancy, but the food is the best," Jake was saying as he slid Edie's chair under her.

"I'm sure it'll be fine," Edie said as she looked at the menu.

Twenty minutes and a cup of coffee later she was feasting her eyes on the pile of pan-fried, "Fresh caught Lake Erie walleye" she had ordered from the menu. Jake settled on the fried chicken, collard greens and mashed potatoes. The place offered the best fried chicken he'd ever tasted.

After the dishes were cleared the waitress brought over their dessert and freshened up the coffees. "I've never had sweet potato pie." Edie took a taste. "It's nice. No, great might be a better term."

To Jake, it tasted a bit like pumpkin pie. Pie is pie. He liked them all.

Edie carried the table-talk, telling Jake about Hillman, Michigan, the town she grew up near. She told him about the dairy farm, cleaning and candling eggs from the eight hundred and some hens they had, picking berries in the summer, and trudging through snow on the way to Reider, a one-room school house, a mile down Truax Road in the winter.

Jake had never heard of Hillman and sure didn't know a thing about candling eggs or milking cows. He just liked to hear the woman talk. They were the last customers at Shakers to leave.

On the ride home, Edie scrunched in beside Jake. "Hope you don't mind, at least 'til the heater gets going."

Jake felt himself turn a shade or two of red as he reached over and grabbed her hand. Within, he was thanking God for a warm hand to hold—Edie's hand. She scooted in closer.

The kiss good-night, after Edie made sure the boys were asleep and Beth was on the way home, hadn't been in Jake's plan. It just happened.

"I'll call tomorrow."

"I hope so," Edie whispered. "I'll be home by five."

Jake drove home wracked with emotions. Flashes of Anne's smile kept reappearing.

———

It was near five and Jake kept looking at the phone. He wanted to call—to hear her voice. *It's not fair.* The phrase kept reverberating in his mind. He showered and got dressed for work, pretending that the phone wasn't there. He tucked his magnum in the holster on his left side, grabbed his keys and headed for the door. The phone rang.

"Hello?"

"Hi, Jake." It was her. The voice he wanted to hear. The voice he was avoiding.

"I'm sorry. I fell asleep. Can I call you tomorrow?"

"Promise me you will?"

"I will." He clicked off and went out the door. *It's not fair. It's not fair.*

Four hours into the shift Jake was looking out into the night and seeing nothing. Jess stopped four cars and two pedestrians. Jake was there, going through the motions, covering his side of the stopped car, or jotting down the information on their log sheet. But his mind wasn't totally on the streets of Detroit.

"You haven't said a word. What's wrong?" Jess waited for an answer. Jake kept looking out into the night.

A half hour later Jess pulled into the lot at Biff's. "I'm going in. You comin'?"

A coffee was all Jake ordered.

"I'll take the half pounder, double the onions and put gravy on the fries," Jess said as he folded the menu and handed it back to Gwen, the waitress.

Gwen, an olive-skinned Greek goddess, was working the tables that night. She brought the two coffees. When she put one of them down in front of Jake, she asked, "You sick or something, Jake?"

There was a long pause until Jess covered for him. "I think he's in love."

"God, I hope it's not me. I've got three kids already and a very jealous husband." With that Gwen wiggled away and started clearing a table. "Jake," she yelled over. "Not that I'd turn you down." She smiled and banged at the kitchen door with her hip carrying a tray load of glasses, cups and dirty dishes.

Silence.

"Now I know something's wrong with you." Jess tinged his fork twice against Jake's cup to get his attention. "Talk to me, partner."

Silence.

Jake slid in behind the wheel to start their drive back into their precinct. Biff's was kitty-corner across from Belle Isle in Number Seven.

"A few years back, in our TMU days, we whipped some asses in the alley behind Biff's." It was Jess making conversation. "Remember that?"

Silence.

"Hey. We stop someone and I need you, you gonna be there?"

"You know I'll be there." Jake whipped a U-turn. "The black Buick. Didn't like the look."

"'Bout fuckin' time you woke up." Jess was flashing the spot light in the face of the driver behind the wheel of the Buick. He pointed to the curb. The Buick pulled over.

Randy Crawford, a white male, 52, had a whore kneeling on the floor on the passenger's side of the Buick. She pinched his limp dick in a zipper as Jess was flashing the spotlight in Randy's eyes—at least that's what Randy said.

Neither Jake nor Jess knew how to write a ticket for driving while getting a blow job. That was never covered in the police academy. Ten minutes later, Jake headed back to the precinct.

Jess said, "No wonder he gave you a strange look."

"I maybe coulda written him a ticket," Jake said, "for driving while sensually impaired." They both laughed.

"I don't carry my ticket book," Jess said.

"Neither do I." They both chuckled.

———

Precisely at five Jake dialed Edie's number. He asked if he could see her before he went into work. "Care to come by my place?" she asked.

"What about the boys?"

"I'll have some coffee on. The boys can play in the yard while we talk."

"I'll bring a pizza. They aren't a bother."

———

Buddy's makes a nice big square pizza. Jake brought one with just pepperoni on it. Hank and Sam took two pieces on paper plates and plopped down in front of the TV. Soupy Sales was on. They were laughing at White Fang and crazy ol' Soupy while Edie poured the coffee.

"I didn't call the other night 'cause I'm a bit messed up."

"No you're not."

"Yeah. I'm chasin' ghosts. Or they're chasin' me."

"Anne?"

"You remembered her name."

"And Debbie, Shella, Mike and Jet too."

"I loved them a lot. Probably still do."

Edie reached over and put her hand on Jake's. "It's not wrong to love them." She squeezed his hand. "There's no rush, Jake."

"But is it fair to you? To the boys?"

"I don't know what's fair or not. I just know I like being with you."

Jake leaned over and kissed Edie. The boys started chuckling. Jake pulled away in time to see Soupy digging whipped cream from his eyes. He'd caught a pie square in the face thrown from off camera. Jake knew he was blushing. He felt it. Then he realized the boys weren't even aware that Jake had been kissing their mom. Soupy was fun to watch. Adults weren't.

"Can I have another piece?" Sam asked. He held his plate out and Edie shoveled another on and put one on Hank's plate too.

"I'd better head for work," Jake said. It's my day to shoot with Jess.

"Here, take some of your pizza. You haven't had any yet." Edie put three squares on a paper plate for Jake.

"Thanks. And thanks for seeing me," Jake whispered. Edie pulled him by his shirt and stood on her toes to kiss him. Soupy had the boys laughing again. Jake didn't pull away this time.

———

"The green Plymouth is hot, Jess. Make a U-turn." Jess put the Chrysler into a power turn. He and Jake liked the response that the 318 engine gave them. Two blocks later Jess was forcing a Plymouth with four teenagers to the curb. Running was not an option as Jake grabbed the passenger side and Jess the other. Jess towered over the driver that he had swinging at the end of his arm while he held the back door closed. Jake had his two on the ground with their hands behind their heads.

"Radio, this is Five-Two-Five. Can you send a car to Mack and Conner? Make it two. We've got four to go."

"Roger on that Five Twenty-five."

Jess was happy that Jake was back playing cops and robbers.

Chapter Twelve

Cops always have a favorite place to eat. In the Thirteenth Precinct, Jake liked the Taystee Barbecue with their rib special—four bones, fries and coleslaw. In Number Five, Jess and Jake had Shakers on Mack Avenue. Shakers was owned by James and Pigeon Tremble.

One day Jake, making small talk, asked James how he and Pigeon met. The story unfolded in bits and pieces over the course of nearly two years, many cups of coffee and who knows how many pieces of pie. James did most of the telling, but Pigeon was there to fill the gaps if he happened to forget an important detail, including how the restaurant named Shakers came to be.

James told them his best friend growing up was a girl who lived across the cotton field behind his daddy's hardware store, The Nail Keg. The Trembles lived in Winona, Mississippi. The store was on Highway 82 just east of where it crosses Route 51. The friend's name was Pigeon. Well, in actuality, it was Tammara, but she said everyone called her Pigeon for as long as she could remember. James and Pigeon did not go to the same school because he was white and she was black. That was just how it was in the late 40s and early 50s in Winona.

The two were the same age when they met—eight. James was spearing frogs along Miller's creek. He was homing in on a gravelly-voiced bullfrog when he spotted a set of black pigtails slowly bobbing up and down in the chest-high reeds in front of him. James just watched and a minute later a brown hand came up with a fat, wiggling green critter.

"Hey, I was gonna spear that guy," he said to the girl, causing her to drop the frog.

"When you spear them, they cain't jump no more!" she shot back. The barefoot girl was wearing a Pillsbury flour sack sewn into a pinafore. She had milk chocolate colored skin.

Pigeon taught James how to slither through the weeds just like she did and catch frogs barehanded. And yes, those old bullfrogs gave them hours of fun with jumping contests. James always named his frog "Boss" and she named hers "Amos." Pigeon had convinced him that they should let them go at the end of the day's contest so they could catch them again. "That way we don't have to feed 'em," she said. The truth was they didn't know what frogs ate anyhow.

They never knew for sure if they ever caught the same frog twice, though James thought he did every time. "See this black spot on the top of his head?" he said pointing one out. "That's how I know this is 'Boss.'" Pigeon knew that all frogs had black spots on their green heads—at least she thought she knew—but never told James.

For the next eight years on warm summer evenings James would use his daddy's key to grab a couple of free ice cold "Coke Colas" from the red machine on the hardware's porch. Daddy didn't mind since James swept up after school every day and helped straighten the bins of screws and nails, putting the right sizes where they belonged. When a delivery came in, he helped stock the shelves. Momma Tremble would always bring supper from home and the men-folk would eat while she tended the counter. Young James liked being considered "one of the men-folk."

What James never told his parents was that his frog-catching buddy was a girl named Pigeon and that she was black. James's junior and senior years in high school put an end to the regular frog-jumping contests except for an occasional summer evening. He was playing baseball, football and basketball and making All-State in each sport for Winona High. Pigeon and James still kept in touch. They met regularly at the old live oak that grew mid-way down Miller's Creek. James was offered a football scholarship at Mississippi State, but a draft notice had him going to Vietnam instead.

In 1965 Daddy and Momma Tremble got in a wreck driving to the rail station to meet James, who had just mustered out of the Army. Both died when a pulp truck missed the curve on Highway 82 and ran over their 1964 Ford. James was 21 when the hardware store suddenly became his. By then, he had peaked out at six foot three, with light brown wavy hair and dark green eyes. He felt like he could play football for Mississippi State, but the metal fragments in his legs imported from Vietnam said otherwise.

When The Nail Keg was built, James's dad, Marshall, had a covered front porch installed the full length of the store. On the rear of the building was an identical covered porch. The adjoining grocery store was built the same way, and so was the dry goods store next to it. That's just the way the majority of the businesses in small-town Mississippi were, with front and back porches.

James thought he'd make some minor changes three months after his daddy and momma died. First off, he hired two blacks, one being Pigeon, to work at the store. That didn't seem to bother his regular customers, but the people of Winona were used to the whites using the store's front entrance while the blacks entered through the back door. There were no signs; it was just the way things always were for all of James's life. He wanted to change that. During the war James learned that Negroes, Hispanics, Orientals and Caucasians ate, slept, and shared muddy foxholes and oftentimes blood if a battlefield transfusion was necessary. A lot even died alongside one another. An enemy bullet had no bias. In war there were no back doors for some and front doors for others. James thought it was time to let Winona, Mississippi, in on such things.

James had a new yellow sign made with black letters and nailed to both sides of a porch post closest to the back door. It read: *Rear Entrance for Delivery and Pick up Only. All Customers, Kindly Use the Front Entrance.* The store's business plunged dramatically. After two years of struggling, James made up his mind. He had to move. He'd outgrown his home, or rather, outgrew the accepted way of life in Mississippi.

During those two years of struggles Pigeon became an important part of James's life. She could do the books and had a personality that enriched what little business they had. Then too, Pigeon had changed from a pigtailed, frog-catching friend into a pretty young woman with a beautiful smile. Pigeon didn't have the tight curly hair like her momma and daddy. It was jet black, but straight and she let it grow, wearing it kind of long but with the sides curling up so her hair would bounce when she walked. Her smile was enhanced with petite lips. Her momma always said Pigeon's "granpappy" was a white landowner and it was his genes that were there "to curse her for all of her life."

James didn't think Pigeon was cursed. When they were 22, he told Pigeon he loved her. Down deep he knew he probably loved her way back during their frog-catching days, but also knew what that meant in Mississippi. Even so, James proposed. They found a minister at a little country church just outside of Vaiden, Mississippi, who'd marry them as long as they had $50 in cash and a bottle of Johnny Walker Red Label. The preacher never asked if they had a license, one he knew they could never get in the state of Mississippi. They left with a signed marriage certificate. Pigeon had an uncle that worked at Dodge Main and he had been writing her that there were jobs to be had in Detroit.

Two weeks later, James sold The Nail Keg and packed everything they owned under a tarp in the back of their '66 Chevy pickup. They moved to Detroit, long before the Carroll County Sheriff might have gotten wind of any biracial wedding.

Within a week after hiring in at the Dodge Plant, James and Pigeon found a little stucco house on Phillip, just south of Mack. It took all of what they made on the hardware store, but they knew it was the place that they could start anew. Some of their neighbors were white, some black, all seemed nice enough. They were at last free from the hate and the bigotry of the south. That was in May, 1967, just two months before the Detroit riot.

Life changed in a hurry for James and Pigeon after that July. The hardest thing for James was to be working on the line at the plant and eating lunch. There were two distinct sides in the lunchroom. The blacks ate on their side and the whites on the other. James thought that the bigotry was worse than it was in Winona. "At least in Mississippi each race knew their place and which door to use. Here, everyone wants to use the same door, but they want to step on you to get there first." James told Pigeon he wanted a better life for her and for him. Working at the plant had too much tension. "I just can't hate people the way they do—both the blacks and the whites."

Pigeon said she had an answer to her husband's dilemma. She had found a small café on Mack for sale and the place was only a couple of blocks from their home. "People have to have a place to eat," she told James. "And I can sure cook."

James knew she could—maybe too good, judging by the thirty pounds he put on in the past two years—and there was no arguing with his wife. They put three thousand down on it. A year later, July 15th, 1971, James put in his notice at the Dodge Plant. Pigeon's fried chicken and sweet potato pie, as well as her other southern recipes had won over Detroit's east side. And both the blacks and the whites were filling the twenty-two tables they could fit in the place. James helped his wife wherever he could; doing dishes, waiting tables, seating customers, whatever, while Pigeon practiced her culinary talents.

They named the place "Shakers." That was kind of a slant on their last name as well as the whispers they often overheard: "Oh you know, the 'Salt and Pepper' couple that live on Phillip." James had to laugh when Pigeon came up with that name. His wife could make a joke out of anything said, even if it was hurtful. She had a gift and he loved her all the more for it.

———

In July of 1974, Jess and Jake were due for a new car. The '69 Chrysler had started rusting to death the year before. Five's cruiser crew had just gotten a brand new set of wheels, a 1974 black Buick Century four-door. Jess and Jake inherited their old four-door, a '71 Buick LeSabre, repainted of course. Jess had three choices for the paint job that was needed to cover the normal black with the old gold wing on the side: Medium blue, dark blue and darker blue. Jess picked the darkest of the lot to be able to blend in better after dark. Both he and Jake knew, that no matter what color, everyone would know they were cops the first time it hit the street. As Jess said, "You can spot a whore no matter what color her dress is."

Jake complained that the seats were broken down from the 300-pound bodies that had filled them for the past three years. Jess just shrugged his shoulders, saying, "Still better than the Chrysler."

"Barely."

Lanny Tucker was standing on the corner of Kercheval and St. Jean the first night they were in the LeSabre. Lanny was the resident cross-dresser who waved his lace hanky at every passing white man that drove by. He was looking for a date. Jake heard his false soprano voice as Jess turned the corner. "Yoo-hoo! Officer, how about a ride?" Jess slid to a stop.

"Jake, you big handsome devil, you got new wheels." Lanny leaned in the open passenger window. "I'm wearing the same color—midnight blue." He flashed his pearly-whites with a broad smile. "I'm talkin' 'bout my lace panties and bra. Let's go somewhere quiet and I'll show you." The smell of Lanny's perfume moved Jake back in his seat while Lanny batted his false eyelashes. "I love the shade of blue you put on the old big four's rig."

"What'd I tell you Jake? No matter what color it is, they'll know it's the old cruiser." Jake was turning three shades of red. Jess smiled, knowing his partner was uncomfortable around Lanny.

Jess leaned towards the open window where the man in a lavender dress was applying a new layer of red lipstick. "Lanny, sweetheart. Got any leads on a pair of young dudes knocking over small businesses in the area?"

"Jessie, my love. You know I stay away from violent people."

"Yeah, but you have ears. What've you heard?"

"Nothing. But give me your number. I'll give you a ring if I hear anything." Lanny walked around the front of the Buick, swaying profoundly as he went to Jess's side. "I'd love to have your number."

Jess jotted down the number at the Fifth Precinct on a piece of paper. "Here, call the precinct and tell them to have me track you down."

"Shit baby," Lanny puffed out his lower lip. "I wanted your home number."

"My wife wouldn't understand. Then too, I'd have to get her a more expensive wardrobe."

"Oh, you like my new dress?"

"Love it. Call me when you hear something." Jess blew Lanny a kiss and drove off.

Jake shook his head. "Jess, sometimes you can be sickening. Blowing him a kiss?"

"Partner, sometimes you gotta go the extra mile."

Jess drove off and caught Lanny waving his lace hanky at another car in his rear view mirror.

Jake left his window down to get rid of the odor of Lanny's perfume. "The holdups. You've seen the same thing I have, right?"

Jess's flashlight hit the car board as he answered. "Yeah. Stores, bars, whatever, all hit near closing time and only one or two customers in the place."

Jake flipped to the circular in their book and read it aloud. "Two black guys. One with a nickel-plated automatic, the other with a blue-steel revolver. There's been hold-ups in Fifteen, Seven, Hamtramck and Number Five. Both in their early 20s. No real outstanding physical characteristics, except that the guy with the revolver is light colored and has either a tattoo over his left eye or a dark scar." Jake put away the binder.

"Well, with the territory they're covering, we know they're driving. Just means we stop a lot of cars and maybe get lucky." Jess checked the plate on the Chevy he fell in behind. Nothing. Two black males were in it. Jess backed off to let them continue on their way. He was waiting to find a reason to talk to them. Five minutes and a mile later the Chevy turned left onto Mack without signaling. He floored the Buick and caught up to them. Jake hit them with the spotlight and motioned for them to pull to the curb.

Again, it turned out to be just something for their log sheet. The two occupants were in their 30s and let Jake search their car. They accepted the fact that Jess and Jake were looking for holdup men with not much to go on. "We've got nothin' to hide," the driver said. They didn't.

"Thanks guys," Jess said as he gave them their IDs back. The blue Buick again hugged the curb on Mack, slowly driving into the night with their headlights off.

———

"Beth tells me you've been coaching Edie's boys."

"Yeah. Little League. Sam's the bat boy."

"Guess you're still seeing her."

"Yep. The boys are neat." Jake went silent. He wasn't picking up too many books at the library lately.

Jess figured Jake's mind was wandering back to his own family. "I swung by Betty Bynum's house the other day. Remember her?"

"And—"

"She's doing fine. Zo and Merrianne said to say hello."

Jake turned onto Kercheval, crawling along the curb, saying, "Saw Betty about a month ago. I took Edie and the boys out for dinner at the Roostertail. Betty came out to the table to meet them. She's still all smiles."

"You tell the boys how you met Betty?"

"No. Edie knows the story. She said she later told the boys that you and I helped her out one night." Jake spotted a car he wanted to stop.

Small talk ceases when business is at hand.

The two black males in the red Corvair weren't as cooperative as the last pair they'd stopped. Jake let the "white racist mutha fucker" crack from Raphael Whitney just slide as Jess searched the car. Whitney and his passenger, Ronny Jones, begrudgingly gave Jake their IDs. The car was clean. Jake thanked them for their time.

"*Our* mayor's gonna hear about this shit," Whitney said as he walked back to his car.

Jess made sure he logged all the information on the stop, saying to Jake, "In case they complain to *their* mayor."

"I thought he was our mayor too," Jake quipped. "Think they know we didn't vote for him?"

"D'ya think Mr. Young doesn't lay claim to us?"

"Let's not talk politics, Jess."

"I was just going to suggest that."

———

August 4th Jess and Jake had three court cases. They went straight from court to the station's range. Fifteen minutes later they were comparing targets. Jess got one more in the ten ring than Jake. "Finally beat your ass," Jess bragged.

"Only because you took your time. This is supposed to be rapid fire."

"Still beat your ass."

"Barely."

"Dinner at Shakers. Winner's choice," Jess said as he updated the stolen car board. "I'm hungry. That Coney dog we had earlier just wasn't enough."

Three stops and three searches later Jake and Jess walked in the front door of Shakers. They'd parked in the alley as usual. It was near eight. A foursome was paying their bill at the register James Tremble was manning. He looked up and acknowledged the plainclothes officers, waving his arm indicating they could take any table in the near-empty restaurant. Another couple went to the register to pay their tab. Jake looked at his watch. *Guess it IS late.*

Jess grabbed a menu and chose a table near the kitchen. He waved at Pigeon through the serving hole. "Got any specials left?" he asked.

"Y'know what the special is?" she replied, smiling.

"If you cooked it, I'll eat it," Jess answered.

Jake called from across the room. "Make that two, Jess. I'm gonna wash my hands."

"Two secret specials," Jess called to Pigeon and sat down. James brought two glasses of water to the table.

"Coffees?" James flipped open his order pad.

"One for me. Jake drinks Pepsi."

"Only got Coke."

"Make it coffee then. He won't drink Coke."

"And two specials," James added as he tore a page out of his pad and hung it up on one of the clips on the wire running the full length at the top of the order window.

A minute later the bell over the front door rang behind Jess just as Pigeon was carrying out the two specials towards his table. She glanced over and saw the two black men that had entered.

"On the floor mutha fuckers!" A nickel-plated automatic and a blue-steel revolver were being waved around by the two.

"Get outta my house!" Pigeon shouted, throwing a plate of food at them.

Jess was starting to lower himself to the floor, grabbing for his .38. The man with the automatic shot at Pigeon as

Jess's left knee hit the floor. Jess shot twice. The man with the autoloader fell. Two shots rang out from the guy with the revolver; these were aimed at Jess who had nothing between him and the gunman.

Jake heard the first shot, pulled his magnum and jerked open the door of the men's room as the second two shots rang out. He saw Jess catch at least one bullet. Before him was a man crouched with his blue-steel revolver aimed at his partner. Jake fired twice. The man crumpled. Jake kept walking. He saw Pigeon on the floor with dishes and food all around her. He fired two shots at the man on the floor holding an automatic. He turned his .357 towards the first man he hit and put another round into him as the man was trying to rise. There was a long pause as Jake reloaded. He put a toe to both men and knew they were dead. Jake sprinted ten feet to the table that Jess lay beneath. Blood was trickling out from under him. He rolled Jess over. Blood was flowing from a chest wound. Jake pulled his hanky, pressing it to the hole.

"James! Help me. Jess's been hit."

Jake looked over to where Pigeon was. She was picking herself up from under a table, broken plates and food were on the floor around her.

"I'm okay. He missed," she said as she ran into the kitchen, reappearing with a handful of towels.

James was on the phone, yelling, "Policeman's been shot. Need an ambulance at 10247 Mack. Shaker's Restaurant. Hurry!"

———

Three days later, Jake was dozing in a chair at Detroit's Receiving Hospital. He was in dire need of a shave. A twitch in Jesse's arm brought Jake upright. He'd hoped to see Jesse with his eyes open. They remained closed. The sounds of the blips and beeps were still there. The tubes were still in Jesse's nose. Jake looked at the readout on the clutter of machines on the opposite side of the bed. The nurse working the first night had explained what the numbers and the red line on the tiny screen meant. The pulse, though weak, was still there. Jake's chin slumped back to his chest. *Fight it, Jess. Fight it.* Jake fitfully slept. Every sound and every movement of air woke him, just enough to check the numbers again.

Jake jerked awake as the door to Room 301 opened. It was Beth. She had two Styrofoam cups in her hands. "Brought you something, Jake." She looked at the machinery. "Any change?"

"Nothing."

"You need to go home, Jake." She didn't get a response. "Did you hear me? You need a break."

Jake looked up at his partner's wife. "Not 'til I know he's all right." His eyes shifted back to the machinery. "His pulse is pretty weak," Jake said in a whisper.

"They've got him in an induced coma." She put one cup down and ran her finger over Jess's forehead. "To help him heal. Rest is what the doctor said would help." She looked back at Jake. "And rest is what you need."

Jake didn't respond. Beth filled his right hand with the second coffee. "You did all you could."

He took a sip of the hot brew. Tears formed in his eyes. "Did I?"

"You did. And he'll make it. I just talked to his doctor. Jesse's getting better—slowly."

Jake checked the monitors again. The pulse was still there. Slow, but there.

"I'm going to call the boys. My mom is staying with them." Jake watched Beth go out the door. He checked the monitors, set the cup on Jess's table and fell asleep.

———

"Jake! Jake, wake up." His eyes opened a slit. It was Sergeant Fox.

"How's Jess?"

Jake's eyes went to the monitors. The pulse rate was in the low fifties. The blood pressure was slowly climbing.

"Better than yesterday, Sarge."

"Jake, you look like shit."

"Coming from you, I'll take that as a compliment."

"You need a shave." The sergeant fingered Jake's chin. "You're gonna scare the hell out of Jess when he opens his eyes."

"Nothing scares Jess."

"The boss needs you to come in. You've got more statements to write."

"I wrote mine. Nothing more to say."

"There's a complaint. A family member of one of the perps. The autopsy report says Jess's two slugs killed him. They pulled two more of yours out of the same guy. Papers are raising hell about you shooting a dead man."

"Fuck the papers."

"The mayor is talking about a full investigation into this. Same old shit. White cops shoot two blacks."

"Then fuck the mayor too."

"Jake, we need you to come in. The Homicide dicks want more paperwork. The department shrink wants to talk to you, too. I need you to come in. Today."

"Not 'til Jess is better."

"Make it tomorrow. I can't stall the brass any longer."

"What about Jess? Who's going to be here if he comes out of it?"

"Jake, you've been here for ten days."

"I'm not leaving him."

The sergeant dropped his head, shaking it slowly from side to side. "I'll pull Southworth off shift. He'll be here at 6:30 in the morning. Is that good enough?"

"I should be here."

Fox looked into Jake's eyes. "Look. Southworth'll be here. You have to be in our Detective Bureau at eight. A couple hours and you can be back doing your vigil."

"What if I say no?"

"This is an order, Jake. The inspector's orders. A department order. Be there."

"Fuck the department."

Sergeant Fox moved around to where Jake sat and squatted down so he could look up into the patrolman's eyes. "I know how much Jess means to you. He means a lot to us, too. Don't toss the job that you and he love by being thickheaded."

"How about you sitting with him?"

"Me?"

"Yeah. It's you or me. I want someone to be here when Jess opens his eyes. Someone he knows. Is that too much to ask?"

The sergeant stood, walked towards the door. He thought for a minute, circled, then said, "Okay. I'll be here at 6:00. But I want you showered and shaved and at Lieutenant Schmidt's desk at eight sharp." Fox smiled. "You do need a shower, Jake."

"See you in the morning, Sarge." The door to room 301 slowly closed. Jake's eyes went to the monitors again. Heart Rate: 52; BP 90/60. *Better.* Jake took a sip of the coffee Beth had brought in an hour or two before. *Tastes like shit.* He got up to stretch his legs. He could see his image in the mirror through the open door to the restroom. *I do look like hell.* He smiled to himself. *Still wouldn't scare Jess, though.*

Jake rummaged through the drawers in Jess's nightstand. Blip, beep. Blip, blip. The monitor updated again. *Same.* He pulled out a can of Barbasol and a Gillette safety razor from the complimentary kit Detroit Receiving supplied. He looked at the numbers again and went into the little room, leaving the door ajar as he ran some hot water.

Twenty minutes later, Jake was back in his chair. Two pieces of toilet paper were adhered to the nicks from the razor; one on the left side of his chin, the other on his neck. Ten days of growth was a bitch to get rid of without a fight. Just when he had gotten settled in and cracked open the previous day's *Free Press,* there was a light tap on the door. Beth's head peeked in.

"You guys decent?" she whispered as she slid into the room. Edie was close behind her.

"Hi, Jake." Edie walked up and touched his hand. "How's Jess?"

Jake shrugged as he stood. He pulled Edie into his arms, put his head on her shoulder and quietly sobbed.

She hugged him tightly saying, "Long time since you've held me."

"Sorry, Eed. Been busy."

"Missed hearing you calling me 'Eed.' Even Edith would do."

"Shoulda called." He squeezed her tighter. "How's Hank and Sam?"

"Missing their coach."

Jake shrugged as he let Edie go so he could look into her eyes. "I miss them too. Tell them that for me."

Beth walked around the bed, touching her husband's foot. "Things are getting better. Doctor Mulenar said Jesse's gonna make it. Maybe another week of heavy sedation." She bent over and kissed Jess on his forehead. "I've got the boys downstairs, but I don't know if I should let them see their dad with all these tubes and stuff hanging on him."

"They're big enough," Jake said. "Want me to get them?" Beth smiled and nodded. Jake knew his partner was in good hands.

———

Nine days later Jess was propped up in his bed. Jake was holding the glass of ice water so Jess could take a swig. He coughed, taking in too much at once. "Easy partner," Jake whispered. Jake looked around for a straw, knowing it would be easier for Jess to drink with one. He hit the nurse's button.

Two days later Jess was talking. "Beth says you've been here the whole time. What day is it?" Jess laid his head back down. "Even forgot what day you were buying me dinner."

"Just over three weeks ago." Jake made sure Jess could reach the glass with the straw in it. "And I'll still buy you dinner. Beth said they're letting you go tomorrow."

"Three weeks? What did you do, take vacation?'

"They call it 'Administrative Leave.'"

"So you could hold my hand?"

"Something like that. I left one day and Fox took over for me."

"Fox? Why?"

"I had a bunch of paperwork to do. Then an interview with the department shrink and some homicide dicks."

"For?"

"The mayor is demanding a full investigation into us shooting those two assholes."

"Did I get one?"

"Of course. Both shots. Left shoulder and next to the heart. Both side by side."

Jess smiled, put his head back down and fell asleep.

Two hours later, Jess woke to the sound of voices. James and Pigeon Tremble were next to his bed. "Who's cookin' at Shakers today?"

"Closed it," Pigeon said. "We're here to help Jake check you outta this place."

Jess looked around as two nurses entered. "We need your bed, big boy." She started pulling wires and putting away the machinery. "Not that you'd been any trouble. Just this partner of yours." She looked over her shoulder at Jake. "Hangin' around and smelling like a two-week old carp."

"I'll miss you too, Lilah," Jake said as he was filling a bag with the cards, vases and stuffed animals that adorned Jesse's room. "How 'bout you girls sharing the flowers?"

A third nurse came in the door with a wheelchair. "Your ride, Officer Scott."

"I can walk," Jess huffed.

"Not 'til you get out the hospital door," the big black woman in white answered. "Don't want you suing the city for falling down." She gently nudged Jess into the seat and flipped down the footrests.

Jake, James and Pigeon followed her to the elevator. A big, dark blue Buick was waiting at the hospital door when they hit sunlight. Remington Southworth stood next to an open door on Five Twenty-Five. Jake smiled as he helped his partner out of the wheelchair. "Fox said we could use it to take you home."

Chapter Thirteen

On September 3, 1974, Patrolman John Anthony Bush stood in front of room 2132 at the City County Building talking with John Aberdash, an attorney retained by the Detroit Police Officer's Association. Patrolman Bush was served with a subpoena to appear before an Ad Hoc Committee formed by Mayor Coleman Young to investigate the shooting deaths of Marcus Ware and Andreas Ford at Shakers Restaurant.

"There's nothing to worry about, Jake," the attorney casually said as he glanced around at the gathering of reporters from the *Detroit Free Press* and *The Detroit News*. Jake was dressed in his blues—a neatly pressed light blue shirt, navy blue tie and dark navy blue trousers—his pistol was worn in regulation cross draw fashion and Sam Browne leathers, his badge displayed above the left breast pocket. It had been awhile since he had been in uniform. "This is just our fine mayor's way of grandstanding," Aberdash continued.

Jake nervously looked around. "With Jess and me being used as his sacrificial lambs."

"You aren't going to be sacrificed. Mr. Young bit off a bit too much with his rhetoric on 'white cops killing poor blacks' splashed all over the newspapers."

"I'm glad you're so confident." Jake looked around and watched the crowd start to go into the room. The blacks far outnumbered the whites.

Room 2132 was the normal council chambers, slightly modified for this occasion. Instead of the twelve members of Detroit Common Council sitting at the main table, the chairs were filled with those appointed by the mayor to conduct this hearing. There were eight men and four women. Of the twelve, only two were white.

John Aberdash led Jake to a table positioned in front of them. As he took his seat, Jake read the nameplates in front of each person sitting before him. Most were members of the prominent churches in Detroit, or by the titles beneath the names, leaders of a civic organization. *This is going to be an interrogation,* he mused to himself.

The three Detroit TV stations, WWJ, WJBK and WXYZ, were represented by the cameras placed around the theater seating for those interested in a council meeting, or like today, an investigation into a shooting by members of the Detroit Police Department. The court reporter, a woman, sat behind her stenotype machine.

The woman sitting in the center of the council table, behind the nameplate indicating her name as Maxine Rabbish, stood and banged a gavel to bring the session to order. "Good morning citizens of Detroit," she started, stating that she was appointed as the chairperson for the committee appointed by "The Honorable Mayor, Coleman Young to investigate the shooting deaths of Marcus Ware and Andreas Ford at Shakers Restaurant on August 4, 1974 at 8:32 p.m."

Maxine went on for the next fifteen minutes introducing each member of her committee, and the credentials of each before adding her own credentials, the President of the Anti-Defamation League, Detroit Chapter. She'd held that position for the past four years. Jake slowly looked at each person as they were introduced. *This isn't going to be an interrogation. It's a crucifixion. Mine.* "I would like to start off by taking testimony from Patrolman John Anthony Bush, badge number twenty-four-forty-one. Would you stand to be sworn in, Patrolman Bush?"

As Jake started to rise, Attorney John Aberdash stood, pressing on Jake's shoulder enough to stop him from rising. "Madam, I'm John Aberdash, Patrolman Bush's legal counsel. In order to conduct this investigation properly, I would suggest you first take testimony from the other persons intimately familiar with the happenings at Shaker's Restaurant on the night in question."

"Mr. Aberdash, this is highly irregular. I've been instructed to take testimony from Patrolman Bush—"

"Madam, Patrolman Bush was the last person involved in what transpired at Shaker's that night and for you and your panel to understand what happened that night, I strongly suggest that you hear testimony as the events took place that night." He paused for a few seconds as he walked in front of Jake. "Wouldn't you agree that this would put things in their proper perspective?"

Maxine Rabbish looked to her left and right and saw the slight nods from her fellow committee members. "For the sake of conducting a thorough investigation, Mr. Aberdash, the floor is yours."

"Ladies and Gentlemen, I call James Tremble, co-owner of Shakers." Twenty minutes later John Aberdash called on Tammarra Tremble. Each was sworn in before they gave testimony. The events of the evening of August 4, 1974 unfolded.

James Tremble was behind the till of the restaurant at approximately 8:30 p.m. getting ready to close. His wife, Pigeon, was in the kitchen preparing "Two Specials" for what they thought were their last customers of the night. Patrolman Jesse Scott, in plain clothes, was sitting at table fourteen against the far wall near the kitchen and his partner, Jake Bush, went to the men's room "to wash up." The bell rang over the door and two black males entered with guns drawn."

James painted the picture for the committee, two men waving guns, ordering everyone on the floor.

One of the committee members, Pastor Lambert Lucas, asked for the floor first as James testified. He asked, "Did you see Patrolman Bush shoot both men as he exited the men's room?"

"Yes sir."

"Even the one that Patrolman Scott had shot?"

"One man fell as Jesse shot, but the guy was trying to get off the floor and still had the gun in his hand. That's when Jake shot him."

When called on, Tammarra (Pigeon) Tremble testified about walking out of the kitchen as the men were waving their guns and yelling, "On the floor mutha fuckers!" She told about throwing a plate of food at the two and being shot at. "I don't know how much he missed me by, but thank the Lord Jesse and Jake were there." She told of Jesse Scott firing two shots, then Jake emerging from the men's room, firing his pistol. "They saved my life. I am sure of that."

Pastor Lucas asked for the floor again. He asked the same question. "Did you see Patrolman Bush shoot both men as he exited the men's room?"

Pigeon did not hesitate answering, "Yes sir. One was the man that shot at me. He might have been hit, but he was still tryin' to get up an' Jake just sent him to hell—right where he belonged."

None of the other committee members had any questions.

John Aberdash thanked the husband and wife for their testimony, and turned, saying, "Madam Chairperson, I'd like to have the testimony of Patrolman Jesse Scott read to the committee. I took the liberty to have a sworn deposition taken from him in the presence of a court recorder since he would not be able to attend this hearing. He is still recovering from the near-fatal wounds he received that night."

The court reporter read the transcripts of the testimony taken from Jesse Scott on August 31, 1974, concerning the events as he remembered them.

John Aberdash was on a roll and he knew it. "Next, I'd like to call Detective Lieutenant Matthew Broadnax to testify."

Maxine Rabbish pounded her gavel once and rose. "I'd like to know why you are calling on a witness who was not at the scene on the night in question."

"Detective Lieutenant Broadnax is in charge of the Detroit Police Hold-Up Bureau. He will be able to give testimony concerning the two perpetrators of the attempted robbery, namely Marcus Ware and Andreas Ford."

"I am sorry Mr. Aberdash, but not at this time—"

"I object, Madam. The mayor, through the news media, has demeaned two valiant police officers who were doing what they took an oath to do—that is, to protect the citizens of this city—and has just about elevated these two men to sainthood; two men who were committing an armed robbery. I wish to remove any doubts in the minds of rational citizens that this is far from being a case of 'white cops killing black citizens' as the media has brazenly branded Patrolmen Scott and Bush. I think the committee, as well as all the people in Detroit, should hear just who Mr. Ware and Ford were."

"And if I grant you this request, will we then hear the testimony of Officer Bush?"

"Yes ma'am."

Maxine Rabbish's shoulders slumped. "Detective Broadnax, please come forward."

Matthew Broadnax walked to the front of the room. The seams on his light green sport coat strained as he buttoned it and tucked in his necktie. His thick black neck bulged over his shirt collar. All 245 pounds of him filled the chair after being sworn in. If there was ever an officer that Jake would want on his side, it was Matt Broadnax. Jake thought the guy could be playing defensive end for any team in the NFL.

Twenty minutes later, Detective Lieutenant Broadnax wrapped up his testimony on the records of the two deceased men, saying, "Not only did the deceased pair, Mr. Marcus Ware and Mr. Andreas Ford, have extensive criminal records, we have been able to make the pair on six very recent armed robberies."

"And may I ask how you did that?" questioned Maxine Rabbish.

"By showing their mug shots, mixed in among a deck of twenty-five, to the victims of those holdups. All of the victims, a total of eight people, picked Marcus Ware and Andreas Ford as the perpetrators of the robberies that were committed in the last five months." The detective looked around the people in the gallery, "One 19-year old black male was shot for not moving fast enough. Most of those victims are here today, if you would like to question them."

The volume in the council room rose as the committee members and the people in the gallery began talking. The TV crews took this opportunity to start packing up their cameras and rolling up the five hundred or so yards of wire they had stretched out over the floor of the council chamber. The circus was over even before Patrolman John Anthony Bush was called to testify. Maxine Rabbish brought order to the room by pounding her gavel and shouting, "Let's take a short recess, reconvening at," she looked at her watch, "10:35."

It was near 11:00 when the panel re-entered the room and took their seats. Half of the onlookers in the gallery before the recess did not return. The TV crews had vanished. The chairperson banged her gavel twice, calling the session to order. "I call on Patrolman John Anthony Bush."

As Jake rose to take the witness seat in front of the panel, half of the people in the gallery rose and started quietly applauding. Maxine pounded her gavel repeatedly, shouting, "Order! Order! Please take your seats." When silence returned, she said, "Please state your name for the record."

"Patrolman John Anthony Bush. Badge 2441." Jake used his police report for reference and stated he heard shots when he was in the men's room. He drew his weapon and exited, seeing his partner and Pigeon Tremble on the floor and two men with guns. Jake said he fired at the men, five shots total.

Less than five minutes later, Jake was excused. Not one member of the panel asked for any further explanation of what happened that night.

"Told you there was nothing to worry about, Jake." John Aberdash patted Jake on the back as they left the council chamber. Jake knew that the attorney had purposely asked for Lieutenant Broadnax to testify. He was very black. The lawyer had known how to counter Mayor Young's stacked panel.

———

Forty-five minutes later, as Jake unlocked the door to his house, his phone was ringing. "Jake, this is Fox. Report for duty, regular time tomorrow. Ditch the uniform. You're working with Southworth."

"The Bobby?"

"Best I can do."

Jake smiled as he cradled the phone. He'd missed *The Job*.

———

A week later, Jake was having coffee at Jesse's kitchen table. "They've got me with Southworth 'til they clear you to come back to work."

Silence filled the room. Slowly Jess put down his cup, reached over and touched Jake's hand. "Remember years ago when I looked you up in Hope?"

"Yeah. When you were working precinct narcotics."

"I said something about hoping I'd catch a bullet—a golden bullet."

"Jess—" Jake squeezed his partner's hand and saw a tear on Jess's cheek.

Jess flicked it away with a finger. "I caught the gold bullet. I'm not coming back. I've only got a half a lung on one side."

Jake stood, grabbing Jess by the shoulder. Jess winced. It was the shoulder where he caught one of the two bullets. "Sorry, partner." Jake felt a tear on his own cheek and knew Jess was doing the right thing. "Keep in touch."

"Will do."

Jake turned to leave, walking past Beth who was listening in the other room. She hugged Jake, sobbing. Jake kissed her on the top of her head as he hugged her back. "Take care of him, Beth."

"I will."

The screen door slammed as Jake walked to his car. He turned the key and drove off, never looking back.

————

"Jake, you're not talking much." Southworth turned left off the ramp at Number Five.

"Lot on my mind, kid."

"Jess Scott?"

"Sometimes." Jake paused. "Sometimes it's just me wondering what the hell I'm doing back in Detroit working for an asshole like the Honorable Coleman Young." Jake's voice tailed off as his light hit the stolen car board. "That Chevy that's going west, it's hot."

Remington flipped a U-turn and gunned the engine. "Maybe it's because you love doing shit like this." He snaked around a cab. "The blue one?"

"Yeah." Jake was cranking down his window and their spotlight fixed on the man behind the wheel. The Chevy gunned it, fishtailing as he cranked a right at the next corner. Remington power-slid around the corner and a half block down nudged the Chevy's rear bumper. The driver braked and broke into a run while the car was still moving. Jake was running too, cutting between two houses, and taking a right in an alley. At the next street the car thief was tackled by Remington Southworth fifteen feet in front of Five-Twenty-Five's idling Buick.

Jake applied his cuffs on the man. "What happened to the blue Chevrolet?"

"It's back there, up against a light pole." Remington stuffed the prisoner into the back of their Buick as Jake slid in beside him. Remington grabbed the mike and called for another car to assist.

Southworth looked at Jake. "I doubt if it's drivable." He hit the mike again, asking for a tow truck. "No wonder my insurance rates keep climbing," he mumbled.

———

Two weeks later, Jake and Edie, along with her sons, Hank and Sam, were sitting at a table in Shaker's. Jake sat with his back to the wall where he could watch the front door. "Jess said I still owed him dinner. Told me to take you and the boys since he can't make it."

"Are they settled in up north?"

"Wanna take a ride up to see on my next set of days off?"

"I'll take that Monday off and find a sitter for the boys."

"We'll take them. They can hang out with Jess's kids."

She pulled Jake close and whispered in his ear. "Afraid to be alone with me?"

"Get the sitter," he whispered, knowing he'd been avoiding being close to her for far too long. On the drive home Jake fought off memories of the past. *Anne would understand.*

Darkness was coming early as fall crept in. Jake was cruising Mack, hugging the curb. On the sidewalk a man was slowly pulling a wagon. His clothes were disheveled and he was bent over, looking only at the sidewalk beneath his feet. "What's the story on the guy with the wagon?" Remington asked.

"Don't know. Never talked to him." Jake looked over his shoulder as he passed the man. "Seen him lots over the past two years. Just goin' to the store or something is my guess."

A car cutting into the alley in front of them ended the conversation. Jake turned to check out the car. No taillights were in front of them. A block down, brake lights flashed. "They're running with their lights out." Jake gunned the Buick to make up some ground. He had his headlights on. "They know someone's behind them for sure."

"Did you see what kind of a car it was?" Remington asked.

"No, did you?"

"Just a dark GM product. Only got a glimpse."

A set of brake lights flashed again as the car turned right. Jake put his foot into the gas to make up more ground. He turned right in time to see the car they were looking for flick on its lights. The car was two blocks ahead and was driving normally. Jake put his foot in the carburetor and made up the two blocks. As he pulled up to the side of the car, he recognized the guy behind the wheel. "Cops."

"Who?"

"Them. The Clean-up crew. Precinct Vice." Jake waved at Tyrone Wynn, the man behind the wheel. Richard Davis was in the passenger seat. Jake headed back towards Mack. "Where were we?" He asked.

"Looking at the guy pulling a wagon."

Jake put the Buick into the curb lane, slowing down to a crawl. "Like I said. Seen that guy a few times before. Didn't look out of place."

"Next time we see him, let's talk to him." Remington flashed his light on the car board checking a plate number. "I thought he was eyeing us from under the brim of his hat."

"Yeah, you've worked with Jess a bit. Picked up some of his traits."

"He said I picked up some of yours too."

"Like what?"

"Talking too much."

Jake laughed. "Betcha he's missing me though."

"How's he doing?"

"Great! Edie and I went up to see him a couple of weeks ago." Jake headed towards the station. It was near quitting time. "Jess's growing a beard. Says deer season is coming and he and his boys are already out scouting."

His mentioning Edie's name reminded him to call her. It had already been eleven hours since he'd last heard her voice.

Chapter Fourteen

Lamar Hunt pulled his wagon into the alley, looking over his shoulder like someone might be watching. *Thought them cops were lookin' hard at me.* He reached the garage behind his house, looked both ways before he pushed the big wooden door to the side. *Maybe they were, maybe they weren't.* He slid the door closed before turning on the light, placed a padlock into the hasp on the inside jamb and snapped it shut. He opened a door on a row of cupboards against the wall and started taking inventory of the day's take. He put three wristwatches in a shoebox and secured the lid with a rubber band. In another, he placed six rings and four necklaces. He opened a second cupboard and put a small Zenith portable TV on a shelf next to two other small televisions. The shelves were getting full. He knew he'd have to make a run to the west side and get rid of some of the stuff. Lamar smiled. *Business has been good.*

He pushed the wagon into the corner near the door to his yard and took his jacket sleeve and buffed a smudge he saw on the black Cadillac's fender next to him. The car took up almost the entire garage. He was thinking that he'd go back to using the car to work further away from home. He lit a cigarette, doused the garage light, locked the door behind him and went into the house. Lamar's workday was over.

Lamar figured he only had a month or so to go in Detroit. He didn't work winters there. He flew to his second home in Miami at the first sign of a snowflake. He was smart enough to get out of the cold. Besides Miami had a lot of rich folks that did the same dumb things that the people around Detroit did. Both left papers on the porch or mail stuffed in the mailbox. The Radio Flyer was his gimmick. The wagon and his old, dirty clothes were the perfect ruse. He looked like some poor old bum, stumbling along the sidewalks in whatever neighborhood he was working.

"So who's this Edie you keep talking about?"

"Someone Jess's wife introduced me to," Jake answered. He was filling out the top of their log sheet with the date: October 15, 1974. "Are you married, Bob?"

"Engaged. She's a bit leery about being a cop's wife. By the way, my name's Remington, remember?"

"Jess said to call you Bob. Get used to it."

"My dad and mom liked the name they gave me."

"Too many syllables. Bob's easier. What's your girlfriend call you?"

Jake could see Remington's face turn a little red as the street lights on Kercheval lit up the inside of the Buick. "Bobbie."

"How about I don't call you Bobbie, but just plain ol' Bob until they put you in charge of this car."

Remington shrugged. "Fair enough." Remington made a quick U-turn. He saw something he wanted to check—the guy pulling a red wagon. He pointed him out to Jake. "Time to get his name and see what he's up to."

Fifteen minutes later Remington and Jake drove off. No name, no address and no information for the sheet. Jake spoke first. "A deaf-mute. Some stop, Bob."

"I think he's faking it."

"What makes you think so?"

"I know some sign language. All deaf people know how to sign."

"And?"

"I signed for him to give us his name. He just looked at me like I was nuts. He can talk and hear too."

"You sure?"

"No, but I feel it," Remington answered.

"So what do we do now?"

"Stop him again, the next time we see him."

"On something you feel?"

"Anything better to do?"

Jake shook his head. "Guess not."

———

Lamar took a week off. The stop by the plain-clothes cops had him rattled until he counted the cash he had on hand. He figured he needed another thousand or so to tide him over until he got to Miami. *Time to go back to work. Anyway, the deaf and dumb routine worked on them dumb white cops.* He laughed to himself. In another month he'd be in sunny Florida.

Lamar pulled the red Radio Flyer down the alley. It was still dark. He left his Cadillac in the Kroger parking lot. Lamar liked crowded parking lots: churches on Sundays or supermarkets the rest of the week. Doctor's office lots worked fine too. The wagon fit in his trunk. He had been using it for two years now. Well, almost two years, take away the winters.

He was a bit pissed off as he left his Cadillac. The fence he'd been using only came up with $500 for the load he'd delivered the day before. *Hafta find another man. Fuckin' thief.*

His plan was to work the river side of Jefferson for a few days. Manistique and Phillip were his targeted streets. He hadn't been in that neighborhood for a year. He remembered making a good haul the last time and the five thousand he got for some jewelry the previous fall. It was enough to give him a good start in Miami.

———

The twang of the screen door's spring stirred William from his nap. *Meals on Wheels had already been here at twelve-thirty.* He tilted his head listening. *Funny, how I depend on their Coming and going to tell time. It's probably my kid.* He kicked the Lazy-Boy upright. "Come on in, Bill. Door's unlocked."

Lamar thought the dark house was empty because the mail box was overflowing. The voice he heard said to come in. He paused. *Who'd be sitting in the dark?* Lamar shrugged his shoulders and pushed his way in the door.

William stood and walked the three steps to his right to the kitchen table. He knew what the first question would be. "They brought a hot beef sandwich and mashed potatoes today with a roll and butter. Didn't like the peas though."

Lamar stood still as the man talked. The last rays of sunset filtering through the windows gave him just enough light to see by. The guy pulled out a chair at the table and sat down.

"Hey, can you find WJR on the radio for me? I musta bumped the dial this morning. I like the news that comes on at six."

Lamar relaxed. *He can't see.* Lamar flicked on his flashlight. M*ight as well see if there's anything worth taking.*

William got a whiff of cigarette smoke mixed with a strong aftershave. "Hey! You're not my son. Who are you?" He jumped up and felt his way around the table towards the door. He could feel the air around him move. "Dammit, answer me!"

William only heard raspy breathing, then drawers opening and closing in his bedroom. "Get outta my house whoever you are!" He felt the air move behind him and stumbled forward against the sink, groping his way around the counter. He felt his way along the wall, then after five steps to the right, his shin found the Lazy-boy. He turned and fell into it. "Don't know who you are or what you want. Just take it and get the hell out." The air moved around him again and the front door banged shut followed by the screen door. William relaxed.

Whew! At least he didn't kill me.

He groped around on the end table, knocking the phone to the floor. He got on his hands and knees, found the cord and pulled the receiver towards his ear. He put his finger in what he hoped was the zero hole.

"Operator."

"Operator, this is Bill Thatcher at 202 Phillip. Someone's just robbed me." He heard the voice of the operator give him the number for the police department. "Please help me. I'm blind."

"Give me that address again, sir. I'll call them for you." He gave the number and let the receiver drop to the floor. He recalled what the man had smelled like: smoke and a strong aftershave—*what was it? Yes! Aqua Velva.*

———

Lamar legged it to his wagon. *Fuck! Shudda never went in. A blind guy. Damn!*

He walked at a fast pace, hoping to get out of the neighborhood. He took a turn heading for the Kroger lot on the corner of Jefferson and Chalmers. His take was a handful of jewelry and an old Philco Radio. *Sure in hell wasn't worth it.*

———

Jake spotted a man pulling a wagon. "Bob. To your right."

"Walking a little faster this time. Let's lay back and see where he goes."

"You're reading my mind."

The man and his wagon went into the Kroger's lot. Jake slowly turned in. In the fifth row the man and wagon stopped behind a Cadillac. The trunk opened and the wagon was placed inside. The man got behind the wheel of the car and backed out of its slot.

Five Twenty-five's radio came to life. "Five-Ten. 202 Phillip, see the man on a B&E."

"Five-Ten on the way."

———

Bill Junior was pulling around the corner towards his dad's house when he saw a police car pulling to the curb. He ran to the house before they could knock. "What's going on?"

"Got a call on a robbery. This your house?"

"My dad's." Bill pulled on the screen door, pushed open the unlocked front door and reached in to turn on the lights. "Dad, you okay?"

"Thank God it's you, Bill. I just called the cops." William sat upright in his Lazy-Boy.

"They're here with me, dad."

———

Jake followed the Cadillac west on Jefferson. "Our man's driving. He's gotta have a license to drive, deaf or dumb." Jake gassed the Buick and caught up to it. Remington hit the car's window with their spotlight and pointed to the curb. "Bob, you take the driver. You're the one who knows sign language."

Remington didn't try to sign; he just opened the driver's door. "Out of the car, mister." He tugged on the man's arm. "And let's see your driver's license." Again, the man motioned with his hands that he couldn't hear or talk. Remington started spelling out with his hands: D-r-i-v-e-r L-i-c-e-n-s-e.

All he got was a queer look from the man. He spun the man around and gave him a quick frisk and found his wallet. Remington nudged the man towards the back of the Cadillac, tossing the wallet to Jake. "He's still playing deaf and dumb. Let's see if he's got a driver's license."

Jake put the wallet on the hood of their car, while Remington stood on the curb watching. "Just so you know, mister. You're not going anywhere until we know who you are. You and I are going to go through your stuff together, so watch closely."

Jake was a little hesitant going through the guy's wallet, especially a man who might not be able to speak or hear. He flipped it open and found a license under the see-through plastic. Jake reached inside the open passenger window on his car for the clipboard just as their radio came alive.

"Cars in Five and all cars. Five-Ten has some info on a B&E dwelling at 202 Phillip—" Jake proceeded to jot down the driver's name, Lamar Hunt, when he caught the tail end of the radio transmission. "—reeked of Aqua Velva shaving lotion."

Jake sniffed the air. "Bob, what street did we see him coming from?"

"Phillip."

"Mister Hunt, you're going to spend some time at the station with us." Jake turned the man around and cuffed him. "Don't start talkin' now, Mr. Hunt, 'cause whatever you say can be used against you in a court of law."

Jake opened the Buick's back door, guiding the handcuffed man into the rear seat. Remington went around and slid in the back seat on the driver's side. Jake called *Radio* to send another car to take the Caddie in. They'd search it in Number Five's well-lit garage. Jake keyed the mike again. "Radio, can you have that car from Number Five with the info on the B&E Dwelling meet us at the station? We have a suspect in custody."

"Roger on that Five-Two-Five. Five-Ten meet—"

———

Lamar Hunt's Cadillac was pulled into the Fifth Precinct's garage and Remington searched it thoroughly while Jake put their prisoner in the "bullpen," the large temporary holding cell at the station. Fifteen minutes later Jake and Remington were listing the items found in the wagon nestled in the trunk.

They and the crew of Five-Ten talked to the Fifth Precinct Detectives covering afternoons. Five-Ten's report basically said that at the present no one knew if anything was taken by the man who was inside the Thatcher house. The father and son were going to go through the house to see if anything was missing. The lead detective, Charlie Byersdorf, called the William Thatcher house. Bill Jr. was still there. The detective asked if they could come down to the station.

A half hour later in the Fifth Precinct Detective Bureau, a very different line up was held. It was not the normal five men standing behind a one-way glass to be viewed by a victim. There were five men standing side by side in the bullpen. Stature or color didn't matter since the victim was blind. William Thatcher Sr. was led by Detective Byersdorf past the men, two times. The first time Lamar Hunt was the third man in the line. They were shuffled into new positions and Byersdorf led William Thatcher Sr. past them again. This time Lamar hunt was the last man in the line. Both times William Thatcher Sr. stopped in front of Lamar Hunt and both times he said, "This is the man who was in my house today."

"You're positive, sir?" Detective Byersdorf asked.

"Positive. I might not be able to see, but this is the guy that was there. I remember what he smelled like. Cigarette smoke and Aqua Velva."

The items found in the red wagon and the Cadillac's trunk were tagged and on a desk ready to be moved to the locked evidence room. William Thatcher Jr. was brought in to view the items since neither he nor his father could say what, if anything, was taken.

"That old, black portable Philco radio for sure," Bill Jr. pointed out. "And that Cameo locket, if it's got my mom's initials on the back. Her name was Mary. She's been dead four years now."

Byersdorf turned over the locket and the initials on the back were an *M* and a *T*.

Bill Jr. looked at some of the other items Jake had tagged. "And maybe that Benrus watch. Dad got one when he retired from Detroit Edison. It'd have his initials on the back and the year, 1965, that's when he retired." The watch belonged to William Thatcher Sr.

Lamar hunt wasn't heading for Miami any time soon. He was booked for B&E Occupied Dwelling, specifically for the burglary at 202 Phillip. Fifteen other items, all watches and jewelry, were tagged as retrieved from the Hunt's trunk awaiting any further B&E reports that might follow.

———

Two weeks later Remington was updating their stolen car board while Jake was checking the teletypes. "Bob, did you see the note in our box from Fox on the red wagon guy?"

"No, but I can guess. They fingered him on some other jobs."

"The dicks got a warrant and searched his place."

Remington cocked his head. "And?"

"He had a bunch of stuff in his garage. And Lamar's fingered two guys who were fencing the merchandise. He's singing like a canary."

"Told you he could talk."

"Yes you did." Jake might have missed his old partner, but Remington was working out just fine.

Chapter Fifteen

October was just about over. It was damp, a bit chilly and the falling leaves cluttered the curbside on Marlborough. Jake was behind the wheel driving slowly. His lights were out. There had been a rash of cars being broken into in a twenty block area west of Grosse Pointe Park and the Detroit River's side of Jefferson. It was just after midnight, and Jake and Remington hoped they might stumble upon some foot traffic. At that time of the night, there was a good chance it might be their burglars. Jake and Remington figured it'd be two or three guys judging by what was taken in a given night.

A dark car to the front of their Buick LaSabre was parked beyond a lone streetlight ahead. "Bob, is that exhaust fumes coming from under that car?"

"Yep," Remington answered.

Jake chuckled within. *The kid was getting used to being called Bob.* Jake applied the parking brake to keep his taillights from flashing. "Might be our B&E men."

"Might be."

Jake killed the engine to wait. An hour passed and the car ahead was still idling. Wisps of exhaust plumes floated into the night.

Remington looked at his watch. "Think I should sneak up and see if anyone's inside?"

Jake was bored too. "Yeah. I'll stay behind the wheel in case you flush somebody out."

Remington slipped out of the passenger door and crept from elm tree to elm tree. Jake watched, his hand was on the ignition key, ready to start their Buick. He could see his partner at the car looking in the windows, then Remington's flashlight came on. Jake hit the ignition and slipped his car into drive, closing the gap between their Buick and what turned out to be a maroon Chevrolet. Remington signaled for Jake to join him.

Behind the wheel was a woman, asleep in the idling car. Jake was standing at the rear of the car while his partner stood on the passenger's side. "She's breathing, Jake." He tapped on the passenger window with the butt of his flashlight. "Ma'am!" He paused, then yelled, "Hey Lady, wake up."

Jake moved around to the driver's side and started banging on her window with the palm of his hand. She didn't move. The button was up on the door and he slowly opened it, reaching in to keep the woman from falling out onto the street. The smell of marijuana hit as Jake propped her up with his right arm. He reached past her and turned off the car. She still didn't stir. "Bob, you might want to call for a car. One with a stretcher." Jake gave her a push to keep her upright and she fell, shoulder first, onto the passenger's side. "She's totally wasted. Marijuana, in case you can't smell it."

Ten minutes later, Five-twelve arrived in their station wagon along with another car to take the woman's Chevrolet to the station. Jake and Remington helped drag her out of her Chevy and onto a fold-down stretcher. They belted her in with her arms to the side. Jake and Remington followed Twelve to Receiving Hospital. It wasn't until they were strapping her onto a hospital gurney when she showed any signs of coming out of her drug-induced stupor.

An hour and a half later Jake was typing up a report on the arrest of a Gloria Rivers, black female, 28, with an address on Marlborough Street, while Remington was tagging the bag of marijuana.

"Ol' Gloria musta bought some good stuff here, the way she was out of it," Remington quipped.

Jake pulled the report out of the typewriter. "Never could figure out what she was mumbling. Something about an ice cream man." Jake signed the report and shoved it towards his partner. "Twenty-eight, a new car and a couple thousand bucks in her purse. Wonder what she does for a living?"

"Whores don't drive Chevrolets," Remington answered as he signed the report. They locked the cash, purse and dope in the evidence room at Number Five.

———

Hank, the oldest of Edie's sons, was playing flag football. The Centerline Parks and Recreation department had two fields for what they called "Junior Football." Again, Jake was the coach for Hank's team. Baseball and now football practice worked well for him to stay involved with the boys. The four in the afternoon practice times worked well with Jake's 7 p.m. to 3 a.m. shift. And, as it was with baseball, any games played later than five o'clock, one of the other coaches took charge. The three who helped Jake with this team were all fathers of one or two of the boys who were playing on the team.

Jake got the coaching job by the normal route for all boys' sports in the early 70s. No one wanted it. It wasn't that Jake was some big-time jock; he just liked working with kids and had played some football and baseball. In 1961 he helped coach a parochial school's football team at his former grade school, Ascension in Warren. Back then he was fresh out of the Marines and waiting to be hired by the Detroit Police Department. Jake remembered a few Sundays when it wasn't raining where Anne would have Michelle in a stroller and Debbie by the hand, watching their dad's football team playing. Mike and Jeanette were not even thought of yet. Catholic grade schools were big into tackle football.

Now, Jake was keeping busy with someone else's kids. His own were just a faint memory. More than once, as he'd help Hank get into his shoulder pads, Jake's mind would drift back to thoughts of his own son, Mike, wondering if he would have liked to play football. *Mike would be twelve—* then his mind would jump back to the present. He forced himself not to dwell on his past.

Hank was just old enough for Little League and junior football—eight—and Sam had been the bat boy for the baseball team and now was the water boy for Hank's flag football team, the Centerline Cougars. He was six.

Jake's thoughts were interrupted with, "Hey Dad. Kin you throw me a ball?" It was Sam yelling and running ten yards away with his short arms stretched to their limit. Jake paused, digesting the word *Dad*, then lobbed a football Sam's way. The kid took a tumble as the ball hit the ground just beyond his reach.

"Nice try, buddy!"

An hour and a half later the boys were loaded in Jake's Ford half-ton, heading home.   "Want to stop for an ice cream?" Knowing the answer, Jake kept his eye out for a corner store on Van Dyke. The sun was rapidly descending on a fairly warm October afternoon.

The three of them were nibbling on an Eskimo Pie, sitting on the Ford's tailgate. Sam sat on Jake's right and Hank on his left. They all had their legs dangling off the ground. Jake elbowed the boy on his right, saying, "Sam, earlier you called me dad. That was a slip of the tongue, right?"

Sam paused for a second, started to take another bite out of his ice cream, then just shrugged his shoulders. "Dad's easier than Mr. Bush all the time. Mom says I can't call you Jake."

Jake looked at Hank. "You feel the same way?"

Hank was right in the middle of licking off the wooden stick that held one last bit of vanilla ice cream. "Uh-huh."

"What's uh-huh?"

"It's easier."

"Your own dad might not like it."

Sam answered, "I don't remember my dad."

"I do—barely." Hank chimed in.

"Okay. You can call me dad. But this is between you guys and me. No telling your mom." They nodded in agreement.

The boys were quiet on the drive home and Jake started looking for some music on the radio when Sam spoke up. "You know, you could marry our mom, then you'd be our dad."

Jake didn't know how to answer a six year old's logic, so he turned off the radio and said, "Let's just let me get used to you calling me dad for a while. Okay?"

"Okay," they answered in unison, both smiling from ear to ear.

Jake's thoughts jumped to their mom. Jake had his own reason to smile as he remembered a pudgy witch dressed in black at Jess's party.

———

Gloria was sitting on a metal cot chained to the wall in a cell at 1300 Beaubien on the eighth floor—the Women's Division holding cells. A car from the First Precinct brought her over once she was released from the hospital. She was awaiting a visit from Nate Goldberg, her lawyer. Gloria's head was drooped, deep in thought. *Dammit girl, I thought you were smarter than that.* She shook her head from side to side and looked through the bars at the clock on the far wall behind a protective screen.

It had been over five years since she'd taken over her daddy's business and Gloria Rivers had prided herself on her business acumen. She was a graduate of Wayne State University, majoring in business law, and was now running a flourishing *Mutuals Business* her daddy had started 20 years ago. Her dad, Ronnie, had died from a bullet to his head— something that tends to happen in the business he was in.

The term "Mutuals Business" meant her daddy was a bookie. He ran a numbers game, a spinoff on what was once called the Mafia Lottery. The numbers racket was big business in black neighborhoods where for fifty cents, one could win $300. All you had to do was match the three numbers for the day, usually based on race track payouts.

Mothers, dads, the mailman, the milkman and an occasional preacher played the numbers and Gloria was glad to oblige them. She had corner grocery stores, bars, and barbershops that took in the bets that covered an area from Grosse Pointe Park west to East Grand Boulevard, and from the Detroit River to Gratiot. Twenty-five runners were on her payroll. They collected the numbers slips and the cash, and then delivered everything to her.

Unlike her daddy, who had his place raided by the police three times and was held up once—the day he had been shot —Gloria did door-to-door service. In other words, Gloria met her runners at prearranged places and times. This was an improvement over the way her daddy had done business. No one can raid a place when no one knows where it is. Gloria was smart and knew how to make a buck.

Gloria bought the house on Marlborough because it had a three-car garage. In it she had a Ford, a Chevrolet and a Dodge, all run-of-the-mill, mid-priced cars she traded in every six months. She knew that a fancy car or the same one would attract attention. She didn't want to do that. After all, she was a business major from WSU.

Except one time, she lamented as she sat waiting for Mr. Goldberg. *One time I let Dusty Heights talk me into coming to his party. Man, that was some strong shit we were smokin'.*

_____

Five nights after their trip to Receiving Hospital with Gloria Rivers, Jake and Remington were staked out watching 203 Marlborough, her home. She had no record. The Detroit Narcotics Squad had charged her with possession and she was awaiting a trial date. She had retained a high-profile law firm to represent her. It was plain curiosity that had Five Twenty-five sitting a block away with a good pair of binoculars. She had told Detective Hasse the cash she carried was from a sugar daddy. Jake and Remington didn't believe her for a minute.

The November nights were long, and, to fill their time, Jake and Remington thought they'd hang around to see just what was going on in Gloria's life. They'd watch her place for three hours a night, alternating from the start of the shift until the last three hours of their shift. This went on for two weeks. They came up dry. The only thing out of the ordinary was that three different cars came and went from the house on Marlborough, a Ford, a Chevrolet and a Dodge. And the plate numbers were all registered to Gloria Rivers of 203 Marlborough. Out of boredom, they gave up watching the house.

_____

1974 came to a close with a blanket of snow covering the streets for those going out on the town for New Year's Eve parties. Sitting on a table in the teletype room was a copy of _The Detroit Free Press_. The front page headline read "Homicide Record Set." In the article, city officials were hoping for quiet, since at total of 710 homicides had already been recorded for the year.

Another article that was featured on page three concerned a court case before a judge where the mayor wanted to trim the Detroit Police Department through layoffs, but wanted to circumvent the normal "last hired, first fired" seniority principle.

It was a Tuesday, and Jake and Remington just finished their routine at the range in the basement at the precinct. Richard Davis and Tyrone Wynn were coming down the stairs to take some target practice. Jake recognized them. "Still working Clean-up?"

The two black officers nodded. Davis spoke. "Yeah, still kicking in doors on after-hours joints, rousting whores, junkies and numbers runners."

"Just coming on duty?"

"No heading home. Some asshole pulled a gun on us today. Kinda got us thinking that we need some time on the range," Wynn answered.

Jake pointed over his shoulder. "If you need any help, the Bobbie here is an expert. He's kicked my butt every time we come down here."

Remington turned a shade of red at Jake's remark.

———

The midnight hour was approaching and Five Twenty-five was parked at the White Castle. They were taking a long break. Any cop with any sense would abandon the streets of the city for about an hour while the residents brought in the New Year. Almost everyone who owned a gun of any sort would be firing a shot or two, even more, into the midnight darkness.

Remington had been reading *The Free Press*. "Did you see how many murders we've had in Detroit so far this year?"

Jake just nodded, slowly sipping his coffee. He was wondering if the gunfire had stopped. He remembered his dad doing the same thing when the clock struck midnight.

"How in the hell is the mayor going to lay off cops when we're setting homicide records?"

Jake didn't answer.

Remington sensed that Jake had something on his mind. "Got woman troubles, Jake?"

"Yes and no."

"Your girlfriend give you the gate?"

"No, Edie and I are doing fine." Jake paused a few beats. "Remember Gloria?"

"The broad stoned on pot?"

"Yeah, that one."

"Why in the hell did she cross your mind?"

"Seeing the guys from Precinct Vice. They might want to sit on her place. She's into something. Dope, gambling, who knows. It'd give them something to do."

"How do we get that to happen?"

"I'll talk to their boss. I worked with him years ago before he made sergeant. Name's John Warneke. I'll see him tomorrow when we go in."

"You need me along?"

"No. Just meet me at the Y at ten tomorrow. I need a spotter."

"Will it be open? It's New Year's Day."

Jake just shrugged. "Never asked. Let's just skip it then."

———

A week went by. Sergeant Warneke said he'd check Gloria out. The holiday bullshit was in the past. And yes, Detroit set a new record with 714 recorded homicides for 1974.

The mayor was still working on a plan to lay off police officers and the Detroit Police Officer's Association was taking the city to court over the way the mayor wanted the layoffs to be determined. Mayor Young wanted the recently hired blacks and women to stay on the job while more senior white officers would be pink slipped.

———

"Did you see them taillights ahead?" Jake asked.

"Uh-huh."

Jake and Remington were crawling along the curb on Lakewood at nearly one in the morning. It was the fifth street they'd checked that night. An earlier dusting of snow had melted, the result of a January thaw.

"Looked like about halfway up the block." Jake said.

"That's what I figure."

Jake slid out the passenger door. Their interior light never went on. Jake removed the bulb the day they took over the Buick.

The streets of Detroit were lined with elm trees and Jake used them to move up the block, stopping behind each one to scan the darkness. He could hear movement ahead, but the heavy clouds hid what moonlight there might be. Two cars lengths ahead he saw the flash of an interior light, just long enough to know someone had gotten into the car.

Jake waited a minute or two, then crouched, slowly duck-walking towards where he last saw the light. As he got to the rear tire of the car, the passenger door opened and a man crawled out. In the brief flash of light he saw a radio with dangling wires in the man's hands. As the door slammed, Jake stood. "Freeze! Police!"

The man dropped what he had and started to run. Jake anticipated it and three steps is all it took to tackle the man. Jake rolled on top, holding his head down and grabbing at a jacket sleeve. He was broadsided as another man jumped on him. Instead of one, Jake was fighting two men.

"He's a cop!" The first man yelled.

"Get his gun! Get his gun!" A voice rang out.

Jake was on his back, his left hand clutching onto a leather sleeve, and with all the torque he could muster he thrust upward towards the man who was repeating, "Get his gun!"

The base of Jake's right palm made solid contact with a nose. He heard cartilage break as headlights flashed and tires screeched on the street.

It wasn't Remington's voice he heard as he took a shoe in the ribs.

"Quick! Get in the fuckin' car." It was a third man. Then the leather-sleeved arm that Jake was hanging onto was wrenched from his grip, followed by metal crunching.

"Freeze! All of you!"

The Bobbie had arrived.

In the darkness Jake heard a thunk. "Freeze means don't move." There was a second or two of silence. "Dammit Jake, that hard-headed asshole broke my flashlight."

Jake was atop one of the men, grabbing an arm and snapping on one handcuff then another. "You okay, Bob?"

"Yeah. I'll cover them. Get some lights on."

Jake ran to their Buick, flicked on the headlights and grabbed his three-cell flashlight, thumbing the switch as he ran back to his partner. Remington was standing over three bodies, his pistol at his side. One man was handcuffed; one out cold and the third on his hands and knees half over the curb, bleeding from his forehead. There was a large dent in the rear door of the car idling on the street.

"I see you've got everything under control." Jake's flashlight beam bounced from man to man.

"Yeah. Did you call for a couple of cars?"

"I will now." Jake called Radio, and keyed the mike when the radio operator answered. "Yes Radio. That's Lakewood, south of Freud. Five Twenty-five needs two cars. One with stretchers."

———

Two hours later, Jake was still typing up the report. They had three black adult males, two 19-year olds and a 20-year old, in custody for B&E Auto. All were being held at Number Five after a stop at Detroit's Receiving Hospital—one with a broken nose courtesy of Jake Bush, another with a minor concussion and a stitched up scalp wound, and a third with a stitched up forehead. The last two had been the result of not freezing when Remington ordered them to. The trunk of their car contained three tape decks, two CB radios and five factory-installed car radios. Remington was tagging the evidence as Jake typed.

"I was wondering where in the hell you were when the second guy jumped me."

"Saw him. But saw a car coming up, too. Thought it might be their wheels." Remington put a fresh cup of coffee next to Jake. "Knew you could handle two for a while." He smiled. "Black and a little sugar, right?"

"Think we ought to make an accident report on how the side of that car that was caved in?"

"It's their car. Let 'em put in a claim when they get out." Remington grinned.

"A forehead with 170 pounds behind it makes a hell of a dent." Jake pulled the report out of the typewriter. "How far did you throw him? Fifteen feet?"

"More like twenty. Remember, I've been hitting the gym with you."

Jake smiled to himself. *Yeah, the kid's probably as strong as Jess.*

"That reminds me. See you at the Y 'bout eleven. I want to get some sleep tonight."

The clock on the wall was showing 5:30 a.m. as they walked past the desk and to their cars. It was a couple of hours past their time to go home.

Chapter Sixteen

Near the corner of Mack and Belvidere, Five Twenty-five had a new, dark-green Plymouth sedan stopped. A recent teletype had a car of that general description used in an armed robbery of a gas station at Woodward and Alexandrine. A crowd had gathered as Remington searched the car while Jake interrogated the two male occupants. Jake overheard a voice in the crowd. "White Gestapo fuckin' wid a black man again." Jake's eyes slowly panned the group of eight men and two women. He didn't see who was talking and went back to writing the names of Richard Weems and Norvelle Sims, along with their addresses, on his clipboard.

Remington checked the trunk and closed it, shaking his head from side to side. That was the signal that everything was good. "Sorry to bother you two," Jake said as he handed their IDs back to them.

Weems, the driver, took his license and registration, nodding towards the group leaning against the front of Simon's Clothing Store. "You always draw a crowd?"

Jake smiled, looking back over to the people milling around. "Comes with the badge."

"Maybe with skin color too," Weems added as he took the car keys offered by Remington. The Fifth Precinct was ninety-eight percent Negro.

"They're all bluster," Remington added. "Nothing we can't handle."

Richard Weems and Norvelle Sims, two midnight shift workers at the nearby Chrysler Plant, climbed into their Plymouth and drove off, knowing the redheaded cop was probably right. The plainclothes officer stood six-five and weighed about 245 pounds with not an ounce of fat, and his partner didn't look like a slouch either, about five inches shorter and pushing 200.

"Show's over, people—unless the one with the mouth's got a problem." Jake looked around at the crowd, heard no response and climbed in the jump seat while Remington got behind the wheel. The dark blue Buick LaSabre drove off into the early evening.

Jake got settled in his seat after logging their last stop. "Getting harder to do our job. One of these days someone's going to jump our ass."

Remington checked his mirror and signaled for a turn. "Especially when 'His Honor' the mayor, spews his racist bullshit every day in the papers."

Jake grunted in acknowledgement. He normally stayed away from talking politics, but he knew Remington was right. Their first black mayor didn't pull any punches when talking to the media. He was making it a black-against-white issue with everything he said and did.

The mayor was known to withdraw city services, like regular garbage collection, from some white neighborhoods. Coleman Young seemed determined to drive the whites from *his city*.

Headlights moved into the night heading east and west. Some drivers were going home from work, some no doubt looking for trouble. Those looking for trouble knew there were cops like Jake and Remington working the streets to minimize what they'd get away with.

"You still with the same girlfriend?" Jake asked, breaking the stillness of the night.

"Yep. Same one."

"You never talk about it. You said you were engaged. Any wedding plans?"

"There's a bit of a hang up with that."

"She leery about marrying a cop?"

"Maybe more about meeting her family obligations."

"What's her name?"

"Jen Li. I call her Jenny."

Over lunch Remington told Jake about meeting his fiancé. She was Chinese, 22, and her family ran a dry cleaning and laundry not too far from where they'd made the stop earlier that night. "It's Wong's on Mack and Cadillac. I walked the beat covering that area. They did my uniforms."

"That how you met her?"

"Yeah. Stopped by to pick up my clothes one day and there she was." Remington brightened as he talked about Jen Li. "She was attending Wayne State and working the shop. A sane man doesn't walk away from a pretty girl like that without asking for a date."

"That's the place where the cops in Number Five get their clothes done."

"I found that out the first week I was on that beat. Cop cars were all over it."

Jake laughed, thinking it must have been the pretty girl that had all the cops stopping. The Chinese weren't into giving *police discounts*. "So what's the problem with getting married?"

Remington motioned for the waitress to bring more coffee before answering. "The family comes from the Guangdong Province in Southeast China. The grandfather was a lawyer back there, immigrated to the states and ended up starting the business on Mack."

"What's your girlfriend studying?"

"Pre-Law. She's in her last year now and already accepted into Wayne State's law school."

"So she's waiting until she gets her law degree?"

"Something like that. She's determined to return the family's name to a place of honor."

Jake pushed himself away from the table and grabbed his tab. "Sounds like if you marry her, you'll be marrying her whole family."

"Probably." He shrugged his shoulders. "She's worth it."

Five Twenty-five went back to cruising the streets of the Fifth Precinct, checking the back of the business places on Mack, Kercheval, Conners and Jefferson.

———

Wong Chung Yun had emigrated from China in 1949. The communists were in full control and his family was among the minority of Chinese who were Christians. Through bribes and favors owed, he was able to move his family to Formosa. He then went by ship to New York without them. His wife, Lee Yun Hung, and newly-married son, Wong Tau, worked in Formosa to save money so they could move to America.

Wong Chung Yun was an attorney in China, but after a week of knocking on doors, the only thing he could find in New York was a dishwashing job at what he thought was a Chinese- owned restaurant named Luchow's. When he went in and applied for the job he was greeted by the owner, August Lüchow, a German, but a job was a job and it did pay seventy-five cents an hour. With the job came a new name. Mr. Lüchow said he had a hard enough time with English, so Wong Chung Yun became David Wong.

David lived with a cousin, Sing Lee, and five other Chinese men who were trying to do the same—earn enough to bring their families to the United States. By living in cramped quarters and working odd shifts, the six men could survive with the three beds available in their tiny apartment.

Ten years later and after a move to Detroit, Wong Chung Yun opened the shop on Mack Avenue. The laundry and dry cleaning business was a far cry from appearing before the courts in China, but it was a living, and a way to bring his family to America, the "Land of the Free."

In 1965 Wong Chung Yun was reunited with most of his family. By hard work he was able to send for his son, Tau and his daughter-in-law, Chang Fang Ting, to America. Regrettably, his wife, Lee Yun Hung, had died two years before. By then his son had his own family, a daughter, born in 1953, and two younger boys. The girl was named Jen Li and the boys, Shang Ren and Shang Yi. They all went to work at the laundry the minute they arrived. That's the way it is in Chinese families.

───────

Little rocks and debris crunched under the Buick LeSabre's tires. Jake was checking the alleys behind the businesses on Mack. It was after midnight and only an occasional night light shone through the barred windows on the back of the empty shops.

"Why don't you let me out," Remington said, breaking the silence.

"Miss walking a beat?"

"No. Just need a little fresh air."

"Take the walkie-talkie. I'll cut across the street and drive that alley."

Remington slid out his door and watched the taillights on the Buick take the next street towards Mack. Winter had broken its grip on the City of Detroit, but the night time temperature was still in the low forties.

Jake doused his headlights after crossing Mack and taking a right in the alley. He lowered his window listening for more than just his tires rolling over crumbled glass and small stones that always littered the concrete alleys. His slow pace took him across another side street, then a second and a third. Jake keyed the mike, whispering, "Bob, you cool?"

"I'm cool."

Some nights the time flew by. Some, like this night, was void of foot traffic and not many cars on the streets. It was plain dead. Jake knew that's why his partner was walking. He did it too every now and then. Sometimes just to stay awake.

Idle thoughts crossed Jake's mind. First it was Hank saying he wanted to play first base this summer, then Sam asking when he could play Little League, and finally, Edie's smile. He knew they were fast asleep in the quiet confines of their home.

Clang!

The sound of metal hitting concrete broke the stillness of the night and a dark figure was running ahead. The lone streetlight a half block down silhouetted the man. He turned right towards Mack as Jake gunned the Buick, flicking on his lights. He grabbed the mike. "Bob, I flushed someone. He's coming your way."

Jake took the same turn. No one was in front of him. He got to the corner and stopped. "I'm at Mack and Newport, Bob. Where're you?" Jake's radio stayed silent for ten, then twenty seconds. "Bob, you out there?"

Ten seconds later, Jake's radio came alive. "I'm on Coplin, Jake. Got your runner."

Minutes later Jake, was backtracking his route with Remington sitting in the back seat of the Buick with Nathan Balfour handcuffed to his right.

"It was somewhere right in here," Jake offered. "I'll get out and walk." He put the car in Park and took his three-cell with him.

Five minutes and three businesses later, Jake located the pry bar. He checked the door and saw the marks around the lock. The door was within one pry from being open. Through the barred rear window Jake could see it was the grocery store about mid-block west of Newport. He drove around the block and grabbed the address.

Jake typed up the report while Remington notified the owner about the attempted burglary. Their night was over.

The routine for the crew of Five Twenty-five continued. Three mornings a week in the weight room at the Y, then Tuesdays and Thursdays at the precinct range. Remington was upgrading his piece from the department-issued Colt .38 caliber to a bigger Smith & Wesson. He had tried Jake's pistol once and like the feel of it. A lot of the guys were buying .44 magnums, but Jake was convinced they were too big for the job. He told Remington about Fred Greening at Number Thirteen. "A guy's got to be able to get more than one shot off."

"Jake, how many times do you hafta tell me that story? I ordered a .357 yesterday."

"Good. I don't want to walk around alleys looking for a pistol."

Southeastern High School had a few problem students, but none worse than Theodore Roosevelt Poet. Theo spent as much time in detention as he did in a classroom and his parents were weary of the weekly trips to visit the school counselors and principal. Mr. Alabaster, the principal, told Marcus and Rena Poet that their six foot tall, 225 pound son, a sophomore, belonged in another institution—a reform school.

Theodore Poet had been bullying his classmates and shaking them down for their lunch money since the sixth grade. Finally, one student had the courage to turn him in and ended up being severely beaten. Though the student refused to name his assailant, the principal knew who it was. Students and teachers were afraid of Theo Poet and the Detroit Public School system had tolerated him long enough. He was expelled.

Marcus and Rena Poet were faced with a real dilemma. They, too, were afraid of their son. Thus, Theodore Poet became the product of the streets of Detroit. His home was just a place for an occasional meal or somewhere to sleep once in a while, and that was all. Street muggings and snatching purses became his main pursuit.

The Detroit Police Juvenile Division became well acquainted with the young man until the Juvenile Court found some room for him at the WJ Maxey Boys Training School in Whitmore Lake, Michigan. His hair-trigger temper kept him in trouble throughout his stay. He spent most of his time segregated from the general training-school population.

Theodore Poet was released on his seventeenth birthday, when he was no longer considered a juvenile in Michigan.

Detroit Recorder's Court Judge George W. Crockett Jr. had seen enough of Theodore Poet over the next two years. On his fifth appearance before the judge, he was given three to five years for *Robbery Not Armed,* a purse snatching. If one counted his juvenile record, he already had ten convictions for felonies.

For the next three years and two months Theo split his time between the Jackson State Prison's weight room and its library. The weight room turned his 300 pounds of body mass into sculpted muscles and trimmed off 15 pounds. The library wasn't really on his list to visit, but Theo's cellmate happened to be a man convicted for embezzling a half million dollars from a charity he'd been running. The cellmate, Randy Rheil, had an MBA from the University of Dayton, and had been going to the library every day. He talked Theo into joining him, after Theo had been put in isolation for putting two guys in the infirmary, just because he could.

Randy convinced Theo he'd be further ahead if he used his brains rather than his brawn. Theo listened, because if a skinny runt like Randy could get his hands on half a million dollars, he might have a point. The trips to the library got Theo into taking correspondence courses as well as learning from his personal tutor, Rheil, on what it would take to run a business of his own.

Two years after his release from Jackson prison, Theo Poet was still carrying a gift from Rhei. It was a three pound, black leather-bound collection of poems written more than a half century earlier by another former resident of Dayton, Ohio—Paul Laurence Dunbar. Dunbar was a noted black poet, one Rheil studied at the University of Dayton. One of the poems in this collection was titled *The Poet*. That poem gave Rheil the idea for the parting gift to his cellmate. The card attached simply said: "A man named Poet should be one."

The six foot two Poet got out of prison topping the scales at 285 pounds of well-sculpted muscles compliments of his time at the gym, as well as possessing a good business mind, thanks to his former cellmate. He wanted to start some type of business—nothing legal mind you, but a business none-the-less.

He returned to his old neighborhood and slowly established what he called "The Poetic Insurance Company." He did not register this business with the city, the Michigan Insurance Commission or the Chamber of Commerce. His type of business was not advertised. It was just a matter of going door-to-door and talking to a corner grocer, a bar owner, the shoe repairman, or the woman running the local bakery. For the small sum of five dollars a week he offered his services to protect their businesses from things like broken windows and late deliveries of their supplies.

Sometimes it took a broken plate glass window or two, and other times just his imposing stature, to sell his *insurance policies.* He never did fully relinquish the use of brute force in his new venture. Though Randy would not have approved, Theo thought pushing his weight around was a good back-up plan.

The list of clients he carried, nestled in Dunbar's book of poetry, grew from five to seventy-five in three weeks. Mom-and-pop type of stores and small businesses on Kercheval were his first targets. They'd be fully protected for a mere five dollars a week.

"Now I can assure you, Mr. Peebles, I could have prevented the cost of your window replacement," the big man would say on a follow-up visit. It didn't take long for a five spot to appear on the counter. It was easy money.

For the stubborn businessman who had the audacity to call the police, two windows would need replacement, or the guy delivering the beer or bread would fail to show for a day or two. Five dollars later, the deliveries would resume. And yes, even the delivery men found it easier to pay the money rather than to come out to a flat tire.

In a short while, Theo's territory was enlarged to cover Mack Avenue as well as Kercheval, from St. Jean to East Grand Boulevard. He had 203 *clients*, as he called them, and was expanding every day. Business was so good, Theo ended up hiring two other heavy-hitters to do the collecting while he was selling his services.

His new recruits were Bo Mosley and Russ Williams, both fresh out of Jackson, both big enough to fill the front seat of the Cadillac Theo provided, and both no smarter than the tire iron they used to make sure payments were made on time. Everyone in the southeast corner of Detroit soon learned Bo and Russ worked for the big man known as *The Poet.*

On Friday, May 9, 1975, a judge named Ralph Freeman announced his decision at the U.S. District Courthouse on West Lafayette. He ordered that the traditional "last hired, first fired" seniority principle be modified so that police officers recently hired under the city's new affirmative-action plan would retain their positions in the face of proposed massive layoffs.

Remington was keeping track of this court case with utmost interest. "D'you think any layoff will get down to me?" Remington was looking to Jake for an answer.

Jake just shrugged. "To be safe, I'd start putting in applications at other departments even though it'll be tied up in court for years.

Chapter Seventeen

The Detroit Police Officers Association did not idly stand by and let Judge Freeman's ruling go unchallenged. They demanded seniority rights for their membership and got an injunction against any changes in the way policemen were hired or fired.

Demonstrators took to the street. More than 500 policemen, mostly white, picketed to protest planned layoffs excluding some blacks and women from the proposed cutback. During an isolated incident, a scuffle between white demonstrators and black policeman occurred. The papers reported that it was cops against cops.

Remington didn't take any chances. He started writing other police departments. He and Jake didn't talk much about what the newspapers described as a "police revolt." They followed Jesse Scott's rule, they didn't talk politics. They were cops and happy to let the DPOA and city lawyers do the bickering.

―――――

Monday morning Jake worked out at the Y by himself. His partner failed to show. When he and Remington parted company at the end of their last shift the plan was to meet at the regular place at the regular time. *Musta had something come up.* Jake showered and left the gym.

His phone was ringing as he got home. It was Edie. She called to see if he could meet for lunch at Demetrio's, a Greek Coney place on Ten Mile. Remington's no-show was quickly forgotten.

Edie was already at a small table in the corner at Demetrio's. It had become a regular meeting place for them. It was close to the Macomb County Community Hospital where she worked as a surgical tech. She spoke as Jake came up. "We're between cases, so I grabbed a booth."

Jake just touched her hand and smiled as he slid in across from her. "Glad to see you, Hon."

"What? A pat on the hand is all I get?"

Jake shrugged, looked around at the crowd, answering, "You know me."

"And a kiss might give them the idea that we're having a secret rendezvous?"

The waitress put a couple of glasses of water on the table interrupting the exchange. "Ready to order?"

They ordered. Kids, the weather and life in general were the topic of conversation until the coney dogs arrived. Jake put away three while Edie did her usual salad. A half hour later, Jake walked her to her car and kissed her—a long mushy one. "Happy?"

"That's a little better. See you after the boys' practice?"

"Of course."

"Good. I'll have dinner waiting."

"What's for dessert?"

"Me." She smiled. "D'you need anything else?" She slid behind the wheel and drove off.

Jake was shaking his head as she glanced at him before pulling out of the lot. A minute later, he was headed for home. He had a lawn to do before ball practice with Hank and Sam, and an evening with the woman he thought he loved, but was afraid to say so.

———

The next day, Jake did his normal Tuesday shooting routine down on the range. Remington didn't show. At 6:30 Jake had the stolen car board up to date and the teletypes checked before the big redhead came in the room. Jake looked up. "Missed you yesterday, and at the range today."

"I was busy."

Nothing more was said until two hours into their shift, and after they'd stopped their third car.

"Feel like talking about it?" Jake asked.

"Nothing I can't handle."

"Sounds like woman troubles."

There was fifteen minutes of silence. Jake did not force the issue.

"Not really."

"What?"

"Woman problems."

"Oh." Jake waited.

"Someone's fuckin' with the Wongs. Jenny's worried."

Jake pulled into Shakers. "Time for a coffee. You can tell me about it."

Over a half hour and three cups of coffee, Remington told the whole story. Someone was trying to shake down Wong's Laundry and Dry Cleaners. Protection money. The grandfather refused to pay and two days later his plate glass window was broken. David Wong had a second visit from the guy "selling insurance" and naturally Mr. Wong wasn't going to part with any of his hard-earned money.

"That's when Jenny called me. The goons said calling the police would be unwise." Remington told Jake he was staking out the place waiting for a return visit. It seemed that there was one guy selling the protection and two other guys who'd make the threats. Remington said he wanted to be there if anyone showed up.

"Jenny said the main guy's as big as me, and the other two are built the same."

Jake just listened.

Remington took a sip of coffee and looked at his partner. "I don't care how big they are. They've fucked with the wrong people. Now they've got me to deal with." "Let's get back on the street." Jake pushed his coffee cup aside and got up and paid for the sandwiches. The coffee was on the house. Remington followed Jake out to their car and Jake slid behind the wheel. "Let's go check out Wong's." "You don't have to get involved." "I am involved. They're messin' with my partner." Jake drove slowly around the block that Wong's was on. All was quiet. He never strayed too far from the area for the rest of the shift. He was thinking the whole time.

The next morning, Jake called his boss. He asked Sergeant Fox if it was okay to work some odd hours for a few days and told him about the protection racket in the precinct. "I know it's not just this one place someone's trying to shake down. Most are paying and keeping their mouths shut."

Fox agreed and said to clean it up as soon as possible. Jake called Remington's house. There was no answer.

He wanted to start early and had an idea where his partner was. Jake drove to Mack Avenue. On his first pass he spotted Remington scrunched down in his mint green 1970 Ford Falcon. Remington was across the street and four doors down from Wong's. Jake parked down the block and walked towards the Falcon and tapped on the window.

"Slide over big boy." Jake grabbed the door handle when Remington made room for him.

"How'd you find me?"

"Guess. Who else would be in a car like this?" Jake smiled and looked around the inside of the car. "How're you surviving?"

"A couple of sandwiches and a thermos of coffee."

"When's the last time you took a piss?"

"There's a mason jar on the floor of the back seat."

Jake glanced over the seat. "A well-planned stakeout."

Remington just shrugged his shoulders.

Jake told him about his talk with Fox. "This has to be bigger than just Wong's. Ninety-nine percent are probably just paying."

"No doubt."

Jake looked up and down the street. Mack was filled with small businesses and saw that across the street from Wong's and to the east was a Rexall Drug store. He knew the owner through an earlier B&E. "Let me go see a guy. I think we can get off the street and out of this ugly car."

"What? You don't like Fords?"

"Mint green. Jezus! I'd be visiting Earl Scheib for one of his cheap paint jobs."

———

Mahendra Patel, the owner of the Rexall Store, recognized Jake as soon as he walked up to the pharmacy counter. Patel's eyes were checking the rest of the store to see if someone was watching. "You have a prescription to fill, officer?"

"No sir. I need some help."

Patel raised his eyebrows.

Jake laid out the plan that was running through his head, using the drug store to "watch a place," not specifying Wong's.

"I don't think that would be possible. My customers wouldn't—"

"It won't be a bunch of us. Just one guy in here at a time."

"I think a police officer might—"

"It'll either be me or my partner. No uniforms."

"I'm sorry, officer. I can't risk—"

Jake looked around to make sure no one was near. He talked in a low voice. "You're already paying them, right?"

"I don't know what you are talking about."

"You do, and you're scared. A big black guy is selling protection. He has two goons working for him."

Patel dropped his eyes. "Officer, I'm from India. There we have to pay for some services. I am trying to do business in this neighborhood. I just want to make a living. No trouble."

"Sir, I'll be right back." Jake went to the front door and took a few steps outside and got Remington's attention. His partner accompanied him back inside.

"Mr. Patel, this is my partner, Remington Southworth."

The pharmacist sized up the redhead. "He's bigger than the last one."

"And just as tough. It'll be him or me in here." Jake went on to talk about using the magazine rack near the front window as a cover. "I'll guarantee you that when this is over; you won't be paying for any extra services."

"I don't know officer."

"Mr. Patel, extortion is a crime. You, and a bunch of people, are paying someone under a threat of harm to your business or your person. We'll put an end to that."

"You sure?"

Remington stepped forward. "Mr. Patel. This will end. Very soon."

"Have you seen this one they call The Poet? He's big."

Remington put his hand on the pharmacist's shoulder. "They make big prison cells at the state penitentiary."

Patel finally agreed. Jake said they'd be back in an hour and that one of them would be in his store, the other in their car. "When does someone come by to collect?"

"Today or tomorrow."

"If they show up before we get back, stall them." Jake shook the owner's hand. "Relax. We'll take care of this."

An hour later Remington was glancing through a *Sports Afield* and Jake was somewhere in their Buick. Remington had a small Motorola radio tucked in his back pocket. *Yeah, this is much better than sitting in my car.* He smiled as he thought about not needing a mason jar. The employees had a restroom in the back. He did bring his lunch and thermos though. He was ready for a long day. He forgot to tell Jen Li what was going on, but he could do that later.

On Thursday morning Theo Poet was going over his clientele list. It was time to start at the top and collect his weekly premiums. His hired help, Bo Mosley and Russ Williams, were kicked back on the couch at Theo's Kercheval apartment, sipping on a couple of beers. They were waiting for orders from their boss.

"That Chinaman ever come across with what he owes us?" Theo asked.

Bo set his empty can down. "No."

"He's had plenty of time to consider the consequences. Swing by there today." Theo looked at his list. "He owes two weeks. Tell him it'll cost him double for the trouble he's caused. If he don't come up with twenty bucks, slam a hand in a drawer or break a finger or two."

Russ Williams stirred off of the couch. He smiled. "What if that nice piece of China, the granddaughter, is working the counter?"

"Hurt her if they don't come up with the money, but don't be thinkin' of doing anything else." Theo then remembered something about the big white bastard he'd hired. *Yeah, he did time for rape or something like that.*

"I mean it, Russ. Keep your cock in your pants. I run a business. You do something stupid, someone's gonna call the cops."

"Relax Theo, we'll get your money." He tossed his empty can towards a basket in the corner of the room. It missed. "Hey Bo, you colored boys ever get any Chinese pussy?"

"Who you callin' boy?" Bo asked as he straightened himself up.

"Cool it, you two," Theo said. "Get your big asses on the road and make that collection. If that Chinaman gets away with holding out on me, others might follow. Meet me at Biff's at two and I'll give you a list of a couple more places that might need a little convincing to sign on with us.

Jake had been looking over the magazine rack in the Rexall Store. There, prominently displayed, was the new *Hustler* magazine next to *Playboy*. He avoided cracking the pages on either and found a crossword puzzle book. Mahendra Patel took the seventy-five cents that Jake offered.

"Got a pen I can borrow?" He looked at the name embroidered above the left pocket on the white lab coat the man was wearing. It said *Mike*. "You change your name?"

"Mike is easier than Mahendra." The druggist smiled. "Now that I'm an American, it's what I prefer." Jake went back to his window, checked across the street and cracked open the puzzle book. Two hours went by with nothing going on across the street. Jake was five puzzles into the book.

"Jake." The voice came from the small Motorola in his pocket.

He grabbed it. "Go, Bob."

"A white Caddy just parked in the alley behind Wong's. Two big guys, one black, one white, heading towards the street."

Five seconds passed and Jake saw the two at Wong's front door. "Got em." Jake reached down and grabbed the laundry bag that he and Remington were using and headed across the street. He'd go in like he was a customer. If everything was cool, he'd wait his turn with the bag. Jake opened the door. A bell rang overhead. The white guy had Jen Li by the arm.

The black guy spoke. "Jes' head back out the door mister. We got private business here."

Jake saw a tire iron in his hand, flipped the small bag of shirts at him and drew his .357. "Two things, guys. You, drop the tire iron." Then he looked at the white guy. "And you'd better gently release the lady."

"You a cop?" The black guy asked.

"The Chinese mafia," Jake answered.

"You ain't no Chinaman."

The bell rang behind Jake. It was Remington. "This guy isn't Chinese either, but we handle their light work."

"He hurt you, Jenny?" Remington asked.

"Just twisted my arm. I'll be all right."

Remington's face reddened. He grabbed the white guy by the collar. "Jake?"

Jake picked up the tire iron and motioned with his head. "Outside, both of you."

The black guy led, Jake followed, then the white guy with Remington holding up the rear. Jake holstered his pistol and handed his partner the tire iron. Jake nudged the black guy. "In the alley. To your car."

"You guys don't know what you're getting yourselves into," the white guy mumbled as he turned around.

Thwack! The tire iron came down across his left collar bone. The man went to his knees. Remington growled, "You don't know what you've gotten yourselves into."

There were tears coming from the man's eyes as Remington reached down and grabbed a handful of shirt and lifted him up. "You so much as look at this building or the people inside again, it'll be the last thing you see."

At the Cadillac, Jake and Remington frisked both, pulled out wallets and laid them out on the hood of the car.

"Just who the fuck are you guys?" The black guy asked.

Jake pulled the driver's license out of the man's wallet and read it. "Bo Mosley, I'd advise you to keep your mouth shut unless I ask you something. Understand?"

His response was just a nod. His partner was leaning against the car, supporting his left arm with his right.

"Bo, who you guys working for?" Jake asked.

Bo started to answer. "The—"

The white guy butted in, "You'd better shut up, Bo."

Thwack! The man's right arm went limp and he fell to his knees again. Remington spoke. "What's your name asshole?"

"R-Russ." His voice cracked as he spoke. "Russell Williams."

"Russ, maybe you'd better do the talking. Your head'll be my next target." Remington towered over the kneeling man. "Who do you work for?"

From his knees Russ looked up to see where the tire iron was. Remington had it in his hand. "Th-The Poet."

"What's his real name?"

"Theo Poet is all I know him by." Russ Williams tried wiping a tear under his left eye, but he couldn't move his arms.

"Where do we find this guy?"

Williams shook his head. He wasn't talking. Remington nudged his right arm with the tire iron. "Yow! Easy man."

"Then start talking. Where do we find Poet?"

Williams mumbled, barely audible. "Supposed to meet him at two."

"Where?"

"Biff's."

Jake checked his watch. It was 1:30.

"Boys, we're going for a ride. Remington, you drive."

Remington got behind the wheel of the Cadillac and Jake opened the door so Russ Williams could climb in the front. "You, Bo. In the back behind your partner." Jake went around to the other side and slid in.

On the way to the restaurant Jake told them how things were going to go down. Bo was going to go into Biff's and tell the guy they called *The Poet* that Russ Williams got hurt and needed to go to the hospital, but first, he had a message for him.

"Your job is to get Poet in the alley." Jake then turned to Remington. "Bob, the windows are on the front and both sides. We don't know where this guy is, so drive in off the side street, Field, and into the alley behind it."

Remington drove down Field and pulled in across from the garbage cans next to a board fence that isolated the alley from the first house behind the restaurant. Bo stiffened when he saw a car he recognized in the lot parked just east of Biff's. Jake sensed it. "Which one's his?"

"The Lincoln. The maroon one with the white vinyl top."

"I'll go in first," Jake said. "What's this Poet look like?"

"Big. Black. He'll be wearing a fancy suit," Mosley answered.

"I'll find him and I'll be sitting nearby. You tip him off and you'll be worse off than your partner here. Understand?"

"Yes sir." Bo tilted his head back and closed his eyes. "This Poet is no one to fuck with. He's big, he's bad. Sometimes I think he's a bit crazy. He ain't gonna like this.

I'm just warning you." Bo shuffled in his seat. "You know my ass is dead if I lead him back to you guys."

Jake answered, "If you don't get him out here, you may not live through the day. Make a choice."

Bo remembered the pistol that he was looking at earlier and he was sure the guy knew how to use it. *Maybe Poet moved into mafia territory?* "All right, let's go."

Jake smiled. "You're smarter than you look." He got out of the Caddy and went around to the front door and entered.

Jake scanned the ten or fifteen patrons and spotted his man. He couldn't miss him. Yeah, he was big. He took up almost the whole side of a booth and was wearing a medium blue suit, a light blue shirt and a narrow red necktie. The guy was watching the door.

Jake spotted an empty stool not too far from him and took a seat. He ordered coffee. Jake had never been in Biff's on the day shift and the waitress didn't recognize him. He breathed a little easier.

Thirty seconds later Bo Mosley walked in. Jake noticed that the man they called *The Poet* sat more erect. Bo walked to his booth.

"Where's Russ?"

"In the car."

"Get his ass in here."

"Can't. He's hurt."

"How?"

"Fell down I guess. You know how clumsy he is."

"What the hell do you want me to do?"

"I'm going to take him to the hospital, but he said he's got an important message from the Chinaman."

"Humph!" It took two moves for the big man to work his way out of the booth. He hadn't been to the gym since he got out of prison. "What kind of a message?"

"I don't know. He's the one that went in to see the guy."

Chapter Eighteen

Remington was leaning up against the Cadillac's front fender; his arms were folded across his chest. He saw Bo and a big man in the blue suit come around the corner of the restaurant and enter the alley. Russ Williams was sitting quietly in the passenger seat with his head down. He was hurting.

Poet barked, "Who's this white mutha fucker?" Pointing at Remington.

Jake was closing the gap behind Bo and Theo.

Remington casually stood tall answering the question. "The guy who's going to stuff your ass down a sewer."

Poet stopped, looked at the man at his side, then at Remington. "You better've brought help."

"He did." It was Jake's voice coming up behind. Jake was flashing his badge. "Up against the car with your hands on the roof."

Theo Poet looked at his man in the car, then at Mosley. "You brought me out here for the fuckin' cops?"

"Boss. I didn't know they were cops. I thought they were some Italian goons."

"Either one look I-talian to you?"

Poet stood in one place too long and Jake gave him a nudge, pushing him forward. Poet stumbled towards the Cadillac, dropping the big leather-bound book he was carrying.

"Up against the car and spread em!" Jake repeated.

Theo Poet crouched, let out a scream and lunged like he was rushing a quarterback, aiming for the big redhead standing in front of him. Remington side-stepped the rush, parried with his left arm, letting the man's own weight carry him sideways and open handed the man on the back of his head. Remington pirouetted and landed with his arms halfcocked and his hands extended, ready for another attack.

It never came. Remington's move had sent the big man head first into the front wheel on the parked Cadillac. When the head of a two hundred seventy-five pound man flying through the air suddenly comes in contact with a steel rim and hubcap attached to a two and-a-half ton car, two things are going to happen. First, the hubcap might get bent a bit. Second, the man's head will receive some pretty severe damage. Theodore Roosevelt Poet was not moving. He was breathing when Jake checked him after calling for an ambulance on his portable radio.

Biff's restaurant was in the Seventh Precinct and the radio operator sent the cars Jake requested. Theodore Poet was still unconscious and went in the first station wagon that doubled as a patrol car. It had two collapsible stretchers. The man was so big he hung over the sides of the one he was strapped to. The next wagon took Russ Williams, but with his collar bones broken, he chose to sit upright in the back seat. Lying on a stretcher was too painful. Both were headed to Detroit Receiving Hospital as police prisoners. Bo Mosley was delivered to the Fifth Precinct along with Jake riding in the back of Seven-three. Seven-five's crew took Remington back to Mack Avenue to retrieve their Buick.

The heading on Five Twenty-five's report read: Three arrests, Investigation extortion and racketeering. In the body of the report were the names of the three men arrested, two of which were being held at Detroit Receiving Hospital. There was a brief description of the attempted extortion at Wong's Laundry and Dry Cleaners with an address on Mack Avenue and the complainants listed as David Wong, Jason Wong and Jen Li Wong.

Dunbar's book of poetry was placed under evidence tag#5-7506011. The book was an important piece of evidence because within the pages were two ledger sheets. Penciled across the top were the names of streets. Mack Avenue headed one, and Warren the other. Down the left column were addresses, then what looked like last names and a dollar figure. A red check mark was in the left margin by five addresses. There were no dollar entries on these lines. Bo Mosley was talking freely, trying to save his ass, and when shown the sheets admitted those were no doubt the places that the Poet wanted him and his partner to visit that afternoon to convince them to pay their *insurance* premiums.

A search warrant was carried out at Theodore Poet's apartment on Jefferson by the Fifth Precinct detectives. Their search turned up five more ledger pages of addresses and names—his customer base. There were two hundred and fifty three businesses on the list in just the Fifth Precinct, and yes, Patel's Rexall Drug Store was there. Jake had copies of the list made before it went into evidence.

The following morning Jake and Remington, were working on Poet's list. The sergeant agreed that it would be a good idea to let those on the list know the shake-down was over.

Jake climbed in the car talking. "Bob, the only thing I just have to ask you is, where in the hell did you come up with those Kung fu moves on that big guy?"

Remington smiled. "Kung fu is Chinese. I practice Aikido. That's Japanese."

Jake looked at his partner. "Chinese, Japanese who cares? All I'm wondering is where did that fancy shit come from?"

"My dad was a fanatic at everything. Guns, martial arts, motorcycles, whatever. I think I was ten when he enrolled me in some classes at a local martial arts studio."

"For how long?"

"Seven years." Remington centered the stolen car board on the dash. "I guess it didn't go to waste."

"What did you say it was?"

"Aikido. It's just using the motion of the attacker and redirecting the force of the attack."

"Redirected into a Cadillac's wheel. Metal and rubber."

"Didn't look like he hit much rubber," Remington countered. He was smiling.

"Japanese. Not Chinese."

"Correct."

"I've never seen you do any Kung fu stuff."

"First time I had someone charge me like that. I just reacted."

"Like riding a bike."

"I guess. And Kung fu is Chinese."

"I know, I know," Jake interrupted. "Let's start visiting the policy holders. Time to tell them their insurance has been cancelled and no more premiums are due."

———

It took three full days for Jake and Remington to check off every entry on the list. Visiting over two hundred business owners takes time. They wanted to assure them that *The Poet* was out of business.

The policy holders weren't so sure until Jake told them that Theodore Roosevelt Poet was in the hospital. The latest diagnosis, according to the detectives, was that he suffered a major concussion and had three fractured vertebrae in his neck. He was wearing a cervical collar, still in the intensive care unit, wearing shackles and still couldn't remember his given name. Charges were pending for extortion and parole violation as soon as he was aware of who he was.

"I don't think he'll be visiting any of you too soon," Jake said.

Russ Williams and Bo Mosley both were charged with extortion and awaiting trial, but in the meantime were returned to Jackson State Penitentiary for parole violations. It would be at least five years before they saw daylight again.

Jake and Remington were heading to the range in the basement of the Fifth Precinct. June had rolled into July. Patrolmen Richard Davis and Tyrone Wynn were just finishing up and checking their targets. Jake took a look at them. "You guys need some coaching." He nodded towards his partner, "The kid'll give you some tips if you want."

Davis and Wynn were still working Precinct Vice. Davis spoke. "Speaking of tips, thanks for putting us on the broad who lives on Marlborough."

"Three car Gloria?" Remington asked.

"Yeah." A wide smile crossed Wynn's face. "She had a pretty big operation."

"What was she doing?" Jake asked.

"Oh, I thought you knew. Numbers." It was Wynn answering.

"We sat on her place for three days or so and didn't see any traffic, just her coming and going." Jake was curious. "What was up with her having three different cars?"

Davis and Wynn filled Jake and Remington in on the twist that Gloria Rivers put to her mutuals racket. She went to her runners, meeting them at certain corners rather than using her house or an office.

"We busted a pretty big operation with her. Thanks to you guys." Davis started for the stairs.

"She'll be operating again. It's just a matter of time," Remington said.

"A shame too. Good looks, a college degree. Figure that one out," added Davis.

"She went mobile after taking over the business from her father," said Wynn. "The old man got shot in the head when someone followed one of his runners and held him up."

Jake knew Davis and Wynn had to get to work and ended their shop talk with, "Risky business, being a bookie."

"Or being a cop," Davis said over his shoulder as he and his partner bounded up the stairs.

Remington outshot Jake again, and Jake was glad they weren't betting lunch on the results. They climbed the stairs to get ready for another shift, and glad to be back on the seven to three watch.

———

Hank and Sam's Little League season was winding down. The only thing left was the All-Star game. Hank made the team and Sam did okay for his first year, even though Jake had to call out his name a time or two when he played right field. A dandelion or two took Sam's concentration off of the game, but boredom often invades Little League outfields when only one or two balls get past the infield during a game.

Jake was enjoying picking up the boys five days a week for practice and, most of all, seeing Edie. Oftentimes he thought he was getting too comfortable sitting at her table and having supper with them, not that he was complaining, just not ready to totally commit to a family again.

Edie was serving up spaghetti and meatballs as Jake finished setting the table with help from Hank and Sam. The boys took their chairs on either side of Jake as Edie sat down at the head of the table. Jake knew the normal routine; the three of them took turns saying the grace. It was Edie's turn.

Before she could begin, Sam said, "Dad, I think it's your turn."

Jake looked up and saw Edie's face begin to redden. "Sam, where did that come from?"

Jake interrupted by starting the prayer. "Come Lord Jesus, be our guest—" Hank, Sam and Edie joined in. The boys were hungry and didn't really pay attention to their mom or Jake. They just dug in. Edie got up and poured the milk, stopping at Jake's side, whispering, "Sorry about that."

———

Jake and Edie were doing dishes after the boys cleared the table. Hank and Sam left to see if the Soupy Sales Show was on TV. The boys loved Soupy, White Fang and the rest of the unseen cast.

"Sometimes Sam just says whatever crosses his mind," Edie said, breaking the silence.

Jake was washing a dish, rinsed it and said, "It's my fault."

"No—"

Jake interrupted Edie. "It started last summer. Sam called me dad by accident and the three of us talked about it after ball practice."

"And?"

"Sam was right. Mr. Bush was cumbersome and you told him he couldn't call me Jake."

"I guess I put you in a bad position."

"Not really. I've enjoyed every minute I've spent with them. They're great kids, and—" Jake paused, wiped his hands on Edie's dish towel. "And I told them they could call me dad, but not around you. So I'm at fault here."

"Kids say things."

"And most of the time they're right." Jake led Edie back to the table. "I remember that talk the boys and I had. Sam had it all figured out."

"Like how?"

"He said I should marry you and then he could call me dad for real."

Edie blushed again. "Maybe we're spending too much time together—"

Jake put his finger on her lips to silence her. "He's right, you know. And for sure we're not spending too much time together, unless you think—"

It was Edie's turn to put her finger on Jake's lips. "Let's just enjoy what we have. You, me, the boys. I think things'll work out."

"Yeah, they will."

Fifteen minutes later Jake kissed Edie good-bye for the night and headed out the door. He stopped long enough to call out to the boys. "Hank, pick you up for practice tomorrow. Sam, you too. You can shag some balls in the outfield."

It was time to head for the Fifth Precinct.

———

The amplifier was playing the tune "Puff the Magic Dragon," as the white Ford rolled down Warren and turned right onto Lillibridge at a snail's pace. The catchy melody had people of all ages running to the curb to buy a mid-day or early-evening treat. The truck had rainbow-colored signs on both sides and the rear of the insulated box, touting "The Happy Hippie—Ice Cream, Frozen Candy Bars and other Treats."

The owner and operator of the truck was Dusty Heights, a name chosen to go along with the new Social Security number that cost him $350. Dusty was an entrepreneur, spending his second summer driving an ice cream truck in a predominantly black neighborhood. His customer base lived on the city's residential streets. He knew the main streets drew too much attention from the cops. A well-established firm, The Good Humor Ice Cream Company, supplied all the frozen treats he carried, while other wholesalers supplied the rest.

Dusty was working a territory bounded by Warren to the north, Jefferson to the south, McClellan to the west and Chalmers to the east. That area was ceded to him by Good Humor after three of their employees were robbed by small gangs of Negroes.

Their most-recent driver, Norman Stillwell, had been shot just beneath and to the right of his black leather bow tie. He survived because only one twenty-two caliber bullet had been fired from the "Saturday Night Special" before jamming. Norm's legs took him fast and far enough from his ice cream truck to avoid further injury. Two hours later, after being patched up at St. John's Hospital, he led the police to where he thought the robbery took place. His ice cream truck was sitting on four rocks, and the steering wheel, battery and radiator were gone. To add insult to injury, every freezer compartment was totally empty. The Good Humor Company gave up servicing that part of Detroit.

Dusty heard about the open territory and took advantage of the opportunity to serve the people of his old neighborhood. He knew he could make a good living on the streets of Detroit.

Good Humor had a fleet of ice cream trucks that were leased to their owner-operators. When Norman quit, that left Good Humor with a stripped-down truck. Dusty got it for a song. The ice cream company was happy to sell what remained of the specially-built truck.

The design of the Good Humor ice cream truck he'd bought was simple. A 1967 Ford F-100 platform was used with the normal pickup bed removed and replaced with a square insulated box with reefer doors on the passenger side and the rear. The truck had a single seat behind the steering wheel, then on the passenger side of the cab, the door and part of the roof had been removed to give the operator easy access to that side of the vehicle. He could stop, move to the right and walk upright onto the curb to greet his customers. The frozen products were kept cold with cakes of dry ice that lined the floor of the insulated box. The music coming from under the hood was Dusty's own idea. He had a friend who connected an eight-track player to an amplifier where the horn normally was and found a music box rendition of *Puff the Magic Dragon,* the song made famous by Peter, Paul and Mary. Dusty didn't want to be ringing bells all day.

Dusty had a grand plan and selling ice cream was just going to be his cover, something that he came up with while serving eighteen months in the Detroit House of Correction under his previous name, Darrel Huggs. His old gig of trying to hustle a buck on street corners peddling a little grass didn't work out. Cops always managed to nail the little guy who was just trying to survive, he said.

Dusty was very thin—boney as a matter of fact—with concave cheeks, set off by a large nose. He sported a bushy Afro, a multi-colored headband and a rainbow-colored muslin poncho. Dusty considered himself one of the last remaining hippies in Detroit. That culture had run its course at least five years earlier, but Dusty was still hanging on. To embellish his peace and free love image he often bragged about spending an August weekend at the Woodstock Music Festival at Bethel, New York, saying he wore himself thin with all the free love available. The fact of the matter the closest he'd ever gotten to New York was Belle Isle on the Detroit River, and any loving that came his way was from the girls working around Brush and Canfield—for a price.

Beside his hippie get-up, Dusty added one other piece of essential equipment as he worked the streets. Nestled in the small of his back was a Colt blue steel .32 caliber automatic pistol in a clip-on holster. He knew a skinny hippie looked like easy prey. He wasn't worried about some nickel-and-dime crook stealing any ice cream or the small change he made from their sales, but was protecting the other *treats* that he carried hidden overhead in the back compartment for his non-ice cream customers. That's where the real money was. Drumsticks, Popsicles and Fudgesicles that sold for twelve cents each were just a part of his cover. Dusty knew he could make some serious money by adding a couple of items like hand-rolled joints selling for a dollar and a half, blotter acid going for two, and a dime bag of marijuana for ten—for the cheap stuff. Acapulco Gold or Panama Red went for twenty dollars. Dusty bought in bulk, so his profit margin was pretty good. Dusty carried about fifty dollars in ice cream inventory at the start of each day and at least five hundred dollars' worth of the other treats.

The last decent days of summer were upon Dusty and he was thinking about parking his truck for the season. He knew September brought colder temperatures and too much rain. *Puff* was playing from under the hood of the Ford, twilight was coming too early and he felt a bit uncomfortable as he sized up what he thought was his last customer. A kid no more than twelve, wearing a Detroit Tigers T-shirt and a rag tied around his head, was standing and waving on the corner of Eastlawn and Charlevoix.

"Got any Dixie cups?" the kid asked.

"Just a few. How many you want?" Dusty took his truck out of gear and set the parking brake. As he stood and moved towards the right side, four other bodies were shuffling towards the truck.

"We'll take all you got," said the tallest of the bunch, smiling, showing his jagged teeth.

Dusty counted five in the group as they started to circle him. "You lookin' for ice cream or trouble?"

A knife blade flashed. "We know your skinny ass ain't gonna give us any trouble." It was Jagged Teeth doing the talking.

Dusty's hand moved under his poncho and the little automatic opened up five sets of eyes. "This'll put a little more weight on my skinny ass, don't you think?"

All five carefully stepped backward before turning and running.

Dusty climbed back behind the wheel, knocked off the brake and put the truck in gear. He turned off the music for the night.

"Always some punk-assed mu-fuckers wantin' somethin' for nothin'," he grumbled as he headed for home. "Damn streets are getting rougher every day."

———

Remington was driving and Jake was filling in the top of their log sheet. "August already," Jake quipped as he put in the date. "Time's just flying."

"Oh, here's something for you," Remington said as he handed Jake an envelope.

It was a standard four by five that usually meant there was a card inside. The writing on the front was very neat and fancy. It was addressed to John Anthony Bush, the Fifth Precinct, Detroit Police Department.

"The last time I got a card through the department mail it was a Spiritual Bouquet, a Catholic thing, offering some prayers for me for giving some broad a ticket." Jake tore at the flap on the envelope.

"This is from Jenny and me," Remington said. "I don't have your address."

Jake pulled out a red card, embossed in silver. "This a wedding invitation?"

"Yep. Jen Li and I are getting married. She got the cards ready before I had a chance to talk to you."

"Talk to me? What, do I need to give you my permission before you get married?"

"No. To ask you if you'd be my best man."

"Whoa, whoa. Let's back up a minute. I thought any wedding plans were on hold until she restored honor to the family name by becoming an attorney."

"Grandpa Wong said honor has been restored by the actions of a man desiring to marry into his family. That's me." Remington headed their Buick into the early evening. "He said he'd shop around for a wife for you, too, saying every good man deserves a good woman."

"Tell him not to worry about me; I've already got a good woman."

Somewhere in the distance, Jake and Remington heard *Puff the magic dragon* playing. It sounded like an amplified music box plucking away at the different notes.

Chapter Nineteen

It was one of those days that Jake felt like just driving around as he reminisced about the past and thought about the present. Thick clouds were hanging low, and a steady summer rain was coming down. He had spent the night with Edie, the woman he knew he loved, but found the words difficult to say. Then, too, he didn't want to scare her off. As usual, he'd left long before the boys stirred.

He had nothing planned and the rain and clouds just made it drearier. He stopped for coffee and went home to read the paper. In an hour he was out driving again. Driving and thinking. He glanced at his watch. It was four hours before his shift started, and still three hours before he was to meet Remington at the basement shooting range.

First he drove by Notre Dame High. It was vacant except for a number of cars way in the back near the football field. Summer practice had begun. He wondered if Mr. Kelly was still coaching. A few turns later he was on Boulder at the corner of Liberal, parked next to the house he and his wife had rented back in 1963. He glanced at its lawn that needed mowing. Memories of kids playing in the yard filled his mind. He drove off, running away from the giggles he imagined he heard. Deb and Michelle had loved the old swing that now stood rusted and empty in the backyard.

Minutes later, Jake pulled into a strip mall on the corner of Kelly at Moross. He saw the barber shop he once frequented. It was when he lived on Liberal that he had found the little one-chair place. He looked at himself in the rear view mirror. He was due for another haircut. Jake paused, remembering why he stopped frequenting the place in 1968.

Dave was an arrogant ass that had an opinion about everyone and everything from the Detroit Lions, to the Tigers, to the Red Wings and any political subject that might hit the news that day. He had all the answers if just someone would listen to him. On Jake's last visit, Dave said something about an article in the newspaper where a police lieutenant had been indicted for taking bribes. Jake recalled Dave's words. "Hell! We all know all cops are on the take." That was the day Jake started letting his hair grow.

Jake was back wearing flattops, getting it cut every two weeks, but still hadn't found a decent barber. He looked in his rearview mirror again. He shrugged his shoulders. It had been seven years since he'd been in Dave's place. *A barber who could cut a good flattop was hard to come by.* He climbed out of his car into the rain.

As Jake opened the door to the shop, he saw it was still Dave Winslow cutting hair. He was about five-six, had dark hair combed straight back and a nose with a slight hook. He wore a white barber's smock, the same as Jake remembered from years ago. There was one customer in the chair. Jake hung up the black nylon jacket he wore to shed some of the rain, grabbed the morning *Free Press* and sat to wait.

The Tigers lost the night before. Nothing new. Two minutes later, Dave finished with the customer and Jake took his place in the chair.

"I like it nice and flat and close on the sides," Jake said.

He didn't get a reply. Dave rolled Jake's collar out of the way, wrapped a tissue around his neck, shook out the white and black pin-striped cape and fastened it. Immediately Dave's one-sided conversation went from the economy to Gerald Ford and Ford's pardon of Richard Nixon. As long as he was getting a good haircut, Jake could always tune the barber out.

Ten minutes later, the front door banged open and a man in a long raincoat entered. Dave was working on the back of Jake's head, thus his chin was against his chest. Jake's eyes rotated up giving him a view of the man only from the waist down. The raincoat parted and Jake saw the distinct oval trademark that was on a Louisville Slugger baseball bat.

"You Dave Winslow?" a deep voice growled.

Jake felt the pressure on the back of his head being released.

"Yeah, I'm Dave."

"I'm goin' to cave in your fuckin' skull."

Jake slowly raised his head, taking in a full view of the man behind the voice. He was a white man with his dark hair mashed down by the rain. Some of the hair curled near his eyebrows. He had dark gray eyes. Jake couldn't tell if it was rain on the man's cheeks, or if he was crying. He wore a knee length black raincoat. It was unbuttoned. The man had the bat in both hands. He was right handed.

"Whoa, man. Who th-the hell are you?" Dave stammered.

"The guy whose wife you've been banging."

The bat started moving upwards as Dave backed away from the chair, edging to the back corner of the small shop.

"You don't want to do that," Jake calmly said, starting to move his hands off the arms of the barber chair.

The man's eyes went from Dave to Jake. "You just stay out of this."

The man was three feet from Jake, the bat cocked back. Jake's head was an easy swing away. Silence filled the room. Jake looked in the mirror behind the man and saw the barber. His eyes were bulging. His back was against the shelf under the full mirror on the backside of the shop. The shelf held all Dave's clippers, scissors, an old cash register and the germ-

264

killing ultra-violet sterilizer. Dave was trying to get as far away from the Louisville Slugger as possible.

When Jake climbed into the chair, as Dave started to pin the striped cape around his neck, he leaned forward, taking his off-duty Colt .38 Detective Special he carried in a holster in the small in his back and placed it between his legs. He could sit more comfortably that way. The move had been so subtle, Dave never realized what was happening. Now Jake was palming the .38 and watching the man with the bat. Jake's finger moved to the trigger.

"No one's going to get hurt if you just walk away," Jake said in a calm voice.

"This is between me and this asshole, so butt out." The bat started to tremble in his hands.

"I can't let it happen." Jake tightened his grip on the pistol just a bit, as he moved the two inch barrel ever so slightly, pointing it at the mass of the man three feet to his front.

"What, you been banging my old lady too?"

"No, I'm just a cop trying to get a haircut." The bat hung in mid-air. "Now put the bat down, button up your raincoat and go home. You've got three seconds." Jake knew he had a bead on the man's belly button.

The bat moved up, then slowly went down. "You really a cop?"

"Really." Jake moved the cape away with this left hand, revealing the Colt. The next sound was the wood bat hitting the linoleum floor and rolling. The man backed up to the door, turned, opened it and walked out into the rain.

"You let the son-of-a-bitch go," Dave yelled as he walked to the window and watched the man climb into a black Dodge.

"Well, I could have arrested him, but then, who's going to explain things to them?" Jake turned, pointing to the family portrait hung on the far wall. The eight-by-ten picture had David arm and arm with a pretty blond. They were sitting behind two boys and a girl, a nice professional pose. "I can still catch the guy if you want to press charges."

"No." Dave turned away from the window and walked behind the barber chair.

"You sure you can finish my haircut?" Jake glanced in the mirror and saw Dave's hands shaking behind him. Jake got out of the chair. "On second thought, I think I'm done."

"I haven't shaved the edges yet," Dave said, his voice trembling as much as his hands.

"If you think I'm going to let you get near me with a razor, you're nuts."

Jake whipped off the cape, walked over to his jacket and put it on. His pistol was already returned to the leather holster in the small of his back. He bent over and retrieved the baseball bat. "Maybe I ought to leave this here for you, as a reminder not to be screwing anybody's wife but your own." He weighed the bat in his hand. "Nah, I'll take it with me. Maybe give it back to the guy." Jake smiled in the mirror so Dave could see him.

"Come back tomorrow and I'll finish it up."

"Maybe. You might be done shaking by then."

"This one's on me, just for keeping my head intact."

Jake walked to the shelf behind Dave and put a five on the register. "No thanks, David. Just doing my sworn duty. Sometimes I even hate myself for having to protect some people." Jake went to the door and grabbed the handle. "Nice looking family you have. I think I did it for them."

Jake slowly walked to his car, the rain washing the clippings from his new flat top down the back of his neck. He was thinking how Hank and Sam would someday grow into the new thirty-two ounce Louisville Slugger the man had left behind.

———

Jake and Remington did their twelve-shot routine in the basement range at Number Five, then went upstairs to get ready for their shift. "What the hell happened to your hair?" Remington asked as they climbed the stairs. Jake told his partner about what happened at Dave's Barber Shop.

"I think the first thing we do tonight is find a barber. Your friend David left a big patch in the back."

"No. The first thing I want to do is drive around and find that ice cream truck we saw a while back."

"Which ice cream truck?"

"The one that was playing the music box tune rendition of *Puff the Magic Dragon.*"

"Why?"

"Something that's in the back of my mind." Jake made sure their radio was on the right channel. "I don't know what, but it'll come to me."

Jake and Remington cranked down their windows and strained their ears. They were listening to the sounds of tires hissing on the pavement, and listening for a music box melody. Just before dark they heard the plinking sounds a block away. They found the "Happy Hippie" heading down Belvidere towards Kercheval in his white Ford truck with a reefer box on the back. When the truck reached the main drag, it turned right and the music died. The Happy Hippie was done for the day.

"See where he goes," Jake said.

"What, tail an ice cream truck?" Remington started to chuckle.

"Nuthin' else pressing is there?"

"Just your haircut. It looks bad."

The Happy Hippie found a garage behind a house on Riverside off of Avondale. The ice cream truck was parked for the night. Remington drove straight to Mack and Beniteau. "Tiny will be open," he said to Jake.

"Who's Tiny?"

"My barber. Tiny Birdsal. He works late on Thursdays."

Five minutes later Jake was under a white and black striped cape and a six foot five black man was cleaning up the back of his head. He buzzed up the patch of hair Dave had left behind and had Jake lathered up to straight razor the edges and sideburns. Tiny weighed about 200 pounds, had bulging muscles, and wore a powder blue smock. He pumped up the chair so he wouldn't have to scrunch down. Jake watched in the mirror as Tiny gently scraped away the foam.

"Nice flat top," Tiny said. "How come your barber didn't finish it?"

"He got interrupted."

"I could cut it flat like that." Tiny vacuumed off Jake's neck and shoulders and unsnapped the cape.

"You sure?"

"Ten years in the Corps cutting officer's hair. They demanded it be flat."

"When were you in?"

"Still am. Reserves."

"Do you screw around with other men's wives?"

"Why do you ask?"

"That's the reason he got interrupted."

Tiny waited a beat. "In answer to your question, no."

"You guarantee it'll be nice and flat?"

"Money back guarantee."

"See you in two weeks." Jake put a couple of bucks next to the register.

"No charge for straightening jobs."

"You don't get it flat the next trip, you can give it back."

"Fair enough."

Jake walked out the door and climbed in next to Remington. There was a hot cup of coffee in a cardboard container waiting for him on the dash.

"Black, one sugar," Remington said as he pulled out away from the curb. "The hair looks a lot better."

"Thanks." Jake took a sip and hit the car board with his light. "The Mercury, going the other way, it's hot."

Remington craned his neck, checked the traffic on Mack and made a quick U-turn. The Mercury was a block and a half ahead. Jake and Remington made the bust. They found a pistol under the driver's seat. The guy said it wasn't his.

———

Their shift ended and Jake grabbed the wedding invitation from behind the visor and looked at it as he headed to his personal car. "I thought wedding invitations were white?"

"It's a Chinese tradition. Just about everything is red around their weddings. Jen Li has been filling me in."

"I won't have to wear a red tux as your best man, will I?"

"No. Does that mean you accept?

"As long as I don't have to wear red."

"Maybe just a cummerbund."

"That won't be too bad."

"Great. Jen Li will be glad to hear that you'll be there. And wearing a tux."

"I'll do anything, no, almost anything for my partner."

Jake paused at his car and called out to Remington. "Hey, remember the broad running the numbers racket on Marlborough?"

"Yeah."

"I just remembered. She was mumbling something about an ice cream man when we busted her that night."

"She was?"

"Yeah. Let's start early tomorrow and find that ice cream man again. I want to watch him for a while."

Remington nodded. "What time?"

"Two?"

"See you at two." Remington jumped in his mint green Falcon and drove off.

At two the next afternoon, Five Twenty-five was cruising the residential streets with their windows open, listening for *Puff the Magic Dragon.* It was after four before they heard the tune. The Happy Hippie was parked on the corner of Algonquin and Goethe. There was a line of customers. It was eighty-seven degrees and ice cream would be a big seller. Jake was parked at the curb a half a block away and Remington had their set of field glasses fixed on the crowd waiting in line. There was a mix of kids and some adults.

"The last guy in line doesn't look like he wants an ice cream," Remington said. He went silent and watched. The guy didn't leave with a cone or a Dixie cup. "He bought something though," Remington mumbled.

The ice cream truck crept ahead, slowly picking up speed. The music box tune of *Puff* kept repeating. At the next corner, another line was waiting and the white truck pulled to the curb. Business was good. This scene was repeated for the next two hours. At every stop, there were one or two people who went up to the truck but didn't come away with anything that looked like an ice cream. But neither Jake nor Remington could see what, if anything, had changed hands.

"How long we gonna do this?" It was Remington talking as he lowered the binoculars.

"'Til he turns off the music and heads for home."

"Jake, how we gonna find out what he's doing?"

Jake shrugged. "Patience and persistence. We'll watch. Something will happen."

Dark was approaching and the music suddenly stopped. The Happy Hippie was done for the night. Jake followed just long enough until he was sure the white truck was heading for Riverside and Avondale.

"Did you get a warrant on that kid we busted last night in the Merc?" Jake asked as he headed for Kercheval to check the alleys behind the businesses there.

"Yeah. His prints were on the piece as we expected. Someone doesn't steal a car that just happens to have a loaded gun in it."

"Forgot to tell you, that was a nice job of driving. Never spilled a drop of my coffee."

"It's your turn to buy." Remington was smiling as he said it.

They stopped for a couple of coffees and some lunch. A half hour later they were cruising Mack Avenue.

———

This was the third afternoon that the blue Buick slowly trailed "The Happy Hippie" in his white truck. Jake was getting tired of the tune that constantly played in the background. Remington started singing the words. Jake asked for quiet. He was watching a man about twenty buy something from the driver of the white truck. The man put something in his right rear pants pocket and slowly sauntered down the street. Straight towards their car.

"Want me to follow the truck?" Remington asked.

"No, let's talk to this guy. He's got something I want to see."

There was no running, just a look of resignation on the man's face as the two white officers climbed out of their car when he got near them. The man was carrying a dime bag of marijuana.

Jimmy Lewis was arrested for possession. He was a used car salesman who said he liked being upbeat as he worked a lot full of old clunkers on Gratiot.

"The only way I can do that is smoke a little weed."

Jake felt sorry for the guy. There were about thirty-five used car lots on Gratiot between Eight Mile and downtown. Business had to be tough. But they took Mr. Lewis off to jail anyway.

"I want the seller," Jake said as he finished the report.

"We've got to make a buy, and the guy's not selling anything to us." Remington was stating the obvious. "Your flattop and my freckles are a dead giveaway. Might as well try buying from him wearing our blue uniforms."

Jake nodded, thought for a minute, then said, "We might be able to borrow Wynn or Davis."

Remington smiled. "Davis would be the guy. Looks like a dope head with those droopy eyes."

"Let's go find their boss."

———

The plan was simple. Jake and Remington would locate the ice cream vendor the next afternoon and the Fifth Precinct Clean-up crew would wait for radio contact. Their radio ID was Five Twenty-six. Money was marked and it was decided that Davis would be the first to attempt a buy. If for some reason, that failed, Wynn would try sometime later. Their sergeant, John Warneke, liked the idea of using his own men rather than recruiting one of their stooges. Sergeant Warneke would drop Davis off a block ahead of the Happy Hippie's route and wait for the buy. Jake and Remington would be watching, as they had been for the last three days. When the buy was made, a scratch of the left ear would be the signal for the clean-up crew to come in from one direction, while Jake and Remington came in from the other. It would be a quick and easy bust *if* a buy was made. Jake had no doubts. Dealers are out there to sell and they don't know all their customers.

———

Peddling ice cream and his other treats had the pockets of Dusty Heights bulging. He had an easy life. Each day during the summer he'd wake, look out to see what the weather was, then make a choice. He could either roll over and get a couple more hours of sleep, or get out of bed, grab some breakfast around the corner at Maggie's Diner and then wash his wheels before starting his route.

He was renting a nice house with a fully furnished kitchen, but never had the ambition to even make a pot of coffee. His excuse was Maggie's had the best coffee around and he hated doing dishes. For $3.95 he could buy a full breakfast with a bottomless cup of coffee. And he could afford it.

Dusty split the slats on the blinds covering his bedroom window. It was bright and sunny as Jac LeGoff had predicted the night before on WXYZ-TV. Fifteen minutes later he was downing his first cup of coffee at the diner. Two hours after that he had his white Ford truck in the driveway, a handful of rags and a bucket of soapy water. He washed it every day before starting work.

He had a big area, so he split it in half. It was impossible to cover it all in one day, especially when the weather was so hot. Dusty would always cut his day short if he ran out of frozen treats. When his cover was gone, his night was over. Dusty was no dummy. Twice he increased his ice cream inventory. The hot weather had too many kids waiting on the corners and ice cream wasn't where his money was.

Dusty liked to get rolling around three in the afternoon and always ended his day before dark. The one run-in he'd had with a guy with the knife and jagged teeth had taught him that. *Get off the street before the assholes come out* was his motto. Then too, he made sure his piece was clean and hidden in the small of his back. *A guy's gotta have insurance.*

At 2:30, on a Saturday, Dusty was running what looked like a small rake through his Afro. He tied the multi-colored headband in place and donned his rainbow colored muslin poncho. The little Colt was where he always carried it. The temperature was near eighty-five, too damn hot for the poncho, but Dusty liked the look.

He fired up the clean white Ford and headed out for his first stop, The Good Humor warehouse. It was on the corner of Alter Road and Jefferson. That's where he got his night's inventory and the dry ice he needed for the compartments in the insulated box behind him. This was the day he'd be working the north end of his territory.

Jake picked up the white ice cream truck as it crossed in front of him on Mack. Remington radioed their position to Warneke and crew. There was no rush. They wanted the guy settled into his routine. A white truck was easy to follow, even at a distance. Warneke kept their car ahead of the target. The sergeant said he'd pick a spot for his man where there'd be a line of customers waiting.

Davis didn't work out on the first attempted buy at the corner of Canfield and Gray. The guy just shrugged when the cop said he was looking for something that wasn't frozen. Davis left empty handed.

Jake dropped the binoculars. "Guess he doesn't look like a dope head."

"What do I know," Remington mumbled.

The plan was to wait at least an hour before Wynn would try. Jake and Remington monitored the movements of The Happy Hippie. The ice cream truck slowly crawled along Shoemaker, stopping at every corner. Business was booming.

Jake had the glasses on the truck as it stopped on the corner of Harding. Two boys with small bikes were waving down the driver. Jake saw some movement just around the corner. Behind a black car were what looked like three teenagers. He moved the glasses back to the white truck, then back to the kids hiding behind the car.

"Oh-oh."

"What?" Remington asked.

"I see a gun. Move it Bob."

Jake grabbed the mike from under the dash, "Five-twenty six. Shoemaker and Harding. I see a gun. Someone's going to rob our guy. We're moving in."

Warneke's voice responded, "Ten-four."

Jake heard the radio blare. "Cars in Five. Harding and Shoemaker. Man with a gun, plain clothes officers at the scene." Warneke had alerted East Side Radio. Blue uniforms would join them.

Harley Jones had his back to a black Ford at the curb. He was picking his jagged teeth with a toothpick. He was nervous. In his waistband was an old .32 caliber Iver Johnson revolver. He pulled it out and made sure all five chambers were full. His two younger brothers were with their bikes on the corner, as planned. He could hear *Puff the Magic Dragon* getting closer. "Payback time," Harley said to his friends. There were three of them. All had guns. Between them the .32 caliber was the biggest. Ricky Evans had a Raven Arms .25 caliber semi-auto that he had borrowed from his grandfather's nightstand. It only had four rounds in the clip. He and Harley fired it once each the night before to make sure it worked. Cecil Brooks was playing with a little black .22 revolver with white plastic grips. Something was filed off of the side of it. Maybe the manufacturer? Maybe a number? It had three rounds in the cylinder. Harley had borrowed it from a guy on Kercheval for Cecil to use. All they knew was he said it worked.

Harley didn't like that "fuckin hippie" pulling a gun on him a while back. It took some time, but they found some guns of their own. Harley said it was time to show the ice cream guy what it would be like looking down a gun barrel. Ricky and Cecil liked the idea. They had heard talk on the streets that the guy was selling dope. It was time to cash in.

———

Dusty saw the two kids standing next to their bikes. He slowed and knew they wanted some ice cream. They were too young for anything else. He stopped, threw the Ford in neutral, set the brake and walked out of his seat to the right and onto the curb.

"What'll you have, boys?"

"Eskimo Pie," they both said in unison.

Dusty turned and reached into the box behind him, grabbed two bars and turned. The boys on the bikes were gone. In their place were three older kids, sixteen or seventeen. Dusty recognized the one with the jagged teeth. He went for his piece.

Remington had the Buick going sideways as he braked hard. The tires were chirping. Jake's door was nearest to the ice cream truck. He was coming out gun first. Remington was doing the same. More brakes were screeching as Davis, Wynn and Warneke in their Plymouth were piling out, guns drawn.

"Police!" Jake shouted. A pistol turned his way.

Jake heard two fast, weak shots. Pop-Pop. His left thigh and side stung. All three kids were shooting. Jake fired twice. More shots rang out. Remington was shooting. Warneke, Wynn and Davis were shooting and the ice cream man was shooting.

Four seconds later the corner was quiet.

The ice cream man was on the ground. He wasn't moving. The three teen-agers were down. They were crying. Sirens could be heard in the background. And Jake was hurt.

Chapter Twenty

At 5:45 a.m., a nurse shook Jake to wake him so she could take his blood pressure and to shove a thermometer under his tongue. He'd been coming in and out of consciousness, the after effects of the anesthesia. Jake didn't quite care for the nurses on the fifth floor at Saint John's Hospital. Every couple of hours they were waking him to take his pulse, blood pressure and temperature. *Like it's gonna change.*

He'd forgotten how working the midnight shift would alter your attitude on life. He recalled how he'd been when working the night shift—a bear. He lay there awake for a few minutes after the witch in white had banged out the door, remembering that he had been shot when all hell had broken loose. He fell back asleep.

Two hours later, Jake picked up his head and looked around as the sun was peeking around the shade on his window. At the foot of the bed he could make out the back of a chair, a set of shoulders and a head lying near his left foot. There wasn't enough light to make out who it was, but he could guess. He wiggled his foot. The head moved.

"How long've you been here?" He asked through parched lips.

The woman just started crying, holding onto his foot. Kissing it through the blankets.

"Eed. I'm okay."

Edie stood, grabbed a couple of tissues out of a box and wiped her eyes. "Jake, you scared the hell out of me." She offered Jake the ice water that sat on the tray next to the bed.

He took a sip and grabbed her hand. "It's nothing."

"The hell it is. Do you know what it's like to get a call in the middle of the night? Then to see you lying there, tubes going this way and that, machines beeping?"

"They shouldn't have bothered you. The boys—"

"Shouldn't have bothered?" Edie interrupted. "Shouldn't have bothered? What the hell am I to you, Jake? I want to be called. I love you. Don't you understand that?" She grabbed a handful of tissues, blew her nose and started crying again.

Jake took the hand as it reached for more tissues. "Edie, I'm sorry." He squeezed it and moved it to his lips. "Sorry to put you through this."

"It's all just part of the job. Right Jake?"

Jake didn't answer. Edie slowly withdrew her hand from his. "I've got to go. I have a neighbor with the boys." She turned and walked to the door.

"Thanks Eed." Jake paused for a few seconds. "Thanks for being here."

She left quietly. Not looking back.

———

Right after the nine o'clock visit from the nurse Jake saw a head peek in the door. It was Remington. "Well, don't just stand there. Come on in."

"Didn't want to wake you."

"How in the hell is a guy supposed to sleep. They wake your ass up every two hours. Put a cold glass tube in your mouth, pump up an arm that stops all blood circulation, then just mumble something about how well you're doing. And I'm hungry. Evidently I don't get fed in this place."

"I guess you are getting better." Remington moved around to Jake's left side. "Are you done bitchin'?" He lifted the blanket and looked at the bandages; one on Jake's left side, just below the ribs, then another on his thigh. "They said you can eat after you take a piss."

Jake looked at the tubes dangling and the wires running to the machinery. "Don't look like I can walk too far with this shit on me."

Remington dug the plastic container out of the small bedside cabinet. "Here, use this. I'll go get the nurse."

"How in the hell—"

"No Jake. I'm not holding anything for you. The bottle or your wanger." Remington smiled and banged out the door.

Five minutes later the door opened and in walked a nurse with a tray. "Good morning, Officer Bush." She started pulling off the silver plate covers. "Ring when you're done." She grabbed the portable urinal on the way out. Remington must have told her he took a pee.

A bowl of oatmeal, one piece of dry toast, a half of a banana and a small cup of lukewarm coffee was on the tray. There wasn't any sugar for the coffee and nothing in the oatmeal. It was overdone—almost a solid. Jake shrugged and downed it all within a minute. He hadn't eaten since noon the day before.

Remington came back five minutes later. He looked at the empty dishes and moved the bed tray out of the way. "The doc's making his rounds. I saw him in the hallway."

"How bad did I get it?"

"Not bad. You're lucky it was a small gun. They dug the slugs out. The digging did more damage than the bullets did."

Jake asked Remington to crank the bed back down. He felt like another nap.

"Want me to get you something else to eat?"

"A large chocolate malt." Jake closed his eyes and fell back to sleep.

———

The doctor had come and gone. Remington brought the malt. Lunch followed. Another nap later, Jake woke to see Sergeant Fox standing at the end of his bed.

"Hi boss."

Fox moved the chair around and sat down. "How you feeling?"

"Who knows? I'd like to get up and stretch my legs."

"That'll be this afternoon. We talked to the doctor. He wants to keep you for a couple of days, just to be on the safe side."

"Anybody figure out what happened?"

It took all of an hour for Sergeant Fox to show Jake a diagram of the scene at Shoemaker and Harding and to explain what happened. First thoughts were that the three guys were going to holdup Dusty Heights, aka Darrell Huggs, who was the ice cream man. Dusty was dead along with a man named Cecil Brooks. Two others, besides Jake, were wounded. Those two, Ricky Evans and Harley Jones, were being held at Detroit Receiving Hospital for murder. "A total of about twelve rounds were fired at the scene," Fox said. "They're running ballistics tests to see who shot whom."

"How old was Cecil?" Jake asked.

"What difference does it make?"

"Because I shot at the guy who was shooting at me. I know I didn't miss the son-of-a-bitch."

"Seventeen," Fox answered. "He was out on bond on a couple of armed robbery charges. Whether you shot him or not, there's one less asshole on the streets."

A day later, Jake was up and walking the hallways on the fifth floor. Remington had stopped by with another chocolate malt. His partner was still doing paperwork on what had happened two days before and off the street until the investigation was over. Fox and two detectives from Number Five had already tape recorded Jake's recollections of what happened that night. Jake was thinking of calling Edie as he walked the hallway. But then she was mad when she'd left. He thought he'd give her some time before he called her.

Earlier that morning, Doctor Brewster, the surgeon who removed the two bullets, said Jake could go home the next day. His wounds were slight. A little muscle damage, but both would heal in two to three weeks.

"But no lifting weights for six weeks, at least." The muscle tone seen during the surgery had told the doctor that Jake was working out.

Jake got to the end of the hall and looked out the window. The sun was shining on the hospital's back parking lot. Little people were walking to and from the cars five stories below. He clutched at the opening on the back of the hospital gown with his right arm to keep his ass from hanging out. As he turned to go back to his room he almost lost one of the paper slippers they'd given him. It was time to call Edie. He missed her and the boys. He wondered how the all-star game went for Hank. He missed that, too. He was in surgery when the game had been played.

As he touched the door to room 517 he heard a voice. "Dad! Oops—Mr. Bush! Wait up." It was Sam. As Jake turned toward the voice. There, walking behind Sam, was Hank, grinning. Jake bent down and held out his arms to catch the boys running to him.

"We were looking for you down the hallway." Hank said.

"Careful Sammy!" It was Edie. Her head was hanging out the door to Jake's room.

Jake was glad she'd brought the boys. "Did your team win, Hank?"

"Yes, and I got three hits."

"He even hit a homer," chimed in Sam.

"Wow! I guess I missed a really big game." Jake led the boys past Edie as she held the door. He stopped and took her in his arms, kissing her. "Sorry, Eed."

"No. It's me who's sorry."

Jake held her for a few seconds and saw the boys checking out what was left of the malt. "Here, let me split that for you guys."

A half hour later Edie and the boys were heading out the door. "I'll call you in the morning," Jake said. "And thanks for bringing the boys."

"It was their idea. Not mine." She turned to follow them.

Jake grabbed her hand. He kissed it. "Don't let this come between us, Eed."

"Your job will always come between us." The door slowly closed behind her.

———

Remington appeared in the room at ten the next day. Jake was being released. Remington drove Jake to his house. His truck was already there in the driveway. "Some of the guys and I got it home last night." He handed Jake his keys. "By the way, you need some gas."

"Thanks." Jake took his keys and walked to his front door.

"You need anything, call me."

Jake waved Remington off. "I'll be fine." He was looking forward to a nap. Then he'd call Edie.

An hour later, Jake was dialing Edie's number. On the third ring he heard someone at the door. He hung up the phone and went to see who was there. It was Edie. She had a couple of bags of Chinese take-out.

"I brought lunch."

Jake looked beyond her to see if the boys were along.

"They're at the neighbor's," she answered when seeing the question in his eyes. "It's time we talked."

Edie took a couple of plates out of the cupboard and added silverware to the settings. "Can you put some water on for tea?"

"I don't have any tea bags."

"I brought some. I can't eat Chinese without tea."

Jake grabbed some spoons to serve up what was in the four boxes on the table. "This sounds serious. What are we talking about?"

"The boys."

"Something wrong?" Jake put a kettle of water on to boil.

Edie started spooning out some rice and shrimp in lobster sauce. "Sit."

Jake did as she demanded. Edie pulled up a chair and served the same for herself.

"I heard Sammy yesterday. At the hospital. He called you 'Dad'. Again."

"It's no big deal."

"Yes it is. I won't have my boys hurt. What happens between you and me, I can handle, but the boys—"

"I'm not going to hurt the boys."

"Sam and Hank idolize you."

Jake shrugged his shoulders. "Probably the same way I feel about you." Jake heard the kettle whistling, got up and shut the burner off. He filled their cups to let the bags steep.

"They need more than a coach."

"Then let's give them a full-time dad."

"You know that they love you. I won't let them get hurt."

"Then marry me."

Edie pushed the rice around on her plate with a fork. "You're all they ever talk about."

"You didn't hear me."

"We're talking about Hank and Sam here." Edie started fidgeting with her tea bag. She wasn't listening. "I'm serious."

"So am I. Marry me."

"What?"

"Sam had the answer a year ago." Jake took a sip of his tea.

"What answer?"

"Marry me and they can call me 'Dad.' Simple as that."

"You want to marry me so the boys—"

Jake put his two fingers on her lips to silence her. "No, marry me because I love you. The boys are a bonus."

"Jake, I'm serious here."

"So am I." He pushed his plate of half-eaten Chinese out of the way. "Will you marry a cop?"

Silence filled the room. Jake waited for Edie to respond. A tear rolled down her left cheek. She finally spoke.

"Jake—" She dropped her head. "Jake, I don't know if I can handle you going off to work not knowing if you'll come home." Edie reached for the tissue box.

"Until the other night, things like that never crossed my mind." She blew her nose and wiped her eyes. "Now I know what Beth was going through when Jess got shot."

Jake took Edie by the hand and held it tight. "Eed, I—"

"I need some time." She stood and started gathering their plates. She never touched her tea.

"Take whatever time you need. I'll be here."

Jake's door closed. He reheated his tea on the stove and started washing the dishes. Edie had left without another word.

Chapter Twenty-one

The doctors cleared Jake to return to duty on a limited basis. Sergeant Fox found a desk for him in Number Five's Detective Bureau, working the day shift. The Detective Lieutenant, Stan Morowski, said they could always use some help. The precinct detectives and the Robbery Bureau were still putting all the pieces together on the shooting that Jake and Remington had been involved in a couple of weeks before. Most of the work was being handled downtown. They kept in touch with the Number Five dicks, and they naturally passed things on to Jake.

The Prosecuting Attorney's Office had ruled a week prior that the police officers had been justified in their actions at the scene of Shoemaker and Harding the night of August 28, 1975.

First, the search of the Happy Hippie's truck had revealed a stash of narcotics. It was easy for the detectives and the Prosecuting Attorney's office to conclude that the officers attempting to make a drug purchase happened to be witnesses at the scene of a planned robbery that had gone wrong. The cache of drugs was no doubt the target.

The facts and ballistics bore out that Dusty Heights was shot three times by Harley Jones who was using a .32 caliber Iver Johnson revolver. Harley Jones was shot and wounded by Officer Remington Southworth.

Officer Bush was shot twice by Cecil Brooks, who was using a .22 caliber black revolver. Ballistics showed that this same pistol was used in a robbery-murder that occurred in the Thirteenth Precinct on June 22, 1975. They were able to deduce that the cheaply-made pistol was manufactured in

Belgium even though its serial number and make were filed off.

Cecil Brooks was shot and killed by two bullets fired from Officer Bush's .357 Smith and Wesson, along with one bullet fired from a Colt .38 caliber Police Special revolver that Officer Tyrone Wynn was carrying. The coroner ruled that either officer's bullets would have killed Brooks.

Ricky Evans was shot by Sergeant John Warneke and Officer Richard Davis. Both Evans and Jones were recovering and being held for murder at the Detroit House of Corrections.

The only loose end to the investigation was that Jones told the investigators that the pistol Brooks was using came from a guy only known as "Digger" who hung out on Kercheval. Discounting Jones' statement they found that Brooks' photos and prints did not put him at the scene of the robbery-murder in the Thirteenth Precinct. The June 22nd robbery-murder scene had prints all over the counter glass, some in blood, then more on the cash register and inside door handle.

Jake continued to work in Five's DB for the next two weeks. He was just shuffling papers, filing old cases that were closed and reviewing unsolved cases. He was completely bored, just biding his time until he could hit the street once the doctor cleared him to return to full duty.

Remington had picked up a new partner, Roberto San Miguel, a recent transfer in from the Second Precinct. Evidently the temporary replacement was working out fine. Remington stuck his head in the dick's office the second week he had been working with San Miguel. He told Jake about an arrest they had the night before. They witnessed a guy named Paul Digsby pulling a street mugging on an old man on Kercheval.

"You know, doing the regular hug the curb, lights out routine. And there it was. Right in front of us." Remington shrugged his shoulders and shook his head. "Then this Digsby guy took a swing at Roberto. That was dumb on his part." A wide smile crossed Remington's face. "I thought I was watching Muhammad Ali. Three jabs and a right cross and that asshole was down for the count."

Jake was happy his partner was doing all right with the new guy. But he did have to say something. "Don't get too comfortable with him. I think I'm back on the street next week."

"Remember, I'm getting married. Then it's off for our honeymoon."

"Thanks for reminding me. I have to get sized for my tux." Jake paused. "Can you out-shoot him?"

Remington just looked and smiled. "Of course."

"You gonna be at the range tomorrow?"

"Yeah, me and Roberto. He's got good fists, but needs some help with a pistol."

"I'll join you guys down there."

Jake went back to shuffling papers. An hour later, he was going over the arrest report on Paul Digsby, hand written by Remington. Evidently Roberto didn't type and Jake already knew Remington didn't like to. The report was hard to read. It was simple enough though. The crew of Five Twenty-five observed one man jump on another who was coming out of a store and tried to steal his wallet.

Jake wished he was back on the street. He missed the action. Edie crossed his mind. He dialed her number. After four rings he hung up. He remembered she'd be at work. He did have her work number, but knew he shouldn't call there. She was probably in surgery. But then, she said she'd call when she was ready. He put her out of his mind.

Jake reread the report on the arrest the night before. Digsby was a strange name. Then another name crossed his mind. *Digger.* He knew Paul Digsby was still in a holding cell. They hadn't run the prisoners downtown yet. Jake went and stuck his head in the door that led to the holding cells.

"Hey Digger," he yelled out.

"Yo!" Came a reply.

Jake didn't have to look to see who answered. There were three men being held. And only one would have answered up to the name Digger. And they had the prints of the three men waiting to be shuttled to 1300 Beaubien, the Police Headquarters main lockup.

Lieutenant Morowski listened as Jake told him about someone named Digger that lent a gun to Cecil Brooks before the shooting on August 28th and the guy Remington and San Miguel arrested the night before. The detective lieutenant said he'd check it out.

———

Working days had Jake getting home in the daylight. He was used to being at the station about this time, getting ready to start his shift. A light rain was falling; his wipers were slowly clearing away the droplets. He pulled into his driveway, wanting instead to head to Edie's. She said she needed time to think. He wanted to give her time, but decided to call her. The phone was answered on the fourth ring. It was Hank.

"Hi Hank. Is your mom home?"

The boy talked like he hadn't heard the question. "Mr. Bush. Football sign-ups are going on. You gonna coach again?"

"I really don't know for sure. Can I talk to your mom?"

"Yes sir. I'll go get her. But I really want you to coach our team. Please?"

"We'll see. Get your mom, Hank." Jake heard the phone clunk on the kitchen counter.

Seconds ticked by. "Hello."

"Hi Eed."

There was silence on the other end. Jake waited to hear her voice. Nothing.

"I had to call. I miss you."

Jake heard a sniff. Then, "I miss you too."

"You okay?"

"Jake, I just need time to sort things out. Please."

"It's about me being a cop?"

The line was silent. Jake hated the silence, but that's all there was. He thought he heard her starting to say something, but she didn't.

After a minute he said, "Call me if you want to talk."

He listened for an answer. Silence. He could hear her breathe. More silence. Finally Jake whispered, "Good-bye," and hung up.

———

It had been quite a while since Jake thought of the family he'd lost four years ago. They were finally in the past, memories that crossed his mind at times, but were no longer as painful. *I have Edie, Hank and Sam,* Except now, he wasn't sure. He was suddenly alone again. But he had *The Job,* if that was any consolation.

She wants time; I can give it to her, he kept telling himself. Yet, inside he hurt. He finally realized just how much he loved Edie. But he also loved being a cop. Now it was her choice if she wanted one in her life.

Jake knew what he wanted—both—Edie and the badge.

———

Jake kept busy shuffling papers in the detective bureau. He finally got caught up sorting the reports on the shootings, robberies, stolen cars and B&Es. He glanced at the clock. It was near two, so he asked the lieutenant if he could go to the range for about a half hour. He joined Remington and San Miguel and took his frustrations out on the target. For once he beat Remington by putting one more hole in the X-ring. San Miguel didn't stand a chance.

"Did you ever go to get fit for you tux?" Remington asked.

"Sorry. Forgot."

"It's the Vanity Room Boutique on Beaubien. They have the style and just need your measurements."

"Got a lot on my mind, partner." Jake made a mental note to get it done after work. Edie crossed his mind. She was on the invitation. Jake knew that if she didn't call, he'd have to go alone.

———

On Saturday, September 27, 1975, Remington Southworth married Jen Li Wong. It was a simple ceremony at St. Anthony's on Sheridan off of Gratiot. The ceremony was set for 4:30. Remington explained the time was a Chinese tradition also. The hands on the clock would be going up, rather than down, had they been married on the hour.

It came as a surprise to Jake that the Wongs were Catholics. Religion never came up in conversation until Jake got the invitation. Father Francis O'Malley was officiating. Jake was there early with the ring for the groom, wearing his tuxedo with a red cummerbund. He was there because he had promised his partner. He didn't really want to be there, especially alone.

A reception followed at the small Knights of Columbus hall on Mack Avenue where friends and family gathered to greet the newly-married couple. Red was the dominant color in keeping with Chinese tradition.

The reception looked like a session of the United Nations with Father O'Malley offering the toast in his Irish brogue, the Wong family and a dozen of their Chinese relatives, and Remington's mom, Carol, with her strong English accent. Stan Wiznewski, Jake and a couple of other Polish cops were there, as well as Tyrone Wynn and Richard Davis, the black officers working the Clean-up Crew. Mahendra Patel, the druggist from India, and his wife were there, too.

As Jake's eyes panned the crowd, he thought that Mayor Coleman Young might be upset with the happy gathering of representatives from just about every race and nationality that made up the City of Detroit in the mid-70s. It seemed the mayor wanted a black town—his town. And yet, this potpourri of happy people were here celebrating Jen Li and Remington's wedding.

No one seemed to notice that Jake was there alone.

———

While Remington and his new bride were off to Niagara Falls for their honeymoon, Jake was back on the street partnered with Roberto San Miguel. Car Five Twenty-five was slowly rolling down Chalmers. The heavy rains of early fall had knocked down most of the Elm leaves and Jake could smell someone burning them somewhere in the neighborhood. He was glad to be back on the streets of Detroit. He knew he'd never make it behind a desk. He loved the feel and the smell of the streets. Even the alleys. That's where he thrived.

"Can I call you Bert?" Jake asked.

"Bob will do," came the answer.

"We already have a Bob on the car."

"Remington?"

"I call him Bob. It's short for English bobby. Remington's too long."

San Miguel shrugged. "Bert or Roberto will work." He looked at Jake. "You got a problem working with a Mexican?"

"Hell no." Jake liked the guy's frankness. "You got a problem working with a Polack?"

"Bush isn't Polish."

"Buszewski was the real name. My dad shortened it so people would pronounce it right."

"Glad he did." Roberto smiled.

"Bob already said you were a good cop."

"He said the same thing about you. We should get along."

Jake settled back in his seat. He already knew the wisps of gray around his partner's temples said the guy had been on the job a bit longer than Jake. Time together would determine what kind of a cop he was.

———

Cars passed going the opposite way and Jake instinctively checked plate numbers against their stolen car board. Computer generated sheets replaced the old hand-written stolen car boards of the sixties. Jake rechecked a number he had just read. Their board had Nora Mary zero-four-three-three. A Chevy that just went north had matching letters with the last pair of numbers just one off.

"Bert, make a quick U-bender. Let's check that Chevy going north."

No questions were raised. The blue Buick's tires squealed on the pavement as the maneuver was made. At the Ford Expressway they saw the Chevrolet duck down the ramp heading northeast.

When Roberto reached the bottom of the ramp Jake spotted the car in the left lane at least a quarter of a mile ahead and it wasn't doing the 55 mile-an-hour speed limit. It was booking it, full bore. Roberto saw the car too.

"We've been spotted," Jake said.

Roberto floored the Buick, the eight cylinders giving him all it had. He cut to the right then back left, sliding around traffic, closing the gap.

Jake slapped the small magnetic blue bubble on the roof and grabbed the mike. "Radio, this is Five Twenty-five, we are in pursuit of a black Chevrolet east on the Ford. Possible stolen car."

The radio operator cleared the air for them. "Your location, Twenty-five?"

"Just went under Cadieux."

They were doing ninety-five, weaving in and out of traffic just as the Chevrolet was doing. They were now less than a quarter of a mile behind. Roberto was cool behind the wheel, weaving in and out of traffic, gaining a yard here, and two yards there.

The radio came alive. "Harper Woods and East Detroit are notified, Twenty-five."

Two cars from the Fifteenth Precinct jumped onto the freeway, lights and sirens helping clear the way for Roberto. The Buick was gaining on the Chevrolet. By it slowing a bit, Jake thought the driver was looking for a way off the freeway. The Chevy dove into the right lane. Sam Miguel was only two lengths behind. Jake spoke into the mike. "Radio, he's approaching Harper heading towards Eight Mile, still heading north." He was trying hard to control the adrenalin-induced excitement in his voice.

"Twenty-five, East Detroit has Harper blocked at the top of the ramp."

The Chevy picked up speed jumping on the Harper off-ramp.

At the top, metal crunched metal, sparks and car parts flew as the driver of the Chevy tried going between a

Macomb County Sheriff's car and two Harper Woods Police cars. Officers scattered. The Chevrolet came to an abrupt stop meeting a telephone pole at Hawthorne. The front bumper was pushed back to the dashboard. The steering column had impaled the man behind the wheel. As the police officers neared the wreckage it became apparent, the chase was over. The driver was dead.

A half hour later, the fire department had finished removing the body from behind the wheel and was hosing down the gasoline, oil and blood from the roadway. The wagon from the Wayne County Morgue hauled away the body. Jake and Roberto were led to the Harper Woods Police Headquarters. The wreck was in their jurisdiction.

Two hours and a pot of coffee later the paperwork was done. The end result was one totaled stolen car and three wrecked police vehicles. The VIN on the Chevrolet confirmed that the car had been reported stolen in the Fifth Precinct the morning of June 22, 1975. It had been roaming the streets for over two months. There was a mistake on the hot sheet.

Jake knew that humans input the license numbers into a machine and humans could make errors, like hitting the wrong key. He always stopped cars whose numbers were close to what he read on his stolen car board, just in case. This car didn't stop. It ran. Now, the driver was dead.

They headed back to the station.

"By the way Bob, nice driving," Jake said. "You've obviously been in a few chases." His heart rate had finally slowed to normal.

Roberto just shrugged. "Don't tell anyone, but I learned to drive while stealing cars when I was fifteen."

Jake sat up tall in his seat. "You're shittin' me."

"I am. Thought I'd get a rise outta you."

Jake knew he found another partner if he ever needed one.

———

Jake gave Edie all the time she needed. He hoped she'd call. She didn't. Two dozen times he started to dial her number, but hung up before he finished. Those on the street paid the price.

"You always stop this many people?" Roberto asked one night as he finished up the log sheet. Both sides were full.

"Sometimes."

In truth, Jake was burying himself in his work. He couldn't think of Edie when he was busy. And you can make yourself very busy in the Fifth Precinct. Then, in his off hours, one hour at the gym turned into two or more. Remington was honeymooning. He needed to fill his time. Twice Roberto joined him at the Y, but gave up.

"You need to get a life, Jake," Roberto said when they hit the shower. He said he had leaves to rake and kids to play with.

Two weeks passed. Jake and Remington were back together. There was a note in the box from the Hold-up Bureau informing them that Roberto San Miguel, Remington Southworth and John Anthony Bush were being recommended for citations. Fingerprints and witness corroboration put Paul Digsby and a man named James LaBlount at the scene of a jewelry store armed robbery on the afternoon of June 22, 1975. James LaBlount was the man driving the stolen Chevrolet, the man who was killed in the chase on the freeway the night of October 1, 1975.

"Talk about a coincidence," Remington said after reading the note. "You, in the dick's office, filing reports. Then back on the street when that Chevy goes by."

"And you and Bert arresting Digsby." Jake chuckled a little. "Things like this always brings Jesse Scott to mind. He was always preaching that I had to keep my eyes open. 'Watch the street people,' he'd say."

Remington folded the note. "Don't you just love being a cop?"

"Yes. And I'm sure a lot of us do." Jake paused a beat or two. "Jess did for sure."

Edie would never understand. Jake just shook his head, clearing his mind as he threw his stuff onto the front seat of their Buick. They were ready to start another shift.

Chapter Twenty-two

Jake retrieved the morning paper off his porch and poured a cup of coffee. He glanced at it. The *Detroit Free Press* ran an article concerning recent interviews with Mayor Coleman Young. Crime in general was the topic, but a question was raised about Halloween and, in particular, "Devil's Night," when a lot of arsons took place. The mayor's response was, "to a unique degree, Detroit has buildings to burn."

As Jake read the paper, he thought of Edie again. It'd be two years the end of the month since he met her, at Beth Scott's Halloween party. *That witch sure put a hex on me.* He wondered what she was doing as he tried to read. He shrugged. The clock chimed eight bells. He dressed, downed another cup of coffee and went for a ride. He wasn't hungry. He was figuring on a lonely Sunday.

A light rain started falling as he cruised by his old neighborhood, first the house on Liberal, then the one on Strasburg. Then he thought about maybe stopping and seeing his Uncle Phil. Jake hadn't really seen any of his dad's family since he moved back to Detroit. He turned the corner onto Goulburn and recognized the brick home that Phil and Ceil lived in. He pulled into the driveway. His uncle and aunt were just climbing into their Plymouth.

"Jake," Uncle Phil yelled out. "We're heading for 9:30 mass. Join us."

Jake was embarrassed. He never gave Sunday morning a thought, especially mass. He hadn't been to one in over four years. Remington's wedding was at a church, but that was just a wedding ceremony.

There's no talking my way out of this. He backed up, parked on the street and jumped in the back seat of Uncle Phil's car.

"And we'll go to breakfast after. You can buy." Uncle Phil smiled as the words came out in his raspy voice. Forty years of smoking will do that to a man.

Yeah, just like my dad. Only Uncle Theophil Buszewski hadn't changed his name. Jake touched Aunt Ceil's shoulder. "Sorry for dropping by so early, forgot it was Sunday."

"Glad you stopped, Jake," Aunt Ceil said. "We can have a good visit after church."

Jake knew all the moves at mass. When to stand, when to kneel. All the prayers. But inside, his mind was flipping from one thing to another—Anne, his four children, then to Edie and the boys. The priest was at the end of his sermon before Jake came to realize that maybe the unplanned visit, the invite to mass, might be what he needed that lonely Sunday in October.

It took all that he had, but he finally prayed God would forgive him and guide him. He then mumbled a short prayer that Edie would call. The mass ended. He was glad he turned onto Goulburn that morning.

At breakfast Aunt Ceil and Uncle Phil were full of questions. Questions Jake knew they'd ask. There was a ton of "Oh my," and, "We're so sorry for you." Jake purposely didn't mention the new woman in his life.

———

Three hours after mass Jake headed for home. He had promised his uncle and aunt he wouldn't stay away so long. Then he thought of his other uncles and aunts. They didn't know Jake had moved back to Detroit, either. But then, he really didn't want to talk about the family he'd lost more than four years ago. He was hoping that maybe Uncle Phil or Aunt

Ceil would spread the word and save him from having to repeat what he had tried to bury for so long.

Jake turned on the TV and opened the paper. A football game was on, but he only used the TV for background noise as he read. He had the sound so high he almost didn't hear the phone ring.

"Hello."

"Hi Jake." It was the voice he wanted to hear.

"Eed—"

"Can you come by for dinner?"

"You sure?"

"Positive."

"What time?"

"Anytime. Come now, if you'd like. We'll eat at five."

"I'll be there."

———

An hour later he was pulling into a driveway on Romeo Plank Road, at Edie's house. He took his time driving, wondering if this was the last time he'd make that trip. He sat in his car for a moment. The rain had stopped before noon and it turned out to be a nice sunny day. The boys weren't in the yard. He thought they'd be out throwing around a football, then realized that she might have shipped them out to her mom's, or a neighbor's. That would save them from seeing Jake for the last time.

As soon as he stepped on the porch, the door opened. Hank was playing the role of a butler, only he had a smile on his face. Inside, Edie was busy at the stove and Sam was setting the table. They both stopped when Jake entered the kitchen. Sam ran up to him and hugged him. Edie stood there smiling.

"The boys have something to tell you. Hank, you first."

Jake turned to Hank.

"I'd like you to be my dad."

That was it. A short statement.

"Sam, your turn." Edie was putting something in the oven.

Sam looked up at Jake; a broad smile was punctuated by a missing front tooth. "Having you for a dad would be cool."

Jake looked at Edie. She was walking towards him.

Edie pulled a pink rose from behind her back. She was wearing pink slacks and a white blouse. She offered the rose to Jake. "Would you consider marrying us?"

Jake scooped her up in his arms and instantly a tear was rolling down his cheek. "I thought—"

Edie kissed Jake hard on the lips, stopping him in mid-sentence, then looked up at him. "I've been doing a lot of thinking, even called Jess's wife twice. Yesterday, I decided to talk to the boys. As soon as I said that you asked me to marry you, pandemonium broke out. They told me I'd better. It was like I had no say in the matter."

"But, how do you feel?"

"I want to marry the man I love. That's you. They like the idea of their dad being a cop."

Jake hugged her, whispering in her ear. "I love you."

She moved away. "Let me finish getting dinner together. Take the boys outside and play some football with them. They've been driving me nuts all morning. 'When's Jake coming? Can we call him dad?'"

"I'd rather hold you for a while. I've missed you."

"We can save the holding until later." She winked. "And we'll have the rest of our lives. Scoot. I've got things to do."

Jake and the boys played for two hours and sat on the porch for another. He was back with "his boys" as he called them.

———

Edie stuck her head out the door. "Come on in. Supper's ready."

She pulled out a tray from the oven filled with fresh rolls as the men came in.

"What's in the roaster?" Jake asked as he took his chair.

"Stuffed cabbage. I called your mother for the recipe. And mashed potatoes."

They all held hands and said grace. Sam led the prayer. Jake joined in. It was their Lutheran grace. He then tried the German girl's cooking—a Polish dish. *Not bad.*

He had a family again.

"Dad—" Sam stopped, looked at his mom, then at Jake. "Is it okay to call you Dad? I'm tired of this Mister Bush crap."

"Sammy!" It was Edie.

Hank, the normally quiet one of the two added, "He's right mom. It is crap."

Edie blushed, whispering. "I guess they need the firm hand of a father."

Jake laughed. "I'm tired of the Mister Bush crap too."

"Jake, don't be encouraging my boys—"

"Our boys." Jake interrupted.

Jake met Remington at the Y Tuesday morning. He told Remington to throw on twenty more pounds for his bench presses.

"Boy, you're full of energy today."

"Just happy."

"Did you get laid?"

Jake stopped for a second, then grabbed onto the bar. He didn't know if he was blushing or not. "Edie proposed to me. Yesterday."

"She proposed to you?"

Jake was pumping iron. Deeply inhaling as the bar came down. He stopped for a second after he exhaled and said, "Yes." He finished his fifteen reps.

"And you thought Chinese traditions were strange." Remington grabbed the bar and set it on the stanchions.

Before starting his next set, Jake told his partner all about the proposal, what she wore, the flower, the meal. That's where the conversation ended.

"You never did answer. Did you get laid?"

"That's none of your damn business."

"You did." Remington smiled and walked towards the shower room.

———

Gossip filled the Fifth Precinct and it slowly got to Jake and Remington. The word was that a directive came down from the mayor stating that three out of four candidates for the police academy were to be black and that only citizens of Detroit were to be considered. The hiring qualifications were also going to be loosened to increase the percentage of minority officers on the department.

Jake said he had no problem with increasing the number of black officers, but didn't agree with lowering the hiring standards. He saw this as the beginning of the end to the department as he knew it. Remington agreed.

There was a note from Fox in Jake's box when he came in. It was a Wednesday. The note read, "See me before you hit the street tonight."

Jake stuck his head in his boss's door. "What's up?" Remington was already there. Jake wondered what they'd done wrong. The bosses usually left them alone.

"Have a seat, Jake," Sergeant Fox said, motioning towards a chair.

"This gonna take that long?"

"It could." The sergeant shuffled some papers. "Another directive came down. Effective immediately, all black officers will be reassigned if they are partnered up with another black officer."

"What's that got to do with us?" Jake looked at Remington, then back to his boss.

"Remington is being reassigned as of tomorrow. He's going back in uniform."

"And my partner will be?"

"Tyrone Wynn."

Jake just shrugged his shoulders. "He's got big shoes to fill." He nodded towards Remington. "Your nephew's a pretty good cop. Hope Wynn is."

Fox smiled. "How'd you know he's my nephew?"

"He mentioned an Uncle Beau one time." Jake grinned, then added, "I'm a cop. I can figure things out."

"Do you have a problem with getting Wynn?"

"Like I said, if he's half as good as this kid here, it'll work."

Jake looked at his partner. "First you're married and a month later divorced—from me. That lawyer wife of yours ask for this?"

"Yeah. She's jealous. Says I talk in my sleep about you." Remington stood, looked at Fox and said, "Can we hit the street now?"

"Yeah. So much for my big meeting with you guys. Stay safe."

Jake looked at the sergeant. "He's got my back. I've got his."

Five Twenty-five was rolling half an hour later. Lights out, slowly driving the curb lane on Jefferson Avenue.

———

Tyrone Wynn was about an inch taller than Jake and a little beefier. He had been a cop for six years by the time he was teamed up with Jake. He had big lips that surrounded a wide smile. There was no question about him being black. He was the darkest man Jake had ever seen. The smile was always there. It put others at ease, but behind the smile was another one-time U.S. Marine who knew the streets of Detroit.

"So what do I call you? Tye?" Jake asked as he got behind the wheel of their Buick.

"Gunny," was the answer behind the smile.

Jake knew the term *Gunny* in the Marine Corps was short for "Gunnery Sergeant."

"You were a Marine Gunnery Sergeant?"

"No, but they all knew me as 'Gunny Wynn.'"

Wynn told the story of when he'd been first assigned to a Marine Barracks at a Naval Air Station. He'd known, being fresh out of boot camp, he'd get all the shit jobs. He said since he had looked a lot older than the eighteen he was, he'd let it slip that he had been a Gunnery Sergeant only to be busted down to Private for bucking a young lieutenant's order.

"They bought your story?"

"They sure did." He chuckled a bit. "You know white boys can't tell how old a Negro is." Wynn smiled, showing all his teeth. "They sucked the story right up." Wynn chuckled again. "One thing I learned growing up in Houston was how to bullshit my way through life."

"Now you telling me you're a Texan?"

"In the flesh."

"You know, I can handle you being black. But a Texan?" Jake shook his head. "I'm gonna have to talk to Fox. What the hell did I do to him?"

Jake checked a plate number on their board. He smiled, looked over at his partner. "Gunny, eh?"

November rolled around and Edie was into planning *the* big day—her wedding. She chose the Friday after Thanksgiving for the date. That's when Jake found out that she came from a large family. A very large family. Four sisters and three brothers. Her Lutheran Pastor met with Jake and Edie and said he'd do the ceremony. Jake didn't care where or when they'd get married. He just wanted it done. The one item on his agenda, though, was finding a best man. He called Jesse Scott to see if he wouldn't mind.

"I hope I don't have to wear a damn tux." That was Jess's way of saying yes.

"No tux. But a suit would be nice," Jake assured his old partner. "Edie'll send you a formal invitation, so plan on bringing Beth and the boys."

Jess closed the conversation with, "Knew you'd like that fat lady in black."

Jake heard Jess laugh as the phone went dead. He didn't ever remember his partner laughing. *He must be enjoying retirement.*

Standard Electric had a three-story brick warehouse just off of Chalmers and Mack. They were one of the major suppliers of electrical parts for the building industry in and around Detroit. Wynn was driving in the alley behind the building. As their headlights bounced on the way up the alley approach he saw something.

"Jake, shine your light on the second-story windows."

"What'd you see?"

"One's open, I think."

Jake grabbed the big spotlight hanging under the dash and panned the building. One window was tilted open—the kind that you unlatch and push out. Wynn and Jake looked as the beam of light moved to both sides of the open window, then down. A dumpster was on the floor of the alley. Just to the right and above it, a tile downspout ended.

"Humph," mumbled Wynn. "What d'you think?"

Jake ran the light up the side of the dumpster, to the downspout and to the open window. "It'd take some skill to climb that thing," Jake said as his beam slowly went up the wall.

"How were you on the confidence course at San Diego?" Gunny asked.

"Taxed the shit outta my arm strength," Jake answered. His light kept climbing the wall and to the window.

"You want to give it a try?" Gunny Wynn smiled. "Might be a burglar in there."

"Might. But you're younger than me, and the rookie on this car. It'd be like climbing a rope. Texans can climb, right?"

"Humph," is all Gunny said as he got out of the car, stepped onto the metal pivot on the side of the dumpster and lifted himself to the top. "You're the guy pumping iron. You should be going up this," he whispered.

Gunny grabbed the drain pipe and gave it a yank. It held. He wrapped one hand around the pipe, then the other a little higher. It was a six-inch pipe he could get his hands around. He pulled. One hand moved up, then the other. His foot dragged against a fastener that held the downspout to the building. He used it to help shinny up the pipe. After a ten-foot climb he was even with the window. Gunny reached over and grabbed the metal window casing and pulled himself to where he could get his left knee on the brick ledge, then his right knee. He took a short break, then slithered into the window. In a second Gunny's head popped out.

"I'll find the stairs and come let you in."

"Okay."

Jake grabbed the mike and called Radio. He asked for some backup and to have the station call the emergency contact number for the Standard Electric warehouse. He got out of the car, leaned on the fender and waited.

"Jake." It was a whispered call. Gunny's head was hanging out the window. "Come on up." He pointed to the pipe.

Jake pocketed a flashlight and followed the method that Gunny had used to climb up on the dumpster, grabbed the pipe and started hauling himself up to the second floor. He reached for the metal casing when he got next to the window, moved to the ledge and put his shoulders in the canted window. Gunny was there to help him in and onto the floor.

"Couldn't find the stairs to the door?"

"Just wanted to see if you could drag your ass up here," Gunny whispered.

"You're shittin' me—" Gunny had clamped a hand over Jake's mouth.

"Listen."

Jake listened. He heard a high whine. "What's that?"

"A drill. It's down the hall to the left. Two guys working on a safe."

Gunny led the way. He had his pistol in his hand. Jake did likewise. In his left hand he held his unlit flashlight. Jake and Gunny used their hands to feel their way along a corridor. The noise got louder as they neared a back office. They peered in.

A small portable light illuminated the door of a safe. Two silhouettes were outlined at the edge of the beam. One man was handling a large drill, the other handling a container of liquid. *Cutting oil no doubt,* Jake thought. They were drilling a hole next to the tumbler. The man paused.

"Here. Take the drill," he said to his partner.

Jake's flashlight went on.

"Freeze! Police!" Gunny barked. His hand was extended, pointing his .38. They froze.

Jake handed Gunny his light. "I'll find a light switch."

Jake found the switch and flicked it on. Two banks of overhead fluorescent lights came to life.

"You can put the tools down. Gently," said Gunny.

They did as ordered. The two men were then handcuffed behind their backs.

"Come on, let's find the stairs," Jake said as he grabbed an elbow and led his man down the hallway towards the office where they had entered. Wynn followed with the second guy. Jake found the stairwell. Two short flights down, he banged open the door. The alarm over the door started clanging.

Five Ten, Remington Southworth and Glenn Poore, were getting out of their black Ford station wagon as Jake opened the alley door. Remington greeted Jake and Gunny Wynn with a smile. "You guys need a hand?" He was yelling to be heard above the alarm.

"Yeah. You can take these two in while we go gather the evidence. They were working on a safe."

Another set of headlights came into the alley. It was the warehouse manager. Gunny Wynn pointed over to the door. "Can you shut that damn thing off?" He had to say it again when the guy got closer.

He nodded and went inside. The bell went silent. He came back out.

"What's going on?" He asked.

"Second floor." Jake said. "They were working on your safe."

"They set off an alarm?"

"No, went through an open window." Gunny pointed his flashlight beam at the upstairs window.

An hour later Gunny was tagging evidence. Jake was finishing the report on the arrest of David Bouma, white and 32 and Cecil Yaeger, white and 35. Neither man was carrying identification and gave varied addresses as Jake and Gunny were booking them.

"They've been around," Jake said as he typed. "Their prints will tell us their story. Might even be phony names."

"I shoulda timed you climbing up that pipe," Wynn said. "You looked kinda slow."

"I beat your time. You might have to join me at the Y."

"That ain't gonna happen. My ol' lady works me hard enough around the house."

Jake handed him the report to sign. "How do you suppose they found the window?"

"Somebody on the inside. No alarms on the windows above the first floor. Somebody left it open for them."

"Glad you spotted it."

"I was taught by the best."

"Who?"

"Jesse Scott. We worked Precinct Vice together."

Jake just smiled. It was time to go home.

Chapter Twenty-three

Theodore Poet had his neck in a brace for three months. The latest X-rays showed that the fractured vertebrae were nicely healed and the brace was removed. He was still being held as a police prisoner at Detroit Receiving Hospital. The man who called himself *The Poet* did not know who or where he was. His medical files passed through the hands of three psychologists, a psychiatrist and two neurologists. They all concluded, after they examined the patient, that he had "traumatic brain injury" that caused his amnesia.

That was causing the doctors and the hospital staff a problem. Three months was longer than they'd ever held onto a prisoner for the police department and Poet had now been shackled to a bed for almost four months.

The Detroit Police and the Wayne County Prosecutor's Office had their own problem. Theodore Poet was being held on a warrant issued on June 25th, 1975 for extortion as well as violation of the terms of his parole. But Theodore Poet could not be arraigned in court on either charge until he knew who he was. It was as simple as that.

The Assistant Prosecuting Attorney, Joseph Paine, recommended that Poet be placed in a halfway house until such a time when he could assist his attorney with his defense in a court of law. Paine found such a place on Beaubien Street, three blocks from the Police Headquarters.

Poet was moved from Detroit Receiving Hospital to the Regis Halfway House on October 10th. That meant he would be no longer shackled to a bed. Paine said that didn't really matter because the man did not have a clue as to who he was.

Three weeks later things changed. During a bed check on November 1st, Theodore Poet was listed as missing from the halfway house. It took the Regis two days to notify John Paine that Poet was gone. Another two days later a runner from the prosecutor's office stopped by the Regis to pick up the files on Poet. They too were gone.

That afternoon Joseph Paine issued a new warrant for the arrest of Theodore Poet for escaping from police custody and reinstating the extortion and parole violation charges.

Inspector Richard Dungy, recently assigned to lead the Organized Crime Unit, was sitting in the Wayne County Prosecuting Attorney's office on November 5th, asking exactly what was in the file that had gone missing from an unlocked file cabinet. Charlie Dane, the second-term head prosecutor, shrugged his shoulders.

"I'm assuming copies of his medical records and the arrest report."

Dungy knew the complainants on the extortion charges would be listed somewhere in that file and the arrest report would have the names of the arresting officers. The inspector made two phone calls. The first was back to his office. He wanted one of his crews to check where Poet lived before his arrest. The second call had him leaving a message at the Fifth Precinct to have Patrolman John Anthony Bush call him.

Jake and Edie had talked a lot since the rose, pink slacks, white blouse and her proposal. The big question was where they were going to live. Edie had suggested that Jake should move into her house. It was close to the hospital where she worked and the boys would not have to change schools.

Edie was very emphatic as she said, "For sure, I'm not moving to Detroit."

"I wouldn't expect you to. We won't disrupt what the boys have out here."

Jake had been living a few blocks outside of the city for three years, violating the police department's residency requirements. An officer's phone number was what tripped up those who were caught living outside of Detroit. Jake still had his old phone number where he was renting. If he moved in with Edie, he'd have a problem.

It didn't take long for Jake to decide what he was going to do. He and Edie were going to get married. He'd worry about the consequences *if* he got caught.

Every now and then, stumbling into relatives you hadn't seen in a while turns out to be a blessing. Uncle Phil and Aunt Ceil lived within the Detroit city limits. Mayor Coleman Young was not going to force them out. The northeast corner of Detroit was still ninety-eight percent white. Jake called them to see if they were going to be free the following Monday. They were. He said he'd bring supper and a friend.

The friend was Edie and they brought a roaster brimming with sauerkraut and fresh Polish sausage—kielbasa. Jake knew all of his dad's brothers loved to eat, especially Polish food. Jake knew of a place in Hamtramck from his early days working in Number Eleven where they made the best fresh kielbasa. Edie's folks had made the kraut in a crock in their basement. Jake had already sampled it.

Jake introduced Edie as Edith Ruth, soon to be Bush, to his uncle and aunt. That was the first time he'd ever called her by her given name. Edie glared at him.

"But she prefers Edie," he quickly added.

After dinner Jake started to tell his uncle and aunt about his dilemma and the residency requirements. Before he could finish, Uncle Phil said, "Just give them my address and phone number. For all they know, you live here. Hang some clothes in the back bedroom. It's empty."

Uncle Phil and Aunt Ceil's kids were grown and gone. Problem solved.

Before Jake and Edie left, Uncle Phil casually asked, "Did Edie make the dinner, or you?"

"She put it together. I picked up the sausage. The sauerkraut was made by her folks. They're German."

"Could be worse. At least she's white."

The women were coming out of the kitchen just as Phil spoke.

"Phil! Watch what you say," Aunt Ceil said, turning to Edie. "Sometimes I have to filter what my husband says. I thought he was going to say something else."

"What? You worried about me saying something about the damned nigger mayor driving the whites outta Detroit?"

"Phil, I told you—"

"What? Can't I say what I want in my own house?"

"See what I mean?" Aunt Ceil raised her hands in resignation and walked away.

Jake never said a word. His dad used to talk just like Uncle Phil until the day he died. Jake knew enough not to tell his uncle that his partner was black and a friend.

An hour later, Jake was making a turn onto Romeo Plank Road outside of the small village of Washington. That's where he'd live after he and Edie got married. Only now, Jake's new phone number was going to be a local call from the Fifth Precinct, and he'd have an address four blocks south of Eight Mile Road within the City of Detroit.

———

Jake and Gunny Wynn were copying teletypes and checking the circulars before hitting the street. "Gunny, here's one on a guy Remington and I arrested—Theodore Poet." He pushed the teletype over the table so Wynn could read it.

"This guy and two others were running a protection racket. They were shaking down half the businesses in the precinct."

Wynn read the teletype. "How'd he escape?"

Jake shrugged. "Last I knew Poet was in the hospital. Remington put him there."

Jake filled in Wynn on the story. "I'll check with the dicks to see what his address was when we arrested him."

On the way out, Jake looked in his box. There was a note to call Inspector Dungy with a phone number.

"Gunny, wait in the car. I've got a quick call to make."

Five minutes later Jake was sliding into their Buick. "The guy's making rank fast. He's now an inspector."

"Who?"

"The guy I called. He's now running the Organized Crime Unit." Jake snickered. "We were patrolmen together at the TMU seven years ago."

Jake told Gunny about Theo Poet walking away from the Regis Halfway House.

"Everyone thought he had amnesia. He didn't know who he was so they couldn't take him before a judge."

"So why did Dungy specifically call you?"

Jake drove off the station ramp. "Poet took his file with him. Stole it. It has the names of the complainants on the extortion charge and a copy of the arrest report. He was thinking the guy might cause some problems for them. He thought I should warn them."

"You know 'em?"

"Remington's wife, father-in-law and grandfather. They own a Chinese laundry. It was just one of a couple a hundred or more places Poet had been shaking down."

Jake was driving towards Mack. "He's already had his men check where Poet lived when we arrested him. New tenants moved in a month after he ended up in the hospital and the manager said he hasn't been back."

Jake pulled to a stop in front of Wong's laundry and dry cleaners.

"I'll be right out. Dungy said Poet might want to come back on them."

"Think the guy'd be looking for Remington and maybe you?"

Jake thought for a moment. "No. We have guns."

Five minutes later Jake slid in behind the wheel and they were rolling again. Wynn checked a number on the board.

"You miss working with the Southworth kid, don't you?"

"Why'd you ask that?"

"I don't know. Just a question."

Jake turned the next corner. "Things keep changing around the department." He drove slowly in the curb lane with his lights out.

"I liked Jesse Scott, but with his wounds, he had to retire. Then Remington came aboard and now you." Jake's light hit the board. No match. "As long as my partner's a good cop, I'm okay with it."

"He ever tell you about saving my ass right after he got out of the academy?"

"Remington?"

"Yeah."

"He never said he worked with you."

"We didn't work together. He and his partner were backing us up on a drug raid. I'm glad he was there."

"What happened?"

Gunny Wynn talked about when he was working Precinct Narcotics, and that his crew had a search warrant on a suspected drug pad. He said they were going in the door to a house on Vernor. They had five people in custody along with some heroin and a couple of guns. Gunny said he was checking a back bedroom when a drugged-out kid jumped him.

"Some spaced out shit-head was on me before I knew it. I dropped my gun, and he was choking me from behind. I couldn't even shout for help. I blacked out. I guess Remington somehow heard the scuffling. The next thing I knew was Remington is on me blowing in my mouth."

"He was giving you mouth-to-mouth?"

"Yeah. It scared the hell outta me."

"What happened to the guy?"

"I guess Remington broke his neck. He was on the floor with his head twisted around and deader than a carp washed up on a Belle Isle beach."

"He never said anything about it to me."

"He was just out of the academy and filling in on a car that night. I'm glad he was. I owe him my life."

Gunny hit the rear of some business places with the spotlight. "I know I'd be pissed if someone took his place if'n he were my partner."

"Rest easy, Gunny. I was the best man at his wedding and he said he'd make me Godfather of his first-born." Jake smiled and pulled into an alley. "We'll always be friends. One day maybe we'll partner up again."

Five Twenty-five rolled into another alley off of the north side of Mack. Jake looked at the back of the darkened businesses that Theodore Poet was shaking down, thinking the guy probably left town. That'd be the route taken by a sane man. He'd have to know every cop in the city would be looking for him, especially Jake and Remington. Yes, if Poet was smart, he'd be anywhere but Detroit.

———

Juanita Comings was an exotic dancer at a club on Jefferson called *The Charging Station*. It was a topless bar frequented by men who wanted their batteries charged after a long day at the office, or maybe by a bunch of cops from the Fifth Precinct who were coming off shift.

Juanita was a tall black woman with long straightened hair who knew how to work her thirty-six double Ds. The pasties she had to wear—by law— didn't take away from the view she gave her audience.

Juanita knew men loved to talk to the dancers and talking meant selling more five dollar drinks that brought the bigger tips stuck in her G-string. Then too, when you're having a beer and getting your eyes filled, it was, *whachya want to know, babe?* Juanita could get any information she wanted out of those horny ol' guys who dropped by the club.

Jake had to buy a suit for the wedding. He didn't own one. He remembered a wholesale place in the Second Precinct that an old partner put him onto. It was called Kaiser's, and it supplied clothes to most of the men's shops in Detroit. That partner was a big-time shopper who knew where all the deals were. Kaiser's sold to police officers at wholesale prices. Jim Breedlove, the one-time partner, took Jake there once back in 1968—just before Jake resigned.

Jake had priced a suit at Jack's Fifth Avenue, a men's store at the Eastland Mall. They wanted $199.95. He found the same suit for a third of the price at Kaiser's. It fit. He bought it. They had shirts, belts and shoes too, so he bought everything he needed for his big night. Jake paid less than a third of what his wardrobe would have cost at Jack's Fifth Avenue.

The next step was to terminate his lease on the little place he had been renting. His rent was paid until the end of

November. He checked that off the list he and Edie had come up with. Jake called Jesse Scott to make sure he had the date, the time and the place. He did.

Now Jake didn't know what to do. He had the three items on his list done. All he had to do was to wait for November 28th, the Friday after Thanksgiving.

Edie sang in the choir at Our Redeemer, a Lutheran Church near Washington, Michigan. She had often asked Jake to come and hear her sing. He always had an excuse. Now he had reconsidered since the pastor, Jim Pettys, was going to marry them. Since the proposal, he drove up to take Edie and the boys to their 10:30 service. If nothing else, the upcoming wedding had Jake going to church.

———

The radio run went out as "Family Trouble." A black car that had *Detroit Police* stenciled in gold on the doors pulled up to the front of 1745 Phillip.

A man hidden deep in the shadows of the house to the south of that address watched the two uniformed officers open their car door, walk to the house and ring the bell. As soon as the car's dome light went on he knew neither officer was the one he was looking for. In less than five minutes the police car left.

The guy in the shadows knew there was no family trouble. He was the one who'd called in the phony complaint. The man shoved the long barreled blue steel pistol in his belt and waited until the taillights on the police car were two blocks away before leaving his hiding spot. He moved quietly to the car parked around the corner. He was looking for a cop who was assigned to Five-Ten. *Maybe it's his day off?*

In a couple of days he'd try again. The cop he was looking for was working afternoons that month. The man checked his mirrors for headlights before he started his car and drove away. A half block down the street he had to shift his weight. The hammer on his pistol was digging into his rib cage. He pulled it out, dropped it to the floor and kicked it under his seat.

The pistol he carried was cumbersome, but it was the one he wanted. It took two days for him to locate a Colt Python . 357 magnum like the one he saw in a couple of Dirty Harry movies, but the one he bought only had a six-inch barrel. The one that Clint Eastwood carried would be way too long. Three days later he bought a silencer for the piece. It cost him four times as much as the pistol. Silencers were tough to come by.

———

Remington passed Jake in the station while booking a drunk driver. Jake stopped to talk for a minute.

"Jen Li, or her family, hear anything from that Poet character?"

"Not a peep. Things are quiet."

"I'll bet he left town."

"You'd think so." Remington started to move his prisoner towards the bull pen.

"Jake, are you getting nervous?"

"Should I?"

"Your time as a free man is getting short."

Jake smiled. Gunny was waiting in the car. He called out over his shoulder, "Take care of your drunk, kid. I've got crooks to catch."

Remington turned away. He missed working the B&E car and missed working with Jake. Now, he was back to writing tickets and answering radio runs.

———

The man had called the police number five different times for five different addresses over a two-week period. His calls were for minor reasons for a police car to show up. He made sure his complaint was minor. He didn't want the dispatcher to send two cars, or for a second car to decide to swing by for back up.

Picking an ambush spot was something he did during the daylight hours. Most of the houses in the Fifth Precinct were built on lots forty feet wide. He liked to find a house he could hide next to it or one with a porch that had the bottom half closed in. Then the house needed to have easy access to a yard—that had no dogs—and the alley. Daylight was the time to find these things out. He did so much walking and looking that one woman asked if he was the city tax assessor. He said he was.

His plan was falling into place. With the narrow lots, one porch was only about ten to fifteen yards away from the other. It was a range the Python could handle with ease. Every time he found such a place he'd note it down. Then well after dark he'd make a call when most of the people were wrapped up in a TV show or in bed. Then he'd wait.

Five calls in a row came up empty. The cop he was looking for didn't show. But he was getting results. Dropping a dime in a pay phone always had a police car arrive. It might take an hour, but one would respond. He was told that sometimes other cars would be sent to an address in Five-ten's territory. He knew that, one day, things would go his way.

Maybe tonight.

He dropped another dime in a phone booth on Mack, then drove around the corner from a number he got off of a house on Grayton.

He climbed up on the porch of the house next door. It had a covered front porch with the bottom half closed in. The house was dark. He figured the lady who took him for a tax guy was probably in bed. If the right cop showed up, he'd shoot from there and wait until the second cop ran to his car to call for help. Darkness was his ally. He'd disappear in the panic.

———

At the start of the shift Remington scratched the date on Five-ten's log sheet. It was November 14, 1975. He and Glenn wrote two movers apiece, answered three radio runs and had lunch. It was dark by the time they called back in service.

"Five-ten. 1822 Grayton. See the man on a stolen bicycle."

"Five-ten, on the way." Remington hung up the mike. He looked at his partner. "That's what I miss about working with Jake. There's none of these bullshit calls to answer."

Glenn headed for the address. "I'll sit in the car while you handle this one."

"No, better come with me. The guy might blame me for his bike being gone."

Glenn just shrugged. He wanted a cigarette. Remington didn't like him smoking in the car. "A stolen bike don't sound that dangerous."

"Jake said partners work together. We'll both go to the door."

"Jake isn't on this car. I am."

"We both go, or you'll find yourself a new partner."

The address was mid-block on the right. Poore glided to a stop.

"Then I'll do the talking," Poore said. "You take notes." He was thinking, *what an asshole.*

He and Remington got out of the car and approached the porch. Glen rang the bell. Remington stood two feet behind him.

Two loud pops broke the quiet of the night as the two men in blue waited for someone to come to the door. Remington fell into Glenn Poore, knocking him down.

A porch light went on and the door of the house opened. The woman standing there saw blood splattered on the side of Poore's face. She screamed. Glenn already had his Colt out as he turned his partner over. Blood was pumping out of Remington's chest. Poore looked into the darkness and saw nothing.

The woman was frozen in place, screaming at the top of her lungs. Poore ran to his car to get to the radio. He needed help.

The big man waited for the right moment, then slipped off the porch in the darkness, cutting through the yard into the alley and around a corner to his car.

In seconds the East Side Radio was blasting out, "All units, Officer down 1822 Grayton."

Sirens screamed from all corners of the Fifth Precinct. Jake floored the Buick, heading towards the address.

The man in dark clothes was driving away forty-five seconds after he'd fired two shots. A half a block later he had to slam on his brakes as two police cars crossed Cornwall in front of him. He knew where they were going. He was heading the opposite direction.

Chapter Twenty-four

The parking lot at the A.H. Peters funeral home on Mack in Grosse Pointe Woods was bulging as car after car filled with men and women stopped by to pay their respects. Jake had spent a good part of two days there. Jen Li needed a shoulder to cry on. Edie relieved Jake so he could go to work. His boss had offered to park the B&E car for a few days. Jake refused. He said he needed to work.

Edie showed up just after four the first day. She didn't say anything to Jake, but just took him in her arms in one of the ante-rooms off the main parlor where the body of Remington Southworth was being shown.

Jake could see that she had been crying. He could feel her tremble as she held him tightly. He wanted to cry too, but prayed for strength. Jake knew what was going through her mind, so words were never spoken until it was time for him to leave.

"I love you Eed."

"I know," she answered.

"Thanks for being here for Jen Li and Remington."

Edie didn't answer. She just let his hand go as he turned to leave.

Jake climbed in his truck. He adjusted his rearview mirror as he turned onto Mack. He glanced at the entryway at the funeral home, then into his mirror. He caught a glimpse of a Lincoln turning slowly into the Peters parking lot as he pulled away. It was white over maroon.

His ride to Number Five was somber. Jake could not understand how one policeman could get shot in the back and his partner apparently not shot at. Glenn Poore had said he only heard two loud pops before seeing the blood.

The lack of loud gunfire told the police one thing. A silencer was used. To Jake, this meant Remington was not killed randomly, but preplanned. The TV news and newspapers didn't say this, but Jake knew.

Gunny Wynn met Jake down in the pistol range. Jake had already fired two cylinders at the paper target by the time Wynn got on his ear muffs. Jake's shots were slow and deliberate.

Wynn took his turn as Jake hung a new paper target and sent it down range. Jake fired two more cylinders, slow and methodically. Most of his hits were in the ten-ring.

Jake didn't speak as they climbed the steps. The teletypes and circulars were read in silence. Jake put the computer-generated Hot Sheet under the clip after he updated it with two recently-stolen cars.

Jake took the wheel of the Buick. Wynn slid in beside him, propping up the car board in the middle of the dash.

"Jake, you shoulda taken Fox up on his offer. Take some time off."

Jake didn't answer. He just drove. November brought an early sunset.

"It wasn't your fault, Jake. Somebody wanted him dead."

Jake looked at Gunny. "Exactly. And I'm going to get the son-of-a-bitch."

"I talked to the dicks today. They have a theory."

Gunny Wynn proceeded to tell Jake they were thinking that maybe this was the work of some Chinese Tong, or maybe Jen Li had jilted someone before marrying Remington.

"Bullshit!"

"Hey, I'm just telling you what they are thinking. They gotta start somewhere."

An hour into their shift their radio came alive. "Five Twenty-five. Return to your station."

Gunny answered the radio message. "Maybe a break in the case," Wynn said as he hung up the mike.

Jake recognized Inspector Richard Dungy immediately. He was getting a little gray above his ears and his Afro was gone, but he was the same Richard, an old friend. Dungy was wearing a dark navy suit, white shirt and a dark red tie. He looked just as sharp in a suit as Jake remembered him in a uniform.

"It was me that had you come in," he said as Jake approached.

Jake looked past his old partner and saw John King. John nodded at him. King was Richard's regular partner back in the TMU days.

Dungy turned to Wynn and King. "Go grab a coffee, guys."

Three minutes later in a back corner of the garage Jake's head was on Richard's shoulder. The tears flowed and kept on flowing. Richard kept silent. Just like there was no more water behind the dam, Jake stopped. He looked at the inspector's wet shoulder.

"I fucked up a good suit, partner."

Dungy just shrugged.

"I'm sorry. He was a friend."

"No apology needed. That's why I came by. For that, and to talk.

Richard led Jake through the station and to the coffee pot in back of the dicks office. The three detectives that were working in there left them alone. Dungy poured two cups of coffee. He let Jake do all the talking.

"Richard, this town's going to hell, fast. Did you know about my old partner, Jess Scott, getting shot just over a year ago?"

Dungy nodded.

"And now, another one of my partners is gunned down."

Richard grabbed Jake's arm, leading him towards the inside of the station. "Him getting shot isn't your fault. You weren't working with him."

"I know. But I broke him in."

"And you taught him everything he knew about the streets. Fox told me."

Jake stopped in mid-stride. "God, I forgot. How's Fox taking this?"

"Hard. Remington was his only nephew. Fox was the one who talked the kid into coming on the job. He won't take any time off, either."

The next hour, the head of the Organized Crime Unit, and more importantly, Jake's friend, talked about the dangers of wearing a badge and what he knew of Jake's two partners.

"If it had been Jess who went to the restroom that night in Shakers, the roles may have been reversed. You might have gotten killed. Ever think about that?"

Jake just shook his head.

"And Southworth had been back in uniform a couple of months. Right?"

Jake nodded.

"So what I'm saying is none of this stuff is your fault. And most of all, you're not some big super hero who's going to save the world. The City of Detroit is a sewer. All your job entails is making sure you do your part so you don't get swept up in that clockwise eddy that's taking this town downwards. Jesse Scott got shot by a couple of hold-up men. Between the two of you, those two pieces of shit are history."

Jake nodded. Richard poured two more cups of coffee.

"As far as Southworth getting shot, I think from what we've uncovered so far, the Chinese Tong theory doesn't hold water. The Wong family has kept to themselves. Nobody in the Chinese community really knows them. We don't see any connection there.

"Then the jealous boyfriend angle isn't working out either. Jen Li said she didn't have any suitors or old boyfriends. I think that angle was all wrong to begin with. An upset boyfriend doesn't go out and find himself a .357 magnum with a silencer. I believe this was a deliberate plan, thought out over a long period of time."

Richard drained his coffee. "John and I will be going through some stuff. Maybe this is some other outfit that thought Remington was stepping on some toes and had to be gotten rid of."

Richard scratched his head. "Were you and him involved in anything that you can think of?"

"I don't think so." Jake tossed his empty cup into a trash can. "I'll think on it for a bit." Jake shook his old partner's hand. "Thanks for coming by."

Gunny Wynn and Jake went back on the street. Jake asked Wynn to make a swing by the funeral home. "Just want to make sure Edie's all right."

She was, and they returned to the Fifth Precinct, slowly driving the curb lane with their lights out. Jake was thinking of the year he had spent with the guy he called *Bob* while Gunny Wynn was looking for whatever lurked the streets of Detroit after midnight. They rode in silence.

———

The funeral mass was going to be held at St. Anthony's on Tuesday the 18th. Jake thought it was ironic, that just a short while ago, Remington was in that church alive and well. Jake's toast that night had been for a long and prosperous life with Jen Li.

About six weeks is all. Jake shook his head as the thought went through his mind.

Friday morning had Father O'Malley leading the rosary at the funeral home before they'd walk past the casket for their final good-bye.

The final good-bye took an hour and a half as men in blue, not just from Detroit, but all corners of the state, came by to say farewell to one of their own. A delegate from the mayor's office and the Chief of Police, Phillip Tannian, were a part of the queue along with three out of five members of the Board of Police Commissioners.

Father O'Malley led the procession from the Peter's display room where Remington Southworth was lying in state. Jake gripped a handle on the left side of the casket, while five other Fifth Precinct officers in their blues wearing white gloves took hold of it. They paused at the back of the hearse as the funeral director had them place the casket on the rollers. The casket was then gently rolled forward, locked in place and the two doors on the back of the black Cadillac hearse were closed.

As the second door closed, Jake spotted a white over maroon Lincoln parked across the street. It looked empty, but he stared at it for a few seconds. He'd seen it before.

A procession of police and civilian cars followed the hearse towards St. Anthony's. Four police motorcycles led the way, two breaking off before every light to stop all traffic. The lead car behind the hearse, a Cadillac limo, carried Jen Li, her father and grandfather along with Sergeant Beauregard Fox and Remington's mother, Carol.

They drove the surface roads, taking Mack back into Detroit to Alter Road, then on to Jefferson to drive past the Fifth Precinct before heading to East Grand Boulevard and on towards Gratiot. The church was just a couple of blocks back to the northeast. It took over forty-five minutes to cover the eleven or so miles.

Jake was driving Edie's Chrysler Newport. Hank and Sam were in the back seat. Edie was quiet.

"Dad," Sam said after ten minutes of silence. "Why'd your partner die?"

Edie tried to shush Sam up, but Jake said, "That's all right. There's some things they need to know."

For the next fifteen minutes Jake talked about why he became a police offer. Yes, he needed a job. He had a family. But it was more than that. He wanted to protect and serve the people of the City of Detroit.

"It's just a good feeling knowing you are helping people like you, your brother and mom.

"Then why would anyone want to shoot a policeman?"

"Well Sam, there are some bad people in the world. I don't know their reasoning, but it's my job to make sure they pay for doing the wrong thing."

"I remember seeing you in the hospital. You were shot, Mom said. Why don't you let someone else be the policeman?"

"Sometimes, doing what I do scares me, like that night I was shot, but if I quit because I was afraid, then the bad guys would win. I can't let that happen."

Edie, Sam and Hank didn't know about what had happened in the alley in 1968, and Jake wasn't going to tell them.

Sam went silent. Edie reached out and squeezed Jake's hand.

Hank was looking at the boarded-up store fronts, remnants from the riot eight years ago, then at the bars and cages on the rest of the businesses. "Mr. Bush—Dad, why do all these places have boards, bars or cages over the windows?"

"The boards are from something that happened a long time ago. Some people didn't have insurance to repair the damage. Some of the business owners just quit and moved away. The bars and cages are to keep people out who want to steal what's inside."

Hank went silent. Jake glanced over his shoulder and saw Hank still looking at the businesses on Mack Avenue the further into Detroit they drove.

Five minutes later, he spoke again. "Our downtown doesn't have bars or cages on the windows."

Jake didn't have an answer for him.

The procession drove slowly past the station house on the corner of Jefferson and St. Jean. The sidewalk was lined with the on-duty staff, the desk lieutenant, sergeant, clerk and the cadet. Behind them were ten detectives. All were saluting the hearse as it drove by.

Random thoughts were going through Jake's mind as he drove. Remington Southworth had been less than two months away from resigning from the Detroit Police Department. Jake knew about it. With the threats of a layoff facing him, Remington applied and was accepted by the Oakland County Sheriff's Department.

At the funeral home, Jen Li told Jake Remington was to start there at the beginning of the new year. He was going to put in his notice in mid-December.

Another six weeks and his papers would have been in. Jake pondered at that thought until Sam and Hank's questions came to mind. He wondered if he shouldn't apply somewhere else. The Detroit Police Department was going downhill fast.

The long line of cars in the procession arrived at St. Anthony's. An honor guard made up of officers from Detroit, the Michigan State Police, as well as fifteen communities in and around Detroit, lined the sidewalk leading up to the entrance of the church. Jake, along with the other pallbearers, donned their white gloves and carried the casket between the honor guards.

Father O'Malley presided over a solemn high mass funeral for Patrolman Remington Southworth. The eulogy extolled the short but valiant career of "one of Detroit's finest," in the words of the priest. Those words echoed in Jake's ears.

Truly one of the finest. At those words Jake couldn't hold his emotions in check. His eyes filled with tears, overflowed, and trickled down his cheeks. Edie reached over and grabbed his hand and held it. She sensed his pain.

———

Jake was sitting atop a desk in the back of the Fifth Precinct's Detective Bureau. Gunny Wynn was in the chair. Fifteen detectives were scattered about the packed office. Inspector Richard Dungy was leading the meeting. They were all gathered for an update on the investigation into the murder of Remington Southworth.

Richard Dungy introduced himself and John King. He went into ruling out any involvement of a Chinese Tong into the death of the officer, as well as eliminating the boyfriend angle. Richard then went into how they had checked further since the "Radio Run" the officers had received was for a stolen bicycle.

"That's hardly a call where an officer might be shot. So John and I looked a little deeper."

The inspector explained how they'd pulled all the afternoon log sheets for that month, and found that there were an odd number of petty complaints made for Five-ten's area. All accept the last one was listed as a "false run," or "no complainant found." The last petty complaint was the only one answered by a crew where Patrolman Southworth was on duty.

"From that information we can gather that Southworth had been targeted. His killing wasn't a random act, and it wasn't committed as a result of a crime of passion." The inspector paused and looked over the police officers gathered in front of him. "What we don't know is why and by whom." He paused again, looking over the men in front of him.

"Your Precinct Inspector and the Homicide Bureau has asked me to stay involved in this since everyone's at a loss for the motive. John's got all the reports for the last six months that have Remington Southworth's signature on it. I am asking for volunteers to go over them and see if there is anything we're missing. Then, if we don't turn up anything, we'll go back another six months."

Six sets of hands went up and Jake and Gunny added their names to the list.

"All of you. Talk to your contacts, your stoolies. See if there's anything being said on the street that's even remotely connected to Southworth."

John King divided up the reports and passed out a stack to each of the four pairs of officers. Dungy looked at the Detective Lieutenant. "Do you have anything to add, Lieutenant Quinn?"

The lieutenant just shook his head. The meeting was over.

———

Jake was waiting for Edie to show up with the boys. They were meeting for dinner that night at Shakers before Jake went in to work. Edie pulled into the lot alone. Jake opened her door for her.

"Where's the boys?"

"Got the neighbor to hang out with them."

Jake took her arm and they walked around to the front door and Pigeon smiled when she saw Jake and Edie coming in.

"James," Pigeon called out. "Jake and his girl are here."

James came out from the kitchen. He was wiping his hands and motioning them to a corner table near the kitchen.

"Sorry for your loss, Jake," he whispered.

Pigeon put two menus on the table, then hugged Jake before he could sit down.

"Sorry, friend." She kissed him on the cheek and left.

"That's why I left the boys at home. The funeral upset them enough."

Jake didn't answer. Pigeon returned with two waters and coffees.

"Catfish, fries and okra's the special."

"That sounds good," Edie said as she gave Pigeon back the menu.

"Make it two." Jake handed her his, too.

Jake slowly stirred in some sugar. Edie liked just cream. They sat quietly, both finally taking a sip on their coffees.

"Jake, I'm scared."

"You want to postpone the wedding?"

"No. That won't help matters. It's just—" Her voice trailed off.

"The boys say something?"

"Sort of." Edie took another sip of her coffee and paused. Pigeon was on the way to their table. She put two plates down in front of them.

Jake waited for her to leave. "What did they say?"

"Well, it's not what they said. It's what they're doing."

Jake nibbled on his food, letting Edie talk.

"They're growing up too fast. The first thing they do when they get home is quickly check the paper. I know it's to see if there were any policemen shot." She took a bite of fish. "They're worrying about you. They haven't said so, but I can see it."

"I'll talk to them." Jake moved his okra around on the plate. "Eed, I won't let the boys down. You neither. Things'll work out. I've just got to finish some things here first."

———

Jake and Gunny did their normal Thursday thing on the range before their starting time. Dungy and King were waiting for them in the teletype room.

"What gives, Richard?"

"Just a quick question. You know a Juanita Commins?"

Jake thought for a moment. "Name's not familiar. Should I?"

Dungy checked his notebook. "A couple of coppers on another shift came to John and said a girl by that name was asking about Remington and you."

Jake just shrugged.

John King asked, "Have you or Remington ever been in a titty bar called The Charging Station?"

"Not me. I don't think Remington would go to one." He paused for a minute. "Where's this going?"

Dungy filled Jake and Gunny in on what they were told. A few cops go there for a beer or two and watch the dancers about once a week. The Commins woman was a dancer there and had been asking about a freckled-faced kid and his partner who wore a flattop. "She wanted to know how come you guys stopped coming in, and what shift you guys were working."

"Then for sure I can tell you that Remington and I've never been in there."

Dungy folded up his notebook. "John and I are going to check this Juanita chick out. The guys said they might have accidentally told the girl that Remington was back in uniform and what car he was working."

King and Dungy started to leave when the inspector stopped. "Let me handle this, Jake. It's just a lead and I'll follow it up. If you go there and start asking questions you might blow it apart."

"You going to the bar?"

"Yep. Don't you think I look suave and debonair in the suit I'm wearing?"

"I didn't think you'd be the type that went to those kinds of places."

"Hey, sometimes a guy's got to make sacrifices." Dungy looked at John King and motioned his head towards the door. "Seriously Jake, we'll keep you posted. It might be nothing."

Chapter Twenty-five

Dungy and King checked out Juanita Commins and got their eyes full. Richard had to excuse himself early in her routine. He had seen enough. Sometimes the way you were raised made it hard being a cop, and the inspector was the son of a Pentecostal minister.

They returned the next day when the owner was there overseeing the cleanup crew. Jack Nicholson was the name listed on the license, but he was a far cry from the movie actor with the same name. This Jack was as thin as a straw, bald with caved-in cheeks. He was wearing a mint green pant suit with broad lapels, a matching shirt and a dull yellow tie. A smile revealed teeth that were nearly the same color as the tie.

A flash of their badges got Juanita's address and her work history along with the names and addresses of all the dancers working at *The Charging Station.* Dungy and King passed themselves off as working for the Liquor Control Commission. They knew bar owners didn't want any heat from the commission so they cooperated as fast as they could, wanting to get any person there on official business out the door before they found any violations that would close them down. You can't make money with a padlock on the door.

"Just a routine check of who you have working here. Nothing to worry about," Dungy told the owner as he and King left.

1022 Cass Avenue, the address they had on Juanita Commins, was an apartment building near Wayne State University. Dungy and King rang the manager's bell. In five minutes the officers were leaving. Juanita Commins had moved out earlier that month leaving no forwarding address.

As usual, the detectives had two things going at once. They were still working on the Theodore Poet escape. The arrest report had information on two cars that were impounded the day that Poet, Mosely and Williams were arrested, a Cadillac and a Lincoln. Since they were in the downtown area, they stopped by the Detroit Police Auto Pound across the street from headquarters.

The city worker behind the desk turned the log book around so that Dungy and King could read it. On November 3, 1975 the cars were released to a man and a woman. The clerk said they presented the titles for both cars, paid the storage fees in cash and drove off. The woman signed for the cars.

"Juanita Commins," King and Dungy said together as they looked at the signature.

The clerk had a note in the book saying the titles for both cars were for a business named The Poetic Insurance Company. The civilian working the desk at the auto pound said he was the one who had handled the release of the cars, but didn't remember anything about the guy with the lady.

"What did the woman look like?" John King asked.

The answer came quick. "She was tall, a humungous set of headlights on her, and—" He paused a few beats, "I think she was black."

"Sounds like your eyes never left her tits." John figured the auto pound clerk had to be pushing sixty-five.

"Sorry officer, but looking at cars and tow trucks all day, a guy kinda needs a break now and then." The man wiped a bit of drool coming out of the side of his mouth. "Boy, she had a dandy set."

"Did she leave an address?"

"Yeah. It's right here." The book showed the Cass Street address they had on Juanita Commins and the information on two cars: a 1974 white Cadillac Coupe DeVille bearing license number PA2750 and a 1975 white over maroon Lincoln Continental bearing the license number PA2751.

Thursday had Wynn and Jake downstairs on the range. Jake fired off four cylinders, two slowly and methodically, the other two as fast as he could empty the Smith. Wynn looked over at Jake's target. The ten ring was obliterated and only two holes were off center. One in the nine ring, the other slicing the line between the eight and seven ring.

"You take your shooting seriously, Jake."

"I didn't until I caught a couple of bullets."

Jake replaced the wad cutter empties with the Winchester ammo he preferred, the 125- grain bullet with a muzzle velocity of 1220 feet per second. The salesman said that particular load would go through an engine block. Jake didn't figure on killing any engines, but wanted to make sure what he hit didn't shoot back.

Dungy and King were waiting in the teletype room for them.

"You always know where I'll be and when, eh Richard?"

"Saves phone calls."

Dungy and King were tipped back in chairs with a coffee in their hands.

"What did you find out?" Jake asked.

Gunny and Jake heard about the Commins woman moving out of the address they had on her, and that she was the one who paid for and signed out the two impounded cars.

The inspector was doing most of the talking. "Somehow, she's tied in with this Poet character. She was handling the transaction. The guy with her never said a word."

King then read off the description on the two cars and their plate numbers.

Flashes of a white over maroon car seen twice around the funeral home just days before crossed Jake's mind. *Couldn't have been.*

Jake took out his small steno pad. "Gimme those plate numbers again."

He remembered Poet's man stiffening when he saw a maroon Lincoln with a white vinyl top a few months back. Now he knew why a glimpse of a Lincoln around the funeral home had caught his eye.

"Any idea where she's moved to?" Wynn asked.

"None."

Jake put away his steno pad and looked at his friend slowly sipping the last of his coffee. "You look kinda tired Richard."

Dungy nodded. "John and I've been going day and night."

"We're just coming on. How about we check out the bar tonight and see if Juanita is working. Maybe we can follow her home, see where that leads us."

Dungy nodded, "Just see if she's there. Nothing else." He stood and motioned to King. "Call me if she's working. I can have a couple of guys on her. You need to stay out of this. 'Specially if Poet is involved."

"If the son-of-a-bitch killed Remington, I want him."

"You gotta cool it Jake." Inspector Dungy was tired. He wanted to go home. "Wynn, make sure he keeps his nose clean out there."

Wynn nodded. Ten minutes later, he was driving into the night. "You think this Poet guy might be the one that got Remington?"

"Makes sense. His two guys said Poet's a little crazy."

———

The night girls started dancing at seven—that's what the flashing neon sign said on the front of The Charging Station. Wynn parked around the corner.

"Let me go in, Jake. Your haircut has cop written all over it. I'll just see if she's working."

"What, you gonna ask for her by name?"

"No, I'll just look for a tall black girl with big headlights. Dungy said that's how the auto pound clerk described her."

"While you do that, I'll check the area. I'll have the portable." Jake got out of the car, pocketing the small Motorola radio. "Don't get all lathered up over the women. We're working, remember?"

Gunny just smiled as he walked around the corner.

Jake called after him. "Meet you back here in ten. It shouldn't take you much longer than that to see if a tall black woman with big tits is working." Gunny frowned. "Okay, I'll give you an extra five to fill your eyes."

Jake stepped out into the night and headed for the alley. He was looking for the lot where the help parked their cars.

Ten minutes later Gunny was back at the Buick. Jake was sitting on the trunk lid.

"She's doing her thing. Them ain't headlights. They're beacons."

"Looks like she's driving the white Cadillac. It's in the lot out back."

Gunny slid in behind the wheel. Jake got in beside him.

"I'll find a phone," Gunny said as he cranked the Buick to life.

"Let Dungy sleep. We can see where she goes tonight."

"He said to call."

"We can see where she's living, then call him."

The club had guys coming and going until last call at two. At 2:30 the Cadillac was still in the lot. At three the club went dark and an ugly green Dodge pulled out of the lot. The only car remaining was the white Cadillac.

"Let's give it another hour, Gunny."

A grunt was all Jake heard in response.

———

Jake had a short night. He called Dungy at home before Richard left for the office. Jake filled him in on what happened; telling him the Cadillac was still in the lot at four in the morning.

"I'll have a crew on it this morning. It's the only thing we have that might lead us to Poet."

"Richard, be honest. You think he's the one who popped Remington?"

"It's a lead. That's all it is. I'm hoping the woman will lead us to him."

"Well, the Cadillac's in the lot. My guess is she's driving it."

"My guys are on it. If it moves, we'll see where it takes us. Get some sleep, Jake."

"Sleep? What's that?"

"Call me when you get to the precinct tonight. I hope to be home. Carolyn's understanding, but it's time I had dinner with her."

The call ended.

———

More than four hours sleep wasn't on Jake's agenda. He opened the Y at eight and pumped iron for an hour and a half, then drove by the bar where Juanita worked. The Cadillac was still there and so were a couple of cops watching it. He headed for Van Dyke. He was meeting Edie for lunch at the Greek place near her hospital. The wedding was a little more than a week off. They needed to discuss a few things.

The talk was all about the wedding and Edie was hoping he'd approve the flowers she'd picked out at a shop around the corner from where they were. "Want to go see what I ordered?"

"I know roses and tulips. That's it. I'll pass."

"Mom's real excited. She's my maid of honor."

"Aren't your sisters jealous?"

"Not really. They know it was my mom who said I'd better marry you before I lose you."

Jake had been wondering what changed Edie's mind. "I like your mom even more."

Edie smiled. "I think it's a conspiracy. The boys are rooting for you; Beth Scott, my sisters and my mom. I don't think I have any say in the matter."

Jake was glad she was back to smiling and giggling. He squeezed her hand, asking, "And how do you feel about getting married?"

"I wish it were tomorrow."

That told him all he needed to hear.

———

Juanita Commins was touching up her makeup in the dressing room down the hallway towards the restrooms at The Charging Station. There were five other girls getting ready for the evening crowd.

The owner stuck his head in the door. "You girls decent?" He looked around at the six girls touching up their lipstick. "Make sure them pasties are on good. I had a couple of guys stop by the other day from the Liquor Commission. I can't afford to get busted for you showing off too much skin."

He stopped by Juanita and watched for a minute. She caught him staring a bit too long.

"Don't you be getting any ideas, Jack. I do appreciate you putting me up the last couple of nights, but you and I are not meant for each other."

Jack blushed a little. "You might be missing out on a good time."

"I saw you peeking in my room last night."

"How in the hell's a man supposed to sleep when in the next room he's got something like you."

"Just a temporary arrangement, Jack. I appreciate you helping me out, but you ain't sliding into my bed. We clear on that?"

"You thinking of going back to that big friend of yours?"

"Definitely not. He's nuts. And remember, you offered me a place to stay until I found another apartment. 'No strings attached,' you said."

"Yeah, but—" Jack made sure the other girls were out of earshot. "You sure make me hard, just knowing you're so close. A little taste would be all I'd need."

"Get outta here, Jack. We got a show to do. We make your register ring. Ain't that enough?"

Jack checked his watch. Fifteen minutes 'til show time. He liked the money they brought in. On the way out he stopped by Wanda and patted her on the ass.

He whispered in her ear. "I could use a little relief before you go on."

The blonde adjusted her G-string, sighing, "How 'bout giving one of the other girls a turn?"

She could see Jack's hollow cheeks in her mirror and the sad look on his face. "Oh, okay. Just a quickie. Your office."

Jack snuck out the door and went straight to his office. Wanda waited a minute, then followed.

Julie walked over to Juanita's dressing table, dabbed a little mascara on while bending over her shoulder. "You ain't doin' Jack after work are you?"

"No, he's just giving me a place to stay for a couple of nights."

"I thought you were cozying up to that big guy who started coming in here."

"Was, until he went berserk. I'm not hanging around a crazy man."

"Didn't he give you a Cadillac to drive?"

"Yep. It's still in the lot. Too much trouble goes along with his gifts. Want it?"

"He's not crazy, you are. I'd be hanging onto someone that'd give me a Cadillac."

Juanita dug in her purse and handed the keys to Julie. "Here. You got the Cadillac and you can have his big ass if you want."

Julie smiled, grabbing the keys. "Trade you even up for my Ford."

"Leave me your keys. I might need a ride tonight. Jack's getting too frisky."

"Don't worry about Jack. Wanda's takin' the wind outta his sails right now."

"Now?"

"Don't tell me that you haven't had to do an interview in his office?"

Juanita stuffed the keys to the Ford in her purse and tossed it under her dressing table. She smiled. "I just had to undress for him while he played with himself. He's got a real small skinny dick."

"You're right there. Real small. Couldn't satisfy me for sure."

The girls giggled and walked out towards the bar. It was show time.

———

The white Cadillac pulled out of the lot behind The Charging Station. Detectives Quinton Morrow and John Hall slowly followed a block back. They were told to tail it and find out where it goes. Hall grabbed the mike and called for another Organized Crime Unit car for a hand in the tail job. Ten minutes later Morrow and Hall were joined by Fred Plantz and Rocco Rossi.

The Cadillac took Mack past Grosse Pointe Park, the City of Grosse Pointe, finally slowing for a turn just inside Grosse Pointe Farms.

"Doesn't look like a neighborhood a black exotic dancer would live in, does it?" Rossi said, passing by the corner the Cadillac had turned on. They knew Morrow and Hall were paralleling the white car and would pick it up at the next corner.

"OCU-one, we've got the white fawn. She's pulling into a gas station on Moross."

"Two, hang back. We'll pull in and get a visual on her." Hall gunned the gray Plymouth and pulled onto the ramp near the white Cadillac. He looked at has partner. "Go in and grab a couple of coffees while I watch her."

Morrow grunted, climbing out into the early-morning air. The attendant was on the way out to the pump where the Cadillac came to rest. Morrow glanced at the driver, turning quickly away and going into the all-night station. He waited to pay for the coffees. The attendant came in and rang up the sale.

"Be with you in a minute," the man in coveralls said as he worked the cash register and left with the change for the driver.

The Cadillac drove off of the ramp into the night.

"Two coffees? That's a buck."

Morrow handed the attendant the dollar. "Was I looking at your customer right? She's a blonde and white?"

"Yep. Pretty too. Stops in about once a week. Drove a Ford before."

"Same girl? You sure?"

"Name's Julie. Lives over on Hillcrest."

Morrow moved to his car with the coffees. He grabbed the mike. "OCU-two. Stop the Cadillac and get an ID. It's not the girl we were looking for."

A half hour later, Inspector Dungy's night was interrupted. His crews were checking in. He was wide awake by the time Morrow told him the Cadillac was being driven by Julie Hutton, a white female, living in Grosse Pointe Farms.

"At seven tomorrow night I want both crews to visit the club and arrest Juanita Commins."

"What'll we charge her with?"

"Aiding and abetting in an extortion scheme. And Quint, the broad's black. Make sure you bring in the right dancer."

Jake knew it was Theodore Poet's Lincoln he'd seen two times the week of the funeral. He couldn't prove it, but he knew it. *He's lookin' for me.*

Jake was checking the teletype machine when Gunny showed up. "Anything new?" he asked."

"Not a peep," Jake answered.

The police cadet stuck his head in the door. "Jake. Dungy's on the phone for you."

Jake followed the kid to the desk and picked up the phone.

Five minutes later, he and Gunny were in their Buick heading for the titty bar.

"Richard's men are arresting Juanita Commins right about now. Seems like she's been playing hide and seek with us. Another dancer was driving the Cadillac last night. The inspector says he's through messin' with the woman."

As Jake turned the corner they saw the four cops leading a tall, black woman to their cars. Gunny took a look as they passed. "Yep, that's her. I'd recognize them tits anywhere."

Jake turned into the alley to go around the block, just in time to see the long, low taillights and extended bumper under a continental kit leaving the lot. He goosed the Buick enough to see the car with a white vinyl top over a dark bottom take the next corner. His heart started pounding. *Now's as good a time as any.*

He hit the street and gunned the Buick heading for the corner. Morrow stepped off the curb with his hand in the air. The Buick's brakes squawked as Jake put his weight on the pedal.

"Dungy wants you two—" were the words Jake heard as he swerved to miss the cop. Tires spun as the Buick lunged towards the next corner. Jake made a quick turn only to see darkness in front of him.

"What the hell you doin', Jake? You almost hit Morrow."

Jake didn't answer; he drove to the next corner to look. Nothing. He raced to the next corner. Nothing again. He made a circle six blocks wide. He only saw darkness. No taillights and no Lincoln. He parked the Buick. As he sat behind the wheel his heart rate slowed. He wondered if he'd been seeing things. *No!*

"Jake, you all right?" Gunny asked.

"I'm Fine."

Chapter Twenty-six

Jake drove to the precinct. He figured Dungy wanted to talk to him and he'd call the inspector from inside the station. Corner phone booths were too cramped for long conversations. Ten minutes later he was back in the car with Gunny.

"Richard says he'd let us know what they find out from the Commins woman."

"That's all?"

"I was hoping he had another address on Poet. He didn't. He just asked how I'm doing and the regular small talk. He knows I'm getting married next week. I think he's trying to get my mind off of that Poet character."

Jake looked in the mirror, checking the headlights that fell in behind them as they went north on St. Jean. He slowed and pulled to the curb. The car passed by and turned left on Vernor.

"What's goin' on Jake? You're acting awfully spooky."

"I'll tell you over coffee." He went back to Jefferson and headed for the Top Hat. At the restaurant Jake went towards a back booth and grabbed the side where he could watch the door.

Gunny didn't stop. "Get me a coffee and a burger. I'm goin' to the john."

While Gunny was gone Jake pulled his Smith and put it on the seat next to him, covering it with his jacket. He sat watching the front windows for lights and movement. The waitress came and he ordered for Gunny and himself.

Gunny just got seated as the waitress dropped the burgers and coffee in front them. "Well, what gives?" Gunny said as he started to eat.

"I think I'm next on Poet's list."

Gunny's mouth opened, half-chewed food hanging there. "What makes you think so?" He grabbed his glass of water and took a slip, waiting for Jake's answer.

Jake proceeded to tell his partner about seeing a white over maroon Lincoln twice around the funeral home. "Something about it stuck in my mind. I didn't know why, just then. And when King gave us the information on the cars that were released to the Commins woman, I knew." Jake took a bite of his burger. "Then the other night, I saw the back end of a Lincoln Continental leaving the lot at the titty bar."

"You sure?"

"No, not positive, but that's why I almost hit Morrow. I was trying to catch up to it. It disappeared."

"You sure about this?"

"No, but I'm on full alert." Jake's eye went to the door as a big black man came in. He relaxed. It was a DSR bus driver in full uniform getting a coffee to go. His big, empty, white, silver and green General Motors coach was at the curb waiting for him.

"I think Poet was watching the bar when Dungy's guys picked up Juanita."

———

Juanita said she didn't need her rights read as she sat in the interrogation room at 1300 Beaubien. "I haven't done anything wrong."

Dungy told her about knowing she signed for and paid the storage fees on two cars and the Cadillac was at the club she worked at. "The cars were registered to The Poetic Insurance Company," he said. "Right now we've got you for aiding and abetting."

"Theo Poet called me for some help. I'm his cousin. His mama and mine are sisters."

"Did you?" Richard asked.

"I didn't see anything wrong with helping him pick up his cars. He said he was working things out with the police to get his life in order." Juanita paused, checking in her purse. "One of you guys got a cigarette?"

King gave her one and offered her a light. She then said her cousin offered her a place to stay. Poet said he had a nice place that was too much for him.

"Did you move in with him?" King asked.

"For a little while. You ain't seen the dive I was living in."

"Yes, we have," added the inspector.

"But I ain't been back since he came in bragging about killin' a cop."

Dungy looked at the woman. "He told you he killed a cop?"

"Sure did. Said it was payback for the guy sending him to the hospital."

"Where's he living?" Richard asked.

"At one of those fancy places on Nautical Way."

Juanita said she didn't know the address, but could show them where it was. "I even have a key if you want it. I'm not going back. I don't want anything to do with a man that'll kill people—'specially a cop."

Dungy and King took her for a ride so she could point out where Theodore Poet was staying. She told them about her cousin asking her to get some information on a couple of Fifth Precinct cops, knowing that cops came by her club all the time.

"I didn't know what he wanted it for. I just got it and passed it along. I thought they were some guys he knew from his old neighborhood. Hold it." Juanita pointed towards a two-story brick house. "That's the place."

King pulled to the curb two houses beyond where she pointed.

"He ain't there," Juanita offered. "He parks his Lincoln right out front so he can watch it. It's gone."

"Got that key, girl?" Dungy asked, holding his hand out. She dug in her purse and gave it to him.

"John, park down the block. I'll take a portable. Call me if you see the Lincoln. Make sure Juanita stays out of sight if he shows."

Inspector Richard Dungy let himself in Poet's house. He didn't know what he was looking for, but he needed to look. The oak desk in the corner of the living room was littered with newspaper clippings. All were about Patrolman Remington Southworth, the shooting and the newspaper updates on the investigation. The obituary was on top of the pile.

He checked the drawers. They were empty. Then Dungy remembered he was looking through the house belonging to a man that had just recently moved in.

Richard went upstairs, giving all the rooms a quick look-over. Nothing was found beyond clothes and the normal sundries in a man's bathroom. He found Juanita's room. She had left a few things in the drawers. He closed the drawer quickly when his finger caught a bra strap.

On the way downstairs, he checked a small closet. It too was empty; all except for a half-empty box of .357 magnum bullets. Richard left the box where it was. He made a mental note to get a search warrant as soon as he got back downtown.

The last place the inspector checked was the kitchen. On the counter near the phone was a note pad. He recognized the Fifth Precinct's phone number. On the table were more notes, some on bar napkins, some on torn pieces of paper. The name

Bush appeared on more than three of them. Another note was scribbled "5-25" and had "7 p.m.-3 a.m." written down.

Dungy didn't move anything. He just looked. His visit confirmed his suspicions. He locked the door on the way out and walked down to the corner, sliding in beside John King.

As they turned down Jefferson, Dungy turned to talk to their passenger. "What I don't know is what to do with you, young lady."

"You can just drop me off at the club."

"So you can let Poet know we're looking for him?"

"I told you, mister, I don't want anything to do with him."

"But, I can't take the chance. We've got a murder investigation going on, and according to what you said earlier, the guy admitted to you that he killed a cop. That makes you a material witness." Dungy scratched his head. "Got any ideas, John?"

"We've got that house on the west side. Could put a couple of cops with her for a few days."

"Policewomen, not men," Dungy said.

"Hey, I don't need no matron watchin' over me."

"It'll just be for a couple of days," Dungy said. "All the food you want, a nice TV, the works. Or we can lock you up on the eighth floor for safekeeping. I need you out of circulation until we have Poet in custody."

"I'll take the TV and take-out. But you'll have to talk to Jack. I need that job."

"Back to the office, John, I have some calls to make." He turned towards the back seat. "Got some clothes somewhere?" Richard remembered that his men had pulled her off of the stage. All they took with them was a long leather coat she said was hers.

"Some back at Theo's. Some at the club."

Richard Dungy made a couple of calls. One was to Mary Fiermonti, who was heading the Women's Division. He got two policewomen to watch over Juanita and to get her some clothes. The next call was to the prosecuting attorney's office. He wanted a search warrant for Poet's house. He thought about calling the Fifth Precinct and asking the desk sergeant to have Bush call him. He decided against that.

A third call had the radio operators re-broadcasting the information on Theodore Poet and the Lincoln he was driving. He told them to add the message: "Wanted in connection with the shooting of a police officer."

He had his clerk call in his units off the streets. Three cars were currently working Vito Groppuso, a mafia lawyer. They normally stayed with him until he went to bed.

The mafia will always be there. I want Poet now.

————

"So whatchew thinking of doing?" Gunny pushed his empty plate out of the way.

"Just what we've been doing. Working. Dungy will find out where Poet lives. I know they'll stake out his place. I think Poet's on the street looking for me. All he's got to do is find me."

"You're a walking target."

"But you've got my back while we're working, right?"

"Always." Gunny smiled as he pushed his plate out of the way. He was thinking, *Maybe more than that.*

————

Theodore Poet thought about having a police scanner put in the '73 Green Lincoln he just bought. He knew that his white and maroon Continental was too recognizable. He almost got caught as he was looking for Juanita at her club. He caught a glimpse of her as she was ushered out of the club by some guys he knew had to be cops.

Fuckin' bitch probably gave them the keys to my house.

A quick deal at a lot on Gratiot had him driving something a little more subtle, but still with a little luxury. After thinking about it, he nixed the scanner idea. He knew for a fact his cop worked from 7 p.m. until 3 a.m. Tuesdays through Saturdays. He could just wait for an opportunity. He was patient.

Watching the Fifth Precinct parking lot from a block away was easy. He only had to watch for headlights leaving the station house in the middle of the night. He knew only two cops worked those hours and he had a fifty-fifty chance of grabbing the right car on the way home.

The previous night he fell in behind a Mercury that had left at three fifteen. Ten minutes later, at a Clark station, Theo saw that it was a black guy driving the Merc. Now he was one hundred percent sure he needed to follow a blue Ford pickup.

Shoulda known the guy with a flattop'd be drivin' a truck.

By following his man home there'd be no partner to worry about. Theodore Poet smiled as he thought about his own ingenuity. With a less obvious car and the Python, it was just a matter of time.

———

The desk sergeant said Gunny was at the range when Jake asked for the key. He trotted down and joined him. Jake noticed that Gunny was taking his time. Jake shot his three cylinders. Gunny shot four. They compared targets.

"Not bad, Gunny," Jake quipped. His partner was getting better.

An hour later they were hitting the street. Gunny was driving. Jake noticed his partner was quieter than usual.

"You okay, Gunny?"

"Fine."

Gunny had nothing more to say. He had been a bit edgy since he'd spotted a white and maroon Lincoln the night before as he stopped for gas. That's when he knew Jake wasn't imagining things. Theodore Poet was looking for Jake. Wynn wanted to end things right then, but by the time he was able to stop the attendant pumping his gas, the Lincoln disappeared into the night. He called Dungy the next morning to let him know what he'd seen. He didn't want to say anything to his partner about seeing the Lincoln.

———

Dungy had three night crews at his disposal. He put Morrow and Hall on the house on Nautical Way. Plantz and Rossi were sent to watch the house on Strasburg that Jake's file listed as his home. Patrolmen Bob Meadows and Darrel Moore were in a third car. Dungy told them to stick with Five Twenty-five while it was on the street without getting caught. He knew Meadows and Moore could do just that since their everyday job was to follow guys like Vito Groppuso and see who they contacted, what they ate, who they talked to, every day from daylight until they went to bed.

"Stay with Jake until he's safely home and in bed. I'll have one of the day crews there when he wakes in the morning."

Dungy had complete confidence in Meadows and Moore. They were pros. The inspector leading the Organized Crime Unit knew that Patrolman John Anthony Bush was Poet's next target after talking to Wynn and the Commins woman. Now, he had to make sure his friend stayed alive until they had Poet in handcuffs.

———

Jake stashed the stolen car board in the precinct locker room. He waved good-night to Gunny as they left the station.

Jake went to his truck, Gunny to his Mercury. Jake went north on St. Jean while Gunny went west on Jefferson.

After Jake crossed Kercheval, he saw a set of headlights fall in behind him a half block back as he casually checked his rearview mirror. He made a right on Mack, planning on taking his normal route, Conner to Gratiot.

Jake bumped across the railroad tracks that fed the Chrysler Plant. They were switching cars in the middle of the night, but left Mack open. A time or two going home, he got caught by them, but that was over a two year period. He made the light at Conner, turning left. There were very few cars on the streets at three-thirty in the morning. He was checking his mirror more often and saw a set of headlights still hanging nearly a block behind. He didn't know if it was the same car, but the lights seemed to be keeping pace with him.

———

As Meadows and Moore neared the railroad tracks, railcars moved to close off Mack. The switchman was swinging his lantern and climbing on a ladder attached to the boxcar.

"Fuck!" Meadows yelled. "We'll lose him."

"Back up, back up," yelled Moore. "Go to St. Jean and head north. Maybe we can get around 'em."

Tires squealed and smoke flew from under their Plymouth as Meadows floored it. He burned more rubber as he power-turned backwards at St. Jean, then north.

"Go to Shoemaker," Moore was yelling. "Take a right. Maybe he's on Conner."

Moore grabbed the mike on his car-to-car. "OCU-three, you out there?"

When they answered he asked if they were where they could give them a hand.

"We're sitting on his house. Can't help you, sorry."

"We lost Bush."

Meadows was flying around the corner at Shoemaker, heading for Conner. "We gotta find him. If anything happens to Bush, Dungy's gonna bust our nuts."

———

The light at Harper just turned green and Jake made a right turn. He pulled out his Smith and Wesson and put it on the seat beside him, only to start thinking about how foolish he was.

He's getting under my skin and I'm letting him.

Jake looked in his mirror and saw a set of headlights make the same turn. As he neared Outer Drive, he pulled to the curb and doused his lights. The headlights continued by. Jake relaxed. It was a dark green Lincoln.

This is stupid. He shook his head, put his car in gear, flipped on his lights and drove into the night. He needed to relax. He saw a Clark station ahead and pulled in. He bought a Pepsi and got back behind the wheel. His wandering mind soon had him on Kelly driving towards his old high school. Just for kicks he turned in the lane that ran between Notre Dame and Regina High. Old memories flooded his mind as he took the left turn between the gym and the football field out back. Another left took him along the north side of his old school. He paused as he reached Kelly, then made a right into the road leading to the Eastland Mall.

Memories of drag races as a seventeen year-old kid on this very same hunk of pavement brought a smile to his face. He threw a rod in his '53 Ford straight six, trying to beat Max Stoll's '52 Chevy. Off to the left the neon sign for Stouffer's caught his eye. He worked there a year during his senior year as a charcoal broil chef before he joined the Marines. Stouffer's had its own memories, like meeting Judy DeMonico, his first love. He'd been shocked when the beautiful, dark haired waitress had agreed to go to the Senior Prom with him.

He finished the last of his Pepsi, crammed the empty bottle under his seat and made a wide U-turn in the parking lot. His headlights caught the corner of the J.L. Hudson store, then the empty lot behind it. He slowed as his headlights settled on a car that was parked on the roadway. It wasn't there when he drove in. He let his Ford creep forward, holding his headlights on the car that was just sitting in the darkness ahead of him. It was facing him. Jake inched forward, his motor running at idle speed, closing the gap between it and his truck. Fifty yards, then forty. His headlights glinted off the grill. The low boxy design along with the chrome around the dark headlamps registered in his mind as a Lincoln—a dark Lincoln.

He was no more than twenty yards from it when two flashes erupted in front and two holes and spider-web cracks filled the F-100's windshield.

In one motion Jake's left hand pulled on the door handle while his right grabbed the Smith. He rolled while his truck continued forward towards the Lincoln. The curb stopped his rolling and another flash erupted. From his prone position Jake fired three rounds at the flash.

The left door was swinging loosely while his truck kept rolling until the sound of metal folding and the tinkling of glass broke the silence of the night. Jake's blue F-100 came to a rest kissing the right half of the parked Lincoln.

It was the distraction Jake needed as he jumped to his feet and cut around the bed of the pickup. His eyes picked up movement. Jake's reflexes took over. Planting his feet, his left palm slid under the butt of his .357 as he fired two rounds in a tenth of a second.

There was a scream. Jake inched forward. He heard a low moan. The distorted beam from the right headlight on the Ford showed a dark heap lying next to the Lincoln.

A flashlight came on, illuminating the figure on the ground. It startled Jake.

"Jake!" It was Gunny's voice. "You all right?"

Gunny's flashlight beam stayed on the prone man who was trying to grab the pistol that was on the pavement.

"I'm good," Jake said as his foot nudged the gun further from the man's reach. It spun on the pavement. It was a Colt Python with a silencer attached.

Jake's eyes locked on the big man while he cocked the hammer on his Smith. His sights were centered in the middle of the large forehead between the man's wide, white eyes. *Theodore Poet.*

There was no mistaking him. It was Poet.

"Please, no more."

Poet's hands went in the air as he struggled to his knees. Jake could see a dark stain growing on the man's light colored shirt. Tears rolled down Jake's cheeks. His hand trembled slightly and he palmed the Smith to steady the bead.

"You ambushed a cop and now you think it's over?"

The big man shrugged. His eyes widened as he saw Jake's pistol three feet from his head.

"The only thing you're going to get is a bullet between the fuckin' eyes."

Jake took another step, his finger tightening on the trigger.

"Jake you can't." It was Gunny's voice.

Jake stood, thinking. His finger tightened on the trigger, then loosened. *No, you're not walking away from this.* His finger tightened again.

"Jake, think about it. You've got Edie and the boys."

Jake closed his eyes, thinking of Edie, Hank and Sam. Then a painful memory crossed his mind—a Suburban burning with Anne, Debbie, Michelle, Mike and Jeanette inside. He quickly pushed that thought away, but then, there was Remington, freckles and all, staring at him.

Seconds ticked by.

Gunny's right. Jake eased the hammer back down.

He didn't see his partner pick the Python off the pavement. A muffled shot broke the silence. Tissue, broken teeth and brain matter splattered all over the side of the Lincoln.

"That's for Remington."

Gunny bent over and placed the python in Theodore Poet's right hand. He looked over his shoulder at Jake. "I don't have a wife or children. And I owed the kid."

———

On November 28, 1975, Jake stood in front of Pastor Jim Pettys in front of the altar at Holy Redeemer Lutheran Church. To Jake's left was Jesse Scott wearing a nice gray suit with a red rose in his boutonnière. The organ was playing in the background as Edie and her mother walked up the aisle. Edie was wearing a white dress with a hat and a short veil. She was smiling as she clutched a small bouquet. Hank and Sam were standing to Jesse's left, both in a suit and tie. Gunny Wynn, Sergeant Fox, and Inspector Richard Dungy with his wife, Carolyn, were sitting in the front pew.

———

Jake was driving Edie's car with Hank and Sam asleep in the back seat. They were heading to Traverse City and a Holiday Inn for a short weekend honeymoon. The brochure had pictures of an Olympic-sized pool, just what the boys requested. Edie was snuggled up to Jake, her head on his shoulder.

Jake kissed the top of her head. "Check the envelope over the visor."

Edie looked up and saw the corner of an envelope, grabbed it and moved the flap out of the way. Jake turned on the dome light so she could see. The letterhead on the page was from the Oakland County Sheriff's Department. She quickly scanned the letter.

"John Anthony Bush is hereby accepted for employment on the Oakland County Sheriff's Department. He is to report at eight in the morning on January 2, 1976." It was signed by the Oakland County Sheriff, John Nichols.

Edie put the letter down. Tears formed in her eyes as she squeezed Jake's hand. "You didn't do this for me, did you?"

"I did this for us. Hank, Sam, you and I." He smiled. "And I'll still be a cop."

———

Wynn checked his mail slot at the Fifth Precinct. He told his new partner, Roberto San Miguel, to meet him at the basement range at 5:30 p.m. There was one piece of mail in the box. It was from the Wayne County Prosecutor's Office. He tore the envelope open.

It read: "On December 3, 1975, a coroner's inquest determined that Theodore Poet died of a self-inflicted bullet wound to the mouth. Ballistic tests had determined that the Colt Python magnum retrieved at the scene was the same pistol used in the murder of Patrolman Remington Southworth."

The letter further stated that their findings were mainly based on the Wayne County Medical Examiner's report. The report stated that Theodore Poet suffered two entry and exit wounds from Patrolman John Anthony Bush's .357 to the left side of his lower rib cage. They also determined that the wound to the head was consistent with a self-inflicted gunshot based on residue and powder burns.

Tyrone "Gunny" Wynn smiled as he read the letter, then put it back in the envelope, slipped it into his back pocket and headed to meet Roberto downstairs.

Gunny had already wished Jake and his new bride a long, happy life, many miles away from Coleman Young's city— one that was slowly decaying from within.

About The Author

The author is a 76-year-old retiree (since the end of 1997). He is a married father of four grown children, has one stepson, eight grandchildren, eight great grandchildren and counting. His wife of 25 years, Edie, is his partner, friend, biggest fan and critic. Her subtle suggestions started the long journey that resulted in his first novel, "Among the Tin Cans and Broken Glass." That novel was based on the experiences he had as a police officer in Detroit during the 1960s.

While enjoying winters in the Southwest U.S. the author joined a writer's group in Lake Havasu City, Arizona. While fulfilling his assignments with the group more police-type adventures evolved. The result is this, his second novel.

The Author and Children